HIS NAME IS JUNSAKU

TENKARA SMART

His Name is Junsaku
By Tenkara Smart

ISBN: 978-0-648-85053-3

Cover Design by George Saad

I dedicate this book to my beloved husband, Mark.
He is my rock, my creative genius, my other half, and
the man who makes all my dreams a reality.

And to my wonderful parents, Dino and Elizabeth, who blessed
me with their love, wisdom, and guidance throughout my life.

*'As I look up the mountain,
my mind casts light on the shadows.'*

Kancho Ookomi

PROLOGUE

FUKANO CLOSED her eyes, struggling to breathe, a strained wheezing sound filling the air. 'Haru, you must go now. You need to get my otosan,' she mumbled, her body shivering despite the sweltering heat that filled the room. Even as sickness attacked her youthful body, sapping her strength, her mind remained in check, and she knew she needed her father by her side.

Haru's sleek, jet-black eyebrows furrowed, forming faint lines on his forehead as he gazed worriedly at his friend. 'I cannot leave you alone. You are too sick.'

'The sooner you fetch my father, the sooner he can help me. I need him here. Do this for me, Haru,' Fukano pleaded.

'Where is he? Do you even know?'

'He is with the shogun at the castle in Kumamoto.' Fukano inhaled sharply and clutched her stomach, the pain cutting her gut like a knife. 'Go, Haru. Tell him of my condition.'

Haru shook his head. 'You should have listened to me when I told you not to trust them. Now I am afraid to leave you. What if you die?'

'If I am dying, I need my father even more. Stop talking and go!' Fukano demanded.

Haru leaned in closer and stared into Fukano's half-open eyes. He reached out and put his hand on her forehead, feeling the heat and dampness of her sweat on his skin. 'I will find him and bring him to you, Fukano. I will go as fast as I can.' Haru cautiously glanced towards the open bedroom door to ensure the others weren't spying or lurking in the hallway. Then, he moved his lips close to Fukano's ear, almost touching her skin. 'While I am gone, be careful,' he whispered urgently. 'If they bring food or drink, offer it to Nikka first and see how she responds. If the dog hesitates even for a moment, do not take it.' Then Haru backed away slightly and cupped Fukano's shoulders. Staring into her eyes, he inhaled deeply, suppressing the rising fear inside him, determined to shield his friend from further anguish, and stated calmly, 'Do not trust anyone. Do you hear me?'

'Hai,' Fukano sighed, looking at him with green eyes dulled like antique bottle glass. 'Find Junsaku, Haru. Bring my otosan. I need him.'

JUNSAKU

ONE

CHIBA KNELT on the tatami mat, clutching the fabric of her white robe to keep the hem from touching the floor. Leaning forward, the new mother fixed her gaze upon the reddish-brown, veiny placenta splayed on the bamboo mat, the umbilical cord still attached to the baby. Two youthful Japanese women wearing long, brown cloaks, their raven-black hair meticulously pulled into tight buns, knelt beside her, supporting her as she regained her strength. Soft, gurgling noises came from the unusually serene newborn as the midwife, dressed in a tea-coloured robe with a white hood, placed him on a sheet of royal blue cotton and expertly cut and tied his umbilical cord before cleansing him with a warm sponge.

Afterwards, she swaddled the newborn and passed him to Chiba just as Goto burst into the room. 'The baby is born! Chiba, are you alright?' he asked, his voice trembling with emotion. He fell to his knees before his wife and reached out, tenderly touching the top of her soft hand.

'Hai, I am fine. So is our son, Saito,' she replied, looking down at the boy cradled in her arms. She smiled, feeling a sense of wonderment as she stared at her baby's dark brown, curious eyes and the black hairs that sprung off the crown of his head like the velvety feathers of a black duckling.

With both hands, Chiba presented the infant to his father like a gift for the gods. Goto took his son and held him near his hard chest. He bent his forefinger, gently stroked his son's soft cheek, then looked at Chiba. 'We will not call our son Saito as planned.'

'But Goto, we said if we had a boy, he would be named Saito as a legacy to your father.' Chiba massaged the back of her neck as she remembered when they first married and discussed having children. They agreed they would name their first-born son after Goto's father, and now, Chiba felt confused by her husband's sudden change of heart.

'Something has happened.'

Chiba cocked her head. '*Wakaremasen.* I do not understand.'

'Leave us,' Goto ordered, deliberately swiping his hand through the air, signalling for the other women in the room to depart. The women stood quickly and obediently shuffled to the sliding door, careful not to glance back at the samurai and his family as they exited.

Cautiously lowering herself to lay on the bamboo tatami mat, Chiba looked at Goto and calmly asked, 'Why would we change his name?'

Goto knew he had to choose his words carefully or risk sounding like he had lost his mind. He took a deep breath. 'Chiba, last night I had a vision. I awoke to an apparition—a boy standing at the foot of my bed. His face looked like he was five, maybe six, and he was extremely tall, with yellow hair and pale white skin.'

'Did the spirit speak?' The candlelight flickered in the amber eyes of Chiba's widened gaze as she listened intently to Goto's story, believing every word.

'Hai,' Goto replied. 'At first, he spoke in a language I did not understand. English, I think. Then, the ghost began speaking in broken Japanese. The spirit asked to see my son, Junsaku.'

'Junsaku?' his wife asked, puzzled.

'That was my response, too. When I questioned the apparition, the spirit told me Junsaku was my son, and he wanted to see him. I told him I had no son, and he laughed, a strange giggle like the tinkling of bells.' Both parents locked eyes, a momentary hush filling the room. Goto placed his hand on his wife's hip and whispered, 'Chiba, do you realise what this means? A ghost visited me and told me our son is called Junsaku.'

Chiba licked her dry lips and sighed. 'Well, Goto, we cannot go against a spirit. We will give our son this name. His name is Junsaku.'

TWO

'YOU ARE A NATURAL!' Goto exclaimed, admiring his son's sword-fighting skills.

Chiba sat on the lush green grass with their five-year-old daughter, Etsuko, nestled comfortably in her lap as she watched Junsaku, muscular yet rail-thin, wield his bokken, his wooden sword, with remarkable ease, his movements as precise as a boy twice his age.

Junsaku stopped his practise, straightened his posture, and stood tall before his father. 'Otosan,' Junsaku said, 'I do not need this bokken. I am ready for a real samurai sword!' Junsaku could see an aura of yellow and orange clinging to his father's figure as Goto laughed at his son's confidence.

'You hear this, Chiba? Your son believes he is already a samurai,' Goto stated loudly. Goto could see that Junsaku possessed extraordinary talent and was a prodigy in swordsmanship at nearly ten years old. However, Goto remained acutely aware of the dangers of fostering his son's burgeoning sense of superiority. He was determined to keep humility at the forefront of their training so that Junsaku would not let his exemplary skills cloud his future judgment.

Chiba smiled and wrapped her arms around her daughter, Etsuko, who sat quietly in her lap. Etsuko's tiny fingers explored the smooth surface of a hand-carved wooden kokeshi doll she held in her hand, a gift from her father. With a look of boredom on her face, Etsuko studied the doll, with its perfectly rounded, limbless body, smooth circular head, and a cheerful, hand-painted smile that exuded warmth, a stark contrast to her disposition.

From her earliest days, Etsuko acted reserved, often shielding her feelings behind a stoic façade, and everyone in the family found it challenging to decipher what was happening behind the glint of her mischievous, defiant brown eyes. Junsaku, in particular, often felt the weight of her negative energy like a heavy blanket. As he gazed at his younger sister, nestled comfortably in their mother's lap, clutching her doll, a memory invaded his thoughts—the painful recollection, months ago, when his sister wielded her doll like a weapon and struck him with sudden ferocity as he tried to play with her, leaving a deep cut below his lower lip that healed into a crescent-shaped scar, a permanent reminder of her extreme dislike towards him. Despite Junsaku's persistent attempts to connect with her, no matter how hard he tried, Etsuko responded with nothing but chilling indifference and bitter anger.

Junsaku's mother interrupted his thoughts, saying, 'Junsaku, when you finally go to samurai school, you will be the head of your class because your father, a cousin of the daimyo and a true samurai, has taught you well,' she remarked proudly.

Standing at six feet with a lean and muscular build, Junsaku's father was the tallest man in the village. He had amber eyes shaped in a perpetual squint and long black hair, which he pulled into a top knot at the crown of his head.

Junsaku turned to his father. 'I will be a better warrior than you someday, Otosan,' he bragged, positioning his bokken before him, prepared for another sparring match. 'When I am older, I will be Japan's most powerful samurai and able to defeat anyone, and all the people will bow to me.'

'I expect that spirit from you,' his father replied. 'Why else would I have given you the nickname Ōkami? I gave you this nickname to remind you to be like the wolf. Though generally non-violent, the wolf will fight when necessary. Be like the wolf, Son. Practise non-violence until there is no other option. Right now, I know some of the boys at school are disrespectful towards you, but trust me, that will change after you leave the village. There will come a time when your dream comes true, and you will be powerful and feared.'

Junsaku smiled, his pride radiating across his face.

'Come everyone,' Chiba said. 'Let us return home and eat.'

Chiba gently nudged Etsuko, who reluctantly stood. She took her daughter's small hand as Junsaku ran to Chiba's opposite side. He interlocked his fingers with his mother's, and the family walked to their thatched-roof house. With each step, Junsaku listened to the rustling of his mother's canary yellow kimono as she moved gracefully, almost like she floated. Junsaku thought his okasan was the most beautiful woman in the world. He liked the feel of her straight, silky black hair against his palm and loved how her eyes arched lightly towards her temples. As they walked through the serene garden, Junsaku observed a delicate, ethereal light reminiscent of a soft halo emanating from the outer edges of his mother's form. Then, Junsaku noticed his sister had the opposite energy. He could see Etsuko had an intense aura that seemed to draw shadows around her, with only dark colours surrounding her body, mostly blood reds and storm greys, clinging to her like an eerie fog.

When the family arrived at their house, constructed of thick wooden beams, woven bamboo walls covered in dried earth, and sliding panel doors, they entered, removed their shoes in the *genkan*, slipped on V-shaped sandals, and went to the kitchen to eat.

***

AFTER SUPPER, Goto made an announcement. 'Ōkami,' he said, 'your mother and I have discussed your training. We believe the time has come for you to go to the *koryū*, the samurai academy, called *Shiraki ryū*. You leave on the next day of the fire. Does this please you?'

'Hai, Otosan,' Junsaku replied, his voice high-pitched with excitement. 'I will make you proud.' Junsaku turned and smiled at his younger sister. 'Are you sad to see me go, Etsuko?' His smirk hinted that he knew the answer and playfully provoked her.

Etsuko grimaced and looked at her okasan. She could see from her mother's tight-lipped expression that she needed to respond to her brother politely. She wanted to be truthful but lied to appease her parents, her words monotone. 'Uh, hai, I am sad to see you go, brother.' Then, Etsuko's whiskey-brown eyes stretched wide as she looked at her mother and begged, 'Okasan, can I have Junsaku's room? It is bigger!'

Junsaku noticed a bright yellow spark in his sister's dark aura, signalling her excitement at his absence.

THREE

B EFORE BED, Junsaku played the shakuhachi for his family. He blew air into the diagonal-cut opening of his bamboo flute as his fingertips pressed against the four upper holes, his thumb covering the opening on the underside. As with most things, playing the instrument came easily to Junsaku, and his music filled the room with a melancholy sound similar to the wail of a loon. While Junsaku performed, Etsuko snuggled between her parents on floor cushions, clutching her wooden doll, a dull expression on her face as she sat obediently, bored by her brother's exhibition.

When Junsaku finished, his mother said, 'Arigato, Junsaku. That was lovely.' Chiba squeezed Etsuko's shoulder and looked at Junsaku. 'Now, time for bed – both of you.'

Junsaku cleaned his shakuhachi, slid it into a soft, worn cloth bag, placed his flute in a wooden cupboard, and then bid goodnight to his family, walking to his bedroom.

***

INSIDE HIS room, Junsaku closed the fusuma panels behind him and lay on his futon. As Junsaku teetered on the edge of sleep, a presence beside his bed woke him. Junsaku opened his eyes and saw the familiar spectre of a tall boy standing near the edge of his bed, looking down at him, the apparition's body nearly transparent. Next to the young spirit, Junsaku could see the ghostly image of an Irish wolfhound with dry, mangled, tan-grey fur sitting in quiet obedience.

The trees outside the open window were visible through the spirit's body. 'Good evening, Junsaku,' said the pale, blonde-haired ghost as he knelt beside Junsaku's futon.

Junsaku felt no fear, and his breath remained steady, his eyes focused on the ethereal image. 'Good evening, ghost. Hello, Dog,' he replied slowly in English.

'How dost thou?' the ghost asked.

'I am well, thank you,' Junsaku responded slowly.

The spirit patted the Irish wolfhound's head and commanded, 'Lay down, Dog.'

The dog lay down on the tatami mat floor of Junsaku's bedroom. Junsaku watched as the Irish wolfhound crossed his paws in the front, splayed his back legs, and opened his jaw slightly, allowing his tongue to spill over his jowls. Then, Junsaku asked, 'Ghost, why do you call him Dog? Why does he not have a name?'

'I could not decide what to call him, and because I called him dog many times, that became his name. 'Tis a funny name, I admit.' The Irish wolfhound let out an eerie bark; the sound muffled as though the animal cried out from deep within a cave. Then, the spirit sat on the edge of Junsaku's futon, his weightless body creating no indentation on the cotton mattress, and he commented, 'Junsaku, your English is improving. You are recalling your old language.'

'What is the meaning of 'recalling your old language'?' Junsaku asked, scratching his head.

'You spoke English in a past life and are remembering well.

Have you also been practising?'

'Hai. Um, yes. My mother give me book,' Junsaku enunciated, pointing at a leather book on a low table. 'I recently told parents you visit me and that I want to learn English, and mother gives me language book to help. My father believe you visit him before I was born. When I describe what you look like, he thinks you may be the spirit that came to him and told him my name.'

"Tis true. I was looking for you, but you had not yet arrived,' the apparition replied.

Junsaku yawned, his mouth stretched wide as he inhaled loudly, then said, 'You know my name, Ghost, but I still do not know yours. Why will you not tell me your name?'

'Because a name is not important, Junsaku. It is our substance that matters.'

'But I want to know your name, and why you visit me.' Junsaku's eyelids blinked sluggishly as he attempted to stay awake.

'I have told you why I visit you. Do you remember?'

'Hai. You tell me, 'Learn from my mistakes.' But what mistakes?'

'You will know when you listen to your soul speak. You will feel a cloud of darkness and uncertainty whenever you go off your path and the opposite when you make the right choice. Learn from my mistakes, Junsaku, and listen so that you may live in the light.'

Junsaku lay silent, his breathing slow and rhythmic.

'Are you ready to go to sleep?'

'Hai. I am tired.'

As Junsaku drifted into slumber, he watched with half-opened eyes as the ghostly boy and his dog slowly faded into his room's shadows.

Just as they were about to disappear, the phantom boy whispered loudly, 'My name is Bartholomew.'

However, Junsaku, deep in sleep, did not hear him.

FOUR

JUNSAKU'S ANTICIPATION had been building for weeks since his parents announced he would attend the samurai school. Each passing day felt like an eternity as he eagerly counted the hours, the excitement of finally leaving his current school keeping his spirits high.

On a sunny morning, Junsaku awoke feeling unusually elated. He rolled out of bed, dressed, and went to the kitchen. He ate a steaming bowl of miso soup and a grilled piece of fish, gathered his things, and headed to school.

Several boys crowded the entrance of the schoolhouse, a one-room building built from dark timber and sun-baked clay. As Junsaku passed a student, Tako Sukenobu, the classmate leaned into him, forcing Junsaku to stagger. 'Learn to walk, peasant,' the ten-year-old mocked.

'I am no peasant,' Junsaku protested, his eyes black as coal. 'My father is a samurai, just like yours.'

'Ha!' Tako scoffed. 'He is nothing compared to my otosan. Your father is a foot soldier, and my otosan is a mounted samurai. My otosan stays overnight in the daimyo's house. Your otosan has not even received an invitation for tea,' he mocked.

'My father is a great man and a blood relative of the daimyo, and it does not matter what you think; you are a fool. One day, I will be Japan's greatest samurai, better than all of you cowards.' Junsaku widened his stance and narrowed his eyes. 'And when I move to Edo and become the shogun's *hatamoto*, you will bow to me.'

As Junsaku finished, his words hanging in the crisp air, the latticed wood door of the school slid open, and the teacher emerged, a scowl on his face. Short and thin as a chopstick, the man wore a full-length, dark blue robe with long, loose sleeves that could hide a small child and a hat shaped like a mushroom cap. He rang a brass bell and announced, 'It is time to begin your lessons. Come inside.'

As the students entered the classroom, Junsaku got as close as possible to the bully and stepped on the boy's canvas shoe, forcing it off at the heel. Tako turned and threw a punch towards Junsaku's head. Junsaku slid to his right, a sly grin on his face, and easily evaded his attacker's strike.

As Tako shifted his stance, preparing for his next move, spindly fingers gripped his shoulder. Time seemed to slow as the boy turned his head, his expression morphing from arrogance to shock at the sight of his teacher looming behind him with a disapproving glare. Junsaku watched, stifling his laughter as Tako bowed low in a gesture of apology, murmured '*gomennasai*,' and then hurried into the classroom, his cheeks flushed.

***

'*YAME!*' SENSEI Ono, the martial arts teacher, yelled to the group, ending the practice.

All the students, including Junsaku, stopped, bowed to their teacher, and slipped their bokkens into the soft canvas belts tied around their waists.

'That concludes today's training. Pack up your things and go home,' the master instructed.

A cloud of disappointment settled over Junsaku as training ended. Although his body occasionally bruised and ached from the rigorous sessions, he treasured each moment spent in practice. During those exhilarating hours, he felt alive, his heart racing with the thrill of pushing his limits, and each demonstration of skill gave him a rush of adrenaline, making every drop of sweat and momentary pain worth it.

As Junsaku bent down to pick up his bag, someone forcefully knocked him from behind, shoving him off balance. He tumbled forward, and his hands smacked the earth as he landed on his knees. He quickly stood back up, coarse dirt clinging to his gi, and looked to see what or who had hit him. His eyes snapped to the figure of Tako standing before him, a mocking sneer twisting his lips.

'Watch where you are going, peasant,' Tako hissed, his voice dripping with contempt. 'You got me in trouble today with the teacher, and you will face the consequences.' Tako's hands clenched into fists at his sides as he stepped closer to Junsaku, determined to make him feel the weight of his wrath.

Junsaku, courageous and determined, moved forward rapidly, closing the space between himself and the bully, their chests nearly touching in a silent standoff.

Sensei Ono's voice suddenly cut through the air like a thunderclap, reverberating across the training grounds. 'I said go home!' he bellowed, causing both boys to startle and break their fierce gaze.

With a wicked smile, Tako growled, 'This is not over, peasant.'

Junsaku watched as Tako strode confidently across the dusty training grounds, his footsteps kicking up small clouds of earth. At the far end of the field, Tako's father sat atop a powerful-looking horse, his hands gripping the reins of a second, unridden steed that stood patiently beside him, its black coat gleaming in the sunlight. When Tako arrived, he effortlessly lifted himself into the empty saddle of the horse and took the reins. With a gentle nudge of his heels, Tako and his horse were moving, matched in pace with his father's mount as they trotted side by side and left the grounds.

***

JUNSAKU STOOD alone at the deserted training field, the late afternoon sun casting long shadows across the green grass. He searched, hoping to see his father emerge from the surrounding trees to walk home with him. As minutes stretched into what felt like an eternity, he released a deep, resigned sigh as disappointment washed over him like a cold breeze. The thought of making the thirty-minute trek home alone stung more than he cared to admit; he cherished every moment spent with his father.

Junsaku shifted his focus inward, seeking to balance his *chi*. Then, he slung his worn bag over his shoulder and began his journey home. As he walked, lost in thought, Junsaku absentmindedly kicked stones, following their path as they skittered to the roadside, hoping he might be lucky to meet his father along the route. Just then, the distinct sound of hooves approaching from behind caught Junsaku's attention.

Junsaku went to the road's edge to allow the horses to pass, and when he saw the riders, his heart sank.

Tako and his father approached him on horseback. A foreboding figure, Tako's otosan dressed in the armour of a mounted samurai, including a blue lacquered breastplate, leather coverings on his legs, an iron helmet on his head shaped like a dome, and his long and short swords, his *daisho*, hanging from the left side of his

17

waist. As the two approached, Tako leaned in slightly and whispered something into his father's ear. Instantly, Tako's father's demeanour shifted; his eyes narrowed into slits as they shot toward Junsaku, burning with an intensity that seemed to pierce the air between them.

When both riders were directly in front of Junsaku, they stopped their horses, slid off the saddles, and hit the dirt with a faint thump.

Junsaku stood frozen in place, his heart pounding in his chest like a drum. Confusion washed over him, and he stood motionless, wondering what would happen next.

Then, Tako spoke. 'Bow to my otosan, peasant,' he demanded.

With a puzzled expression, Junsaku bowed deeply, his brows furrowed as he struggled to comprehend the situation.

Tako's father stepped forward, very close to Junsaku, and said in a low grumble, 'You have caused my son dishonour, boy. This sort of behaviour will not be tolerated by a farmer's brat.'

Junsaku's confusion turned to rage as he straightened his posture. He lifted his chin defiantly and allowed his chest to puff out, a subtle attempt to project an air of strength despite his youth. 'My father is not a farmer,' he declared, his voice steady and unwavering. 'Like you, he is a samurai.'

Tako and his father laughed loudly, making Junsaku's blood boil. Junsaku clenched his fists, the heat rising in his chest, and then inhaled deeply, attempting to calm the storm brewing inside him. As he tried to steady himself, he recalled his father's words: *Practice patience and fight only when necessary.'*

'We will settle this now,' Tako's father stated. 'Tako, use your bokken and teach this peasant a lesson in respect.'

Tako slid his wooden sword from the worn belt around his

waist. The boy's dark eyes danced with anger as he stepped toward Junsaku. Junsaku instinctively pulled out the wooden sword secured in his canvas belt, the smooth handle familiar in his palm, and knew he had no choice but to fight.

Suddenly, a commanding voice yelled, 'Enough!', the words shattering the tense atmosphere. Instantly, all eyes turned toward the source. Junsaku's father, Goto, approached the group, holding his walking stick. A steely determination settled over Goto's face, transforming his usual calm demeanour into the fierce intensity of a tiger. 'What is the meaning of this, Nagao?' Goto demanded, his tone resonating with an unmistakable authority. In the bright sunlight, Junsaku could see a bonfire behind his father's brown eyes, a reflection of his warrior spirit, and Junsaku felt proud and confident that his father would support and protect him.

'Watch yourself,' Tako's father replied sharply. 'I am Nagao-sama to you. Your boy has insulted my son's honour at school today, and now they will resolve it with their wooden swords and fists.'

Goto's face flushed bright red as he stated sternly, 'Junsaku, come here.'

Junsaku dashed towards his father, who protectively positioned himself in front of his son, blocking him. From behind, Junsaku peered around his father's hip towards where Nagao stood, curious how the situation would unfold.

'There will be no fighting,' Goto declared.

Nagao rested his hand on the hilt of his katana sword and replied to Goto, 'There will be a fight, and it will be them or us. Which do you choose?'

Goto's right hand inched towards the swords secured at his left hip, silently preparing for what could come next.

'Wait!' Junsaku exclaimed, grabbing the hem of his father's

jacket and yanking on it. 'Otosan, this is my fight. Let me win my own battle.'

Goto slowly relaxed his arms at his side, his eyes locked intently on his son. A surge of pride filled his chest, accompanied by an unsettling knot in his stomach as he contemplated Junsaku's abilities as he neared ten years old, wondering whether or not his boy could win this fight. Then, his thoughts drifted to Tako, a boy physically larger than his son, and a wave of anxiety washed over him. Taking a steadying breath, Goto met his son's intense, dark brown eyes, recognising the resolve of a young warrior, and posed the question, 'Ōkami, do you truly feel prepared for this? Keep in mind, there is no room for mistakes.'

Junsaku stood tall, squaring his shoulders as he looked his father in the eyes. 'I am certain I will win, Otosan,' he responded firmly. 'This bullying needs to end now.'

Goto sighed and touched Junsaku's shoulder assuredly. Turning to Tako and Nagao, Goto spoke with determination. 'They will settle their dispute with bokkens, and no matter who emerges victorious, this fight will end their conflict once and for all.'

Nagao waved his hand dismissively and said to Tako, 'Ready yourself.'

As Junsaku stood with his wooden sword, taking deep breaths, Goto whispered, '*Mushin*: no mind. Look to the mountain beyond,' before nodding and stepping away from his son.

As the two boys faced each other, bokkens ready, Junsaku bowed to his opponent.

'I do not bow to insolent peasants. I crack their heads,' Tako said smugly.

'Without warning, Tako lunged at Junsaku with his wooden sword raised high, confident he would end the fight with one blow.

As he let his bokken fall to deliver a powerful strike aimed at Junsaku's head, Junsaku swiftly sidestepped to the left and, in one fluid motion, raised his wooden sword to the right, intercepting Tako's bokken and stopping it with a resounding crack. Next, Junsaku deftly lowered his wooden sword and swept it between himself and his opponent, executing a smooth pivot to the right and landing an upward strike on Tako's right elbow.

Tako let out a pained cry as his right hand slipped from the wooden sword's hilt while his left hand managed to maintain its grip on the bokken. This unexpected display of Tako's skill slightly impressed Goto, who had anticipated that the boy would drop his weapon. Yet even though Tako still held his sword with one hand, he did not have time to reposition; Junsaku had already moved behind him.

Junsaku launched forward, executing a powerful downward swing that struck Tako's left shoulder. The sheer force of the blow caused Tako's fingers to slip from the hilt of his bokken, and he lost his grip. Tako's wooden sword followed him to the ground as he fell to his knees and released a gut-wrenching howl of pain. As Junsaku advanced toward Tako with his sword raised, intent on delivering the decisive blow to end the fight, a sudden grip on the collar of his gi lifted him off the ground.

Junsaku found himself hanging in mid-air like a piece of laundry hung out to dry. As Junsaku's feet hovered inches above the dirt, he turned and looked to see who trapped him; he saw Nagao, Tako's father. Then, off to his right, Junsaku witnessed his father charging towards Nagao at lightning pace. Goto, filled with fury, bent slightly at the waist and swiftly maneuvered his left arm under Nagao's right arm, extending it across the man's chest. At the same time, he skilfully positioned his left leg behind Nagao and exerted force, delivering a powerful slam into the samurai's right side. The energy and impact of Goto's move caused Nagao to lose his grip on Junsaku, and he dropped the boy, who hit the dirt with a thump before quickly jumping to his feet, shaken but unhurt.

The sudden impact of Goto's attack caused Nagao to crash to the ground, landing on his back and knocking the air out of his lungs. The samurai lay momentarily still, steadying his breathing, then slowly rose to his feet, regaining his balance. Locking eyes with Goto, he could see his fury mirrored in Goto's steely stare, and Nagao reached for his sword.

'No,' Goto commanded, shaking his head as he raised his hand, palm facing outward, signalling for the fighting to cease. 'I will not fight you with a sword.'

Ignoring Goto's attempt for peace, Nagao unsheathed his katana and attacked. Junsaku's father remained eerily still as Nagao charged him. Then, Goto sprang into action, moving with incredible speed and agility, so fast that Junsaku struggled to keep track of his movements.

Before Junsaku could fully comprehend what had happened, the katana slipped from Nagao's grasp and arched through the air, landing near where Junsaku stood. Then, Nagao collapsed facedown onto the dusty earth with a forceful grunt, defeated.

Stunned, Tako looked at his father lying on the ground, motionless.

Junsaku's stomach formed a lump as he thought worriedly, *'My father killed him.'*

As the boys stood in shocked silence, their eyes locked on Nagao sprawled motionless on the road, Junsaku observed no sign of blood. Suddenly, Nagao writhed on the ground as Goto stepped forward, towering over him, peering at the defeated samurai, his walking stick held upright at his side, its tip planted firmly on the ground.

Junsaku noticed Tako's pained expression and approached him. 'Your father is still alive, Tako,' Junsaku reassured, gently placing a hand on the boy's shoulder to comfort him. 'My otosan did not raise his sword. There is no blood. He defeated your father with his walking stick.'

Tako blinked rapidly before rushing to his father's side, dropping to his knees, and assisting his father in rolling onto his back.

As Nagao and Tako looked up at Goto, who stood tall and imposing, Goto's eyes flashed with a mixture of anger and authority as he delivered his stern warning: 'Nagao, never lay a hand on my son again, or your boy will be carrying your head home in a basket.' Then, Goto turned and said, 'Come, Junsaku. Let us go home. Your mother will have supper ready.'

***

GOTO DRAPED his arm over Junsaku's shoulders as they leisurely walked home.

'You could have killed him, right?' Junsaku questioned.

Goto redirected the conversation. 'What did you learn today, Ōkami?

Junsaku paused momentarily, contemplating his response to the question, and, after a brief silence, declared, 'Do not mess with my otosan!' looking at his father affectionately.

Goto laughed heartily, his eyes sparkling with amusement as he reached out and playfully flicked Junsaku's top knot with his fingers. In a voice light and teasing, he said to his son, 'Junsaku, you are intolerable.' As they walked the final few minutes to their house, Goto placed his hand on Junsaku's upper back. 'Junsaku, I am proud of you. You stood up for right and fought with honour and skill.'

Junsaku's face lit up with a radiant smile, and his cheeks

blushed as if coloured by the soft pink of the setting sun that dipped gracefully behind the rugged mountains.

FIVE

DAYS BEFORE his tenth birthday, the time came for young Junsaku to leave for the samurai training academy, *Shiraki ryū*, in the town of Hirosaki in the Aomori prefecture. Despite feeling sad at being several days away from his family, Junsaku could hardly contain his excitement at knowing he would become a samurai. Adrenaline coursed through him as he filled a small trunk with his clothes, wooden sword, gi, and once-white karate belt, now a dark shade of grey because of years of hard work and dedication to learning martial arts.

Ready for his new adventure, Junsaku closed his bedroom door and joined his family in the front yard. 'Otosan, Okasan, and Etsuko, I will miss seeing you each day. But, as a warrior like Otosan, I must follow my path,' Junsaku said, standing tall, his posture straight and proud.

'Hai, Ōkami. You are on your way to becoming a great samurai,' his father replied.

A single tear escaped his mother's eye and trickled over her high cheekbone like water over a ledge. She reached out, pulled Junsaku to her, and held him tightly. 'Junsaku, I will miss you. Your otosan will visit you often, and when Etsuko and I can make the journey, we will join him.'

Junsaku gently lowered Etsuko to the ground, and without hesitation, she darted towards her mother, her tiny arms outstretched. Chiba scooped her daughter up, holding her at her side, and Etsuko settled on her mother's right hip. Junsaku shook his head, an amused smile on his lips. He felt the familiar confusion wash over him as he tried to understand why he had upset his sister. Yet, he had become indifferent to her outbursts and now laughed it off.

'Junsaku, it is time,' his father stated.

'Hai, Otosan,' Junsaku replied, nodding. Junsaku went to his mother and wrapped his arms around her slender waist, deftly manoeuvring to keep his distance from his sister, who still balanced on his mother's hip. Then, he released his embrace, looked her in the eyes, and said, 'I will make our family proud, Okasan. I promise.'

'I know you will, son,' she replied gently, resting her fingers lightly on his cheek, her eyes shimmering with unshed tears.

Junsaku went to the sturdy wooden cart, where his father sat on the front bench wearing a straw, conical hat on his head, holding the reins. With a burst of energy, Junsaku scrambled into the carriage and plopped beside his otosan, and his father flicked the leather straps, signalling the ox to walk. As Junsaku's wooden box of belongings rattled in harmony with the cart's movement, he turned to look back at his home. He could see his mother and sister standing on the cobblestone street. His mother enthusiastically waved goodbye while his sister, clutching her beloved doll tightly to her chest, stood beside her, motionless. At that moment, Junsaku felt a bittersweet tug at his heart, a twinge of sadness at leaving his home mixed with exhilaration for his journey ahead

SIX

SIX YEARS passed, and Junsaku had worked hard at *Shiraki ryū*, rising to the top of his class by age sixteen. Junsaku's father made the long, arduous journey from their home as frequently as possible to visit his son, and today Goto stood in front of Junsaku's teacher, a probing gaze on his face, and asked, 'How is his progress, Eizo-san? Is Junsaku ready to become a samurai in Daimyo Suketoki's guard?'

'He is my best student, Goto-san. He has the fearless soul of a warrior. He trains all hours of the day, meditates, and follows instructions. I have heard rumours that Suketoki will be coming soon to view the students, and I am confident the daimyo will want Junsaku to join his samurai guard.'

'*Subarashī*. Excellent,' his father responded, standing tall, his hands cupped behind his back. '*Domo arigato gozaimasu, Eizo-san.*'

Goto made his way to the dojo, the sound from the training room reverberating in the wooden beams of the hallway as he walked. He found Junsaku sparring with another boy inside the dojo, both wielding wooden swords. Watching his son, Goto couldn't help but feel a swell of pride as he admired Junsaku's impeccable technique, a testament to Junsaku's self-discipline and dedication.

'*Konnichiwa*, Otosan,' Junsaku said, sliding his bokken into the black obi tied around his waist.

'Konnichiwa, Ōkami,' his father replied, putting his right hand on Junsaku's shoulder. 'Your sensei tells me you are excelling in your studies.'

With a bright grin, Junsaku responded, 'Yes, and I live by the code, Otosan.'

'The code?' Goto understood what Junsaku referred to, yet he felt his son needed to articulate the answer to reinforce his learning.

'Bushido. The way of the warrior,' Junsaku declared. He then enthusiastically recited the fundamental values: justice, courage, benevolence, politeness, sincerity, honour, loyalty, and self-control.

His father leaned closer, studying his son's face. 'And which of these values poses the greatest challenge for you, Ōkami?'

Junsaku sighed thoughtfully. 'Self-control, Otosan. I often struggle with impatience and must constantly remind myself to rein in my emotions.'

'Hai,' his father replied with a nod. After a momentary pause, he asked, 'What about justice, Ōkami? Do you recall our conversations?'

'Yes, Father. I will never forget what you told me. Like ōkami, the wolf, you told me to practise non-violence and engage in battle only when necessary. You explained that my actions must be rooted in pursuing peace and justice and that I should never take a life for greed or wealth.'

'*Kashikoi*, Junsaku. You are wise, my son. When you are

serving the daimyo or, if fortune smiles upon you, the shogun, you may not always be able to choose, but in your heart and soul, you must always choose justice. Do not kill for the sake of killing.'

'Hai, Otosan. Also, I am learning English here and am good at it. As a boy, I practised at home. Do you remember? I even spoke English with the spirit boy who visited me as a child, though he has not appeared in a long time.'

Goto tilted his head, his brows furrowed. 'Ōkami, I never understood why you want to speak English. Why not Portuguese? Or Chinese?'

'During the visits from the ghost, he told me that English was my old language. If only Okasan were still alive, I would love to share with her how much I have improved in English and discuss the other wonderful things I am learning at school. I can picture her sitting by the fire, delighting in my stories.' Junsaku's words drifted off, and his gaze turned toward the ground. With a look of sorrow clouding his expression, he softly murmured, 'I miss her so much. I wish I could have been at home when she passed on.'

'Son, your okasan felt your presence even though you were not physically there. Your mother's death came quickly—much sooner than any of us could have foreseen.' He swallowed, struggling to hold back his emotions. 'Even though she is physically gone, Junsaku, your okasan will always be close to you, watching over you.'

'Hai, Otosan.' With a subtle shift in tone, Junsaku steered the conversation in a different direction. 'Now, tell me, what has become of my sister, Etsuko?' he inquired, his eyes shimmering with curiosity and subtle disdain.

'Stubborn as ever. Etsuko does well in school, learning flower arrangement, calligraphy, and even tea service, and the teachers are preparing her to become a fine wife. Etsuko also told your mother she wants to marry someday. In the village, a young man named Onishi has taken a liking to her. However, at seventeen, he is several years her senior, and Etsuko, only eleven, is still too young. Nevertheless, I cannot help but wonder if, as she matures into a teenager, she might develop feelings for him. I suspect if Onishi continues to be interested in her, they could end up together in the future.' Goto pressed his lips together, sighed deeply through his nose, and said, 'Now, let us talk about you again. Your teacher says you are doing well in all areas of study, especially martial arts. The daimyo will be coming soon. Remember, our ancestors are descendants of the Tochigi clan, the same as the daimyo himself. When he sees your talent and finds out you share his bloodline, I am confident he will make you one of his guards, and then you can continue my legacy.'

He felt a deep sense of purpose swell within him. 'I am ready, Otosan. I will be most honoured to serve his lordship.' Junsaku's path was solid in his mind, and he longed to fulfil his destiny and become a legend, a samurai whose name would echo through the ages.

SEVEN

JUNSAKU ENTERED the dojo wearing his white gi and black hakama, skirt-like trousers. He loved training in the sprawling space, with its natural, earthy colours, tightly woven tatami mats, thick beams of burnt cherry wood with ochre-coloured walls, and the numerous large windows that lined the room, providing abundant natural light and views of the garden. A painting of cranes standing amidst bamboo stalks spanned an entire wall, and adjacent to it, on the ceiling, a striking painting portrayed two magnificent, fire-breathing dragons in vibrant shades of red, orange, and gold, their jaws wide open, revealing sharp teeth and forked tongues.

Yasafune waited for Junsaku inside the training room, his hand resting on the hilt of his wooden bokken. The young men, both similar in stature, had their jet-black hair tied in a knot at the crown of their heads. They bowed toward each other, slid their wooden swords from their belts, held them vertically in front of their torsos, and remained still for several seconds. Then, their weapons flew into action, and the sparring began, their swords slicing the air.

Junsaku bent and twisted, dodging Yasafune's wooden

bokken as his opponent targeted his head, neck, and chest, his mouth curved into a sly grin. Both fighters were light on their feet, gliding over the bamboo floor in all directions. At one point, Yasafune took rapid steps backwards, stopped, and steadied his body. Then, he raised his sword and exploded, lunging at Junsaku, who angled his blade in front of his forehead and blocked Yasafune's wood sword before it reached his face. They pressed their weapons together, both young men using their power and weight to hold off their opponent, and then Junsaku shot out his right leg, whacked his rival with a low spin kick, and cut him down like a tree, sending Yasafune's sword spiralling through the air before it landed on the mat.

Junsaku stared down at Yasafune, who lay flat on his back. He placed the blunt tip of his wooden sword in the centre of his rival's neck, looked directly into his deep-set eyes, and said, 'Not bad. You are improving.' Then, Junsaku slid his bokken into his belt and held out his hand, helping Yasafune rise to his feet.

'Give me another chance. I am a better fighter than you!'

'You keep practising, and maybe someday you will be as good as me, but I doubt it,' Junsaku said with a teasing smirk, a light chuckle escaping his lips. Then, something caught Junsaku's attention near the spot where Yasafune's wooden sword lay on the mat. Junsaku saw a ghostly figure near the wall, towering eight feet tall with the broad shoulders of a man, obscured by a shroud of darkness from head to toe as though encased in the black smoke of a fire. Junsaku had encountered ghost's before, but this spirit was different, sending shivers down his spine. Junsaku stood frozen, his bokken hanging limply at his side, and stared at the ghostly figure, which gradually dissolved before his eyes and vanished. 'This may sound like a strange question,

Yasafune, but did you see something over there?' he questioned, pointing to the spot where the spirit appeared.

Yasafune drummed his fingers against the thick, cotton pants of his gi. 'Do not try to change the subject, Junsaku. Admit that I am improving, and someday I will beat you.'

At that point, Junsaku knew only he had seen the ghost. Junsaku shrugged, smiled at Yasafune, and said, 'You are delusional, friend. A cup of sake will bring you back to reality.'

EIGHT

JUNSAKU'S SCHOOL sat at the far end of the main cobble-stone street of Hirosaki, the road shaded by trees bursting with gold, green, and red leaves. Wood and thatched-roofed houses and shops lined the roadside, including seventy-five exclusive samurai homes. Perched atop a small hill at the opposite edge of town stood the daimyo's fortress, constructed from Japanese cypress wood and stone. A moat surrounded all sides of the castle's steep, piled-stone walls, with a single orange-red bridge leading to a massive wooden gate, and within the tallest structure of the castle complex lived Daimyo Suketoki.

Eleven years earlier, upon assuming power, Daimyo Suketoki commissioned the construction of a prestigious samurai academy to train the local warriors. Labourers built a grand central hall, ten dedicated training rooms, fifty student living quarters, and beautiful gardens. When construction finished, the daimyo christened the academy *Shiraki ryū* and entrusted its leadership and operations to Shihan Eizo, the foremost martial arts instructor in the Aomori region, who dedicated himself to honing the students' martial prowess and preparing them to serve as formidable warriors in the daimyo's army.

Recently, Shihan Eizo received word that the daimyo would be conducting a surprise visit to the school to gather recruits, and he began preparations to be ready. One mid-day, while teachers and students ate soba noodles with dipping sauce for lunch, they heard marching feet in the distance, growing louder as the daimyo and his accompanying samurai approached.

'Hurry, he is arriving,' Shihan Eizo announced. 'Clean this up, and have the women prepare tea and sake.'

The students cleared the tables and wiped the polished wood surfaces with damp cloths, finishing just as the daimyo entered the school grounds with his army.

The infantry lined up in rows of four, ten rows deep, followed by sixteen samurai on horseback, each soldier with their daisho, a matching set of long and short swords, hanging near their left hip. All the samurai wore black lacquer chest plates called dou, their arms and legs covered by thick leather flaps, and iron helmets displaying the shamrock emblem of Daimyo Suketoki's Tochigi clan painted with gold leaf.

Daimyo Suketoki, an average-sized man with narrow shoulders and hips, entered on the lead horse, dressed in the same body armour as his samurai warriors, except the eboshi on his head, a hat made from starched, black fabric, moulded and lacquered to look like a dolphin's fin.

'Yasafune, are you excited?' Junsaku asked his friend.

'Hai. I want to join the daimyo's samurai guard.'

'As do I. I will be going with the daimyo today. There is no doubt in my mind.'

'How do you know?'

'Because I have trained for this moment my whole life. More importantly, I have envisioned working for the leaders of Japan since as early as I can remember. And, the truth is, I am the best,' Junsaku boasted, raising his right eyebrow. 'No one is better than me, not even you.'

Yasafune laughed aloud before stifling his amusement for fear of reprimand from Shihan Eizo.

The daimyo dismounted his horse, stood on the gravel path, and said to a foot soldier, '*Rirakkusu.*' The samurai repeated the phrase to the other warriors, and the small army of soldiers relaxed, dropped their shoulders, and rested their hands at their sides.

The daimyo removed his outer armour, handing it to a waiting foot soldier, and revealed a bright blue jacket and loose-fitting pants underneath. He approached the group of teachers and students lined up and standing obediently, their torsos slightly bent, their eyes aimed downward, and said to Shihan Eizo, 'Konnichiwa, Eizo-san. It is good to see you, old friend. Let us share *nihonshu* before the exhibition.'

'Of course, Suketoki-sama. You are our most honoured guest. Come and sit.'

The daimyo followed Eizo to a small outdoor space adjacent to the main hall. They sat at a low table, and Daimyo Suketoki sat on the floor cushion, folding his legs, as Shihan Eizo rang a small brass bell. A teenage girl dressed in a turquoise kimono embroidered with red cranes arrived carrying a tray with a carafe of sake. Both teacher and daimyo held their small cups while the girl poured the drink, her fingers delicately touching the neck and base of the carafe.

'Beautiful,' the daimyo said, his voice filled with admiration as he looked at the girl's petite frame and pale golden skin.

The young girl smiled demurely and bowed, a blush kissing her cheeks, before hurrying away.

'So, Eizo-san, who do you think I will choose to join my guard?'

'Suketoki-sama, you can select from eight of my best students. I suspect the son of your cousin, Goto Aoyama, will be your top choice. His name is Junsaku.'

'I look forward to seeing how he performs in the demonstrations. Can he ride a horse?'

'He is an excellent rider. He is also highly intelligent, an exceptional martial artist, speaks some English, and strongly understands and appreciates bushido. He will make a fine samurai,' Shihan Eizo praised. 'Now, let me tell you about the demonstrations today. You will witness four challenges by the students. First, they will recite haiku and afterwards demonstrate their skills in archery, hand-to-hand combat, and finally, the bokken.'

'*Kanpai*,' replied the daimyo, lifting his cup and tipping rice wine down his throat.

***

AFTER INDULGING in two carafes of sake, the daimyo's spirits soared. 'Time to find my next samurai!' he announced.

The daimyo followed Shihan Eizo to a large room with a sign above the door that read *The Hall of the Crane*. The men replaced their shoes with straw slippers, slid open the paper-covered shoji panels, and entered the hall.

Forty-two spectators crowded the edges of the tatami mats inside the exhibition room. The eight chosen competitors stood across from the main entrance, their backs near the wall, each wearing baggy black pants, a loose-fitting white jacket tied with a black sash, and carrying no weapons. The competitors bowed to the daiymo and their master before standing at attention, waiting for their command. '*Chūi!*' Shihan Eizo declared. 'I will divide you into two groups. Junsaku, Kime, Matsu, and Orochi, move to your right. Yasafune, Botan, Hideki, and Yamato, step to your left.'

With the boys assembled, Shihan Eizo continued. 'Your first demonstration is haiku. Your poem must reflect bushido and be new to our ears. We will start with you, Yasafune. Please step forward and honour our daimyo with your haiku.'

Before Yasafune left the group of boys, he turned towards Junsaku and bent at the waist. Junsaku returned his bow, and Yasafune walked towards the daimyo.

Yasafune bowed to the daimyo, who sat in an oversized wooden chair, the wide sleeves of his royal blue haori jacket draped over the edges. Then, sixteen-year-old Yasafune straightened his spine and inhaled deeply.

As Yasafune opened his mouth to recite his haiku, the daimyo interrupted. 'Why did you bow to your opponent before sharing your poem?'

Yasafune's mahogany brown eyes widened. 'Suketoki-sama, even though I am in the biggest competition of my life, and I know winning will bring great honour to my family and my teacher, Junsaku is a samurai at heart, and we are brothers of bushido. For these reasons, I show him honour and respect.'

The daimyo rubbed his bristly chin and squinted his eyes, staring intensely at Yasafune.

Yasafune's heart raced.

After several seconds, Daimyo Suketoki said, 'Arigato, Yasafune-kun. Return to the group. There is no need for you to recite a haiku. No poem could capture the essence of bushido better than your actions.'

Yasafune bowed, straightened, thrust out his chest, and raced back to the boys, his joy evident in his sparkling eyes.

Junsaku, already jittery, felt a surge of anxiety quicken his pulse. He initially planned to present a haiku about the tree frog. However, based on what he witnessed between the daimyo and Yasafune, he knew his poem would need to be more meaningful to win, and he had to think fast.

'Junsaku, step forward and recite your haiku,' directed Shihan Eizo.

Before approaching Daimyo Suketoki, Junsaku bowed to Yasafune. As he walked towards his lordship, he invented a new poem. Before beginning, he turned to the daimyo, bowed, then stood tall and delivered his haiku, his voice deep and powerful, the words clear in his mind.

> 'Fire, ice, steel, tension.
> Wind, water, willow tree bends.
> Sword does not control.'

A satisfied smile spread across the daimyo's face. 'Very insightful, Junsaku-kun.'

Shihan Eizo lifted his chin, impressed by his two top students. 'Botan, come forward. Share your haiku,' the master said, inviting the next student.

Boton, inches shorter than Junsaku and smaller framed, bowed before his judges and then straightened. He tipped back his head, met the gaze of the seated daimyo, and began his haiku.

> 'Deer drinking water.
> Cool and fresh it is.
> He is barely thirsty.'

The daimyo twisted his lips, cocked his head, and stared at Boton, who seemed to shrink in place, his shoulders melting towards the floor. After several seconds of silence, Boton bowed, turned, and walked briskly back to join the competitors, knowing he failed his test.

'Yamato, your turn,' Shihan Eizo announced.

The demonstration of haiku continued until all eight boys completed the exercise. Shihan Eizo and the daimyo whispered to each other, periodically glancing at the anxious students. Then, Shihan Eizo rang a bronze bell and announced, 'Boton and Yamato, you are both eliminated.'

The boys left the competition, their heads slumped in defeat as they joined the spectators.

'Now, each group has three members. Round two will eliminate one member from each team. You will demonstrate *kyujutsu*. You are all skilled with the bow and arrow, so it is time to impress the daimyo.' Shihan Eizo signalled to several boys to prepare for kyujutsu. Two students placed round, cork targets on easels at the far wall, while six boys presented the competitors with their bows and arrows. 'You will only have three arrows. Your goal is to hit the white mark in the centre. Matsu, you go first.'

Fifteen-year-old Matsu positioned his feet, grabbed an arrow from the pack hanging over his shoulder, and placed it in the bow, drawing the bowstring to his ear before letting the projectile fly. The arrow failed to hit the white dot, a spot no bigger than a walnut, and landed on the outer edge of the target. After shooting all three, Matsu could not land an arrow in the bullseye.

Hideki took his turn next, proving unsuccessful in hitting the centre target. Then, Kime and Orochi demonstrated their archery skills, each boy landing one arrow into the round, white bullseye. Yasafune followed Orochi, and two of his three arrows landed in the centre of the target, putting Yasafune in the clear lead.

The spectators whispered excitedly, the humid air electrified.

Junsaku's turn had come. He bowed to the daimyo, faced the

target, turned his body marginally, and breathed deeply, balancing his energy. He loaded the first arrow into his bow, pulled back, and released the string. The projectile flew forward, slicing through the sticky, summer air, and the arrowhead landed in the centre of the round target, piercing the circle on the hard cork. Junsaku repeated the exercise, and his second arrow landed on the bullseye again. His last arrow went straight through the two existing shafts, landed in the centre, and all three of Junsaku's arrows sprung from the target like reeds from the earth, mesmerising the crowd.

A low hum of curious voices filled the hall as Shihan Eizo and the daimyo whispered to each other. Again, Shihan Eizo rang the brass bell and said, 'Matsu and Hideki, you are both eliminated. Join the others. Junsaku, Yasafune, Orochi, and Kime, you are in the top four. You will show us your ability in hand-to-hand combat. Whoever avoids getting knocked out or held in submission will go to the final competition using the bokken. Yasafune and Kime, you will fight first.'

The boys bowed to the daimyo, turned to each other, assumed their stance, and prepared to fight.

Shihan Eizo shouted, '*Hajime!*'

Kime threw the first punch. Yasafune blocked with his left arm, sending Kime's arm to the right. Kime tried again, this time a hook punch. While Kime's fist moved towards Yasafune's jaw, Yasafune slid forward and to his left, avoiding Kime's powerful strike. Then, Yasafune twisted to his right and delivered a left elbow strike to Kime's jaw, causing the inside of his opponent's mouth to bleed. Kime delivered a right, backhand strike to Yasafune's face, which Yasafune blocked with his right arm before executing a straight left punch to the centre of Kime's sternum. Yasafune quickly wrapped his right arm around Kime's neck and attempted to drag him to the ground in a submission choke. However, Kime slid his foot forward, maintained his balance and posture, and wrapped both arms around Yasafune's torso as if hugging a tree. Kime pushed with his hips and forced his head against Yasafune's shoulder, using his whole body to avoid falling to the floor. It worked, and Kime escaped Yasafune's attempted chokehold. Yasafune delivered another straight punch to Kime's chest, and Kime blocked before hitting Yasafune in his right cheek with the back of his fist. Kime used both hands and clamped Yasafune's arm, attempting to get him into a lock. Yasafune bent his arm, creating strength in his elbow, and used his body weight to force Kime backwards.

The fight continued for almost ten minutes, each competitor taking blow after blow as they attempted to escape locks and chokes. Junsaku could see from the sidelines that Kime appeared tired. His movements were sluggish, his breathing rapid, and he looked fatigued. Yasafune took advantage of his opponent's weakness and performed a perfect shoulder throw. As Kime fell to the floor, his arm in Yasafune's grip, Yasafune shifted his body. Kime landed on his stomach, his chest hitting the mat, and with Kime's arm clenched in Yasafune's hands, Yasafune forced his competitor into submission. Facedown and powerless on the tatami mat, Yasafune subdued Kime in a wrist and shoulder lock until Kime tapped his fingers on the golden bamboo floor.

Shihan Eizo tinkled the brass bell, ending the fight, and said, 'Yasafune is the winner. Kime, you are eliminated.'

Yasafune helped Kime to his feet, and they bowed to each other before separating.

'Junsaku and Orochi, take your place on the mat.'

Junsaku stood on the tatami, is eyes as dark as a starless midnight. As he waited to start, he contemplated his strategy, thinking about all the hand-to-hand combat scenarios he played and re-played in his mind. Despite Orochi being as big as a barge, confi-dence coursed through Junsaku, and he anticipated a swift victory. The boys bowed to Daimyo Suketoki, and Shihan Eizo rang the bell.

Orochi charged Junsaku in hopes of mowing down his op-ponent. Junsaku stood firm, his toes curved towards the floor. As Orochi rushed forward, Junsaku lifted his right leg and executed a savage front kick square in Orochi's sternum. The power of Junsa-ku's kick stopped Orochi in his tracks and forced the air from his lungs. While Orochi tried to regain his breath, Junsaku delivered three lightning-fast knife hand strikes to his neck and jaw before moving forward swiftly and executing a powerful forearm strike to his upper chest.

Orochi fell backwards, hitting the bamboo mat with a thud, and a dead silence blanketed *The Hall of the Crane*. After Orochi lay on the floor for ten seconds, unmoving, his breathing shallow, Shihan Eizo ended the contest by ringing the bell.

Junsaku went to Orochi. The boy's eyes were open and glazed over, and he appeared to be steadying his breath. Junsaku reached out his hand, and Orochi accepted Junsaku's help and stood. Orochi sighed and bowed weakly to the daimyo, Shihan Eizo, and Junsaku before hobbling to the spectators, knowing he had lost the fight.

The moment had arrived. As Junsaku predicted, he would bat-tle his friend for a coveted spot as a samurai in the daimyo's guard. Junsaku focused on his mental and physical strategy to ensure a win.

'Junsaku and Yasafune, you will now participate in the final demonstration with the wooden sword. Go outside, get your bok-ken, and return.'

The boys bowed before leaving the hall.

Two younger students waited outside and handed the competitors their swords.

'Yasafune, you have fought well,' Junsaku remarked as he gripped the bokken tightly in his right fist. Then, with both hands, he began to slice the air, warming up for the challenge ahead.

Yasafune copied Junsaku's movements. 'You fought well, too. No matter who wins, let us promise to remain friends.'

'You have my word.' Junsaku smiled as he slid his bokken into his belt with a fluid motion.

The two warriors returned to the grand hall, where Shihan Eizo and Daimyo Suketoki awaited them. The competitors bowed deeply, stood straight, and awaited instructions, the air thick with the tension of the upcoming sword fight. Junsaku knew his strategy: force his opponent into submission or draw blood.

'Ready,' Shihan Eizo said. Both boys drew their bokkens and assumed their fighting stance. A moment later, Shihan Eizo yelled, 'Hajime!'

Immediately, it was clear that neither boy would allow the other an advantage as they fought with their wooden swords, each strike carefully calculated. Their bodies moved in all directions as they avoided contact, attempting straight lunges to the centre of the chest and crosscuts, moves that could have been lethal if the fighters had wielded real swords. The daimyo stood up from his chair, his mouth slightly open, riveted by the flawless techniques demonstrated by the two students. As they performed strikes, blocks, and counterstrikes with their bokkens, it appeared neither would be the victor. However, Junsaku finally saw his opening. Yasafune held his sword high over his right shoulder as his front foot angled, giving Junsaku the clue he needed. Junsaku knew that most of the time, Yasafune's posture, footwork, and hand placement gave nothing away, causing Junsaku to be unsure of where exactly Yasafune's wooden sword would land. However, right before his opponent delivered a downward strike, Junsaku noted that he continually moved his front foot in a particular way, and this slight movement provided Junsaku with everything he needed to predict his opponent's next move and plan his counterattack. Junsaku successfully blocked Yasafune's attempted downward strike before delivering a powerful shin kick to his opponent's mid-calf, causing Yasafune to drop like a felled tree. As Yasafune dropped towards the floor, Junsaku's wooden sword followed, and when Yasafune hit the tatami mats, Junsaku struck him hard on the neck, creating a purple-red welt on his skin.

The bell sounded. 'Junsaku wins this round,' announced Shihan Eizo.

The crowd erupted, cheering as Junsaku extended a hand and helped Yasafune to his feet.

'Congratulations, friend,' Yasafune said, massaging his neck. 'Good fight.'

'Hai,' Junsaku replied.

Shihan Eizo moved to the middle of the tatami mat. 'You will have tea while we discuss who Daimyo Suketoki chooses. Leave us, and we will call you back when his decision is made.'

The students exited the hall and entered the school's garden.

'Well done, Junsaku,' congratulated a teenage classmate. 'I did not think you would beat Yasafune with the bokken. Do you think you will be Daimyo Suketoki's choice?'

Junsaku put his arm around the boy's shoulders. 'I know I will be, Makoto. My whole life has led up to this moment.'

Junsaku could hear the lively chatter of students nearby. One boy said, 'I think he will pick Yasafune; he has truly earned his respect,' while another debated, 'No, it has to be Junsaku; he has excelled in everything.'

Then, the bell's low, resonant chime echoed through the air, and the students returned to *The Hall of the Crane*. The daimyo and their master sat in ornate wooden chairs as the teens approached. Junsaku and Yasafune bowed deeply, their hearts racing, then stood tall and waited to hear the daimyo's selection as a hush fell over the crowd.

The daimyo leaned back in his chair, both arms resting on the armrests. 'You both demonstrated great skill. I will tell you who won in each category. First, Yasafune is the haiku winner. Even though he did not recite a poem, his actions spoke louder than words. Though, Junsaku,' he commented, 'I did like your poem. Now, for the next three demonstrations, there is an obvious winner. Yasafune, who is the winner?'

Yasafune wanted to lie but could not. 'Junsaku.'

'Hai.' The daimyo looked directly into Junsaku's rich brown eyes. 'Junsaku, you showed outstanding skill in hand-to-hand combat, archery, and the bokken. I pick you to become a samurai in my guard.'

Junsaku smiled, his grin narrowing the moon-shaped scar near his lip. However, despite his happiness, the moment felt bittersweet; he felt disappointed for Yasafune, knowing how much his friend wanted to join the daimyo's samurai army.

The crowd of students loudly whispered until the daimyo's commanding voice silenced them. 'Quiet!' Suketoki's sharp gaze fell upon Yasafune. 'You will also join my guard. You proved you have the skills to be a great samurai, and the spirit of bushido is within you. You and Junsaku will leave for my castle this evening. Prepare your things. We leave at sundown.'

NINE

DURING HIS first two years working for Daiymo Suketoki, Junsaku made several journeys back to his family's village home in Kakunodate, mainly to visit his aging father, whom he cherished deeply. Within weeks of returning from his most recent trip home, Junsaku received a letter from his sister.

> *Brother,*
>
> *Otosan is dead. He became sick days after you left the village, unable to eat or drink. We tried to save him but could not. He is buried next to Okasan at Kurodani. My husband, Onishi, will move us to his family home in the village of Mibaru on the island of Okinawa. I will take what I want from our parents' possessions and sell any valuables so that Onishi and I have money. I will leave any items I do not want in the house, which you can have, though I expect there will be little left for you.*
>
> *Etsuko*

Junsaku felt no surprise at his sister's blunt harshness. Despite the passing years, the truth remained painfully evident: his sister remained unchanged, her cold heart shut to him even after the loss of both their parents. With his mother and father gone, Junsaku realised that the only things that mattered now were his friend Yasafune and his burning desire to continue his pursuit of becoming Japan's greatest samurai.

***

IN THE first years of living at the castle, Junsaku shared a modest, cramped room near the outer wall with Yasafune. The decades-old room held the scuffs and marks of hundreds of occupants who had come and gone, with uneven walls constructed from weathered timber and clay and worn tatami mats covering the dirt floor. A single, solitary square window allowed light to filter into the room, and the air smelled of the pungent aromas from the nearby horse stables, a mixture of sweat, manure, and ammonia. Junsaku woke at sunrise each day and went to bed after dark, exhausted from his daily routine. He was assigned to spend twelve hours each day standing guard at the castle gates, dressed in heavy leather armour and a metal helmet that strained his neck. To further prove his ambition, he also purposely sought personal, one-on-one training from the daimyo's most accomplished masters and drilled daily.

At eighteen, Junsaku and Yasafune became foot soldiers and moved to a more spacious room in a building at the heart of the castle complex. With its solid dark wood walls, this impressive structure sheltered nearly two hundred and fifty of the daimyo's highly trained guards, and each private chamber featured clean tatami mats and large windows that allowed the residents views of the meticulously maintained gardens.

As part of Suketoki's aggressive war strategy, Junsaku and Yasafune participated in four successful battles over three years, which added more land and wealth to the daimyo's growing network. Amidst the chaos of war, Junsaku outshone hundreds of fellow foot soldiers on the battlefield, gaining further notice from the army leaders and, at age twenty-one, Junsaku's talents earned him a prestigious new rank as a mounted samurai, receiving a horse and a private residence in the village, a symbol of his new position. Yasafune, also twenty-one and still a foot soldier, fell in love and married a seventeen-year-old girl from the local village named Kurakawa, who, after one year of marriage, gave birth to a baby boy named Nobushida.

Junsaku achieved a captain's rank in the daimyo's army by twenty-four. Tall, lean, and muscular, Junsaku pulled his shoulder-length black hair into a high knot, emphasizing his high cheekbones and dark, penetrating eyes, giving him the fierce look of a wild tiger. In Junsaku's new role, he also wielded the power to propel Yasafune's career and, in recognition of his friend's exceptional skills, Junsaku promoted Yasafune to the role of mounted samurai, including the benefit of a private residence in the village for him and his family.

One chilly afternoon in autumn, Junsaku planned a training session with Yasafune.

'Konnichiwa, Yasafune,' Junsaku said as he entered the dojo.

'Konnichiwa, Captain.'

Slim, muscular, and slightly shorter than Junsaku, the top of Yasafune's head reached the centre of Junsaku's forehead. His amber eyes, set high above sharply contoured cheekbones, stretched wide as he said, 'It is still strange for me to call you Captain. It seems like just yesterday we were students at *Shiraki ryū*.' Then, Yasafune's eyebrows raised and pulled together. 'Before we start training, could I have a word?'

'Of course.'

'Join me,' Yasafune said, sitting cross-legged on the tatami mat. 'It is about my family.'

'What of your family?' Junsaku asked.

'If I die, Junsaku, would you care for my wife, Kurakawa, and my young boy, Nobushida? When I am gone, I am unsure how my wife will get by, especially because she has no family, and I fear something is wrong with her health. She is not physically strong. I know she may remarry, but until then, could you please watch over them if something happens to me?'

'Nothing will happen to you, Yasafune,' Junsaku reassured, his voice steady.

Yasafune rubbed the back of his neck and replied, 'But it might, and I cannot bear to go to the next life knowing they may struggle.'

'Fine,' Junsaku said, standing up and extending his arm. 'I will take care of your family if something happens to you. Now, get up, and let us practise hand-to-hand combat.'

Yasafune took hold of Junsaku's outreached hand and allowed him to lift him off the mat. 'You know we are going to war against Daimyo Yamaguchi in the Iwate prefecture, right? I knew the day would come when Daimyo Suketoki would attempt to overthrow Yamaguchi and seize his castle in Morioka,' Yasafune commented, crossing his arms.

'Hai, this is true.'

'Deep in my soul, I feel this next battle will be my last, Junsaku, so I need your word that you will care for my family if something happens to me.'

'For the last time, Yasafune, I will care for your family if you die. Maybe I will kill you now and get it over with,' he joked, assuming a fighting stance, dismissing his friend's worry as battlefield jitters, a common reaction to the looming threat of war.

AFTER PRACTICE, Junsaku and Yasafune left the castle and walked down the main cobblestone street to their homes. They arrived at Yasafune's house first, surrounded by a high stone wall with a single wooden gate for entry. Yasafune opened the thick gate as Kurakawa walked out of the house wearing a pink kimono that hugged her straight, curveless body, holding the hand of their little boy, Nobushida. She stopped next to a water basin and bowed, her eyes aimed at the ground, as the little boy stared at Junsaku with wide, brown eyes framed by long lashes. Kurakawa gently tugged her son's arm, and Nobushida bent into a lopsided bow.

'Konnichiwa, Kurakawa. Konnichiwa, Nobushida-san, and you can stand straight now,' Junsaku said, grinning at the toddler.

'Konnichiwa, Junsaku-san,' Kurakawa responded politely, her high-pitched voice reminiscent of a teenage girl. 'Would you like to come inside for tea or nihonshu?' As Kurakawa finished her sentence, a violent cough erupted from her throat. She quickly turned her head away and covered her mouth with her empty hand, the fingers of her other hand tightening around Nobushida's delicate fingers. Yasafune rushed to her side, wrapped his strong arm around her waist, and supported her frail body until the coughing gradually subsided. 'Gomennasai. My apologies,' she said shyly to both Yasafune and Junsaku.

'I hope the doctor can help rid you of that cough,' Junsaku said, his voice tinged with concern. 'And, as for sake or tea, thank you for the offer, but I will go home and rest after a long day. Yasafune, I will see you tomorrow at the castle.'

'Hai. Enjoy the rest of your night.'

Junsaku waved at little Nobushida with both hands, and the boy lifted his hands and wiggled his tiny fingers. Junsaku turned and left Yasafune's house, listening to the musical chirping of cicadas as he walked the short distance home, silently praying for Kurakawa's health to improve.

TEN

THE FOLLOWING morning, Junsaku went to the castle. As he approached the main gate, crossing the fiery orange bridge that spanned the moat, ice crystals from the changing season shimmering on the water's surface below, he heard a guard yell, 'Open the gate!' Junsaku stepped through the heavy, wooden gateway and walked briskly towards the castle tower at the centre of the complex to meet with the daimyo.

Passing through the courtyard, Junsaku noticed hundreds of samurai sitting on stone walls or directly on the ground, polishing breastplates and armour and sharpening katana and wakizashi blades, preparing for combat. When Junsaku reached the entrance to the castle tower, he touched the handle of his long sword and ordered a foot soldier to announce his arrival to Daimyo Suketoki. The samurai disappeared momentarily, then returned, saying, 'You may enter.'

Junsaku removed his shoes and slipped on V-shaped sandals. He walked down the main hallway and entered the room where the daimyo waited. Painted murals of bright green trees, azure lakes, and golden birds decorated the walls, and bamboo tatami mats covered the floor. In the centre of the room, a low, dark wood table had been placed, with ornately carved legs surrounded by rose-coloured silk cushions.

The daimyo sat on a floor cushion, his legs tucked beneath him, wearing a bright blue silk yukata. 'Ah, Junsaku! Sit,' he instructed. 'Tell me, are we ready to take ownership of the land in the Iwate Prefecture and Daimyo Yamaguchi's riches?'

'Hai, my lord, just a few final preparations,' Junsaku replied, removing his swords and placing them on the floor within arm's reach before folding his legs on a cushion. 'Also, I sent the scout Kito to Morioka. He will give us a report when we intercept him in the mountains. Our army will leave today at the high sun.'

The daimyo looked pleased. 'Hai, Junsaku. I will prepare for battle.'

***

ONE HOUR later, the daimyo exited the massive wooden doors of the central tower dressed in full battle gear and wearing a distinctive headpiece resembling the dorsal fin of a dolphin. In the field adjacent to the castle, eight hundred samurai waited, prepared for war. Among them were six hundred infantrymen, one hundred of whom carried red battle flags bearing the Tochigi clan's three-leaf shamrock emblem embroidered in yellow silk, and perched atop steeds were two hundred mounted samurai, their horses clad in protective chainmail, the sound of metal clinking lightly as the horses shifted in place. All the samurai wore black-lacquered metal breastplates adorned with the Tochigi clan emblem painted in lustrous gold leaf, leather flaps protecting their limbs, and metal helmets distinguished by a brass piece shaped like a crescent moon, firmly welded to the top.

Junsaku, Yasafune, and the daimyo climbed on their horses and joined the mounted samurai. Daimyo Suketoki turned his black stallion and faced his army, his horse jittery, as Junsaku rode up on his dapple grey and stopped at Suketoki's side.

'Kōgeki!' Junsaku yelled, his voice deep and guttural like the roar of a lion. Per the captain's orders, a soldier blew into a conch shell and trumpeted the beginning of the advance to Morioka.

For several hours, the army travelled on the road. As night approached and the sky transitioned from shades of blue to burnt orange and violet, a boy in loose pants and a tattered grey robe appeared from the trees. With urgency in his voice, he yelled, 'Captain!' as his eyes nervously scanned the surrounding forest.

Junsaku raised his arm high in the air. 'Tomaru!' he commanded. 'Do not attack. Kito is a scout. He is one of ours.'

The Japanese teen approached Junsaku and the daimyo. He bowed, his loose, black hair falling over his forehead, then stood rigidly with his arms at his sides. With a serious tone, he reported, 'Junsaku-san, the enemy knows you are coming. When I was in the village near the castle at Morioka four days ago, I saw samurai gearing up to fight, and I followed them into the mountains. They are waiting for you in Nibetsu. They have set up camp in the valley at Taehei. I watched and listened to as much as I could without being caught, and they expect your troops to enter via the road. It is there they plan to attack.'

Junsaku's rough fingers brushed against the stubble on his chin as he rubbed his jawline, pondering the situation, his brow furrowed in concentration. Then, he turned to Daimyo Suketoki, gestured toward the roadside, and spoke decisively: 'Suketoki-sama, instead of the road, we will use the secluded country paths that wind their way to the top of the mountain. From there, we will sneak up on the enemy encamped in the valley and strike.'

Daimyo Suketoki nodded.

'Also, we will keep additional samurai on elevated ground, enabling them to survey the valley below and fortify all sides, killing any samurai who attempt to flee. We will cover all sides, lock them in, and secure another victory for you.'

The daimyo tipped his head forward, signalling his agreement. Junsaku gestured to Yasafune to relay the message to the samurai leaders. Yasafune squeezed his calves, applied pressure to his horse, and left to share the plan.

After thirty minutes passed, he rode back to Junsaku, declared the men ready, and Junsaku commanded the army to march towards Nibetsu.

***

DAIMYO SUKETOKI'S samurai army followed narrow, winding paths carved between towering trees and dense canopy. Rich, green moss clung to the roots and rocks, the air cool and heavy with the earthy fragrance of damp soil. Finally, three days later, Daimyo Suketoki's army reached the rugged mountain ridge. From their high elevation, the samurai could see the enemy encampment in the valley below, their campfires flickering ominously in the darkness.

'Set up for the night; make sure the men stay quiet and no fires,' Junsaku whispered to his leaders. 'We attack at dawn.'

As dawn broke, casting a grey haze over the landscape, Junsaku assembled the army into five groups, with Yasafune, Morihiro, Okabe, Matsubara, and Shio leading the charge. Every samurai fastened a *menpō* to their helmets, hiding the lower half of their face. Made from thick leather and painted bright red, each mask featured a large, bulbous nose and a wide-open mouth displaying jagged, white teeth made from tiny animal bones. Four of the groups positioned along the rugged perimeter of the valley, their eyes scanning the terrain as they awaited Junsaku's command to attack and initiate the chaos of battle. Meanwhile, Shio and one hundred samurai positioned themselves along the jagged ridgeline of the mountains where they crouched low, blending into the rocky landscape, and waited, prepared to kill any man who attempted to flee the valley. Junsaku remained by the daimyo's side, accompanied by fifty mounted samurai, each ready to act in a final assault if required. Junsaku understood that his primary responsibility was to protect the daimyo from injury or death, and the burden weighed heavily on him.

As the army waited, the mountain breezes hummed lightly through the battle flags, and a samurai with a *horagai,* a large conch, stood quietly near Junsaku, awaiting the captain's order to blow into the shell and announce the start of the battle. The soldiers stood in tense silence, their breaths steady, while the horses shifted restlessly, their hooves scraping softly against the earth as they stomped and shuffled.

'Now, Junsaku?' whispered the daimyo.

'Hai. *Hajimeru,*' Junsaku commanded.

The samurai with the horagai brought the shell to his lips and, with a powerful exhalation, unleashed a rich, resonant *om* sound that reverberated through the crisp morning air, echoing for miles. In the valley below, the sound ignited a frenzy, the enemy scrambling like ants as the army of Daimyo Suketoki surged forward, unleashing a storm of arrows into the sky as they charged the valley floor.

Within minutes, the enemy army of Daimyo Yamaguchi had donned their armour and weapons and began fighting back. Warriors fought in close combat on the valley plain, samurai killing samurai. They speared their opponents with *naginata,* a polearm sword, piercing through bodies, and used katanas and wakizashis swords to decapitate, remove limbs, and stab the enemy.

Each time Junsaku saw one of Daimyo Suketoki's flags disappear from view, he knew another samurai had fallen and that his engagement in the battle drew nearer. After a short time, Junsaku said gravely, 'We must fight, Suketoki-sama. Are you ready?'

'Hai,' he replied, taking a deep breath.

'Hajimeru!' Junsaku shouted. The riders gripped their horses tightly, their thighs pressing against the warm, muscled bodies of the steeds, and, with a powerful surge, the horses galloped forward, their hooves thundering as they charged toward the lush valley below. When they reached the valley floor, Junsaku pulled his katana from its sheath and the first enemy samurai he encountered lost his head in one fell swoop, the soldier's body collapsing like a paper doll. As Junsaku stared at the decapitated body, he wondered if the man was a husband or a father, and the thought caused bile to rise in his throat which he swallowed back before shaking his head, returning his focus to the fight.

As Junsaku killed man after man, he noticed a fierce mounted samurai charging with alarming speed in the direction of Daimyo Suketoki. As Junsaku spurred his stallion towards his lordship, he watched the assailant's horse collide with the flank of Suketoki's mount, sending the daimyo and his horse crashing to the ground. As Junsaku neared, he watched in horror as the rival samurai dismounted, drew his katana, and raised the sword, intent on stabbing Daimyo Suketoki through his heart and delivering the blow that, if successful, would end his lordship's life and the battle itself.

Then, the enemy samurai heard the unmistakable sound of Junsaku's fast-approaching horse, the equine's hooves hammering the ground. As the soldier swiftly pivoted to face the threat, Junsaku, with fierce determination in his eyes, unleashed a mighty swing of his sword. As Junsaku watched the soldier's still-helmeted head tumble mid-air, he felt the familiar, hypnotic detachment he always felt when sending a soul to the next world: killing for Junsaku generated as much emotion as brewing a cup of tea.

Suddenly, Junsaku's gaze fell on the image of a giant, cloaked spirit of a man standing in the middle of the battlefield, his imposing figure encased in black from head to toe. Junsaku watched in disbelief as arrows, swords, and even combating samurai moved effortlessly through the ghost as though passing through a mass of dense, black smoke. Junsaku squeezed his eyes shut, a dry choke escaping his throat, and when he reopened them, the figure dissolved, blending into the dust and chaos of the battlefield. Junsaku took a deep breath and exhaled loudly to balance his chi, then turned to the stunned daimyo, still on the ground, and demanded, 'Get back on your horse, Suketoki-sama!'

The daimyo stood quickly and mounted his steed, and he and Junsaku returned to the fight.

***

AFTER COUNTLESS hours of fierce combat, the familiar melodies of birds and the gentle hum of insects finally replaced the once-deafening noise of battle. As Junsaku scanned the battleground, the terrain littered with bodies, he saw men lying lifeless on the ground, relieved that most were enemy combatants, dead in the hundreds, who had either been killed by Daimyo Suketoki's samurai or by *seppuku,* death by their short blade to avoid capture.

With his hands cupped at his mouth to amplify his naturally commanding voice, Junsaku yelled, 'Where is their leader, Daimyo Yamaguchi? Is he still alive?'

Junsaku saw a nearby samurai point. 'Captain, he is here. I can confirm he is dead.'

Junsaku raised both arms above his head, clenched his hands into tight fists, and cheered as his men joined the celebration, their exuberant cries echoing across the landscape.

Daimyo Suketoki dismounted his horse. With his helmet in hand, he went to where Junsaku sat atop his steed and stared up at him, his stance wide. 'Domo arigato gozaimasu, Junsaku-san. You saved my life. I will never forget your bravery.'

'I am your loyal servant, Suketoki-sama. I swore to protect you.'

Junsaku suddenly felt a sense of dread. His pulse quickened as his eyes scanned the war zone. His words came out barely louder than a whisper: 'Where is Yasafune?' As the daimyo's sharp gaze swept over the now-stilled battlefield, Junsaku's voice rang out, repeating the question more urgently: 'Where is Lieutenant Yasafune?' Junsaku's chest felt heavy, the weight of his armour multiplied by ten as he slid off his horse. 'Yasafune! Yasafune, *dokoni imasuka?* Where are you?' he bellowed, his voice desperate as his eyes scoured the battlefield.

'Captain, over here!' a samurai yelled, waving his arms and pointing at the ground.

Junsaku ran, jumping over bodies, and found himself standing in front of the corpse of his friend. Junsaku stared at the pool of blood that oozed from the edge of Yasafune's chest plate, and then his gaze moved to his friend's face, whose eyes were still open, drained of life.

Junsaku's legs buckled, and he sank to the ground. With gentle fingers, he closed Yasafune's eyelids and murmured, 'You should not have died here, friend.' As he held Yasafune's hands, he lowered his head and whispered a prayer, then quietly promised, 'I will take care of your family. Do not worry. Transition peacefully, brother.' Junsaku wiped a tear from his dirty, blood-stained face. To Lieutenant Matsubara, who stood near, he ordered, 'Arrange for his body to be prepared and delivered to his family. Tell his wife, Kurakawa, to give him a proper burial and that I will pay. Yasafune was one of Daimyo Suketoki's best samurai and a true disciple of bushido, so ensure he receives the respect he deserves.' Then, Junsaku mounted his horse, his head hung low.

The daimyo, back atop his horse, gazed at Junsaku. 'He has passed to the next life, Junsaku. He fought bravely and died with glory.'

'Hai, Suketoki-sama, he was a brave warrior and like a brother to me. I will miss him. Now, I must fulfil my promise to keep his wife and child safe,' Junsaku sighed.

'Do not worry, Junsaku. I will reward you for your bravery and for saving my life, and I will make sure you have plenty for yourself and Yasafune's family.'

'Domo arigato gozaimasu,' Junsaku replied, tipping his head in appreciation.

'But, before we leave here, Junsaku, you need to organise a burial for our samurai before we go to the main town of Morioka. We will bury our men here, but we will not show the same respect to the enemy: those men will remain where they died. Afterwards, I will announce to the villages that I am now the lord of the Iwate prefecture and, as my retainers, I demand their loyalty and respect.'

Junsaku closed his eyes, took a deep breath, and filled his lungs as he settled into momentary silence, wishing Yasafune peace. Then, Junsaku ordered the army to collect and bury the bodies of Daimyo Suketoki's samurai guard.

Several hours later, the still-living soldiers finished digging a massive hole. They filled it with seventy-three of the daimyo's deceased samurai, stacking them gently and with dignity, leaving the enemy soldiers untouched, left to rot in the field. The warriors prayed for their lost brothers as wild lavender burned, and when the ceremony ended, men shovelled dirt into the grave and hid the bodies below the earth.

Junsaku gave the command, and, with Suketoki-sama at the lead, the army marched towards Morioka to announce Daimyo Suketoki as their new lord. Having conquered another region of Northern Japan, the daimyo's overall wealth and power increased again, giving him notoriety with the emperor and favour with Japan's most influential person, the shogun.

ELEVEN

DAIMYO SUKETOKI entered Morioka village followed by his army. Though the daimyo removed his mask, he instructed Junsaku to keep his samurai hidden behind their frightening face coverings to instil fear in the citizens, a reminder of the consequences of rebellion. As the daimyo's army traversed the narrow, cobblestone streets and headed to the castle at the far end of the village, the townspeople lowered their heads in reverence of their new ruler, and Junsaku noticed Tochigi clan banners already hung from the windows of homes and shops, demonstrating the people's allegiance to their new lord.

That night, Junsaku dined privately with Daimyo Suketoki in the castle. 'Junsaku,' the daimyo said, setting his chopsticks on the holder, 'you saved my life and have been instrumental in growing my landholdings and wealth, improving my standing with the shogun. Because of your exemplary service, I am promoting you to the highest rank in my personal guard: General.'

Junsaku felt warm in the centre of his chest. 'Domo arigato gozaimasu, Suketoki-sama,' he replied, lowering his head. 'I am honoured.'

'Well deserved,' he responded. Then, the daimyo lifted his

hand and said to a female attendant standing quietly near the wall, 'Bring nihonshu. We must celebrate! Junsaku, are you aware you are the youngest general in the history of Japan? No one at the age of twenty-four has ever achieved this rank. You should be immensely proud.'

'Hai,' Junsaku replied, watching the young woman pour sake into his cup.

While they sipped rice wine, Suketoki asked, 'Junsaku, you have a home, wealth, and now a general's rank; why have you not taken a wife? You should marry a woman who can care for you and eventually give you a son.'

'I have never met a woman who could satisfy me for the rest of my life. I like my courtesans and my freedom,' Junsaku replied with a playful glint in his eyes.

'I understand, Junsaku, but think of it this way: one special woman can care for your needs at home while you still enjoy the company of courtesans outside the house.' A sly grin pulled on the corners of Suketoki's lips.

'I will never commit to one woman,' Junsaku replied, his voice steady yet firm. After a pause, he continued, 'I understand why my father committed to my mother. She was perfect, and when he met my okasan, he told me he never wanted another woman. I have yet to feel this for any woman, and I do not believe I ever will. Also, bushido is more important to me than anything else. Warrior life is all that matters.'

'Well, time will tell. Maybe there will be a Japanese woman who will steal your heart when you least expect it. For now, kanpai, General!' the daimyo exclaimed, raising his cup.

When the evening ended, the daimyo told Junsaku to organise the men to return home.

The following day, Junsaku prepared for the army to return to Hirosaki. He also organised one hundred samurai to remain in Morioka to guard, recruit, and train new warriors, building a strong army presence in the region and ensuring the protection of Suketoki's latest conquest.

***

WHEN JUNSAKU returned to his house in Hirosaki one week later, he cleaned up and then walked down a narrow cobblestone lane to the local inn. Inside, he set his swords on the wooden table as a curvy Japanese courtesan slid onto the bench beside him and poured sake. Silky black hair slid over the shoulder of her bright pink kimono, and a suggestive smile curved her red-painted lips. As Junsaku savoured each sip of the rice wine, relishing the smooth and sweet taste that filled his mouth, he flirted with the courtesan, his eyes mischievously twinkling as he anticipated soon ascending the stairs to one of the private rooms. The courtesan giggled as Junsaku whispered in her ear, and as he went to kiss her neck, a teenage boy approached the table and bowed. 'Junsaku-san,' he said, his breathing rapid, 'I have come with a message.'

'From whom? I am not interested if it is not the daimyo or the shogun himself. Can you not see I am busy?' Junsaku said sharply, his roughened thumb caressing the courtesan's velvet-smooth hand.

'I have been sent by a friend of Kurakawa, Yasafune's wife.'

Junsaku's posture stiffened. 'Is Kurakawa alright? What of the boy, Nobushida?'

'The boy is fine. However, the mother has passed to the next life.'

Junsaku's thick, bushy eyebrows shot upwards, deepening the lines on his forehead. 'Dead? Where is the boy?'

'The boy is with a family friend called Yasuda, and he is safe.

Yasuda-san asked me to find you and tell you of Kurakawa's death. Yasuda said he will care for Nobushida until he hears from you.'

'Good,' Junsaku said, inhaling deeply and standing from the bench. 'How did she die?'

'Yasuda told me of a sickness she had been fighting for some time. Recently, she could no longer eat or drink, and nothing would stay inside her. It worsened over the days, and while Nobushida played in the garden this morning, she died.'

Junsaku's lips tightened as he sighed wearily. Then, he glanced at the courtesan before returning his attention to the teen, saying, 'Tell Yasuda I will come in the morning to fetch the boy. I am busy this evening. Tell him Nobushida will live with me, and I will care for him as I promised his father.'

The messenger bowed to Junsaku and ran from the inn.

Questions swirled in Junsaku's mind: *Am I now a caregiver? Will this boy stay with me forever? Will I teach him the ways of bushido as my father taught me?* Junsaku knew one thing: he had promised his friend, Yasafune, to care for and protect his son, which meant today, Junsaku had to embrace his new role as a father and caregiver, but tonight, he would concentrate on the pleasure of a courtesan's company.

TWELVE

YASUDA, A SMALL, frail man with ashen hair, held Nobushida's hand as he led the boy out of the house to meet Junsaku. With sleek, jet-black hair cropped closely to his head, Nobushida rubbed his bloodshot eyes with his tiny left hand; his cheeks flushed a deep rose as he gazed at Junsaku, his expression a mixture of curiosity and exhaustion. Junsaku smiled and held out his hand. 'It is alright, Nobushida. Do you remember me? I am your father's friend, and you have nothing to fear. Your parents are now with your ancestors, and until you are reunited, you will live with me, and I will protect and care for you.'

'Okasan told me you would come for me one day,' the boy replied solemnly. Nobushida's skinny arms folded at his chest as he stood like a statue for several seconds, staring at Junsaku. Then, Nobushida reached out his right hand, his tiny fingers curved slightly, and when his hand met Junsaku's scarred fingers, he touched the samurai's calloused skin. Junsaku outstretched his hand, and Nobushida's soft fingertips grazed his rough palm.

Nobushida slid his hand forward, and Junsaku gently curled his fingers and held the boy's hand. 'Are you ready to see your new house?'

Nobushida stared at Junsaku, the sunlight warming his eyes to dark honey, and he nodded.

'You are brave. Your otosan and okasan would be proud of you. Do you want to walk with me to my, uh, to our house, or should I carry you?'

Nobushida stomped his right foot on the ground. '*Iie!* I walk like a samurai, like my otosan,' he demanded, his voice piercing, his posture defiant.

'Hai. You are courageous, Nobushida,' Junsaku replied, a twinkle of amusement in his eyes as he watched the boy's antics. 'And, Yasuda, take this as my thanks,' Junsaku said, pulling a canvas bag from his pocket and handing it to the older man, the coins jingling lightly.

As Junsaku and Nobushida left Yasuda's home, the boy turned and waved at Yasuda, who stood bent at the waist.

After several minutes, Nobushida and Junsaku arrived at the sturdy earthen wall surrounding Junsaku's home. He pushed open the wooden gate, and he and Nobushida entered the yard. At the house entrance, Junsaku instructed, 'Sit. I will help you with your shoes.'

Nobushida sat on the front step of the wooden deck, and Junsaku knelt before him. He removed the boy's cloth slippers, leaving only tabi socks on his feet. 'Now, go inside.'

Nobushida stood up and ran clumsily into the house as Junsaku removed his shoes and slipped on his sandals. Inside, Junsaku asked, 'Would you like to see where you will sleep, Nobushida?'

Nobushida turned in circles, taking in his new surroundings, his cheeks round like small red apples, his eyes wide with wonder, and replied, 'Hai. Uh, um...'. Nobushida opened his mouth again but suddenly clamped his lips shut, unsure of what to say.

Junsaku observed the boy's expression and recognised the uncertainty in his eyes as he wondered how to address Junsaku. Junsaku thought quickly. Speaking gently, he said, 'Nobushida, from now on, you shall call me Ojisan. Since I loved your father like a brother, you can consider me your uncle. We are family now.'

'Hai, Ojisan,' Nobushida responded. The toddler glanced around the house, the dark wood beams and sand-coloured walls providing a comforting warmth, and asked, 'Where do I sleep?'

'Ah, excellent question!' Junsaku said, slapping his hand on his thigh. 'Let me show you to your room, Master.'

Nobushida's lips curled into a smile as he eagerly followed Junsaku. They walked past the kitchen, down a short hallway, and slid open a fusuma panel. 'Here is your bedroom,' Junsaku said, gesturing with his hand.

The room had hay-coloured bamboo flooring and a futon with a fluffy, blue, feather-stuffed kakebuton for warmth. Nobushida could not contain his excitement; he dashed across the room and threw himself onto the futon, exclaiming with a bright smile, 'This is soft! Arigato, Ojisan.'

'I am glad you approve. Now, you should rest.'

'Oh, iie!' he squealed. 'I want to play in the yard. It is still day. Pleeaassee!'

'Alright, you can explore for a bit, and afterwards, you will need a short sleep while I figure out what to feed you and give you to drink. Do you like nihonshu?' Junsaku asked teasingly, his eyes twinkling with mischief. Nobushida looked bewildered. Junsaku chuckled, shaking his head. 'That was a bit of humour, Nobushida. No sake for you. You will have water, barley tea, or milk.'

'Hai, Ojisan. I like those,' Nobushida agreed, his head bobbing rapidly. 'Especially barley tea.'

THIRTEEN

JUNSAKU EMPLOYED a live-in nanny named Yui to care for Nobushida, who came highly recommended. Twenty-three-year-old Yui, a petite woman with delicate features and an air of timidity like a shy field mouse, kept her gaze downcast and rarely made eye contact with Junsaku. Yet, after interviewing Yui and speaking to her references, Junsaku recognised her intellect, politeness, and respectfulness and hired her, confident that she would be an excellent caretaker and provide a nurturing environment for Nobushida's growth.

On a crisp morning, several weeks after Yui had accepted the role of Nobushida's nanny and moved into Junsaku's home, Nobushida sat across from Yui at breakfast. While Yui sipped tea, actively listening to Nobushida as he chatted excitedly about the adventures he had planned for the day, Junsaku set off for the temple. When Junsaku arrived, he passed through a two-tier gate crafted from thick timber beams painted bright vermilion. At the end of the straight pathway, he saw his destination: a large, wooden building with massive, cylindrical pillars supporting the roof, expertly cut and fitted joints, and eaves that extended generously beyond the roof's edge, diverting rainwater, ensuring the interior remained dry. Junsaku passed under woven straw banners that dangled like golden lightning bolts above the doorway of the inner shrine, removed his straw sandals, placed them next to another pair already on the shelf, and bowed at the entrance. He went to the *chozuya*, lifted the metal ladle with his right hand, and poured water over his left hand before switching and repeating the process. Once both hands were clean, he cupped water and brought the liquid to his mouth, slurping it before spitting it onto nearby rocks. Then he entered the temple, walking in his socks towards the altar, and found Koji sitting with his legs crossed, a peaceful aura surrounding him.

Koji's eyes were closed, and an enigmatic smile played on his lips. 'Konnichiwa,' Koji said to Junsaku, opening his eyes. 'Come.'

Junsaku removed his swords, placed them on the floor, and sat before the monk.

'Have you thought on the koan?' Koji asked.

'Hai,' answered Junsaku.

Greyed eyebrows, dense as the feathers on a bird's wing, framed the monk's narrow, monolid eyes as he stared intensely at Junsaku and said, 'I asked you to think on this koan: *When the student is ready, the teacher appears.* I have contemplated this paradox for almost seventy years and often have new insight.'

Junsaku nodded slowly.

'However, before we go further, tell me about your recent battle; how did you feel?'

After a moment of contemplation, Junsaku took a deep breath and began to speak, his voice steady, as if carefully choosing each word: 'I felt obligated to protect my master, and while I killed, I felt detached, as though completing a duty like sweeping the dojo. For a moment, I felt emotion as I removed a samurai's head, wondering if he would be leaving behind a wife or child. These thoughts lasted only seconds before I refocused on my duty to protect and serve my master.' After an extended silence, Junsaku took a deep breath, his face showing the weight of his emotions, and said, 'My most troubling feeling came after I found out my good friend, Yasafune, had been killed. Koji, I felt despair like I had never felt before. Later the same day, when we went to the town and announced Suketoki as their new daimyo, I felt heavy in my soul as I looked at the faces of the broken-hearted. For the first time, I felt unsure of my purpose, questioning whether or not it was right or wrong to kill in the name of the daiymo only to make him more prosperous.'

Junsaku stared at the monk with intense eyes, dark as coal.

'Continue, Junsaku,' Koji coaxed gently.

'I sometimes wonder if the daimyo already has enough, and is it greed and selfishness that drives him, or does he genuinely need the resources to care for his people? I also thought of what my otosan told me when I was a boy. My father gave me the nickname Ōkami, the wolf. He told me to practise non-violence, only to fight when needed, and to never kill for money or riches. My otosan also said when I work for the lords of Japan, I may not be able to choose my battles, yet in my heart, I should always choose justice.'

'What do you feel here?' Koji asked, poking his index finger into the centre of Junsaku's hard chest.

'Though I know I must serve the daimyo, sometimes it feels wrong, and that is when I see him.'

'Do you mean the hooded man?'

'Hai,' Junsaku said, lifting his shoulders, the tension in his posture betraying his inner turmoil. 'At least, based on the ghost's shape and size, I think it is a man. Sometimes, I also see the spirit in my dreams or when I meditate, but he appears mostly during combat, especially after I have taken another's life.'

'Are you sure you do not recognise this soul, this spirit?' Koji asked.

'Iie. He keeps himself shrouded, and I cannot see beneath the black that covers him from head to toe. I have been fearless my whole life, Koji-san, but I am filled with fear when I see this spectre.'

After a short pause, Koji leaned forward, curiosity glimmering in his eyes. 'Maybe you know him?'

'I do not think so. However, there is something familiar about the spirit's energy. It reminds me of the ghost who visited me when I was younger, but this hooded phantom is different; the vision overwhelms me with dread.' Junsaku scratched his head.

'Maybe it is the boy, now a man, underneath the hood?' Koji inquired, his eyes searching Junsaku's for a hint of agreement.

'Iie. This phantom is not the same spirit. If it were, why would he hide from me now? It does not make sense.' Junsaku tilted his head before straightening his neck and stating confidently, 'This spirit is powerful, possibly evil, and I believe it has driven away the ghost who visited me in my youth. I do not know who this phantom is, Koji.'

'Look to the mountain beyond,' Koji said thoughtfully. 'Maybe this spirit is a teacher, and you are the student.'

Junsaku sat silently.

'These are things for you to think about, Junsaku. Now, it is time to begin meditation. Let us focus on our third eye. Hajime.'

The men sat in meditation for two hours, their breaths deep and rhythmic. Junsaku felt as though gravity had relinquished its hold on him when the hooded man suddenly appeared in his mind, and he felt his weight come crashing down. The apparition's black hood cast a shadow that obscured his facial features and sent chills through Junsaku. Behind Junsaku's closed eyes, the giant man stood before him, vividly real, all eight feet of him, holding a long-handled axe, the blade shaped like a half-moon, and Junsaku grew uncomfortable, fidgeting, struggling to steady his breathing as his mind's eye stared at the cloaked figure.

Then, a rippling vibration travelled through Junsaku's spine like the floor hit him from below, and his eyes popped open. Koji's amber eyes stared intensely at Junsaku. 'Did you see him? Did you see the hooded giant?' Junsaku questioned urgently, leaning towards Koji, his hands gripping his knees.

'Iie,' the old man replied, 'I saw no one. However, I could feel the energy. It reminded me of you.'

FOURTEEN

THE DAIMYO slid open the shoji doors and entered the dojo wearing a bright green yukata embroidered with gold and royal blue dragons, fastened at the waist with a black sash. 'Junsaku,' he announced, 'we travel to the capital tomorrow.'

'Hai, Suketoki-sama,' Junsaku replied, bowing.

'We will stay in Edo for several weeks, so ready yourself. Ren, you will also travel with us,' the daimyo said, addressing Junsaku's sparring partner. 'Our group will be fifty soldiers, and we need supplies and gifts for Shogun Fusakage.'

'Hai, Suketoki-sama,' Ren replied, bowing to his lordship.

After the daimyo left the dojo, Ren and Junsaku looked at each other.

'Women and sake in the capital of Edo,' Ren said jovially. 'Sounds like a much-needed holiday.'

Junsaku's grin etched dimples into his stubbled cheeks. 'I must go home and tell Nobushida. I have been teaching him martial arts, and I promised we would train today. Please arrange fifty samurai to accompany us on our journey, organise the supplies, and prepare gifts to present to the shogun.'

'Hai, General, I will make it happen. Go to your boy.'

When Junsaku stepped through his front door, Nobushida, dressed in a small white jacket, matching pants, and a white belt tied at his waist, dashed towards him, slamming his little body into Junsaku's muscular legs. 'Ojisan, I am ready for training,' he exclaimed enthusiastically.

'Hai, Nobushida. Today, we will practise *sanchin kata* outside in the sunlight. It is a beautiful day.'

Behind Nobushida, in the dim light of the kitchen, Junsaku saw Yui bowing in the doorway. 'Yui,' Junsaku said, 'you can stand straight.'

The young woman stood upright yet kept her gaze fixed on the floor before her.

'Yui,' Nobushida chirped, 'you do not need to be nervous around Ojisan. He is not going to chop off your head!'

Junsaku patted the boy between his shoulder blades. 'That might be a bit much, Nobushida. But Yui, he is right. You are part of our family, and though I appreciate the respect you show me, you do not have to bow every time I enter a room. Now, continue with whatever you are doing. We are going to the garden to train.' Yui smiled demurely, straightened her kimono, and returned to the kitchen as Junsaku draped his arm over Nobushida's bony shoulders, and they walked outside.

In the garden, Junsaku sat on a large boulder. 'Show me what you have practised, Nobushida.'

Nobushida straightened his six-year-old frame, spread his feet apart in a sanchin stance, his pose resembling an hourglass, and tensed his muscles. His skinny forearms formed a loose V-shape in front of his chest like he carried an invisible log, and he slid his right foot forward, his toes pointing inward. He used his left arm to punch with a closed fist, then returned to the blocking position. Nobushida repeated the move with his left foot and right arm, continuing to alternate sides, sliding, punching, and blocking an invisible assailant with focused movement as he breathed deeply, in and out.

When Junsaku finally said, 'Yame,' Nobushida stopped, slid his feet together, and bowed to his sensei.

'Good, Nobushida,' Junsaku said. 'Now, do it again – but with your eyes closed this time. No peeking! Use your other senses to find and return to your exact starting point when you finish the *kata*.'

Nobushida breathed deeply through his nose, exhaled loudly, bowed to Junsaku, and repeated the movements, this time with his eyes shut tight.

After hours of training on various katas, Junsaku stated, 'That is enough for today. You have practised, and it shows. I am proud of you, Nobushida. Keep training while I am away.'

'What? You are leaving, Ojisan?' he said, his mouth forming an exaggerated frown.

'Not for long. I am going to meet the shogun in Edo.'

'The shogun!' Nobushida exclaimed. 'He is the best warrior in all of Japan!'

'Iie, Nobushida,' Junsaku said, gently shaking his head. 'Your Ojisan is the greatest warrior in all of Japan. Soon, I will step into the role of protector to the shogun, a position that carries great responsibility and honour, which means we will move to Edo, the heart of Japan. Would you like that?'

Nobushida hopped in place on the mat, yanking on the ends of his white belt. 'Hai, hai, Ojisan! I want to go to Edo.'

Junsaku grinned. 'Let me first meet the shogun and wait for his invitation to join his samurai guard, and then we go!'

***

SHORTLY AFTER sunrise, Junsaku approached the imposing gates of Daimyo Suketoki's castle. Upon entry, he noticed samurai guards making final travel preparations and the hustle and bustle of servants loading supplies and provisions on horse-drawn carts for the daimyo's trip to Japan's capital, Edo, and his audience with the shogun. Within an hour of Junsaku's arrival, he and the daimyo joined twenty other mounted samurai on horseback. The remaining thirty in the entourage travelled on foot, fifteen carrying giant red banners with the Suketoki clan's kamon embroidered on the fabric, and the small army left Hirosaki for Edo.

The trip from the Aomori Prefecture to the majestic Edo Castle in the Musashi Prefecture took twelve days. The travellers followed roads that meandered alongside the shimmering East Sea before crossing through the mountains towards the capital. As the samurai neared central Japan from the north, the once crisp and cool air and post-winter mud transitioned to fertile green grasses and lush, densely leafed trees that swayed softly in the warm breezes. When they reached the Oshu Kaido, the main thoroughfare leading directly into Edo, they saw the cyan waters of the inner sea surrounded by towering mountains in the distance. Japan's capital, Edo, came into view with its tightly packed, dark wooden buildings and roofs adorned with cypress bark or blue ceramic tiles that reflected the sunlight, and the pulse of the big city seduced Junsaku, increasing his desire to join the shogun's army and achieve his lifelong dream.

As Daimyo Suketoki and his samurai entered the bustling city of Edo, they smelled the fragrance of sweet rice, spices, grilled fish, meats, and livestock. They saw banners made from royal blue fabric hanging gracefully from the wooden buildings, each proudly displaying the intricate family crest of the Fusakage clan, the extended family of the shogun, embroidered in rich yellow silk thread; the elaborate kamon featured a striking design that looked like three hearts, their points touching at the centre and blossoming outward like a flower in full bloom, and within each petal were depictions of dragonflies adorned with twenty sword-like wings.

As the daimyo, Junsaku, and other accompanying samurai approached Edo castle, a hush descended on the cobblestone streets, and citizens parted the road and bowed, their eyes cast downward in deference and respect. However, the shogun's samurai stood still in watchful vigilance, their hands poised on the hilts of their swords, ready to draw their weapons at a moment's notice.

At the castle entrance, the daimyo's army crossed a curved bridge stretched over a moat and stopped at a massive gate. Junsaku heard shouting, followed by the thick wooden doors opening inward. Daimyo Suketoki entered first, followed by Junsaku and the other mounted samurai, and then the foot soldiers stepped into the castle's inner grounds before the gate closed behind them.

Junsaku noticed a man wearing a silk kimono with a blue and green pattern that looked like the swirling waters of a deep lake approaching. Based on his commanding movement and the samurai response of bowing and remaining in place until the man passed, Junsaku immediately knew this man as Shogun Fusakage. As he neared, Junsaku could see he had a straight nose, angular jawline, prominent cheekbones, and ink-black hair tightly fastened at the crown of his head, creating a silhouette reminiscent of a pinecone.

'*Irasshaimase,* Daimyo Suketoki. Welcome,' said the shogun as Suketoki dismounted his horse.

'Domo arigato gozaimasu, Fusakage-sama,' the daimyo replied, bowing. 'I am honoured to be invited.'

'I have a guest house ready for you. Which of your guards will accompany you?'

The daimyo pointed to Junsaku. 'Junsaku will stay with me, and if I grant him time off, I will have Ren take his place,' he finished, pointing at Ren.

'Fine. Let me show you where you will stay. You can bathe and prepare to join me for a meal. Your samurai can follow my captain; he will lead them to their quarters and direct them to one of my many dojos for training.'

As the shogun and the daimyo strolled along the gravel path leading to the castle's imposing main keep, their voices barely audible as they spoke in low volume, their hands clasped neatly behind their backs, Junsaku trailed close behind them. His gaze swept over the meticulously maintained castle grounds, admiring the cherry blossom trees, their branches heavy with pink and white blooms, and he felt a profound sense of accomplishment, envisioning that he would soon work within Edo castle and serve the shogun directly.

FIFTEEN

EFORE THE evening meal, the daimyo granted Junsaku several hours to train in one of the castle's dojos. As Junsaku
practised martial arts, the daimyo and the shogun met privately in
the opulent audience room in the castle's main keep, drinking sake
poured by Japanese women with faces as pale as porcelain and lips
of vibrant red.

Shogun Fusakage reclined on a red cushion embroidered with
gold flowers, one of his thick legs bent at the knee while the other
stretched out. 'Tell me, Suketoki, who is your best samurai?'

'I have many skilled warriors, but none can compare to my
cousin's son, Junsaku Aoyama, from the Akita Prefecture. Because
of his outstanding talent and leadership qualities, I elevated him to
the rank of general in my army.'

'I have heard this man holds the title of the youngest general in
history,' the shogun commented, a knowing glint in his brown eyes.

The daimyo nodded respectfully. 'Hai, Fusakage-sama. He is
an exceptional warrior and even saved my life in battle.'

The shogun let out a low grumble. With a raised eyebrow, he
asked, 'And who is second best?'

'That would be Ren Ogawa. He is a fine samurai in his own

right.'

Shogun Fusakage sipped his sake. When he set it down on the low, polished wood table, one of his attendants refilled it immediately. 'I am glad you have Ren,' he stated matter-of-factly, briefly glancing at the young woman.

'As am I,' replied the daimyo. Curiosity flickered across Suketoki's face as he tilted his head slightly. He gazed earnestly at Shogun Fusakage, searching for clarity, and with carefully chosen words asked, 'Fusakage-sama, with respect, why does my possession of Ren bring you gladness?'

'Because Junsaku will remain in Edo and will not return to your custody. You can retain Ren, but I will take this warrior, Junsaku, in my service. I need strong, capable men and leaders, and I want to bolster my ranks with samurai from the northern prefectures. I have not had a samurai leader from the Aomori or Iwate Prefectures stationed here in Edo, so, given that you govern those territories, and I hold power over you, I will take what is necessary to strengthen my forces. A clan in the north poses an ongoing threat, and Junsaku's intimate knowledge of the area will prove invaluable in maintaining peace throughout Japan.' Fusakage's lips curled cunningly at the edges as a young girl gracefully filled his sake cup, seemingly oblivious to the conversation as she poured.

Daimyo Suketoki sat quietly, attempting to suppress his anger to avoid disrespecting the shogun. However, despite his best efforts, the shogun sensed his displeasure. 'Is there an issue?' the shogun questioned, the tone of his voice like the low rumble of a bear.

'Iie, Fusakage-sama. No issue.' A light perspiration glittered on the daiymo's forehead. 'Junsaku will join your samurai guard as you command.'

'Excellent. I will meet privately with Junsaku following our evening meal and share the news. He can return with you and the others to Hirosaki, but you make sure he reports to me by the next full moon.' Then, the shogun raised his cup and cheered, 'Kanpai!'

***

FOLLOWING THEIR meal, Shogun Fusakage ordered everyone to leave. Just as Junsaku stood from his floor cushion and prepared to exit, the daimyo gripped his muscular upper arm and whispered, 'You will stay here. The shogun wants to speak with you privately.'

Flooded with euphoria, Junsaku felt immense pride in knowing that his invitation to join the shogun's samurai guard was imminent and that he would finally fulfil his destiny. Junsaku turned towards Shogun Fusakage, averting his gaze and avoiding direct eye contact as he waited for the leader to speak.

When the room emptied, the shogun said, 'Junsaku, Daimyo Suketoki tells me you are an excellent samurai. I understand he even promoted you to a general's rank. Why would he do this?'

Junsaku looked in the shogun's direction but avoided eye contact. He aimed his gaze just above the shogun's top knot, staring at a gold-painted wall with the image of a green bonsai tree with a thick trunk just behind where the leader sat. With a confidence bordering on arrogance, Junsaku lifted his chin and responded, 'Fusakage-sama, I live by the code of bushido. I am unmatched in my swordsmanship, archery, hand-to-hand combat...'

Before Junsaku could finish his sentence, Fusakage interrupted: 'Look me in the eyes when you speak,' he commanded.

Junsaku met the leader's piercing gaze, his heart pounding as he purposely slowed his speech. 'Every military operation I have commanded for Daimyo Suketoki has been a massive success, and because of my outstanding leadership and unparalleled skills, the daimyo has quadrupled the size of his domain.' Junsaku's face tensed with intense concentration. 'But do you know the true reason why I have been so successful, Fusakage Shogun? It is the warrior blood flowing through my veins. Since my first breath in this lifetime, my destiny has been to serve you and Japan. For me, nothing else matters.'

The shogun remained silent, his expression contemplative, his eyes narrowed as he absorbed every passionate word leaving Junsaku's mouth.

Junsaku breathed deeply, slowly released the air, and with conviction said, 'I am the most skilled samurai in the region, the youngest general in history, and the greatest warrior in all of Japan. Long after I transition to the next life, my legend will live on.'

The shogun's laughter erupted like thunder. With amusement and disdain, he said, 'Junsaku, you do not lack confidence; you are arrogant! Lucky for you, I find these qualities admirable.'

Junsaku felt a wave of emotion rush through him, his cheeks warmed. At that moment, he longed for his father, imagining how proud his otosan would be to hear that his son, Junsaku, had joined the shogun's army.

The shogun leaned back and rested on his elbows. 'You will join my army and retain your rank of general. However, it will be your responsibility to safeguard your position,' the shogun remarked, his tone challenging. 'You must accompany me on journeys, engage in battle, and ensure my protection. And remember this—any misstep on your part, I will revoke your title and position.'

'I will live up to my commitment, Fusakage-sama. Joining your guard is my dream come true,' Junsaku replied, bowing.

'And what about your wife? Will you bring her to live in Edo?' The shogun leaned forward and relaxed his bent arms on the low table.

'Iie. I have no wife. But I do have a boy: Nobushida. He and his caregiver will live with me.'

'Very well. I will provide you with a fine house in the city, near the castle, where your family can live.' The shogun's expression darkened as he straightened his back. 'Although we have enjoyed several years of peace across Japan, I have concerns about the Daichi clan from the north. I have heard rumours they are amassing an army.'

Concern flickered in Junsaku's dark eyes. 'I know this clan and have also heard they are expanding their army, attempting to reclaim lost territory. However, at present, they are not an immediate threat.'

The shogun shrugged. 'Though there is peace throughout Japan right now, you must stay vigilant, Junsaku, and be ready for an attack from rival leaders.'

'Hai. I understand, Fusakage-sama, and I will protect the shogunate with my life.'

Fusakage sighed, then gestured with his hand, saying casually, 'You may go.'

Junsaku bowed before exiting the dining room. His heart swelled with joy as he walked toward Daimyo Suketoki's guest house, the full moon above casting a silvery glow over the cobblestone and gravel pathways. When he arrived, he asked the guard at the entrance, 'Is the daimyo awake?'

'Hai. I will announce your arrival.'

When the foot soldier returned, he moved from the doorway and allowed Junsaku to enter. Junsaku passed Ren, standing guard at the inner door, and entered a small room with golden bamboo floors, cherry-wood walls and ceilings, and a large banner made from silk with the shogun's kamon hanging on the wall.

'Junsaku, join me for sake,' Suketoki invited.

Junsaku bowed and sat at a low table across from the daimyo.

'Congratulations on being chosen personally by none other than the shogun himself.'

'Domo arigato gozaimasu, Suketoki-sama. Though serving you has been a tremendous honour, my path takes me in a new direction.'

SIXTEEN

MONTHS AFTER settling in Edo, Junsaku, Nobushida, and Yui became accustomed to the city's vibrant and fast-paced lifestyle. Junsaku even enrolled Nobushida in a prestigious school designated for the children of samurai, which included lessons in martial arts and an English language class, which Junsaku specifically arranged.

'Yui, no dinner tonight for Nobushida. It is my night off, so I am taking him to the inn to eat near the hearth,' Junsaku stated as he sheathed his daisho swords, sliding both into his canvas belt.

Nobushida beamed. 'Arigato, Ojisan. I like eating next to the big fireplace.' Grabbing Junsaku's *jō*, his wooden staff, which leaned against the wall in the genkan, Nobushida asked in English, 'Can we go now?'

'Yes. It will be a pleasant walk. The night air is cool and crisp,' Junsaku responded in English, putting his strong hand just below the nape of Nobushida's neck.

As they strolled through the streets, the air buzzed with chatter and movement. In the near distance, towering above the city, Junsaku could see Edo castle with its dark grey, hipped and gable roofs and white exterior walls that seemed to absorb the setting sun's golden glow. As Junsaku and Nobushida passed, the citizens, and even samurai, bowed deeply in respect, keeping their faces turned downward and remaining bent until Junsaku disappeared from view. When Junsaku and Nobushida entered the inn, a wave of silence swept over the room as patrons abruptly stood and bowed, only relaxing when Junsaku lifted his hand in a subtle gesture.

'Junsaku-san, sit over here. This is our best table,' said an older woman, her light tan skin still radiant with the youthfulness of someone half her age. She gestured towards a rustic wooden table where three men were seated. As her hand moved, the men caught sight of her signal, quickly snatched up their cups and plates, and left the table, the bench legs scraping against the uneven floor.

'Kiko-san,' Junsaku said to the woman, 'bring barley tea for Nobushida and nihonshu for me. As for our meal, *omakase*. Tell the cook to serve us whatever he selects.'

'Hai, Junsaku-san,' Kiko replied. Then, the woman gracefully retreated from the table, taking small steps in her wooden sandals as she walked towards the kitchen.

'Nobushida, tell me about school today. What did you do?' he asked as he placed his swords next to him on the wooden bench.

'Today, Ojisan, we studied...'

'General!' a man bellowed, his tone laden with insolence, startling everyone in the inn and interrupting Nobushida's speech. 'Why are you here? Shouldn't such a powerful samurai be eating with the shogun? Maybe you are not as good as they say,' the man laughed, picking up his tin cup and dumping warm sake down his throat before slamming it back on the wooden table.

Junsaku stared intently at the man, curious about his dishevelled appearance and aggressive behaviour. Junsaku observed that the stranger wore tattered, mismatched clothing, the fabric frayed at the edges, and he had straight, black hair that reached his shoulders, wild and unkempt, the colour matching his angry eyes.

'I was once a great samurai working for Daimyo Toyama Kochi in the Gunma Prefecture until your shogun killed him and took our lands and riches,' the man declared. 'Even though I am now a ronin, I am still powerful, and tonight, I will kill you.'

Junsaku took a sip of sake and looked at Nobushida, whose eyes were as round as coins. Junsaku winked at the boy, then turned toward the stranger and said gruffly, 'You may have been a good samurai in the past, but today, you are a masterless fool. Go back to your drink and leave me alone, or suffer the consequences.'

'Ha,' the man scoffed. With a burst of energy, he pushed the wooden bench away from him, stood up, and rested his right hand on the hilt of his long sword. Tall as Junsaku with a slightly larger frame and a deeply tanned face full of pockmarks, giving his skin the appearance of lava rock, the rogue threatened, 'I will kill you tonight so you cannot return to the bed of the boy's mother, and then I will find your house and lay with her instead.'

'I have no mother! My okasan is dead,' shouted Nobushida angrily, rising from the bench and holding Junsaku's jō perpendicular to his body, the wooden stick matching his height.

Junsaku, seeing Nobushida's rage, took a deep breath, stood, and faced the assailant. 'You have no respect, ronin. Learn your place, apologise to my son, and do it quickly before I lose my temper. I have no desire to kill anyone today,' Junsaku stated, his eyes as dark as storm clouds.

The ronin slammed his hand on the table and released a bois-terous laugh that echoed through the room. 'Tonight, only one soul will meet its fate, and when my blade kills the mighty Gener-al Junsaku Aoyama, I will be famous,' he proclaimed, spreading his arms wide and turning in slow circles, surveying the crowd who watched with open mouths. Then, the man demanded, 'Grab your sword, General, and prepare to meet your death. You will pay for what your shogun did to my lord,' he declared, his voice laced with fury as he walked briskly toward the inn's exit.

'Pass me my jō, Nobushida.' Junsaku reached out his hand.

'Ojisan, you must take your swords,' Nobushida replied, his voice shaky. 'How can you beat him with only a stick?'

'Nobushida,' Junsaku replied, gold sparks flickering like em-bers in his eyes, 'I am Japan's greatest warrior. This disrespect-ful ronin, this masterless samurai, will learn a lesson in bushido tonight. You stay here. I need you to guard my swords.' Junsaku gulped down another cup of sake. 'Also, have Kiko bring me more nihonshu and ask her for miso soup. I will be back before the soup gets cold,' he declared confidently, lifting his eyebrows and flashing a knowing grin at Nobushida.

Junsaku walked towards the front door of the inn. Deathly quiet as he passed the patrons, Junsaku wondered if they were breathing. Exiting the inn, he saw the ronin waiting for him, the assailant's long and short swords in either hand. Junsaku placed his jō perpendicular to his body, the tip resting on the cobble-stones, and breathed into his tanden, balancing his chi.

'Where are your swords, General?' the ronin asked, his tone sharp as a blade.

'I will only need my staff to teach you a lesson. Now, make

your move. I do not want my miso to get cold.'

The ronin charged Junsaku, holding his long sword high in his right hand and his short sword low in his left. Junsaku stood motionless, waiting for the strike to come. Junsaku watched as his opponent pretended to use his long sword but attacked with the short blade, bringing it up and attempting to cut Junsaku from hip to shoulder. Junsaku raised his jō, moving with lightning speed to the right, and with a quick turn to his left, brought his wooden stick down hard on the ronin's left wrist, breaking it and rendering the man's left arm useless. Junsaku's strike sent the enemy's short sword to the ground, and the sound of steel striking cobblestone echoed through the quiet streets.

The man stared at Junsaku, who stood tall before him, his posture perfect as he rested the tip of his jō on the cobblestones. 'I am feeling generous, fool,' Junsaku said. 'I will give you two choices: you can either go into the inn, bow before my son, and apologise for your rudeness, or attempt to defeat me with the one arm you have left, and die.'

The ronin remained silent as he raised his long sword above his head with his right hand, then yelled, lunged forward, and brought the blade down in a final attempt to kill Junsaku. Junsaku slid to the left and easily avoided the strike, curving his neck just enough to prevent having his top knot sliced off. He pivoted right and, with the wooden stick, delivered a strike to the ronin's still functioning right arm, breaking the bones in his forearm and causing the man's long sword to tumble to the ground and clatter on the stones. Junsaku pivoted left and delivered another strike, this time hitting the ronin with his jō on the left side of his head, fracturing his skull. The ronin's body hit the ground, blood flowing from his nose, and as the ronin's breathing slowed, his vision blurring as his body died, he heard Junsaku say, 'There is your lesson in bushido, you fool. I gave you choices, and you chose poorly.'

The ronin drew a sharp breath like a fish yanked from the water, and then his breathing ceased.

With the attacker dead in the eerily quiet street, Junsaku returned to the inn. As he walked inside, no one spoke or looked in his direction.

Nobushida jumped from the table, ran to him, and hugged his legs tightly. 'Ojisan, you have returned,' he said brightly. 'Look!' He pointed to Junsaku's swords on the bench and a steaming hot bowl of soup on the table. 'I protected your swords and got you miso soup like you asked.'

Junsaku sat at the wooden table and picked up the bowl of miso, feeling the heat emanating from the ceramic. He smiled and tousled Nobushida's hair. 'Well done, Nobushida. See, I told you I would return before the soup got cold.'

CECELIA

SEVENTEEN

C ECELIA STOOD in the foyer wearing a sheer pink blouse with a white camisole underneath, with a turquoise silk sarong wrapped around her lower half, held in place by a knot tied at her hip. Tall and lean, Cecelia, named after her mother, let her long, brown hair cascade down her back, her caramel-coloured waves highlighted by the sunlight that penetrated the large windows in the house. 'Hello, Father!' Cecelia exclaimed when Lucas entered, her captivating, bright green eyes mirroring her mother's, sparkling with life and reflecting her inquisitive nature.

Lucas set papers on the table next to the front door and glared disagreeably at his daughter. 'Put on a proper dress, Cecelia,' he said dully, his nose squinched like he smelled rotten fish.

'Oh, Father, this is what the people in Batavia wear.'

'I do not care what they wear! Do as I say and take that off,' Lucas replied sternly.

'Yes, Sir,' Cecelia replied, her voice subdued as she lowered her gaze, her shoulders slumped. In her room, she changed into a long, starchy white skirt and a tight cotton blouse, cursing the sweat enveloping her body as a familiar wave of melancholy washed over her. It seemed to her that her father's only concern was that she had the essentials: shelter, food, water, and proper education. His absence of affection left her with an emptiness, though her innate zest for life allowed her not to wallow in self-pity. Before living with her father in the Dutch East Indies, Cecelia spent her first sixteen years in Lithuania, raised by her grandparents, who told her stories about Lucas when he was younger, describing him as vibrant, joyful, and humorous. Though Cecelia regretted never knowing that side of him, she understood that the weight of losing his wife changed him, and she wondered if things would have been different had she not so strikingly resembled her mother.

EIGHTEEN

LUCAS HARTGERS grew up in Rotterdam in the Netherlands, working most of his life for the Dutch East India Company, trading spices, gemstones, metals, and anything else of value. On his seventh voyage with the company, Lucas sailed from the Netherlands to Lithuania with thirty-six other crew members, including three merchants like himself, aboard a wooden sailing ship called *Diemermeer,* with funds from the Dutch government to procure amber, garnet, and sapphire for intercontinental and overseas trade. When the boat arrived at the Baltic seaport in Klaipeda, Lithuania, a carriage transported the men to the capital city of Vilnius, and three days later, they arrived and began their trade negotiations. Darijus Ventus, a local shop owner, excited to make a deal to sell gemstones to the Dutch, invited the merchants to dine that evening with his family at his white stone mansion in the centre of town.

Darijus gushed with pride over his daughter, Cecilia, a sixteen-year-old beauty and the centre of attention in Vilnius. With her long, caramel-honey hair and bright, expressive green eyes, Cecilia turned heads wherever she went, and, since reaching marrying age, suitors pursued her, inviting her for leisurely tea or romantic strolls along the city's picturesque streets. Cecilia loved the attention but consistently declined their offers; she had never met anyone who sparked her interest or made her heart race.

But everything changed the evening Lucas Hartgers came to dinner.

When Cecelia followed her mother into the dining room, she saw Lucas standing behind a dining chair, his posture stiff and alert. Her face grew hot as she noticed his light-blue eyes, red-blonde hair, beard matching his hair colour, and towering six-foot-three height.

Cecelia's beauty equally struck Lucas. He admired her luminous, porcelain skin, intensely green eyes, and tall height, the top of her head reaching his chin. At supper, the dinner party communicated in fluent English, and then, following their meal, the group retired to the drawing room for drinks and conversation. While the men collected on one side of the room, smoking cigars and drinking *midus* made from grain, honey, and water, Cecelia and her mother sat on a floral sofa opposite the men, quietly conversing.

As the ladies discussed the weather, Lucas approached. He stood close to where Cecelia sat, his left hip brushing her right arm. 'I hope I am not interrupting. You have a lovely home,' Lucas said politely, smiling at Cecelia's mother.

'Thank you, Mr. Hartgers.'

'And dare I say, your husband is a lucky man to have two beautiful women to adorn his surroundings,' he said, a warm smile illuminating his face as he directed his gaze towards Cecelia.

'You are too kind,' Cecelia's mother responded, observing her daughter's flushed cheeks.

'I am most genuine,' he said, staring into Cecelia's vibrant green eyes, sparked with excitement.

'*We gaan nu.* Time to go, Lucas,' announced one of the other merchants as he smashed the tip of a cigar into an ashtray.

'Yes, yes, alright,' Lucas replied tersely. 'Mrs. Ventiene, may I have your permission to call on Cecelia again tomorrow, that is, if she will allow it?' he asked gently. Lucas leaned down and whispered in Cecelia's ear, 'May I see you again?'

His warm breath stirred the nape of her neck, sending a spark of electricity through her body, igniting every nerve. 'I would be delighted,' Cecelia responded with a light exhale.

'Then it is agreed, Mr. Hartgers,' her mother replied. 'Please come for tea.'

'With delight.'

Lucas drew Mrs Ventiene's hand to his mouth, lightly grazed the top with his lips, and said, 'Thank you for a wonderful evening.' Then Lucas took Cecelia's hand, brought it to his lips, and kissed her delicate skin as he stared into her emerald-green eyes. As he softly glided her hand back down, he leaned closer and whispered, 'Until tomorrow.'

'Goodnight, Mr. Hartgers,' Cecelia replied, rubbing her palms on her dress.

Later that night, in their large feather bed, Cecelia's mother told her father about Mr. Hartgers request to see their daughter. 'Darijus, I have never seen her so smitten,' her mother said with arms folded across her chest, the crisp, white sheets bundled near her neck. 'What should we do? What if he....'

'What if he asks her to be his wife? If she selects him, we should not stand in her way. She can make her own choices. That is what we have always said, right?'

'Yes, Darijus. We must trust Cecelia will make the right choice. But I am not fond of his job. He sails worldwide as a merchant, so we would not see Cecelia or our grandchildren. However, if she falls in love with him, as I did with you, that is what matters in the end. You cannot stand in the way of true love.'

***

IN THE DAYS after their initial meeting, Lucas devoted every spare moment to being with Cecelia, captivated by her beauty and intellect. Lucas knew Cecelia had ensnared his heart and could not imagine a life without her; he was in love. After eight days in Vilnius, on the day before his return to the Netherlands, they sat on the sofa at Cecelia's home having a pleasant conversation full of laughter when a shadow suddenly seemed to roll between them and Lucas' expression darkened, the weight of the moment altering an otherwise light-hearted atmosphere. 'Cecelia, you know I leave tomorrow, and I need to speak to your father urgently. Could you please fetch him for me and then give us privacy,' he said, his tone urgent.

Lines appeared on the soft, smooth skin between Cecelia's eyes. Stunned, wondering what caused the sudden shift in his affection toward her, she replied, 'Very well, Mr. Hartgers. I will find him and send him to you. If I do not see you before you leave, safe voyage.' Cecelia left the room with slumped shoulders and closed the door behind her, her eyes burning with oncoming tears.

Minutes later, Darijus burst into the room. 'What is it, Lucas? Why the urgency? I thought we completed our business transactions.'

'Darijus, there is no issue with our agreement. There is something else I must speak to you about.'

'If you want to discuss exclusive rights, I am open to negotiating a deal.'

'No, no. That is not it, either. I want your permission to ask Cecelia to be my wife. She is the first woman I have ever loved and will be the last. I cannot imagine life without her.' Lucas paused, took a deep breath and continued, 'I am a Catholic and will take care of her and our children,' he said, wringing his hands near the hem of his jacket. Then, with a deep sigh, he asked, 'Do I have your blessing?'

'What about your job, Lucas? How can you be a good husband or father when you are often away?'

'I will resign within the year and move here, to Vilnius, to be with my wife and family.' Lucas stared directly into Darijus' intense hazel eyes and pleaded, 'Please allow me this chance. I want to make your daughter the happiest woman alive.'

'If she will have you, Lucas, we will be honoured for you to become our son.'

Lucas smiled as he took Darijus' hand and shook it vigorously, sealing the agreement. Then he said, 'Could you ask Cecelia to return?'

'Of course,' Darijus replied, smiling as he exited the room.

Moments later, Cecelia entered.

'Cecelia, will you walk with me?' Lucas asked, beaming.

'Yes,' Cecelia replied, her voice barely as a whisper. She felt confused, assuming he planned to end their relationship before embarking on his voyage. She quickly wiped away a single tear running down her cheek and hoped that Lucas did not notice the redness that circled her eyes as she wove her arm into his.

The pair strolled into the centre of town, their conversation sparse. Lucas suddenly stopped before the sunlit, pale ochre walls of the University of Vilnius. With a deep breath, he sank to one knee. Then, taking both of her hands gently into his, he gazed up at her and, at that moment, proposed marriage.

'Oh, yes, Lucas!' Cecelia chirped.

Lucas pulled a ring from his pocket, a band of white gold with a velvety, deep red garnet gemstone in its centre. He carefully slid the ring onto Cecelia's finger, then wrapped his arms around her, pulling her close as if to shield her from the world. Their hearts raced as Lucas leaned in, and for the first time, their lips met in a gentle kiss.

***

TWO MONTHS after Lucas proposed, he returned to Lithuania, and he and Cecelia were married at The Chapel of Saint Casimir in Vilnius Cathedral. Three weeks later, Lucas set sail once more, embarking on what would be his final assignment. After just one month at sea, he received a life-changing message: Cecelia was pregnant. Nine months later, Lucas' ship returned to the Netherlands, and he resigned, eager to return to his beloved wife and child. He rode in a horse-drawn carriage through quaint villages and rolling countryside toward the bustling port of Travemünde, Germany. There he boarded a sturdy merchant ship bound for Lithuania, its sails unfurling to catch the brisk wind. Days and nights of choppy waters lapping against the ship's hull finally ended when he reached the coast of Lithuania and rode in another carriage to Vilnius and Cecelia's parent's home. Standing at the heavy, wooden front door of their house, he knocked. A servant greeted and escorted him to the sitting room, where he sat and waited patiently. Finally, a baby's cry pierced the air, sharp and sweet. His heartbeat quickened, and a wave of pure joy washed over him, lifting the corners of his mouth into a broad smile as the door to the sitting room swung open.

Lucas stood as Cecelia's mother, Danute, walked in carrying the baby wrapped in a white cotton blanket. Without smiling, Danute crossed the threshold, stopped, and stood in place, her eyes red and puffy. Cecelia's father entered the room behind her and wrapped his arm around his wife's shoulders, offering what little comfort he could. The couple's faces were etched with grief as they gazed at their son-in-law, whose eyes remained on the doorway behind them, seemingly willing his wife to appear and break the heaviness in the room.

'We are so sorry, Lucas,' Darijus said softly. 'Cecelia did not survive childbirth. She fought bravely, but it was too much for her. The doctor could not stop the bleeding.' Darijus dragged his palm across his cheek.

Lucas's blue eyes clouded, and his lips parted, implying he would speak, but no words came out. His mouth hung open as he stared, frozen in disbelief, his face a mixture of shock and confusion as he attempted to make sense of the scene before him.

Danute approached and handed him the baby. 'This is your daughter, Lucas; Cecelia, named after her mother.'

He stared at the baby, utterly bewildered, as if he had come face-to-face with an entirely new species. He scrutinized the girl's small, delicate features and dark, feather-like hair, his mind in a fog, his eyebrows knitted in perplexity, and then abruptly demanded, 'Take her from me. Take her back!'

'What? Lucas, you can hold her for as long as you want,' Danute responded caringly.

'I just need time, that is all. Please, take this baby away!' Lucas begged.

Danute took the infant and exited the room, sobbing.

'Lucas, we all miss her,' Darijus said, moving closer to his son-in-law. 'We loved Cecelia very much. Parents should never outlive their children, and you should never have become a widower at such a young age.' Darijus placed his hand on his son-in-law's shoulder. 'Childbirth can be difficult, Lucas, but God blessed you with a daughter and us, a granddaughter.'

'Yes, and thank you for caring for the child, Darijus,' Lucas choked.

'What of your job? Have you resigned?' his father-in-law inquired.

Lucas lied. 'No. I have not yet resigned. I am still under obligation to the company. I must return to Amsterdam tomorrow morning to sail to Batavia and possibly Africa. I do not know when I will be back.' As Lucas wondered if the Dutch East India Company would rehire him, concerned that he would not be able to get his job back and escape this nightmare, he implored, 'Darijus, can you care for the child? I will give you money to buy the girl the things she needs, and I will visit when possible. Will you do this?' His words hung like a storm cloud, everything quiet around him.

Darijus stared at his son-in-law in disbelief as though he were seeing a ghost. After a momentary silence, he said solemnly, 'If you must leave, Lucas, then so be it. We will care for our granddaughter, but she is your flesh and blood. You are her father.'

Lucas stood. 'Thank you, Darijus. I apologise for my short stay, but I must leave now and organise my immediate return to Amsterdam.'

Lucas ran from the house, stepping into the sweltering heat, the oppressive, muggy air intensifying his feelings of suffocation. Tears streamed down his face as he hurried toward the city centre, feeling the pressure of the uneven stones beneath his feet, and he focused on finding a carriage to help him escape Lithuania and distance himself from the love and loss that had destroyed his soul.

NINETEEN

CECELIA'S GRANDPARENTS raised her in the same centuries-old house in Vilnius where her mother had grown up, while Lucas travelled with the Dutch East India Company. Annually, Lucas came to Lithuania, usually only for a few days, bringing spices, silk shawls, coffee, tea, and other gifts for the household. Whenever one of Lucas' occasional visits happened to fall on a Sunday, he would find himself seated beside Cecelia in the echoing church, sitting stiffly next to his daughter, the unopened liturgical book pressed against his thighs.

The time Cecelia spent with her father was formal and awkward. Unlike the man from her grandparent's stories, she found him distant and lifeless. She consistently sought to learn more about her mother, but Lucas avoided the subject no matter how persistently she tried to get him to talk about her.

One morning, on one of her father's infrequent visits, Cecelia broached the subject of her mother in a different way. Smiling brightly, she brought a painting of her parents - a beautifully painted portrait of her mother and father on their wedding day that hung in the drawing room. 'Father, could you please share the story of this day with me?'

'There is not much to say.' Cecelia had to lean in to hear her father's words, his voice faint. 'I loved your mother and planned to spend my life with her, but God or something else had a different idea.' Listening to her father, she noticed his blue irises flickered like a lightning storm behind his eyes. Then, he became silent again and sipped his tea, hiding his face behind a newspaper.

Cecelia changed the subject. 'Father, Grandfather said you will continue to spend most of your time in Batavia. Is this true?'

'Yes,' he muttered, crossing his legs.

'I am turning sixteen soon, and I know what I would like for a gift.'

'Oh,' he grumbled as he folded the paper and set it on the table. 'Well?'

'I want to live with you in Batavia.'

He smirked, shaking his head. 'Out of the question.'

'Why? I will be sixteen and want to expand my understanding of the world. Please, Father, take me with you. I will be no trouble.'

'No, young lady. Plus, your grandparents will never allow it.'

'You are my parent, not them,' she replied sternly. 'I have already asked them, and they have given me their blessing.'

He gazed intently at his daughter, his eyes as cold as glacier ice. 'Silly girl, do you realise how difficult the journey will be? There will be minimal food and drink, sickness, fever, and possibly death. Have you thought of this?'

'Yes, I have, Father. I am strong, and I want to see the world. Please, as a gift, take me with you to Batavia. I have never asked you for anything.'

'You are foolish,' he murmured. After pausing several minutes, Lucas said, 'Fine, you can come, but you will learn to run the household as I am absent much of the year. You must behave as a proper lady, and I expect you to go to the Dutch school and church.' Looking directly at Cecelia, with a tone of disbelief, he asked, 'Is this really what you want?'

'Yes, father. More than anything.'

His daughter's emerald eyes danced with the same intensity and energy he had seen in her mother's gaze, forcing Lucas to look away, overwhelmed by the bittersweet reminder of what he lost. 'Fine. Pack your belongings. We leave in three days to board the ship in Amsterdam.'

TWENTY

A FTER A YEAR of living in Batavia, Cecelia's self-confidence grew. With her father gone for months, she made friends and immersed herself in the local customs and culture. Because of her knack for languages, she continued practising English and learned to converse in Dutch and Malay. She spent countless hours in the kitchen, cooking alongside the staff, developing her passion for traditional dishes, such as marinated and skewered chicken or goat satays, and fried whole fish smothered with a generous coating of hot chilli sambal. Cecelia also enjoyed strolling outside, even in the sweltering humidity, marvelling at the groves of dense, leafy breadfruit trees, papaya plants with plump, melon fruit clustered near the tops of their trunks, and the tall palms that lined the river's edge.

Despite her rare beauty that made people stare, Cecelia remained remarkably humble and down-to-earth. She had a relaxed, independent spirit, and though uninterested in marriage at this point in her life, she projected just enough warmth to keep men intrigued without creating a fire.

One evening, on a rare occurrence when her father stayed in Batavia, Cecelia and Lucas ate dinner together. Lucas remained seated at the far end of the long, eight-seat table, his demeanour distant. When he finally broke the silence, he stated, 'Cecelia, I am leaving soon on a trade mission.'

'Where will you go this time?' Cecelia asked politely.

'The Japans.'

'Oh, Father, take me with you!' Cecelia pleaded. 'I will stay out of your way and be no trouble. It will benefit my education greatly. Please!'

Lucas looked up, his soup spoon hovering over a bowl of laksa. 'Why would you want to go there? They are barbarians, and it would not be safe.'

'I will follow your direction to ensure my safety. I have longed to visit these islands and can help cook and clean the ship if needed. I will make myself useful.' Silence enveloped the dining room, only the sound of birds heard chirping beyond the windows. 'Father, I beg of you. Please take me,' Cecelia finally said. 'I yearn to go to Japan. I never felt such a deep desire to visit anywhere; it is like a fire burning in my soul.'

Lucas' eyes widened. He looked down at his soup bowl and said, 'Fine. I will expect you to study. And make sure you pack enough clothes. We sail on Tuesday.'

'Thank you, father!' Cecelia squealed, wishing she could leap from her seat, run to him, and wrap her arms around his neck with gratitude. Instead, with a gentle smile, she lifted her soup spoon and quietly swallowed the laksa.

TWENTY-ONE

CECELIA STOOD at the bow of the *Fortuyn*, gazing at the horizon and the approaching land as the vessel glided smoothly into the calm waters of *Edo-wan*. Its wooden hull cut through the gentle waves, and as the sun cast a radiant glow on her cheeks, in the distance, Cecelia saw a towering mountain, its conical shape capped with white snow. As they neared the shore, Cecelia could see the city buzzed with life, a hive of activity and teeming with people moving purposefully about, some pulling carts and others carrying cargo secured to poles across their shoulders. Cecelia noticed soldiers scattered throughout the docklands, clad in gleaming metal armour and distinctive helmets that shimmered in the sunlight, and she recognised them: the renowned samurai of Japan.

Twenty-nine days earlier, when Cecelia and her father set sail for Japan, Cecelia dreamed the emperor himself would greet them when they arrived in the capital city. So today, she dressed in a clean, white top and petticoat, and brushed her hair, pulling the top half back on her head and securing it with a pink ribbon, leaving the rest to flow over her shoulders and down her back.

Cecelia's father approached her from behind. 'Cecelia, you

will accompany me to the office after we disembark. Walk behind me and stay close. Do not speak or engage with anyone. Do you understand?'

'Yes, father,' she obeyed. 'Are we meeting the emperor?'

'Of course not, silly girl. We will check in at the port office, where they will arrange security for us while we are here.'

As Cecelia followed her father down the gangplank, stepping down the wooden ramp that creaked beneath her feet, she noticed a strong-built Japanese man staring at her. He wore loose-fitting navy-blue pants, and a matching jacket cinched at the waist with a black belt. The man had high cheekbones and dark, upward-arched eyes that gleamed like polished obsidian, and he stood tall, his height the same as her father's. On his left side hung two swords that glinted in the sunlight, and Cecelia wondered if this man happened to be one of the barbarians her father had warned her about.

As Cecelia trailed behind her father along the sun-drenched pier, she felt the unsettling sensation of being followed. Upon arriving at the office, her father told her to sit on the dark wood bench and wait. She smoothed her skirt and sat down, straightening her back as she glanced at the bustling surroundings. Suddenly, the Japanese man she saw when she disembarked the ship stood directly before her. Her green eyes widened in surprise as the man said, in English, 'Hello.' Cecelia's breath caught in her throat. She swallowed hard, then responded softly, 'Hello,' shifting on the wooden bench, her senses heightened as she waited for what would come next.

TWENTY-TWO

ARLIER THAT day, Junsaku sat on a futon, his face damp with sweat. The recurring dream, a chilling vision of a towering figure draped in black dropping an axe towards the alabaster neck of a woman, had once again disturbed his slumber, jolting him awake, the image lingering in his mind even as the morning sun began to fill the room. Maiko, his favourite courtesan, lay beside him, her fair-skinned knee poking out from the edge of a goose-down quilt. Junsaku took several deep breaths, gave Maiko a soft kiss on her cheek, and slid out of bed. He dressed in navy-blue pants, as loose as a skirt, and a dark blue jacket with generous sleeves, crimped at the waist with a black obi.

'Junsaku, *anata ga iku?* Leaving so soon?' Maiko whispered sensually. 'You are still young. Do you lack the energy for one more time?' The courtesan exposed her long, lean leg from the edge of the blanket and pointed her toes, hoping to entice the samurai to stay.

'Iie. I must go. But do not worry, Maiko. I will be back. You are my favourite,' he said with a flirtatious wink.

As he grabbed his short sword, his wakizashi, from under the bed pillows, he pulled the covers off Maiko, exposing her nude body. He bent down, kissed her neck, and gently slid his rough-ened fingers along the curve of her hip before walking away from the bed. He approached his katana, the blade leaning against the wall, and, with ease, slid both swords into the leather sheaths attached to his belt.

Junsaku left the room, stepped down the steep, dark wood-en stairs, and exited the inn, a light mist lingering near the cob-blestones. The rising sun warmed the capital city, and windows began to glow pale gold from lanterns inside houses and shops, signalling the town of Edo awakened. As Junsaku strolled, peas-ants, workers, and samurai stopped in their tracks, respectfully bowing as he passed, keeping their gaze fixed on the ground until the general moved out of sight.

As the new day's sunshine cloaked the city in warm hues, Junsaku's eyes were drawn to the silhouette of Edo Castle, with its towering walls and curving rooftops rising against the hori-zon, the grand residence of the shogun. With hours to spare be-fore he needed to report to work, Junsaku relished his solitude and decided to stroll to the waterfront.

When he arrived at the docks, Junsaku went to a large mer-chant ship and watched European men pull on ropes the size of tree trunks before wrapping and knotting them to metal cleats. After the men secured the vessel, they lowered the plank to allow the passengers to leave. The male crew members were the first to disembark, wearing striking blue and white striped uniforms, followed by a man with reddish hair. Junsaku chuckled when he caught sight of the man's peculiar attire: he wore short pants that tightened at his calves, a navy-blue jacket with sleeves adorned in gold brocade, white socks, and polished black shoes. However, his amusement quickly turned to awe as his gaze shifted to the girl behind him. She stood tall and elegant, with a slender, shapely figure and caramel-brown hair that cascaded down her back like glistening liquid honey. Her emerald-green eyes sparkled with curiosity, and her soft, pink lips curled into a radiant smile as she surveyed her surroundings. Junsaku stood mesmerised by her beauty and the colours surrounding her body, her aura rippling with waves of purple and fireworks of yellow. As she stepped off the gangplank, Junsaku moved closer, and he discerned the faint sound of her sharp inhale when their eyes locked. Momentarily, they stared at each other, each with an astonished look on their faces. Then, the girl averted her eyes and obediently followed the man accompanying her.

Junsaku experienced a pull, unlike anything he had ever felt, as if an invisible thread tethered his soul to hers, urging him to follow her every step. As the trio moved towards the port office, locals and other samurai cleared a pathway for Junsaku, bending at the waist as he passed. Junsaku smirked as he noticed the funny-dressed foreigner's smug expression when he noticed people bowing, believing the gesture was aimed at him, not realising Junsaku was the object of their respect.

The group arrived at the dockmaster's office, and the man said something to the girl. The young lady went to a wooden bench, smoothed her dress with her hands, and sat down to wait while the red-headed man conducted business inside the office.

Junsaku approached and stood before her, staring. He could see her eyes, the colour of jade, a beautiful contrast to her pale, smooth skin, which glowed in the sun's warmth. Gazing at the girl, he said in English, 'Hello.'

The girl's green eyes widened, and she gasped softly before responding, 'Hello.' Then she shifted on the wooden bench, her expression puzzled and uncertain.

Junsaku thought of a phrase in English, bent down, and whispered in the girl's ear, 'I want you.' As he moved away, he trailed his velvety lips over her earlobe, across her soft cheek, and near the edge of her mouth before standing upright.

The girl's head jerked backwards, and her lips tightened. Then, she spoke in a rapid cadence, and Junsaku could not translate fast enough to keep up with what she said. He did pick up some words, like 'no', 'go away,' and 'father', and based on what he heard, Junsaku figured she told him he could not have her, which made him more determined.

The red-headed man returned from the dockmaster's office just as the girl finished speaking. 'Come, Cecelia,' he commanded, snapping his fingers.

'She is called Cecelia. That man is her father,' Junsaku ascertained.

As Cecelia and Lucas passed Junsaku, Lucas looked the samurai up and down, his chin raised. As Cecelia followed her father, she glanced at Junsaku with an inquisitive expression before smiling shyly and then turning away.

After they disappeared into the crowd, Junsaku entered the dockmaster's office and approached a skinny man with thinning black hair who bowed behind the counter. 'Who is that foreigner?' Junsaku asked.

Bent at the torso, the man answered, 'He is a merchant on the ship which has just arrived from Batavia. He is a Dutchman travelling with his daughter.'

'Did you assign him security?'

'Hai,' the man responded, still bowing.

'English-speaking samurai?'

'Hai. I assigned him four men, including one who speaks English.'

'Fine. Tell the English-speaking guard to bring the woman to the Festival of the Sakura tomorrow at nine in the morning. Instruct him to deliver her to the Ryōgoku bridge on the river. He is to tell her father he will show her the capital city and that a female escort will join them. The guard must not share where he is taking her. If he fulfils my wishes precisely as I have told you, I will spare your life. Now, where are they staying?'

The man, still bowing, inhaled loudly before answering, 'They are staying at Sukeroku-no-Yado in Shitamachi.'

'Good.' Junsaku reached into his pocket, grabbed a coin, and tossed it onto the counter. 'Make sure the woman is at the festival tomorrow...or else,' he finished.

'Hai,' replied the dockmaster, his voice quivering.

TWENTY-THREE

'YUI, OJISAN is home!' Nobushida yelled as he ran towards the front entrance, his socks brushing the tatami mat floor. After Junsaku put on his slippers and entered the house, Nobushida's six-year-old body slammed into his thighs, and the boy wrapped his arms around Junsaku's legs and squeezed as hard as he could.

'Ah,' Junsaku said, his hands on Nobushida's bony shoulders, 'it is good to see you, too.'

'Ojisan, I have been practising my strikes, and I am ready to show you!' he exclaimed. 'Can we go now?'

'Have you cleaned the dojo today?'

'Hai,' he said, standing tall, rolling back his shoulders.

'Good job.' Junsaku tousled Nobushida's soft, short-cropped black hair. 'Let us change into our gis and train.'

When they arrived at the doorway of the dojo, they bowed before entering. Once inside, they faced each other and bowed again. 'Good,' Junsaku said. 'Now, let me get in position for you to show me your strikes.' Junsaku lowered himself to his knees, his head slightly higher than Nobushida's. '*Kime,*' Junsaku stated.

'*Osu,* Sensei. I will focus.'

'Hajime,' Junsaku instructed, putting his palms in front of his chest, creating targets for the young boy. Nobushida lunged, lifted his left knee, and struck Junsaku's right palm. He repeated this movement until Junsaku said, *'Gyaku,'* and Nobushida performed the drills with his opposite leg. Tiny pearls of sweat clung to Nobushida's lightly tanned skin, and his eyes showed the intensity of his concentration.

Junsaku stood. 'Yame,' he said, ordering his student to stop. Nobushida halted and stood with his hands by his side. 'You have practised well, Nobushida. I am proud of you. Now, show me *joden tsuki.'*

Nobushida beamed, his smile lighting up the room. 'Osu, Sensei,' he said, addressing his teacher with deep respect.

'*Kamae.* Find your stance.'

Nobushida spread his legs apart. He clenched his right hand and pulled it back to his underarm, then formed a fist with his left hand, stretched his left arm parallel to the floor, and bent at the knees, turning his body slightly.

'Hajime,' Junsaku said, standing away from Nobushida as the boy began his demonstration.

Nobushida took his right foot from the back and brought it forward quickly, turning at the hips as his right fist punched forward and his left fist moved back towards his chin. Returning his right foot to its original position, Nobushida performed the joden tsuki repeatedly until Junsaku told him to switch sides.

After two hours passed, young Nobushida demonstrated all the punches and kicks he practised.

'Nobushida, you have done well,' Junsaku complimented.

'Arigato gozaimasu, Sensei.'

'As a reward, I will have Yui make your favourite.'

Nobushida jumped in place, clapping his hands. 'Crispy rice balls!'

'First, let us finish properly,' Junsaku said. He and Nobushida stood opposite each other, their eyes locked in mutual respect. Then they lowered their gazes, allowing their hands to rest at their sides, and, in unison, performed a deep, respectful bow, saying, 'Osu.'

After changing out of their gis, they met in the kitchen where Yui served them miso soup, grilled white fish, and pickled vegetables. After their meal, Junsaku played his shakuhachi. Breathy and solemn, almost painful, each note of the bamboo flute seemed to linger in the air like the light grey smoke from the kitchen fire. As the notes formed, Junsaku remembered years earlier playing *The Crane's Call* for his mother, father, and younger sister, Etsuko; he recalled his mother's delight, his father's respect, and, most of all, his sister's disgust. For a fleeting moment, Junsaku yearned for his parents, but he did not feel the same longing for his sister, who lived in Okinawa with her husband. Despite sharing the same childhood home, they had never bonded, and Junsaku had no interest in seeing her again, even if she was his only remaining blood relative

When Junsaku finished, he set the shakuhachi in his lap and said, 'Yui, give Nobushida crispy rice cakes. He deserves a reward for practising.' Yui's lips curled into a warm smile. 'Also, I have exciting news,' Junsaku announced, his voice brimming with enthusiasm. 'I have met a woman—the most beautiful woman I have ever seen.' Junsaku leaned closer to Nobushida and looked into his brown eyes, the boy's gaze mirroring his excitement. 'She is from a distant land, Nobushida. She is from Europe, a land called Lithuania. She speaks English, so you will have to continue to learn so you can talk to her. I will see her tomorrow and, I hope, every day for the rest of my life.' Junsaku's smile lit his face as he asked, 'Nobushida, would you like her to become your mother? Someone who would care for you deeply and love you just as I do?'

'Hai. I would like it very much, Ojisan. I will wish for her to become part of our family.'

'I can tell you I wish for it more, Nobushida,' Junsaku replied with a chuckle, noticing Yui's gentle smile as she washed dishes, staring happily at the bowl she cleaned with a rag.

TWENTY-FOUR

DRESSED IN black pants and a black jacket embroidered with gold dragons, Junsaku tied his jet-black hair into a knot on the crown of his head and strolled to the river to meet Cecelia. He purposely arrived early and secured a spot in the shade of a cherry blossom tree. He placed a blanket near the river's edge and set down a carafe of rice wine and two small clay cups. Several minutes later, he saw the samurai guard walking towards the bridge with Cecelia trailing behind him, a youthful bounce in her step. She wore a brilliant red kimono with a purple neckline and embroidered white cranes, the robe bound at the waist by a wide, bright green belt, and wooden sandals from the inn. Junsaku thought Cecelia looked more vibrant than the thousands of blossoming sakura flowers surrounding him. Junsaku smiled as he thought about his life's unexpected twist; when he saw Cecelia disembarking the ship the day before, his heart said, 'There she is.' Junsaku never wanted to be with another woman for as long as he lived.

Junsaku stood as they approached, and Cecelia beamed when she saw him.

'Here is the girl, General,' the samurai guard stated, bowing.

'Hello again. I know you are called Cecelia. My name is Junsaku. I am top samurai to the shogun,' he said in thickly accented English.

'It is a pleasure to meet you, Junsaku.' Cecelia stared curiously, her green eyes shimmering in the golden sunlight, and she was surprised when a feeling of calm washed over her despite the reality of standing before a man she had just met in a foreign land.

As the samurai guard began translating her words into Japanese, Junsaku stopped him. 'Silence! I know what she said. Go.' The samurai bowed and hurried off, disappearing across the wooden bridge while cherry blossom flowers drifted around him like snowflakes. 'Sit,' Junsaku said, pointing at the blanket. Cecelia knelt. 'Beautiful kimono,' Junsaku remarked.

'Yes, it is. One of the ladies at the inn brought it to me this morning and helped me dress. My father arranged it.'

'No, not father. I arrange,' Junsaku replied, playfully thumping his chest with his fist.

'Oh,' she responded shyly. 'Thank you. It is lovely.'

'Kimono is nice, but woman in kimono is what makes it lovely,' he said, pointing at her. 'Now, nihonshu; sake,' Junsaku said. He took Cecelia's hand and placed an empty clay cup on her palm. 'You hold while I pour nihonshu,' he said. Cecelia delicately gripped the base with her fingers as Junsaku filled it with rice wine. 'Now, put down, and you give sake to me,' Junsaku said, grabbing an empty cup and holding it towards her with two hands.

Cecelia placed her filled cup on the blanket and poured sake for Junsaku. When she finished, Junsaku motioned for Cecelia to pick up her sake cup.

'Kanpai,' Junsaku said, tapping his cup against hers.

'Kanpai,' Cecelia repeated, sipping her drink. She licked her lips, looked at the sake in the cup, the drink as clear as fresh water, then raised her eyes and stated happily, 'I like this.'

For minutes, the two sat on the blanket, speechless, refilling each other's cups with sake when emptied. Junsaku observed Cecelia admiring the flowering trees and could see a yellow aura emanating from her skin like an angel. 'Cecelia,' he sighed, 'you are the most beautiful woman Junsaku has ever seen.'

Cecelia's face reddened. 'Thank you,' she replied, twisting a strand of hair around her index finger. 'Junsaku, why did you send for me?'

Junsaku took a deep breath. 'I do not understand the question?'

'Why...um, why did you want me to come here today? Why did you want to see me again?' she stammered, hoping he could figure out the meaning of her question.

'Ah, you want to know why I ask you here!' he exclaimed. 'I can feel your energy, Cecelia. It is same as mine.'

Cecelia inhaled, then replied, 'Oh, I see. I feel something, too.'

'Hai,' he nodded. 'You feel Junsaku's energy.'

They gazed into each other's eyes, and then Junsaku pointed at the cherry blossom trees and asked, 'You like sakura?

'Sakura. Is that the name of this flower?' she asked, picking up a pinkish-white blossom from the ground and spinning it between her thumb and index finger.

'Hai. This time of year, sakura flowers come to life in Edo.'

'Then, yes, hai. I like the sakura very much.'

'I like you very much,' Junsaku announced loudly.

'You do not know me, Junsaku.' Cecelia felt giddy and light-hearted, even with the unfamiliarity of her current situation. She should have been scared to be alone with a strange man, a samurai, in Japan, but instead, exhilaration flooded her body, and she never wanted it to end.

'I do know you,' he replied, his dark onyx eyes glimmering with intense emotion as though he could see into the depths of Cecelia's soul. 'You are my other half.' Junsaku took Cecelia's right hand and placed her palm in the centre of his hard chest. 'You stay with Junsaku forever.'

Cecelia allowed her hand to linger while her body tingled everywhere, a buzzing energy surging through her. 'I wish I could, but I cannot, Junsaku. My father will not allow it.'

'Father has no say. I am top samurai, a general. I take what I want,' he bragged.

She pulled her hand away. 'I have heard of the samurai, and I am sure you are important, but my father will not agree.'

'I can kill your father if I like, but I do not want to kill your otosan,' he stated casually, as though deciding between a meal of either chicken or fish.

Her green eyes widened. 'Junsaku, killing my father would not please me.'

'Cecelia, no worry. I will not hurt father.' Junsaku changed the subject. 'You stay at inn; Sukeroku-no-Yado?'

'Yes, that is the name.'

'Tomorrow, I come to inn and take you to shrine.'

'My father has said I can only go with Hiroshi, the guard who brought me here today.'

'I tell guard to bring you outside inn to meet me tomorrow, and we go to shrine together.'

Cecelia smiled. 'That would be wonderful. I will see you as much as possible before I leave Japan, Junsaku,' Cecelia replied, blushing, feeling bittersweet, knowing her joy would end as soon as her father told her the time had come to leave the country.

'Cecelia will not leave Japan. You will stay with me forever,' he said confidently. Then, Junsaku gestured to the sake carafe. 'Now, we drink more sake.'

TWENTY-FIVE

CECELIA WOKE and stretched her limbs on the futon mattress as the sun forced its light through the edges of the sliding wooden panels that covered the windows. As she got out of bed, she looked at the red and purple kimono lying on the low table, thinking of how kind Junsaku had been to give her this gift. Still, she decided she would not wear it for a second day and chose a simple, white-cotton dress instead. The dress's long sleeves hugged her lean arms, the skirt falling mid-calf, and she buttoned the collar high on her neck before rolling cream-coloured stockings up her long legs. She walked across the tatami mats to the shoji doors, slid them open, and found her slippers placed side by side at the door's entrance. She put them on, walked down the hall to the dining room, and joined her father for breakfast.

Lucas did not acknowledge Cecelia when she entered, preoccupied with reading papers as he sat on a floor cushion before a low table. Nearby, the four assigned guards sat eating breakfast, drinking tea, and conversing in Japanese.

'Good morning, Father,' Cecelia said cheerfully in English.

'*Goedemorgen,*' he mumbled in Dutch.

She sat across the table from him. A Japanese woman

brought over a sectioned tray, its compartments filled with white rice, a piece of cooked mackerel, and pickled vegetables. Cecelia felt happy; she enjoyed eating food like this for breakfast. 'Father,' Cecelia said, 'the cherry blossom festival yesterday was wonderful, and today, Hiroshi has agreed to take me to visit a shrine.' Cecelia noticed Hiroshi stopped eating. She could tell he listened to her conversation as he stared at the rice bowl cupped in his hand, his chopsticks still in his fingers.

'Fine,' her father replied gruffly. 'I will be in meetings or on the ship, so stay with Hiroshi and the female escort, and do not get into trouble. Make sure you return by sundown.'

'Yes, father,' she agreed, feeling a sudden pang of guilt for lying to her father while, at the same time, her heart raced with excitement to see Junsaku.

Her father put down his teacup and stood. 'I am leaving now. Remember, you are in a foreign country with customs vastly different from ours, and these people do not see the world as we do – they are barbarians,' he said. 'I have a lot of work to do, so if I do not see you this evening, I will see you at breakfast tomorrow.'

'Yes, father.'

He left the dining room and Cecelia quickly finished her food, looked at Hiroshi, and nodded. The samurai stood up, grabbed his two swords off the tatami mats, and slid them into the sheathes attached to his belt.

Cecelia got up from the table and straightened her dress. 'Are you ready to go, Hiroshi?'

'Hai...ah, yes, Lady,' the samurai responded.

They left the dining room and went to the front entrance. Before exiting, Cecelia removed her sandals and replaced them with her buckle-up shoes. She followed the guard outside, and several meters ahead on the cobblestone street, they turned the corner.

Junsaku leaned against a building of thick, dark wood and mud-coloured walls, wearing a bright blue silk kimono with matching hakama pants, the hilt of his swords protruding near his left hip. He smiled and bowed in her direction. The guard immediately bent at the torso as Junsaku approached Cecelia. Ignoring the samurai escort, Junsaku took Cecelia's hand, raised it to his lips, and kissed it gently.

'Good morning, Junsaku,' Cecelia said, a slight tremor in her voice.

'*Ohayō gozaimasu,*' he replied. Junsaku looked at the guard still bent and said, in Japanese, 'Leave us. You will not be coming along. I will bring Cecelia back to the inn myself.'

'My father said I must be back before sundown,' she told Junsaku.

Junsaku laughed. 'For now, we let Father pretend he is the most important man and make rules, like Shogun. But Father is not Shogun, and only Fusakage Shogun tells Junsaku what to do.'

Cecelia felt torn because she had always obeyed her father. Yet, with Junsaku, she felt independent and rebellious, sensing her life had changed forever.

Junsaku held Cecelia's hand, and they strolled down the road, every person bowing as the general passed. 'Edo is a busy city,' Junsaku remarked as they walked. 'Many nice things, like sake, vegetables, fish, ceramics, and...'

Before Junsaku finished his sentence, he heard someone yell, '*Gaijin!*'

Junsaku stopped abruptly. Everyone, from peasants to samurai, remained bent at the waist, staring at the ground as Junsaku scanned the crowd, searching for the person who yelled this derogatory word, meaning 'foreign outsider'.

'What is it?' Cecelia asked, confused by Junsaku's behaviour, feeling fear for the first time.

Junsaku frowned. 'Someone called you gaijin. Not good. You wait here, Cecelia.' Junsaku approached a low-ranking samurai who bowed, his face downcast. 'Stand up,' Junsaku commanded.

The samurai stood upright, remaining still and rigid, refusing to meet Junsaku's gaze.

'You dare disrespect the woman who accompanies me?' Junsaku threatened.

The samurai tightened his lips.

'I know it is you,' Junsaku growled. 'I can see your energy. Do not be weak. Admit your stupidity.'

Perspiration bubbled on the samurai's forehead.

Junsaku touched the handle of his sword. 'Tell me now or die.'

'But she is a gaijin!' the samurai proclaimed, his tone a blend of exasperation and desperation.

Before the man could take his next breath, Junsaku bent his elbow, swung his arm, and delivered a back fist strike to the side of the samurai's head, causing the soldier to fall to the ground. Junsaku drew his short sword and placed the razor-sharp edge on the samurai's throat as he lay in the street. 'You are lucky I am in a good mood, fool, or your life would end today. Now, get to your feet and apologise to the lady before I change my mind.'

'Hai,' the samurai replied weakly.

Junsaku returned his sword to its scabbard.

The samurai stood and, with heavy feet, walked to Cecelia. Cecelia found herself face to face with the samurai, a fierce expression on the man's face, his gaze piercing through her like sharp daggers. Then, the soldier diverted his eyes and bowed deeply, saying, 'Gomennasai.' Cecelia could not understand what he said, but his words made her shiver; however, despite her fear, she summoned her courage and nodded in acknowledgment.

Junsaku offered Cecelia his right arm, his elbow bent, and she accepted, her heart pounding. Cecelia placed trembling fingers around his forearm, and, with Junsaku leading the way, Cecelia clutched his arm as they walked past the hushed crowd and continued down the street.

＊＊

WHEN THEY arrived at the shrine, the late-morning sun added to the heat of their bodies. They passed under the first gate, the *torii,* its heavy beams painted bright orange-red, and continued to walk on massive, rectangular, block-stone stairs leading to the main shrine. When the couple walked under a second gate, the tower gate built in the same style as the torii, they entered a courtyard and found a handful of visitors wandering the garden just in front of the large shrine. As soon as the people saw Junsaku, they bowed.

'Why do they do that when you are near?' Cecelia whispered.

'*Ojigi*—I do not know this word in English,' he said, his brow furrowed as he repeated the movements several times.

'I understand,' she replied. 'The word in English is bow. But *why* do they bow to you, why ojigi, when you pass?'

'It shows respect, Cecelia.'

Junsaku held Cecelia's hand as they ascended more rock steps towards the shrine's main hall, the pathway lined with short, red lanterns. At the stairs landing, Junsaku showed Cecelia the purification fountain and how to cleanse by filling the long-handle cup with the basin's water and pouring it over her hands to wash.

Next, taking her clean hand, Junsaku curved it into a concave shape, and then he filled it with water. He told her to drink the water and then immediately spit it on the ground, which she did. As they continued forward, Cecelia noticed fierce-looking statues guarding the main hall, part dog, part lion, their bodies painted red with white manes, and further inside, a small structure that looked like a mini-shrine with a small brass bell hanging inside.

Junsaku and Cecelia entered the shrine. They stepped onto the massive stone-paved floor and walked between thick wood pillars extending from the ground to the ceiling. Cecelia noticed straw-coloured woven objects shaped like zig-zag lightning bolts dangling from the ceiling, and Junsaku explained, 'Those are *shide,* Cecelia. They hang from a straw rope, *shimenawa.* This is sacred space. No evil may enter.' Junsaku went to the altar, bowed, straightened, and clapped twice before praying. Several minutes later, he stood and smiled at Cecelia.

'That is quite different from how we pray at the Catholic church,' Cecelia observed.

'You want to pray?'

'Not this time, Junsaku.'

'Then, we go.' Junsaku took Cecelia's hand and led her out of the shrine and into the courtyard.

As they strolled down the lantern-lined pathway, Cecelia asked, 'Junsaku, where did you learn to speak English? Did you learn in school, like me?'

'Hai, some learning in school,' Junsaku said, nodding. 'And, also, I learn English as a boy from a ghost.' Junsaku noticed Cecelia's mouth drop, her eyes wide with astonishment. 'When I was young, a spirit, a boy, came to me. This boy look like your father: light skinned with blue eyes. This ghost teach me how to speak English. Because I am very smart, I learn quickly.' Junsaku boosted. 'Boy visit for many years but stop coming when I grow older.'

'Fascinating,' Cecelia replied, impressed. 'You believe in ghosts—do you also believe in God?'

Junsaku laughed lightly. 'Well, Cecelia, not *one* God. For me, there are many Gods in many things, and I believe I have lived and died many lifetimes,' he said, staring deep into her eyes. 'Do you also believe?'

'Actually, I do,' she replied thoughtfully. 'I was raised a Catholic and taught to believe there is only one God. However, deep down, I have never felt this to be true. Like you, I believe we live and repeatedly die, reborn to learn more until, at some point, we hopefully have nothing more to learn.'

Junsaku slapped his thigh and raised his voice, saying, 'Hai! *Satori!*' Then, he lowered his volume. 'Satori is experience of mind, body, and seeing beyond, Cecelia,' he said, lightly poking her forehead with his index finger. Suddenly, Junsaku pulled her against him, so close she had to lean her head back to avoid her nose bumping his chin. 'Cecelia, you are my other half,' he said, staring directly into her eyes. He wove his fingers through her long hair, drew her lips to his, and kissed her passionately, his tongue entwining hers, igniting her body. When he stopped, Cecelia could hardly breathe, unable to speak, mesmerised by the fiery gold embers that seemed to float in the darkness of his eyes. 'Maybe shrine not good place for this, but I had to kiss you,' Junsaku declared.

Cecelia kissed him gently on the lips then moved away, resting her hands on his broad shoulders. 'I would like to kiss you more – away from the temple.'

'We go to my house. You will meet Nobushida,' Junsaku announced excitedly. He held her hand as they walked towards the road, passing underneath the brightly painted gates and heading towards the city centre.

'Junsaku, who is Nobushida?' Cecelia asked.

'He is the son of my dear friend, Yasafune-san. My friend died in battle, and Nobushida's mother also went to the next life, so I became the boy's Ojisan, like uncle. I now love and care for him like my own son. And Cecelia, Nobushida is very smart, trains hard, and will be a great samurai one day, like me. I want you to meet him. You will love him as I do.'

'I look forward to it, Junsaku. How old is he?'

'Nobushida is six.'

TWENTY-SIX

A S JUNSAKU and Cecelia made their way to Junsaku's home in the samurai district, Junsaku seemed oblivious to the attention the couple attracted. At the same time, Cecelia blushed as she noticed people staring at her, the tall, foreign woman with bright, green eyes walking beside a samurai general. Eventually, Junsaku stopped before a solid, dark wood gate, lifted the iron handle, and opened the door. On the other side, Cecelia saw a pathway leading to a single-level wooden house with sliding, latticed shoji doors across the facade. A lush, green-moss and pebble landscape with meticulously placed rocks, boulders, and ruby-leaved trees surrounded the home, and, in the yard sat a large, rectangular box full of golden sand, its surface etched with lines and swirls created by the teeth of a wooden rake.

As Junsaku and Cecelia approached the front entrance, the shoji doors slid open. Yui came out holding Nobushida's hand, a big smile on the boy's face, his dark walnut-brown eyes sparkling.

'Nobushida, Yui,' Junsaku said in Japanese, 'this is Cecelia.'

Yui and Nobushida bowed, and Cecelia returned their bow.

'It is nice to meet you,' Cecelia said in English, her cheeks a blooming pink, a blend of excitement and nervousness.

Yui looked puzzled as she tried to understand the woman's English words. Junsaku noticed her confusion and translated. However, Nobushida understood Cecelia and responded, 'Nice to meet you.'

'Nobushida, you speak English?' Cecelia asked excitedly.

'A little,' the boy replied shyly.

Then Junsaku said something directly to Nobushida in Japanese. The boy nodded, went to Cecelia, took her hand, and said, 'Come.'

'He wants to show you something,' Junsaku told Cecelia, his face the expression of a proud father.

'Alright,' she replied, smiling as she followed the boy.

Nobushida stopped at the genkan inside the house and pointed at Cecelia's feet. 'Off, please.'

'Ah, yes,' Cecelia said, remembering the custom. She removed her leather and buckle shoes, and Nobushida gave her zori slippers before placing her shoes on a small shelf near the front door. Again, Nobushida took her hand, clasped his fingers with hers, and led her to a room with golden tatami mats covering the floor, stopping at the entrance. The young boy looked Cecelia in the eyes and said, 'This is dojo,' pointing inside.

'That is our training room, our dojo,' Junsaku said, standing behind Cecelia, a full head taller than her. 'Nobushida is proud.'

'Someday, I will show you everything my sensei has taught me. You will be impressed,' Nobushida stated in rapid Japanese, speaking as though Cecelia understood every word he said.

'Nobushida says he wants to show you what he knows in the dojo and that you will be very...ah...imp...imp...'

'Impressed?' Cecelia asked.

'Hai, impressed! He is confident like his ojisan,' Junsaku

said, his eyes gleaming with admiration.

'Nobushida,' Cecelia said, bending at the knees to be eye level with the boy, 'I would like to watch you train in the dojo very much.'

Nobushida's cheeks lifted as a radiant smile spread across his face, revealing his slightly crooked teeth. His expression reflected his happiness as he replied, 'Thank you.'

TWENTY-SEVEN

ON A SUN-DRENCHED afternoon, four weeks after she arrived in Japan, Cecelia sat with Junsaku on a blanket beneath a cherry blossom tree on the riverbank of the *Sumidagawa,* the sound of running water and bird song filling the air. 'Junsaku, I must tell you something,' Cecelia said, her words catching in her throat.

'What is it?'

'My father has told me we leave Japan tomorrow. He has completed his trade, and we sail to Batavia in the morning,' she finished, her voice shaky, tears forming in her eyes.

'No. Cecelia does not go,' Junsaku stated adamantly.

'I must go, Junsaku. I cannot stay here. I do not want to leave, but I have no choice.' Cecelia shrugged. 'He is my father.'

'Cecelia, you always have choice. You must be with me. Become my wife.'

Cecelia looked surprised. 'You want to make me your wife?'

As Junsaku looked into her eyes, he noticed gold rings encircled her pupils, the colour seeping into the bright green of her irises.

'Hai,' he whispered as he grabbed her hand and rubbed her

smooth skin with his calloused thumb.

'How can I be your wife if I am not Japanese? It will never be allowed.'

'Nobody tells Junsaku what to do. If I want you for my wife, you will be my wife.'

With a dry mouth, Cecelia replied, 'My father will not agree.'

'Junsaku will tell Father tonight that Cecelia will be my wife. Leave it to me. Most important, Cecelia, *watashi no ai?* Do you want to be my wife?' he asked, his dark irises laced with golden threads.

'All I want in the world is to be with you,' she said, her heart pounding.

Junsaku smiled, wrapped his arms around her, and let her cheek rest against his chest. 'Cecelia, not to worry. I will go to ship tonight to tell Father the news. Cecelia will be the wife of Junsaku.'

TWENTY-EIGHT

JUNSAKU DRESSED in black striped hakama pants, a black kimono embroidered with the shogun's emblem, and a haori, a waist-length overcoat made from black silk. He carried both swords in the belt around his waist as he walked purposefully to the harbour.

When he arrived at the *Fortuyn,* he strolled up the gangplank and entered the ship. The samurai guarding the entrance bowed.

'Where is the merchant, the girl's father?' Junsaku demanded.

'Go straight through that doorway,' the guard replied, pointing down the short hallway.

Junsaku walked forward and pushed open a wooden door. Inside the room stood three samurai who bowed when they saw Junsaku. Lucas, Cecelia's father, sat at a desk, a pointed quill between his fingers, and he looked up at Junsaku, whose figure filled the doorway. Lucas noticed all the samurai in the room bowing. 'Can I help you?' he groaned.

'I am General Junsaku Aoyama, the shogun's top warrior.' His voice resonated with authority and power, and his thick, black eyebrows arched dramatically above his black, piercing eyes. Wisps of black hair escaped his top knot and framed his face, highlighting his high cheekbones and strong jawline covered in stubble, hiding the moon-shaped scar near his lip given to him by his sister when he was just a boy.

Lucas settled back into his chair, crossed his legs, and with a mocking smirk and raised eyebrows asked, 'And what can I do for you, top samurai?'

'Not 'top samurai'. You call me Junsaku-sama,' he commanded.

'Fine, Junsaku-sama. Why are you here?'

'I have seen daughter, Cecelia, every day since you arrived in Japan. I love her and want her as my wife,' he declared.

Lucas squinted his blue eyes and shifted in his seat. 'You cannot be serious?'

'Junsaku serious. I love her and will have Cecelia as my wife. She also wants this.'

'Preposterous,' he muttered, shaking his head. After a long pause, Lucas stated, 'Sir, your request is ridiculous, and I forbid a marriage between you and my daughter. You don't even know each other.'

'I know Cecelia as I know myself. She must stay with me forever.'

'No, sir, I will not allow Cecelia to marry you or stay in Japan. She will return with me.'

'Father has no choice,' Junsaku said, spreading his legs hip-width and lightly touching the hilt of his sword. 'Junsaku is telling you how it will be.'

'Excuse me? I decide what my daughter will do. Not you. Cecelia will not marry a Japanese man.'

'You are wrong. Cecelia *will* marry a Japanese man– me.' Junsaku poked his chest with his thumb.

Lucas' pale face turned bright red. 'Sir, you will not tell me how or what to do with my daughter.' He looked at the samurai guards standing rigidly, their eyes looking down at the wooden floor, and commanded, 'Remove this man!'

One samurai glanced at Lucas and immediately turned away.

'You heard me, guards! You were assigned to protect me,' Lucas said, his tone a pitch higher. 'Remove this man at once.'

The samurai, Hiroshi, did not move and said in English, 'We cannot remove him from the ship. If we try, he will kill us.'

'Nonsense,' Lucas said, beginning to stand. But, before he could rise, Junsaku moved towards him as fast as a cheetah, drew his sword, and placed the blade's tip at the centre of Lucas' chest.

'I beg your pardon?' Lucas said, exasperated.

'You are not in charge,' Junsaku growled. 'Junsaku in charge.'

Lucas' face turned a deeper shade of red, strikingly contrasting his ice-blue eyes, and he puffed out his chest. 'You don't even know my daughter. She will never be accepted here.'

'I will make sure Cecelia has a good life. And you are invited to the ceremony,' Junsaku stated joyfully as he returned his sword to its sheath.

'Fools, both of you,' Lucas hissed. 'My daughter is making a terrible decision she will have to live with. I will not condone her behaviour, yet it appears I have no say.'

'Right. Father has no say. Only Junsaku and Cecelia decide.'

Junsaku left the ship, grinning as he breathed in the salty air, and headed to the inn. He could barely hide his excitement at the thought of Cecelia's radiant smile lighting up her face when he shared the excellent news: they were to be married.

TWENTY-NINE

CECELIA LAY on the futon mattress wearing a cotton nightgown, crying softly, the cool night air seeping into her room as she listened to the rhythmic chirping of crickets. After falling asleep, the sound of creaking wood on the other side of the shoji doors awakened her. She sat upright and gripped the collar of her nightgown near her chin, unsure if she should yell out or remain quiet. She looked at the parchment-covered door, the paper glowing soft yellow from lantern light, as a shadowy silhouette appeared before the panel slid open. Cecelia could see the outline of a man standing in the doorway, and she relaxed as she recognised the figure.

'Cecelia, may I enter?'

'I will get in trouble, Junsaku. You cannot be here.'

'You will not get in trouble. Your father has not returned from the ship.'

'Then yes, come in,' Cecelia replied.

Junsaku entered her room and slid the doors closed behind him. He came to her bed and sat on the edge of the futon mattress, facing her, their hips touching.

Staring into Junsaku's eyes, Cecelia asked, 'What did Father say?'

'Father have no say.'

'Well, did he say yes? Did he approve our marriage?' she insisted, pulling her knees to her chest.

'Iie. But I told Father we did not need his agreement, that we would marry, and you would have a good life. We belong together, Cecelia.'

As Cecelia's eyes filled with tears, Junsaku gently squeezed her foot below the blanket. 'Tomorrow,' he said, 'we will breakfast in the morning with your father and discuss the ceremony. Rest now.'

Junsaku kissed her lips and left the room, closing the doors behind him.

THIRTY

IN THE DARK of morning, Cecelia heard her father's voice from the other side of the shoji doors. 'Cecelia, get up,' he whispered loudly. 'We are leaving.' Roughly, the doors slid open, and Lucas stood in the entryway. 'Get dressed now,' he ordered.

He motioned to someone in the corridor. A Japanese woman entered Cecelia's room and began collecting her belongings, packing them into her travel case.

'But father, I am not going with you. I am staying in Japan and marrying Junsaku.'

'Now!' he barked. 'You will not disgrace me by staying here with these people, especially marrying one.'

'No,' she responded, her voice timid.

'Get dressed and be outside this door in ten minutes, or I will personally drag you out of this inn by your hair, embarrassing you in front of everyone in Japan,' he said, seething.

Her father slid the shoji panel closed, and Cecelia listened as he walked down the hallway.

Cecelia got out of bed and dressed slowly, sobbing, her vision blurred by tears. When she finished, she left her room and went to the front of the inn wearing the red kimono Junsaku had given her.

'What in heavens are you wearing?' her father scorned. 'You look ridiculous. However, there is no time to change. Follow me,' he said, walking away.

'Father, I am not going.'

Lucas turned to his daughter, his face crimson. 'You are coming with me, you foolish girl. You will board the ship, and when we arrive back in Batavia, you will be on the next boat to Lithuania. I should never have taken you with me,' he grumbled angrily.

'Father, I have accepted Junsaku's marriage proposal. I love him, and I am staying in Japan.'

'Impossible!' he shouted. 'How could you embarrass me like this?' he said, his anger visible in his blue, bloodshot eyes.

Cecelia cried, tears streaming down her face. 'Father, I did not ask for this to happen. I do not have a schoolgirl crush. I am in love with Junsaku.'

Hiroshi, the English-speaking samurai, stood near the wall, trying to be inconspicuous.

'Take her,' Lucas commanded the soldier. 'She is coming with us, even if by force.'

Hiroshi reached out and gently gripped Cecelia's forearm. Cecelia saw the concern in the samurai's brown eyes and sighed, not wanting to escalate the issue.

'Follow me,' Cecelia's father ordered, leaving the inn.

Hiroshi held Cecelia's arm as the three walked towards the harbour, the uneven, cobblestone roads still shrouded in morning darkness. When they arrived at the *Fortuyn,* the captain waited for them on the dock.

'Board the ship, Cecelia,' Lucas demanded, gesturing for her to walk up the gangplank.

The samurai guard let go of her arm, and Cecelia shuffled up the wooden ramp.

THIRTY-ONE

LATER THAT MORNING, after Cecelia had been taken to the ship by her father, Junsaku went to the inn, expecting to see his future bride. However, she and her belongings were gone, and, in her room, a low, black-polished table replaced the futon mattress she slept on the night before. Junsaku ran down the hall. 'Chako,' he yelled. A Japanese woman hurried towards him. 'The woman? Where is she?' he demanded.

Bowing and looking at the ground, the woman answered nervously, 'Her father took her just before sunrise. They were going to their ship.'

Junsaku ran from the inn and headed towards the harbour. When he arrived at the pier, he could see the Fortuyn leaving the bay, the crew still hoisting her sails as the vessel slowly moved toward the open sea. Junsaku found a cargo skiff with long sculling oars, a tenmasen, next to the pier, jumped in, and began rowing towards the ship.

Standing at the stern of the *Fortuyn*, Cecelia saw Junsaku paddling the wooden boat furiously, trying to catch up with the sailing ship. A smile spread across her face, her green eyes glittering like emeralds in the morning sunlight, and she quickly glanced around. Noticing the crew busy with the rigging and her father nowhere to be seen, Cecelia removed her shoes, climbed onto the ship's railing, and jumped feet-first into the harbour.

'Man overboard!' bellowed a deckhand, tossing a life ring into the sea.

'Who is it?' yelled the captain.

'It's the girl!' the deckhand announced as he watched Cecelia swimming towards the shoreline, her arms and legs powered by determination as the waves lapped around her. 'She jumped. I saw her as she crawled onto the railing, but I could not grab her.'

Lucas arrived on deck. He stood next to the captain. 'Is it my daughter? Is it Cecelia?'

'Ja,' the captain replied. 'No need to worry. We will fetch her. Lower the sails!' the captain yelled, ordering the crew to slow down the vessel.

Lucas moved to the ship's railing and watched his daughter swimming away. 'Captain,' Lucas stated, 'we will not retrieve her. She has made her decision. She has chosen to stay in Japan. God save her soul.'

With those words, Lucas vanished into the belly of the ship.

***

WHEN JUNSAKU reached Cecelia, he lifted her into the ten-masen, her kimono heavily saturated. She turned and looked at the ship while Junsaku held her in his arms, trying to warm her. The captain, deckhands, merchants, and cooks all stood at the railing, waving. Cecelia waved back, searching for her father, and realised he was not there, knowing she would never see him again.

'I knew you would not leave me,' Junsaku sighed, holding her tight.

'I will never leave you, husband,' she said, her cheek resting on his warm chest.

Junsaku rowed them to the dock, and they exited the boat, Cecelia's water-logged kimono weighing her body. 'Bring a blanket,' Junsaku yelled to a small Japanese man carrying a rope over his shoulder. The man threw the line onto the wooden planks, ran to a nearby rowboat, and returned with a sheet of heavy wool. Cecelia shivered, her teeth chattering lightly, as Junsaku wrapped her in the scratchy grey sheet. With his arm draped over her shoulders, Junsaku said, 'Let us go home. We need to get you dry and warm,' holding her close as they walked, her hair dripping wet.

***

WHEN THEY arrived at Junsaku's house, Yui greeted them at the front door.

'Yui, take Cecelia to our room. Did you arrange clothes for her as I asked?'

'Hai,' she said, gesturing for Cecelia to remove her wet shoes in the genkan before entering the house.

Cecelia removed her shoes and slipped on sandals. She stepped inside the house and followed Yui to Junsaku's room. Yui pointed at a black jacket embroidered with pink roses, matching loose pants, and tabi socks placed on the futon. She motioned to Cecelia, then at the garments, gesturing with her hands, trying to communicate to the foreign woman to change outfits. Cecelia understood, removed her wet clothes, and handed them to Yui, who carried them from the room, leaving Cecelia alone to dress.

Cecelia changed into the wrap jacket, which she secured at the waist with a black belt, and the loose, flowy pants that hung like a skirt. She put on tabi socks, slid on straw zori sandals, and opened the partition doors. In front of her stood Junsaku. He looked her up and down and smiled. She stood with her arms at her sides as he moved towards her and led her back into the bedroom. He slid his hand underneath her long hair and gently clamped the back of her neck, pulling her to him and kissing her, his tongue sliding into her mouth. She wrapped her arms around his neck and kissed him back, her body pulsing with excitement, as Junsaku shut the opaque fusuma panels for privacy.

THIRTY-TWO

'ARE YOU HAPPY?' Junsaku asked, the tip of his index finger tracing patterns on Cecelia's bare chest as they lay naked on the futon.

'Yes. And you?'

'Hai, so happy,' he smiled. 'Happiest ever in my life.'

'I still cannot believe I am here. It is like a dream,' Cecelia said, shaking her head lightly. 'I do regret disappointing my father.'

'Have no regrets. Be present and here with me,' Junsaku said, stroking Cecelia's cheek with the back of his rough finger. 'Soon, you will become my wife, and Father was wrong for not accepting our love.'

'I suppose. And what about your family, Junsaku? What will they think?'

'Parents are in the next life,' Junsaku said, his eyes softening. 'Only my sister, Etsuko, lives. She is in Okinawa with her husband, Onishi. I do not like her husband much. Something off,' Junsaku said, squinching his nose. 'But sister strange, too. She always thought of herself first and was never kind to me. She even gave me this mark with her toy,' he said, pointing at the crescent-shaped scar near his lip.

Cecelia sighed as she took Junsaku's hand in hers and squeezed it. 'Maybe someday I will meet your sister,' she said. Then, following a short pause, she stated, 'I do not think I will ever see my father again.'

'You never know the future, Cecelia. For now, you have new life; Junsaku's wife,' he replied.

'Yes, my love,' she said, gently stroking his chest with her fingertips. 'Junsaku, I have not asked you, but how did you become a general?'

'For many years, I serve a daimyo,' Junsaku responded. 'He was a powerful feudal lord in northern Japan, with riches and many lands. He noticed Junsaku, the best warrior. Also, I saved his life. Daimyo Suketoki made me a general, the youngest general ever in Japan. Then, Fusakage Shogun take me to work for him and continued my title as general, and again I prove myself in many battles.'

Cecelia sighed loudly. 'You are important, Junsaku, and should be very proud. How can you marry me? I am not Japanese.'

Junsaku leaned on his elbow and looked into Cecelia's green eyes. 'No one can keep us apart, Cecelia. We will be married, and you and Nobushida will live in Kakunodate, where I grew up. It is best for you and all our children instead of living here in Edo. The capital city is too busy and has too many eyes. It is not safe here, and I must protect my family. You will be accepted in Kakunodate.'

THIRTY-THREE

THE COUPLE awoke the following morning with Cecelia's leg draped over Junsaku's muscular thighs.

'Ohayō gozaimasu, Cecelia. Let us have breakfast, and then we leave for Kakunodate,' Junsaku said.

Cecelia pouted. 'I do not want to go because after you take us there, you'll leave and return to Edo, to the shogun.'

'I will visit and stay with you in Kakunodate as much as possible,' Junsaku replied. He pulled her to his chest and felt her soft cheek against his skin, her body warming his. To his surprise, Cecelia straddled him, the ends of her long hair hanging near his face, and he felt himself stir as she kissed his neck and ears.

***

AFTER MAKING love, they dressed in tan kimonos, slid zori sandals over their tabi socks, and went to the kitchen.

'Yui,' Junsaku said, 'serve breakfast. And tell Hira to prepare the ox wagon, as well as two horses. We will leave for Kakunodate today. Get Cecelia a hakama and a *jingasa* hat for her head.'

'What did you say to Yui?' Cecelia asked Junsaku shyly.

'I told her to arrange the ox-drawn wagon, and to dress you in the same clothing I wear when I travel.'

'Junsaku,' Cecelia said, 'I am grateful you speak such good English. I do not know how I would get by without you translating.'

'The boy who visited me would be proud,' he boasted.

'The boy?'

'Hai. Remember I told you about the ghost who visited me when I was young and helped me learn English? The spirit boy?'

'Oh yes, of course! I remember.'

'I have not seen him for many years. If I see him again, we will have a good English conversation. Now, Cecelia, time to go, so you must dress in travel clothing,' Junsaku finished, gesturing towards their bedroom door.

***

CECELIA EXITED the bedroom, the heavy fabric of her pants rustling as she moved, and together, she and Junsaku walked to the house's entryway.

'Yui, Nobushida, we are leaving now,' Junsaku announced, touching the hilts of his swords at his hip.

Nobushida ran out of the house, burst through the gate, and clambered onto the front seat of the cart, excited for their trip to begin.

'Nobushida,' Junsaku said, 'Cecelia sits in the front with me, and you sit with Yui on the bench behind us.'

'Ah,' he frowned, 'but I like to sit next to you.'

Junsaku squinted his eyes, and Nobushida crawled off the front bench and into the back.

Yui came out of the house carrying the last burlap bags full of supplies and placed them in the cart bed. 'We are ready to leave, Junsaku-san. Everything we need has been loaded, including food, drink, and sake.' Yui climbed onto the back bench and sat beside

Nobushida, her hands in her lap.

'*Ikimashou*,' Junsaku said. He turned to Cecelia and whispered in her ear, in English, 'We go.'

The chocolate-coloured ox shifted in place, awaiting the command to begin the trek to the Akita Prefecture, while two *kisouma* horses tethered to the cart also waited for the signal to start the walk to the village of Kakunadate. When everyone settled in the wagon, Junsaku flicked the reins, and the ox pulled the cart, sauntering towards their new home.

THIRTY-FOUR

FOLLOWING TEN days of travelling, the ox-drawn cart arrived at the village of Kakunodate in the northern region of Japan, a small town surrounded by lush green forests and towering mountains. As the cart slowed, Junsaku's childhood home came into view, a modest yet charming house with walls made of plastered earth, a dense, thatched roof, and sliding, lattice and paper shoji panel doors lining the exterior.

Junsaku secured the reins, jumped out of the cart, and went to Cecelia, who waited on the front bench. He grabbed his future bride around her waist, lifted her, and placed her gently on the cobblestones. He reached out his hand and helped Yui to the ground before grabbing Nobushida underneath his armpits and removing him from the back bench. Junsaku handed Nobushida a small bag to carry into the house, and he and Yui brought in the remainder.

'Yui, let us all have nihonshu,' Junsaku said.

Yui found the rice wine and ceramic cups. Junsaku, Cecelia, and Nobushida sat around a low table in the kitchen as Yui brought a carafe, three empty cups, and a glass of well water for Nobushida. Yui gave the boy his drink and poured sake for Junsaku and Cecelia. Afterwards, Yui held her glass towards Junsaku, gesturing for him to pour her rice wine.

'I will do it,' Cecelia smiled, taking the carafe and filling Yui's glass.

'Domo arigato gozaimasu,' Yui replied graciously.

After several cups of rice wine, Junsaku said, "Yui, go to the local stable and have them send someone to take the horses and the ox while I go to the shrine to discuss tomorrow's marriage ceremony. Nobushida, you will be our witness.'

Nobushida beamed. 'Arigato, Ojisan!' he exclaimed. 'Thank you, Cecelia-san,' Nobushida said slowly, practising English.

'You can call her obasan, Nobushida, and trust that she will love you like I do,' Junsaku told the boy. Then, in English, Junsaku said, 'Cecelia, I told Nobushida to call you aunt, obasan, and that you will love him as I do.'

Cecelia smiled and looked at Nobushida. She reached out her hand and stroked the boy's straight, black hair with her long fingers. 'Aishiteimasu,' Cecelia said in Japanese. 'I already love you, Nobushida.'

'I love you, too, Obasan,' Nobushida responded in English, his brown eyes sparkling affectionately.

***

JUNSAKU VISITED the shrine, met with a priest, and made all the arrangements for their wedding ceremony to occur the next day. As he returned home, walking down the main road, he heard a male voice call out his name. He turned and saw a uniformed samurai bowing.

'Stand up,' Junsaku ordered. 'Who are you?'

At least three inches shorter than Junsaku with a bony face, the man replied, 'General Aoyama, you may not remember me, but we were in school together as boys. I am Tako Sukenobu. I work for our daimyo as a samurai, much lower rank than you, but still a warrior.'

'I vaguely remember you,' Junsaku lied. Junsaku could distinctly recall him as the school bully he had once defeated in a bokken fight when he was only ten. He also remembered when Tako's father wielded a sword and attacked Junsaku's father and how his father emerged as the victor using only a walking stick.

'I hear you are a general in the shogun's army,' Tako said.

Junsaku breathed deep, expanding his chest. 'Hai, I reside in the castle at Edo.' Then, Junsaku asked, a smirk on his face, 'Tako-san, do you remember when I told everyone at school that I would become Japan's greatest samurai?'

'Hai,' Tako responded, nodding with his eyes.

'Well, I am,' Junsaku boasted.

'Junsaku-san, we are honoured to have you back in Kakunodate. What brings you here?'

'I am marrying tomorrow and have brought my future wife, my boy, and his caregiver to live here while I am in Edo.' Junsaku looked down at the samurai. 'Tako, I need my family safe and protected when I am away and expect your loyalty.'

'Of course,' he said, straightening his spine. 'Whatever you need. I honour and respect your command, Junsaku-san, and will help ensure your family's safety. And what is your future wife's name?'

'Cecelia,' Junsaku said.

The samurai's eyebrows angled towards the bridge of his nose. 'Cecelia? Unusual name. Is she from the south?'

'No. Cecelia is not from Japan. She is from a European country called Lithuania.'

Tako frowned. 'You are not marrying a Japanese woman?'

'No, I am not. Do you have a problem?' Junsaku growled.

'Iie, Junsaku-san,' Tako replied, physically shrinking in stature.

'I expect you and everyone else in this town to respect and protect my family. Do you understand?'

'Hai. I will do all I can to ensure their safety, General.'

THIRTY-FIVE

YUI HELPED Cecelia dress for her wedding. She assisted her into a white underrobe covered by a white kimono with wide triangular sleeves that hung near her hips, only the bride's finger-tips visible below the silk. Around Cecelia's lean waist, Yui tied a broad, white sash followed by a thinner ribbon, both belts made from white silk. Yui braided Cecelia's long, sun-kissed brown hair and secured the hairstyle high on her head with wooden sticks and an ivory fork, then placed a large, white hat shaped like an upside-down fortune cookie on her head, completing the bridal outfit.

'*Anata wa junbi ga dekete imasu,*' Yui said.

Cecelia smiled, her green eyes sparkling, understanding Yui's meaning: she was ready for marriage. 'Thank you, Yui. Domo arigato gozaimasu.'

'Hai,' Yui replied, her hands cupped at her waist. 'Go,' Yui said in English.

Cecelia grinned.

As Cecelia moved towards the door in her wooden sandals, Junsaku flung open the panels. He wore a black kimono with white-striped, black trousers and a coat with the fern leaf-shaped

kamon of his family's clan embroidered on the breast of his outer jacket. Junsaku stared at his future wife, her womanly figure
lost beneath layers of fabric, and said, 'Cecelia, you are beautiful.
Today, you wear white so you can take on the colours of my life.'
Junsaku reached out his roughened hand, slid his fingers along
Cecelia's soft palm, and held her hand lightly. They left the house
and went to the ox-drawn cart, and Junsaku lifted Cecelia onto
the front seat. 'Yui,' Junsaku announced, 'bring Nobushida.'

Yui came out of the house holding Nobushida's tiny hand.
Yui dressed the boy in loose-fitting grey pants and a long, tu-
nic-style outer jacket of grey, tied with a black belt. The young
boy wore wooden platform sandals, adding inches to his height,
and he had to move slowly in the strange shoes to avoid falling
over. When Nobushida reached Junsaku, he lifted the boy, set
him on the back bench, and went to the driver's seat. Then, Junsaku climbed up, sat beside Cecelia, and flicked the reins, signalling for the ox to walk.

They arrived at the shrine within minutes. Junsaku stopped
the cart in front of a set of stairs and plucked Nobushida off the
back bench, setting him on the ground. Then, he went to where
Cecelia waited. 'Come, bride,' Junsaku grinned, putting out his
hand to help her exit the carriage.

Holding hands, Junsaku in the middle, the three walked on
the tree-lined pathway to the main temple, their footsteps echoing on the paved path. At the orange-red torii gate at the top
of the stone staircase, a Shinto priest and a young woman met
the wedding party. The girl, a maiden in her late teens, wore a
bright red kimono and a white jacket embroidered with light grey
flowers, and the priest, dressed in all white and wearing a black,
dome-shaped hat, held a paddle inscribed with words written in

kanji.

'Welcome, and congratulations to you both. Let me explain the ceremony,' the priest said. 'I will enter the shrine first, followed by the maiden, and the couple will follow her. In the shrine, we will stand before the gods, and you will declare your love.' Then the priest glanced around and asked, 'Is it only the boy attending your wedding ceremony?'

'Hai,' Junsaku replied. 'He is our only family and our most important guest.'

Nobushida stifled a giggle, covering his mouth.

The priest turned, the hem of his white, wide-sleeved robe touching the ground, and he held the wooden paddle upright at his waist as he walked towards the shrine, the wedding party following.

Inside the shrine's pavilion, Junsaku and Cecelia approached the altar. They lowered to their knees in front of a short, rectangular table. The priest raised the sacred wand above their heads, chanting ancient verses to dispel all negativities and cleanse their spirits, preparing Junsaku and Cecelia to present themselves to the gods. Just then, a Japanese man entered the pavilion playing a bamboo shakuhachi flute, producing hauntingly beautiful melodies that filled the air as the maiden began to dance, invoking the favour of the deities.

When the girl's dance concluded, she placed a small cup on the table before Junsaku. With a copper pot attached to the end of a long handle, the maiden poured sake into Junsaku's glass. 'When it is your turn to drink, you must drink three times from each cup. *San,* three, will bring happiness, so three from each cup,' Junsaku told Cecelia.

'Hai,' she replied.

When Junsaku finished taking three sips of sake from the first cup, the maiden removed it, gave him a larger cup, and poured him more rice wine. Junsaku sipped three times until the sake emptied. The girl filled a third, slightly larger cup, and Junsaku drank three times again, finishing the nihonshu. Then, the maiden repeated the process with Cecelia. Afterwards, the priest had the couple stand. Junsaku picked up a leafy branch on the table before him and gestured for Cecelia to do the same. The couple held the greenery in front of their chests, bowed their heads, and offered a deity the stem of a sacred tree. Afterwards, the maiden presented cups to everyone, including Nobushida, filling them with sake, only putting a small amount in the boy's glass.

'*Omedetō,*' the priest said, congratulating the newlyweds, and they all drank simultaneously, symbolizing the support the couple would receive from others in their married life together.

THIRTY-SIX

JUNSAKU LISTENED to the rhythmic clip-clop of hooves approaching his home before stopping at his gate. As the riders dismounted, Junsaku appeared out of thin air. With a stern expression and a tinge of annoyance, he barked, 'Why are you here?'

Two samurai, dressed in red leather armour and black undergarments, exited their steeds, bowed, and stood at attention.

'General,' replied a samurai, 'Fusakage Shogun has sent us to inform you that you must return to Edo immediately.'

'Hai,' Junsaku responded gruffly. 'Do you have supplies for our journey?'

'Hai, General. We have everything we need.'

Junsaku went into the house. Cecelia and Nobushida stood in the kitchen doorway, Cecelia's long arm draped across the boy's shoulders. Junsaku embraced his wife and whispered in her ear, 'I must leave.' Then, Junsaku stated gently, 'Nobushida, go to the front garden and play.'

'Hai, Ojisan,' he said, skipping towards the front door.

'When will you return?' Cecelia asked, her voice trembling lightly.

'I cannot say,' Junsaku replied, squeezing her trim waist.

'For the shogun to have sent for me means something is gravely wrong. I promise to return as soon as possible. Do not worry,' he said. With his hands on his wife's hips, Junsaku kissed her, hoping his passion would sustain her for months. Then, he checked on Nobushida, who posed in a fighting stance at the front gate, challenging the two samurai. 'Nobushida,' Junsaku yelled, 'come here. You can teach those samurai a lesson another day.' Nobushida rushed to Junsaku. Junsaku knelt before the boy, bringing himself to eye level, and gently grasped Nobushida's slender shoulders with his battle-worn hands. 'Nobushida, I must return to Edo. While I am away, you must protect my wife and property. Can you handle this responsibility, my young samurai?'

'Hai, Ojisan,' Nobushida answered confidently.

Junsaku ruffled Nobushida's black hair, looked at Yui near the front door, and said, 'Yui, gather my belongings. I must return to Edo immediately.'

Yui darted to Junsaku's room to pack his bags.

***

WHEN JUNSAKU arrived in Edo, he entered the castle on horseback, greeted by a samurai who said, 'Fusakage-sama waits for you in his private residence.'

Junsaku rode a short distance through the fortress grounds and dismounted his horse.

As he handed his reins to a guard, he heard the voice of the shogun from behind. 'Welcome back, General. Follow me. We will drink nihonshu in the garden and talk.'

The two men went to a small table beside a koi pond and sat on red cushions atop green grass. As Junsaku waited for the shogun to speak, he could see the man's aura, the colours of an over-ripened lemon, bright yellow mixed with spots of dark green.

'I have received word that the Hiroki Clan is organised and plans to attack Daimyo Shigeru's castle in the Tōhoku region,' the shogun said. 'If they are successful, Junsaku, we will lose five of our biggest landholdings.' After a short silence, Fusakage grumbled, 'This cannot happen.' The shogun held his cup, and a young girl with smooth, porcelain skin poured sake. 'Drink, Junsaku,' Fusakage ordered, and Junsaku lifted his glass of rice wine.

The two men sat quietly for some time, and Junsaku knew he needed to wait and speak only when the shogun was ready. Junsaku continued to sip sake, and when the second carafe of rice wine emptied, the shogun broke the silence. 'The Hiroki Clan is sizable, Junsaku. They have been recruiting ronin and even active samurai for years. We will be overwhelmed and lose the battle unless we send our best samurai to the Tōhoku region. Yet, as you can understand, we cannot leave the capital, or Edo castle, unguarded and in such a precarious situation.' Shogun Fusakage inhaled, sighed, and stated firmly, 'Junsaku, I need your plan to stop this aggression towards me and to annihilate the Hiroki Clan. Your plan must not fail, even if we fight outnumbered. You will prepare a small but powerful army to march to Daimyo Shigeru's castle in Yamagata, and we will destroy these traitors.'

***

THREE DAYS later, in the early morning, Junsaku, the shogun, and a carefully selected group of five hundred of the deadliest and best-trained samurai arrived in Yamagata in the Tōhoku region. The shogun met with Daiymo Shigeru in the castle's courtyard while Junsaku assessed the environment. Junsaku could see the fortress grounds were small and compact; the outer walls formed a square that could fit fifty buildings within, each the size of a village home, and, inside the fortress, a complex labyrinth of high-walled corridors spread out like a web, meant to confuse intruders. Watching as soldiers sharpened swords and prepared weapons, Junsaku estimated the daimyo's samurai army to be approximately three hundred soldiers.

When the shogun and the daiymo's conversation ended, the shogun turned to Junsaku and demanded, 'General, tell me your strategy.'

'Fusakage-sama, Daiymo Shigeru's castle grounds are small, and his army is prepared to defend the castle's interior. We will add one hundred of our samurai to protect the inner grounds and leave the other four hundred outside to protect the exterior so the enemy cannot infiltrate.' The shogun nodded his approval. Then, Junsaku turned to his captain. 'Come with me, Hirakawa,' he commanded. 'We must organise the men.'

'Hai, General,' the captain replied.

***

JUNSAKU RETURNED to the castle's inner courtyard after completing battle placements. As Junsaku watched soldiers making final preparations for war, he felt a tingling sensation at the nape of his neck, and, from the corner of his eye, Junsaku saw a flash of bright light as though lightning had struck nearby, impossible on this cloudless day. His focus shifted to a spot where he saw a group of the daimyo's samurai crouched, huddled close to the ground, speaking in low whispers, their eyes cast downward. Then, looming over the group, Junsaku saw the ghost, cloaked in black from head to toe, his head tipped towards the men, his face hidden inside the shadowy recess of his hood. As Junsaku approached the group to find out what they were doing, a samurai shouted from nearby, 'General, your command is required with the archers.'

'I will be there in a moment,' he replied, turning toward the soldier who yelled, waving him off.

When his attention returned to the cloaked apparition and where the men gathered, everyone, including the spirit, had disappeared. Junsaku went to the area and noticed a pile of sand on the ground. It became clear to him that the men had used the loose dirt as a drawing board, and he could see that a person's palm had wiped the surface, destroying any details. Junsaku strained his eyes, his gaze tracing remnants of kanji symbols and drawings in the loose dirt. Then, a faint series of lines caught his attention - a sketch outlining the sloping edges of the roof of the castle's main keep.

A sense of dread filled Junsaku's soul, and his thoughts turned to the unsettling image of the ghost shrouded in black who hovered ominously over the men earlier. *'Why was he here? There has been no battle and no death. Why would the ghost visit me now?'* Junsaku wondered. Then his mind cleared, and his instinct took over. Junsaku ran to the castle's tall, central tower. 'Where is Fusakage-sama?' he asked a guard.

'He is with the daimyo in the hall,' the soldier replied, pointing down a corridor.

Junsaku went to the shogun. *'Sumimasen.* I am sorry for the interruption, but Fusakage-sama, I must speak with you urgently.'

'Hai,' the shogun replied. 'Shigeru, leave us.'

Daiymo Shigeru left the room.

'What is it, Junsaku?'

'Fusakage-sama, I witnessed a small group collaborating secretly on the castle grounds. They disappeared before I could ask them what they were doing. These were not our men, and I cannot tell you anything about them except my instincts tell me you are in danger. You need to trust me.'

'What is your plan?'

Junsaku rubbed his chin, then replied, 'I will relocate the daiymo to a secret location outside the castle, and you will move to a secure hiding place within the grounds until I know more.'

'What exactly are you concerned about?' the shogun inquired.

'I am not completely sure,' Junsaku replied gravely. 'However, I have a strong suspicion the enemy is within, and we need to hide you somewhere safe until I can gather more intelligence.'

Fusakage's eyes widened. 'Of course, Junsaku. If this is what you think is necessary.'

Junsaku left the shogun briefly, returning thirty minutes later, accompanied by four of the shogun's most talented samurai. 'Fusakage-sama, the daimyo has left the castle with several of his guards, and now, you need to follow us. But, before we go, put this on,' Junsaku said, handing the shogun a uniform to wear as a disguise so he would blend in with his mounted samurai and look like one of the warriors.

After the shogun changed into his disguise, he followed Junsaku through the castle grounds to a room inside a small, windowless building, the entrance only accessible by a single passageway flanked by towering walls.

'Fusakage-sama, you will hide here,' Junsaku instructed. 'If there is a threat to your life, we have placed one of your guards, dressed like you, as a decoy in the central tower where the enemy believes you wait. That way, if someone tries to harm you, they will not find you there, and they can fight Kasi Hitosi instead.'

The shogun solemnly shook his head. Junsaku turned his attention to the four samurai assigned to guard Fusakage's hideout. 'Guard Shogun Fusakage with your life,' Junsaku ordered, confident in each warrior's preparedness to kill anyone who dared enter. 'Lock the door, and do not let anyone inside this building unless it is me.'

***

JUNSAKU RETURNED to the area where he had seen the group of the daiymo's samurai conspiring earlier. He tried to find the men but could not identify them amongst the hundreds of soldiers within the castle grounds. Junsaku swiftly assembled six of his elite guards. 'Follow me and be prepared for an attack,' he ordered, leading the way to the castle's main gate.

Their katanas drawn, the six soldiers moved in unison behind the general. As they neared the imposing wooden door at the castle's entrance, Junsaku directed two samurai guards to remove the iron drawbar. As the guards went to lift the heavy metal beam that stretched across the entrance, blocking the two massive doors from opening, Junsaku's heart sank; he could see the iron drawbar chained and locked, the heavy metal connected to a sturdy steel eye bolt embedded in the stone wall.

Immediately, Junsaku knew his suspicions were correct: the attack was from within the castle, and the shogun and his samurai were locked inside.

'Norihiko, Minato, get that chain off and open this gate!' Junsaku barked.

'Hai, General,' the soldiers replied obediently, putting their swords on the ground and rushing to the lock.

'The rest of you find a way out. Locate Captain Hirakawa on the outside, report to him what is happening here, and get our troops back inside these castle walls - no matter what!' Junsaku ordered.

'Hai,' the samurai stated before sprinting away.

Just as Junsaku moved towards the shogun's hiding place, a booming sound rang in his ears. Junsaku watched as a section of the central tower exploded into flames, black smoke pouring out of the many small, rectangular windows.

'Norihiko, Minato, change of plans. One of you stay here and get this door open. The other, gather all our warriors in the centre courtyard. The shogun is in grave danger. This attack is from inside the castle.'

Junsaku left for the shogun. He rounded a corner and ran down the high-walled alleyway to the small building where Fusakage hid with his personal guard, sighing with relief when he saw the building untouched by flames. Suddenly, four enemy soldiers stood in front of him. Based on their clothing, Junsaku could see they were rogue warriors, ronin, prepared to kill him. Drawing his katana, Junsaku dropped low and to the right as a sweeping strike from one of the attacker's swords barely missed his head. As Junsaku slipped past the ronin's left side, his sword sliced the man's midsection, opening his torso from hip to hip, and his internal organs spilled into the alleyway. Before the dead man's body hit the ground, Junsaku engaged in combat with the remaining three men. As the trio tried to overpower the general, Junsaku, quick and natural, moved like a predator toying with his prey. However, Junsaku was not playing; he was learning his enemy's moves and observing their weaknesses. With a clear plan in his head, Junsaku parried left then right, his movements purposeful, orchestrating every move, and he forced the three assailants close together, corralling them like fish in a net.

Junsaku pulled out his wakizashi sword, held it in his left hand, and with a straight lunge, pierced one of the enemies through his heart, the tip of his blade protruding near the man's spine. As Junsaku pulled his short sword out of the man's chest, the katana in his right hand struck upward. The razor-sharp blade sliced through the next attacker's groin, severing the man's leg. The man fell to the ground, howling with pain, and watched his detached leg lay lifeless next to him. Junsaku spun to his left and swung his sword, the metal of his blade only a flash as it cut through the last living ronin's neck. The enemy stood momentarily, his head still balanced, before the man dropped to his knees and his head toppled face-first to the ground.

Junsaku took off running towards the shogun's hideout. As Junsaku approached, he witnessed the samurai guards assigned to defend the shogun in a fierce battle with ten of the enemy. 'Enough. This ends now,' Junsaku murmured as he entered the fight.

***

ACROSS THE CASTLE grounds, while Junsaku fought beside his men to protect the shogun, the rival clan leader, Ishioka Maki, met with his invading army. Almost three hundred enemy soldiers awaited instructions from Maki, each man dressed in a mixture of clothing, from stolen armour pieces to haori jackets and loose, tattered pants.

The clan leader stood in the centre of his men and turned in slow circles. Then he stopped and addressed a stocky built ronin with a broad frame and the sharp eyes of an eagle, saying, 'Captain, take fifty men to the main gate and ensure no one gets inside.' Then, with his katana raised high, he announced, 'The rest of you will stay with me. The shogun was not in the main keep. He still lives, but not much longer; the shogun dies tonight!'

His men cheered.

***

WHILE JUNSAKU and the four samurai assigned to defend the shogun fought the enemy attack at the shogun's hideout, six more of the shogun's samurai heard the raucous and joined the fight.

After Junsaku and his men killed the attackers, Junsaku gathered his small army of ten. 'Because there will be further attacks, you must listen to my plan,' Junsaku said, his voice a low whisper. 'As you know, there is only one narrow road to this building, lined with high walls. We will wait and attack the enemy as they try to enter the alleyway. As we dismember and kill these traitors, their bodies will fall near each other, pile up, and create a blockade that will slow the enemy's forward movement until Captain Hirakawa and our troops have successfully infiltrated the castle grounds and arrive to support us.'

When Junsaku finished, the samurai took their positions.

Minutes later, the first assailants approached. Just as the enemy entered the narrow corridor, Junsaku's soldiers attacked. As Junsaku's samurai fought the rogues, injured men began to fall, creating an obstacle of bodies, making it increasingly difficult for the enemy to clamber over the pile of the maimed and dead.

Finally, with a heap of bodies blocking the entrance, the attack ceased, and it seemed the traitors had given up their assault.

'Now, we retrieve Fusakage Shogun and get him to safety,' Junsaku commanded. Then, Junsaku heard more enemy soldiers approaching, ascertaining at least one hundred men based on the echo of their marching feet in the narrow, high-walled corridor. 'Prepare for another assault. Today, we fight and die with honour,' Junsaku announced, raising his katana above his head.

With swords in both hands, Junsaku watched twenty enemy soldiers begin to step over the human-body blockade. As Junsaku prepared to fight in what he believed would be his final battle, arrows struck the attackers from behind, piercing their throats. Junsaku knew reinforcements from the shogun's army had arrived, and he ran forward, stepping on the bodies as if they were stones used to cross a river. Just beyond, he could see Captain Hirakawa, and at least two hundred of the shogun's samurai embroiled in battle. Junsaku and his small army joined the fight with renewed vigour.

As they fought, Junsaku and Captain Hirakawa noticed Ishioka Maki, the clan leader, running away from the scene, attempting to escape. 'Kill him!' Junsaku ordered, and Hirakawa followed the traitor.

Minutes later, Ishioka Maki stopped in his tracks, an intense burning sensation in his sternum. When the clan leader looked down, he saw the point of a sword protruding from his leather chest covering. Then, behind him, someone roared, 'No honourable death for you,' as the sword slid out of his body. Maki turned and looked into the dark eyes of Captain Hirakawa, and seconds later, his body collapsed to the ground.

Hirakawa cleaned his blade using the pants of the now-dead clan leader, then returned to the battlefield. When he arrived, the fighting had ended, and any still-living traitor now knelt in surrender to the shogun's army.

'Lock up these men until the shogun decides their fate,' Junsaku ordered. Then, the shogun approached Junsaku from behind. 'Fusakage-sama, you were supposed to remain inside the building until I came for you,' Junsaku said.

'Hai, Junsaku, that was the plan. But did anything today go

to plan?' the shogun stated. 'I am still alive. I did not burn to death or get killed by the enemy, and you have again helped us win a battle that will go down in history as one of our greatest victories. Congratulations, men! You have secured the shogunate.'

The samurai army erupted in jubilant celebration. Their shouts of triumph echoed through the castle's stone walls as the soldiers revelled in their hard-fought victory.

While the samurai cheered, Junsaku said, 'Fusakage-sama, I request Captain Hirakawa join us for nihonshu. He saved our lives. Let him tell us how he defeated the enemy.'

'Hai, Junsaku,' the shogun replied as the central tower, bombed earlier, continued to smoulder in the background, dark grey smoke and trails of ash floating towards the sky.

Junsaku, Hirakawa, and Shogun Fusakage left the other samurai and entered the small building where the shogun hid earlier. Inside, the three sat at a low table and poured sake.

'Captain Hirakawa,' the shogun said, 'Junsaku tells me it is because of you that we were victorious. Tell me more.'

'The first part was easy,' Captain Hirakawa began. 'Norihiko found the castle blacksmith to remove the chain and iron lock. Our men were inside before the enemy could relock the gate, and we quickly won the battle with the first group of traitors. Afterwards, we made our way to your secret hiding place, Fusakage-sama. Along the way, we met heavy resistance from many of the daimyo's rogue soldiers, and sadly, a few of our samurai died.' The captain paused momentarily, then continued, 'We reorganised our advance toward your hiding place, and when we turned down the alleyway, we saw the backside of the enemy as they attempted to climb over the mound of injured and dead bodies. My archers quickly loaded arrows and shot the traitors through the neck, and then the remaining rogues turned on us, and a new fight began.'

'Excellent work, Captain,' Junsaku commended. 'And you killed Ishioka Maki, the clan leader?'

'Hai, General,' Hirakawa said. 'When you ordered me to kill him, I caught him quickly and skewered him through his heart like a wild beast; a death befitting such a traitor,' he spat.

'Hirakawa, you and your men fought bravely, and rewards will come,' the shogun said. 'Go back to your men and congratulate them while I have a private conversation with the general.'

Hirakawa stood, bowed, and left the room.

'The prisoners?' the shogun inquired.

'Hai, Fusakage-sama. We have them locked up in the stables and await your instruction on their punishment,' Junsaku replied.

'It is simple: every man must be dead by his own knife before the sun rises tomorrow. See to it.' The shogun lifted his sake cup and poured rice wine down his throat. 'Also, Junsaku, you and the army will not return to Edo immediately. Your job now is to track down and kill every traitor still alive in the Hiroki clan, ensuring none are left breathing.' The shogun set down his sake cup and stood. Junsaku jumped to his feet and bowed as Fusakage exited the room and left Junsaku alone.

Junsaku poured several more cups of rice wine as he contemplated the death of the prisoners and hunting and killing any remaining traitors in the surrounding villages. He thought of when the now-captured men dropped their swords and fell to their knees in surrender, fear and remorse engraved on their faces. *Murder them?* Junsaku thought. His father told him to be like Ōkami, be like the wolf, and practise non-violence until there is no other choice. *'There must be another way?'* he pondered. *'Yet, I serve the shogun, and he commands me.'*

Junsaku left the building and moved through the dimly lit, stone-paved streets of the castle grounds on his way to force the prisoners to kill themselves or to be killed by the shogun's samurai. As he walked with his head hung, his shoulders slumping further with each step, he heard, 'Learn from my mistakes.' As the phrase filled his mind, the hooded spirit suddenly appeared before him, his gigantic, ethereal body covered in black, his facial features indistinguishable within the dark recess of his hood.

'Tell me the meaning!' Junsaku growled. 'What mistakes am I to learn from? I am honour-bound to the shogunate and have no choice but to kill these men. Why do you haunt me when I must follow orders?'

'You must listen before it is too late,' the spirit said, his voice a low rumble.

Then, the apparition vanished.

Junsaku felt ill. As he took deep breaths, balancing his chi, one of his samurai approached and said, 'General, follow me. I will show you where we placed the prisoners.'

When they arrived at the stables, Junsaku gathered his leaders. He cleared his throat and said, 'The rebels will die tonight. Make sure each rogue has a tanto knife, and they will commit seppuku outside the burned section of the main keep. Within the next thirty minutes, I want them lined up on their knees. And, if they do not commit seppuku, we will cut off their heads. These traitors must be dead and gone before the sun rises in the morning. And men,' Junsaku continued, 'more work is still needed to end this rebellion. We will scour these lands, visit every prefecture, and find and kill every soul who is a traitor to the shogunate.'

THIRTY-SEVEN

AFTER TEN LONG, GRUELLING months apart, Cecelia could scarcely believe her eyes as she watched her husband dismount his horse in front of their house in the quaint village of Kakunod-ate. With her heart drumming, Cecelia rushed forward, embraced Junsaku, and kissed him passionately, desperately trying to make up for their lost time. Finally, she stepped aside and made room for Nobushida, who leapt into Junsaku's arms. Junsaku hugged him tightly before setting him back onto the pathway, and then Cecelia took Junsaku's hand in hers and said, her voice brimming with joy, 'Come inside. I have a surprise.'

Junsaku laughed as he looked at Nobushida, whose seven-year-old eyes sparkled. With a playful grin, he leaned down and spoke to the boy like old friends sharing a secret. 'I am not often the one to get surprises, Nobushida. Usually, I am the one bring-ing the gifts.'

'Hai, Ojisan,' he replied cheerfully.

As they strolled along the gravel path to the house, Junsaku turned to Nobushida and asked, 'How are you doing with your English language?'

'Very well, Ojisan,' the boy responded, his voice clear and

confident. 'My teacher says I am a quick learner, and Cecelia helps me every day.'

Inside, after they replaced their shoes with sandals, Cecelia pulled on Junsaku's hand and tugged him towards the kitchen. 'Come, Junsaku,' Cecelia chirped, walking quickly and pointing. 'Look at your surprise!' In the dim light of the room, Junsaku's eyes fixated on a wooden crib sitting on the worn wooden floor. He felt an overwhelming surge of emotions wash over him as he stood speechless. 'It is our baby, Junsaku,' Cecelia said, weaving her arm into his. 'While you were away, I delivered a girl.'

Junsaku's eyes gleamed with wonder as he took a deep breath. 'What is her name?' he asked, each syllable laced with awe.

'That is for you to decide. The baby has been nameless for weeks while we waited– and hoped – for your return.'

Junsaku kissed his wife and tousled Nobushida's hair. Then, with gentle hands, he carefully lifted his baby girl from the crib, holding her in his arms for the first time, feeling a profound surge of love wash over him. 'She is beautiful, like her mother. What should we call her? Do you have any ideas, Cecelia? Nobushida?'

'Iie, Ojisan. Obasan told me it would be your decision, so hurry up! What do you want to name her?' Nobushida urged, his voice tinged with impatience and excitement.

'I have always liked the name of my mother's mother,' he told Cecelia.

'Your grandmother,' Cecelia replied affectionately.

'Hai. I will name our baby after her grandmother. Our daughter's name will be Fukano.'

Cecelia and Nobushida glanced at each other, both with broad smiles, revealing the happiness of their shared moment.

Then Cecelia enthusiastically stated, 'A beautiful name for our daughter.' She stepped forward to where Junsaku held Fukano, leaned over, and kissed her baby on the forehead, smelling the infant's scent of jasmine, vanilla, and strawberries.

'We can call her Ka for short,' Junsaku stated happily. Junsaku placed his palm on the crown of the baby's head and said, 'Ka, you will grow up to be a strong and powerful woman, just like your mother, and I will always protect you.'

FUKANO

THIRTY-EIGHT

JUNSAKU DISMOUNTED his dapple grey and tied the horse's reins to the fencepost. Nobushida, now ten, walked briskly towards him, his black hair pulled into a knot at the crown of his head. 'Ojisan,' he said, smiling, 'welcome home. We have missed you.'

'Hai,' Junsaku said, resting his muscular forearm over Nobushida's shoulders. 'I have missed you all, as well. You have been practising English, Nobushida?'

'Yes, Ojisan.'

'And your sister?'

'Fukano's English is as good as her Japanese,' Nobushida replied.

'Fine. We will all keep speaking English for Cecelia.'

'Obasan's Japanese is getting better, too. She practises with Yui and even speaks to the local villagers,' Nobushida told Junsaku.

Junsaku saw his wife run towards him from the house. Behind her, in the doorway, Yui stood holding Fukano's tiny hand in hers. Turning four within days, Fukano glowed like an angel, with molasses-coloured hair and light toffee skin that complimented her vibrant green, arching eyes. Fukano observed as her father enveloped her mother in a warm embrace, tenderly gazing over his shoulder at his young daughter, who waited patiently for her turn to hug her father.

Cecelia's hands cupped the back of Junsaku's head, and she pulled him towards her, kissing him deeply like they had been apart for a lifetime rather than just a few months. 'Welcome home, Husband,' she said as Junsaku's hands gripped her waist.

'I have missed you, my love.'

'I have missed you every minute. I know I should not kiss you on the street, but I could not help myself. Let's go inside so I can kiss you some more,' she giggled, grabbing his hand and pulling him towards the house's entrance.

'Konnichiwa, Junsaku-san,' said Yui, bowing near the front door.

'Konnichiwa, Yui,' he replied.

With a wide grin on her face, Fukano extended both of her arms towards her father, eagerly awaiting his embrace. 'Otosan!' she exclaimed as Junsaku gently lifted her, cradling her with his strong arms as she nestled against him.

'Hello, my little Ka,' Junsaku said, gently squeezing.

Her arms curled around her father's neck. 'Otosan, I am so happy you are home,' she said gleefully, her shoulder-length, feather-soft hair tickling the skin on his face. 'Did you know it is my birthday soon? Did you bring me a present?'

Junsaku chuckled and looked at Cecelia, whose green eyes rippled with gold. 'Our daughter wants presents, Cecelia.' Junsaku turned to his daughter, stared into her wide green eyes, and said, 'Hai, Ka, I have a present for you. I also have something for Nobushida, Yui, and a gift for your beautiful mother.'

Fukano clapped her tiny hands, turning to her mother. 'We all get presents!'

'Yes, Ka,' she replied softly, her heart light as she looked at her husband holding their daughter. 'Your Otosan spoils us.'

'Let us go to the kitchen and celebrate my visit home. Yui, prepare sake, and you must join us,' Junsaku said in Japanese.

'Arigato,' Yui replied, bowing before entering the house.

As Junsaku held Fukano in his left arm, her tabi sock-covered feet bounced lightly near the hilt of his swords. He gently put his right arm around Cecelia's waist, and with Nobushida following close behind, the family entered their home.

In the kitchen, a rectangular, wood-burning firepit crackled in the centre of the room, casting a warm glow and heating the room. The aroma of miso soup and slow-simmering pork wafted through the air as Junsaku carefully placed Fukano on the floor and settled down at the low table. He folded his legs beneath him, and his daughter sat next to him so close that their bodies slightly overlapped.

'You are getting so big and heavy, Ka. If you sit this close to me, how can I rise to get your present?' Junsaku teased.

Fukano cocked her head to the side and jumped up. 'Ha-ha, very funny, Otosan. Please, may I have my present now?'

'Let me at least enjoy one cup of sake after my long journey,' Junsaku said, watching Cecelia pour him rice wine. He quickly drank the nihonshu and placed the polished tin cup on the wooden table before springing to his feet. 'Time for presents!' Junsaku announced. He left the kitchen and returned with five parcels wrapped in brown paper and tied with string. 'Yui, you first,' Junsaku said, extending the gift towards her. 'You take such good care of our family.'

'Domo arigato gozaimasu, Junsaku,' she replied shyly, taking the parcel in her hand.

'What is it?' Fukano asked merrily, running to Yui's side.

'*Watashi wa shiranai*. Let us find out,' Yui replied, untying the string. Yui removed the wrap and inside she found a hair comb with a silver, ornamental design on one end, the metal bent and twisted to form three roses. 'Beautiful,' Yui said slowly in English, bowing towards Junsaku. 'Thank you.'

'My present now, Otosan,' Fukano begged.

'Iie, Ka. I want to give Nobushida his next.'

'A present for you, brother!' Fukano exclaimed.

Junsaku handed something long and thin to Nobushida, the wrapped item the length of the boy's forearm. Nobushida weighed it in his hand, smiling as he tried to guess the contents. 'A jō?' Nobushida questioned.

'Nobushida, if I wanted to give you a jō to defend yourself, it would not be that small. Open it and see what it is.'

Nobushida unwrapped the paper and found a bamboo shakuhachi flute inside. 'Arigato, Ojisan. I have always wanted a shakuhachi to play beautiful music like you.'

'Me now!' Fukano chirped.

'Not yet, Ka. The next present is for Okasan. While she opens it, you need to continue to practise patience,' he said playfully.

Fukano crossed her thin arms and feigned upset. However, she could not continue her façade for long and covered her mouth to hide her giggles.

Junsaku took another wrapped package and, with both hands, presented the gift to Cecelia. 'For my beautiful wife.'

'Thank you, Junsaku. Ka, come and help me.' Fukano ran to her mother, her tabi socks lightly swishing the surface of the tatami mat, and she plopped down in the centre of her mother's crossed legs. Cecelia placed the package in front of Fukano. 'Pull on the string,' Cecelia said, her head tipped towards her daughter, her chin resting near Fukano's cheek. Fukano pulled on the string, and it loosened. 'Now, rip the paper.'

Fukano dug her little fingernails into the wrap and made a tear, revealing something colourful inside. Then she tore off all the paper and shrieked, 'It is a kimono! Oh, the colours are so pretty. Red, yellow, and oh, there are birds. White cranes!'

'I am going to stand, Ka,' Cecelia said, gently pushing Fukano off her lap. She stood, lifted the garment, and held it before her. 'It is gorgeous, darling,' she said to Junsaku. 'Aishiteimasu.'

'I love you, too,' Junsaku replied.

'Me! My turn,' Fukano begged. 'I have been waiting so long and practised patience.'

'Yes, Ka, your turn. Close your eyes,' Junsaku said. Fukano stood and put her arms stiffly at her sides, closing her eyes so tightly her entire face scrunched up. Junsaku stood in front of her. 'Fukano, you may open your eyes now.'

Fukano's eyes popped open, and she saw her father holding a brown, paper-wrapped package tied with a purple ribbon. 'For you,' Junsaku said, handing it to his daughter.

She snatched the parcel, sat on the floor, and unwrapped the gift. Inside were three white, heavy fabric pieces: a jacket, a pair of pants, and a belt. 'What are these, Otosan?' she asked, her lips pulled to one side.

'Your very own gi, Ka,' he replied. 'You will wear this when we train.'

'You will train with me like you do with Nobushida? Will I be a samurai someday, like you?'

'For now, our focus will be to teach you to defend yourself and be strong, like Nobushida and me,' he said, hitting his chest with his fist and winking at Nobushida.

Fukano smiled. 'I would like that, Otosan. Are there any more presents for me?'

'Hai,' Junsaku replied. 'One more.'

Fukano jumped with excitement.

Next, her father presented her with a dress made from ivory-coloured silk with bright pink cherry blossoms embroidered in the fabric.

'Oh, Otosan, it is pretty,' Fukano proclaimed.

Junsaku winked at his wife.

'It is lovely, but Junsaku, do you realise you have brought so many dresses for your daughter that I am running out of space? We may have to get a bigger house,' Cecelia joked.

'Arigato, Otosan,' Fukano said, swinging the dress back and forth before her. 'May I put it on?' she asked in Japanese.

'Yes. You may put on the dress,' Junsaku replied in English. Junsaku listened to the light, squeaky sound like a rusty hinge coming from the hallway flooring as Fukano ran to her room. He felt comforted by the nightingale floor, designed with clamps attached to the underside of the dry-wood boards that rubbed together and caused a chirping sound. Junsaku knew that no matter how dim the sound of someone walking on the floor, he would hear it, alerting him to intruders. Junsaku moved close to Cecelia and put his arm around her, kissing her cheek as he looked at Nobushida and said, 'Try your shakuhachi, Nobushida.'

Nobushida positioned his fingers on the flute. He blew into the hollow centre of the bamboo but only achieved the hissing sound of moving air. He repeatedly tried, moistening his lips before each blow, and finally, a single note emerged.

Cecelia's face lit up with delight as she gazed at Nobushida and said, 'Yoku dekimashita. Good job! You will be as good as your ojisan in no time.' Cecelia's lush, chestnut-coloured hair tumbled down her back in waves, draping over one shoulder as she tenderly clasped her husband's hand, their fingers entwined.

THIRTY-NINE

AFTER SUNDOWN, Fukano curled up next to her father on the tatami mat, the flickering lantern light making shadows that danced mischievously on the walls. Junsaku held his daughter close while Nobushida stretched out on the floor nearby, his head rested comfortably on his hand.

'Otosan,' Fukano asked in English, 'will you tell us the story of Ōkami, the story your father used to tell you?'

'Ah, the wolf's tale,' Junsaku replied in Japanese. 'Yes. Then afterwards, you and Nobushida must go to bed.'

As the moonlight outside the shoji doors cast a cool glow on the faces of his children, Junsaku began the story.

Ōkami, a wolf with a black coat and blue eyes, was clever. Rather than hunt for his food, he liked to sneak into the village and steal goats, pigs, chickens, and ducks. The villagers disliked Ōkami and tried different methods to stop the wolf from stealing livestock. Still, the wolf was too sly and cunning.

One day, the villagers gathered, discussed how best to trap the beast, and devised a plan. They would bring a live animal to the nearby field where a fire had swept through and burned everything in its path, leaving it barren. Then, with live bait to entice Ōkami into the open, the hunters would strike him dead with their bows and arrows.

Four men agreed to the scheme.

On the night of the planned killing, a bright, full moon illuminated the open space. There were no shadows in the clearing as there were no trees or shrubs, only dried earth and a solitary, charred reed, so the men were confident there was nowhere for the wolf to hide.

The men tethered a goat to a peg in the centre of the deadened landscape, then hurried to the meadow's edge, hiding behind the only boulder on the property, intently watching the silhouette of the standing goat visible in the moonlight. As the moon arched slowly across the night sky, the men waited silently, their eyes fixated on the goat.

Hours later, with no sign of Ōkami, the rising sun began to light the ground, and the men noticed the goat was missing.

'Where has it gone?' one man asked.

All four men walked to the centre of the barren field, their mouths agape, baffled by the disappearance of the live animal.

'It is impossible. We were watching the whole time. I never turned my eyes away.'

'I never stopped looking either,' another man testified.

All four men agreed they never took their eyes off the trap.

Frustrated, the hunters returned to the village. They called a meeting and shared the news that they could not kill Ōkami, and the wolf had taken the bait and escaped unharmed.

'How could this have happened?' demanded a villager. 'You men must have fallen asleep.'

'We did not!' a hunter scorned. 'We never stopped searching for Ōkami.'

The room fell silent except for an occasional heavy sigh.

Finally, a trim, petite man who appeared to be in his eighties spoke. 'You misjudge Ōkami,' he stated with a slight grin. 'He is clever, smart, and sly. Was there anywhere for him to hide?'

'Nowhere. The landscape was barren. There were no trees or grasses, and we hid behind the only boulder in the meadow. The fire destroyed everything except for a charred reed,' he scoffed, bitterness in his voice.

'Ah, that is where Ōkami outsmarted you,' the old man chuckled. 'It is Ōkami. The wolf can hide even where there is only a single reed.'

Fukano looked up at her father, her jade eyes sparkling. 'Ōkami is clever, Otosan.'

'Yes, Ka, the wolf is clever and smart.'

'Tell me the meaning again, Ojisan?' inquired Nobushida.

'I will tell you the surface meaning. At its core, it is a powerful message about the unwavering nature of the wolf. Despite being hunted, Ōkami did not try to be deceptive or trick *the* hunters; the wolf attempted to avoid conflict.' Junsaku took a deep breath. 'However, this tale is far from simple, so continue to think about it and unravel its many meanings. But do this tomorrow or in your dreams because now it is time for sleep!' Junsaku kissed his daughter's smooth forehead, then reached over and squeezed Nobushida's upper arm, smiling. 'To bed,' he told his children.

Fukano stood, went into her room, and lay on her futon. Junsaku followed and covered her with a down feather blanket as Cecelia entered.

'Oyasumi, Otosan. Good night, Okasan,' Fukano said as she turned on her side, put her cheek on her palm, and closed her eyes.

'Oyasumi,' Junsaku replied.

Cecelia bent down and kissed her daughter's temple. 'Goodnight, Ka. Sweet dreams.'

Junsaku and Cecelia left the room holding hands, walking across the hall to say goodnight to Nobushida.

FORTY

THE LATE-NIGHT air became motionless and still, and the skin on Junsaku's body felt clammy as he held Cecelia in his arms. The humming of insects in the garden had stopped hours ago, and now Junsaku could only hear the light breathing of his sleeping wife. As Junsaku stared at the shadows on the ceiling, he heard the distinctive sound, the alert—the chirping of the nightingale floor in the hallway. Junsaku lightly touched Cecelia's mouth with the tip of his forefinger, signalling her to remain quiet. Cecelia's green eyes sprang open, and she stared at Junsaku with rounded eyes, her pulse racing, each beat echoing in her ears as he pressed his finger on her lips. Junsaku pointed towards the hallway and then to the ceiling. Cecelia understood. They had practised this drill many times before. She needed to gather the children and hide.

Junsaku rose from the futon. He slipped on loose-fitting pants and grabbed both swords, holding the longer katana blade in his right hand. Junsaku walked into the hallway and stood alert, watching his wife emerge from their bedroom wearing a flower-print robe. Cecelia moved swiftly and quietly toward the children's bedrooms, her light footsteps barely audible. The moon's pale glow streamed through the windows and doors, casting eerie blue-grey shadows that stretched across the floors, walls, and ceiling. Junsaku kept his senses sharp, scanning the surroundings, trying to pinpoint the intruders' whereabouts. After a short while, Cecelia reappeared, leading two children by the hand, both bewildered and frightened, with Yui cautiously following behind. Junsaku followed the four of them as they quietly moved down the hallway, hardly breathing. He noticed Nobushida had grabbed his bokken, his wooden sword, the tip almost touching the ground as he walked. When they arrived in the kitchen, Junsaku pulled on a string dangling from the ceiling. An attic hatch opened, a wooden ladder dropped to the floor, and Cecelia, Yui, and the children climbed up. Once inside, Cecelia retracted the ladder, closed the hatch, and made the entrance to the hideout invisible in the dark wood ceiling. Junsaku yanked the string, broke it loose from the fastener, and tossed it out of view. Junsaku knew if he died in this fight, the attackers would find his family and murder them, so he promised himself they would not leave his home alive.

Junsaku crept towards the front of the house and could hear the distinctive chirping sound from the corridor's floorboards, which helped him to pinpoint his attacker's location. With his back pressed against a wall, he could see three slender male silhouettes behind the thick, translucent paper attached to the shoji screens. *'Ninjas,'* Junsaku thought as he stood in complete stillness, feeling the rhythmic rise and fall of his breath while he discerned the subtle movements of the invaders.

Suddenly, Junsaku saw a ninja run straight at him from the corridor, holding his sword low, his obsidian eyes peering through a slit in the black mask that covered his face. Junsaku inhaled a slow, deliberate breath, ready for a fight. Then, in his peripheral vision, Junsaku noticed another invader advancing on his right, this assailant with no sword visible in his hands. As Junsaku contemplated what weapon this other attacker might use, the ninja who charged from the hall was upon him, swinging his sword from low to high. Junsaku moved forward, then to his right, his motions blurred, and he successfully avoided the assassin's attempt to cut him in half before slicing upward with his long sword, cutting the attacker from hip to shoulder. As his blade exited the man's body, Junsaku heard a dull thud near his ear. He turned and saw a throwing star stuck in a wood beam, the metal shape reflected in the dim light, and he took a deep breath, knowing this weapon would have lodged in his head had he not moved to avoid the other ninja's sword.

Junsaku swiftly turned to face the ninja who had hurled the throwing star at him. As he did, he caught a fleeting glimpse of the assailant's back as the attacker vanished down the corridor, heading towards the kitchen. Panic gripped Junsaku as he thought, *'My family. I must get to them.'* As he sprinted towards the kitchen where everyone he loved hid in the ceiling, the third invader, a ninja carrying two short swords, one in each hand, attacked. As Junsaku fought, he heard the ladder from the hiding space in the kitchen ceiling hit the floor, and then Cecelia screamed, 'Nobushida!'

Junsaku gritted his teeth and charged the man standing in front of him. The clang of steel hitting steel drowned out everything as the two men fought in a flurry of blades. Junsaku pivoted right, first striking high, then low. The ninja easily parried, counterattacking with countless attempted strikes, and then suddenly, Junsaku felt warm blood flowing down his arm from a shoulder cut. Enraged, Junsaku attempted two quick blows that missed the assassin's head before delivering a powerful sidekick and knocking the ninja backwards. Before the enemy regained his balance, Junsaku landed two fatal strikes with his sword, one across the ninja's mid-section and the second through the man's neck.

With only one ninja left to fight, his whereabouts unknown, Junsaku ran to the kitchen. As Junsaku entered the room, he saw Nobushida's bokken hit the ground as the boy's body crumpled to the wood floor. Junsaku's gaze shifted and locked onto the third assassin, who stood across the room, a blowpipe clenched between his pursed lips. 'Aargh!' Junsaku bellowed as he rushed the assailant, the fierce, guttural roar rising from deep within him as if it had come from a vengeful oni demon.

Before the ninja could draw his sword, Junsaku reached him. With primal savagery, Junsaku carved the man's body into pieces. The man lay dead on the kitchen floor, one arm severed below the elbow, a leg cut in half, a separated hand, and Junsaku's katana buried deep in his chest.

Junsaku turned and saw Cecelia holding Nobushida's limp body in her arms as Fukano and Yui peered down from the hiding place in the ceiling, their tears falling like rain. Junsaku knelt next to Cecelia and Nobushida; he could see the pinprick in the boy's neck and knew the poison from the dart would be too intense for someone so small to survive. Junsaku slid his arm under Nobushida's neck and lifted his head slightly, noticing the boy's eyelids fluttered, his skin pale and cool.

'I tried to stop him,' Cecelia said, tears streaming down her cheeks, her green eyes clouded with despair. 'He was too fast. He was down the ladder before I could grab him.'

Junsaku looked into Nobushida's barely open eyes.

'Ojisan,' the boy whispered, 'I could not let you fight alone.'

'I am proud of you, Nobushida,' Junsaku replied, taking the boy into his arms. Smiling softly, he continued, 'You will be reunited with your parents now. Tell your father of your bravery and tell my dear friend, Yasafune, how much I love you.'

Nobushida's eyes widened, his warm brown irises illuminated by a solitary beam of silver moonlight that snuck through a narrow gap at the edge of the closed wooden shutters. Then, a rush of warmth washed over his body, and he melted into Junsaku's embrace, a delicate pink blush blooming across his cheeks, and he was gone.

FORTY-ONE

FOLLOWING NOBUSHIDA'S death, Junsaku, Cecelia, Fukano, and Yui returned home, each holding a walking stick, symbolising their grief and need for support following the boy's death. On a table just off the kitchen, Cecelia and Fukano placed Nobushida's shakuhachi, his folded gi, and his karate belt. They then lit sandalwood incense, filling the air with a sweet wood and spice aroma.

That night, while Junsaku and Cecelia lay in bed, she asked, 'Junsaku, when must you return to the shogun?'

'I have sent him a message telling him I postponed my return. I must stay with you and Fukano.' Junsaku sniffled. 'This is a sad time for those of us still living. I should be with my family now. Eventually, however, I must return to Edo and my duty.' After a momentary silence, he stated, 'I will leave after one lunar cycle when we no longer burn incense.'

As Junsaku cradled Cecelia in his arms, a sense of dread overcame him. Momentarily, he reconsidered his choice to return to the shogunate's service, but then pushed his thoughts aside, taking deep, calming breaths, hoping that sleep would soon take over.

***

AS THE WEEKS passed, Junsaku and Cecelia paid close attention to their daughter and her behaviour. Her parents held her hand, hugged her often, wiped away tears, played with her, and, as much as possible, tried to make her smile.

'Ka,' Cecelia asked one night at dinner, 'how are you feeling? We know you miss your brother.'

'I am fine,' she replied, stabbing a piece of grilled fish with her chopsticks. Then, Fukano's green eyes welled with tears, and she cried, 'I miss him so much!'

'He was a brave young man,' Junsaku said, 'and will remain close to us. Though we all miss him, let us be happy as he passes to the next life.'

'Do you think he will be with us again?' Fukano asked, her jade eyes glistening.

Cecelia gazed at her daughter, her matching green eyes filled with genuine curiosity. 'What do you believe?' she asked, eager to understand her daughter's thoughts.

'I think his soul will return someday in a different body,' Fukano answered as she picked up a tiny flake of fish using her chopsticks and placed it on her tongue, staring at her plate with a distant, contemplative look.

Cecelia reached out, gently grasped Junsaku's hand, and gave it a reassuring squeeze, which Junsaku instinctively returned.

FORTY-TWO

CECELIA LAY naked on her back, her arms outstretched, as she nestled underneath the thick blanket covering the futon.

'Ah, my wife waits for me,' Junsaku whispered, entering their bedroom. He placed the lantern on the tatami near the doorway and approached Cecelia. He removed his clothes and slid onto the bed next to her, allowing his body to press against hers, her toes touching his ankles. Cecelia moaned lightly and wove her fingers around his neck, pulling him close.

After making love, they checked on Fukano, asleep in her bed, before returning to their room for the night.

The following day, Junsaku awoke to sunshine illuminating the trees, rocks, and flowers visible outside their panoramic bedroom window. As Cecelia slept beside him, softly breathing, Junsaku gazed into the garden. Behind a Japanese maple tree, its gently rustling leaves the colour of ripe plum, Junsaku noticed a giant, ghostly figure, a dark shadow shrouded in black. Obscured by a hood, the ghost's face remained hidden, but a faint glow emanated from beneath the headcover, and Junsaku sensed the ghost studying him, its fixation pressing on his chest like a weight.

Cecelia woke, angled herself onto her hip, and rested her head in her hand. 'Ohayō, love,' she said. Cecelia noticed her husband's paled face and could sense his rapid heartbeat. She placed her palm on his cheek. 'What is it, Junsaku?'

Junsaku inhaled deeply. 'Bad dream,' he uttered, realising he could no longer see the spirit. Turning his focus to Cecelia, he tenderly reached out and gently caressed the soft skin on her shoulder. 'I am fine.'

'Let us go back to sleep,' Cecelia moaned. 'I do not want it to be today because this is the day you return to Edo. I want it to be yesterday.'

'Hai. I wish I did not have to leave, Cecelia, but I must return. It is my duty. I promise you I will come back to Kakunodate as soon as possible. I have arranged with the local daimyo to have a samurai team patrol the perimeter of our house all hours of the day when I am gone. I am the target of these rogues, Cecelia, and it is me they wish to harm. When I am not here, you and Fukano will be safe.'

Cecelia's eyes shimmered with unshed tears, the soft light flickering in them as if mirroring the storm of emotions swirling within her mind. 'Hai. Please come back sooner this time. I do not want to be apart. May we come live with you in Edo?'

'No, Cecelia. I am a samurai general, and you will not have an easy life there because you are not Japanese. The people of Kakunodate have accepted you and Fukano, and I believe our family is safer here. I would not be confident in the capital city because they do not easily trust foreigners, even if you are my wife.'

'*Kvailas!*' she complained in Lithuanian. 'It is stupid, Junsaku. I am the woman you love and who loves you. People should accept this and move on.'

'I agree, Cecelia. I am sorry, but I will not put you and Fukano at risk. I want my wife and daughter safe and happy.'

Cecelia pouted and pressed her naked body against her husband. She placed her hand between his legs and felt him stir. 'You must make me happy right now.'

'Ah, Cecelia wants to make a baby,' he said playfully, flipping her onto her back. He moved on top of her and held his weight off her body with his muscled arms. Looking into her green eyes, he said, 'I wish for us to have a son, Cecelia. I want to train him in bushido and the way of the samurai as my father trained me.'

'I know, Junsaku. I want that, too. Though Ka is strong, I know she can never be a samurai. Until we have a boy, you must continue to train your daughter, and when Fukano has a brother, she can teach him what she has learnt. Just as Nobushida taught Fukano, Fukano can teach her future little brother.'

'On my next visit, I will focus on Fukano's training. For now, I must focus on you.'

***

AFTERWARDS, WHEN Cecelia and Junsaku left the bedroom, the house no longer smelled of incense. The tribute to Nobushida as he transitioned to the next life had ended, the woody, floral, lightly medicinal scent of lit sandalwood replaced by the pungent odour of fresh fish cooking on the open fire.

'Ohayō,' Fukano said as her parents approached.

'Good morning,' Cecelia replied in English as she and Junsaku sat at the table.

'Otosan,' Fukano said, holding her miso bowl near her chin, her elbows on the table, 'I have a gi, and you said you will teach me the ways of a samurai. When you return, what will we do first?

Sword? Bow and arrow?'

'Iie, Ka, those are for later. First, you will learn karate, do katas and tai sabaki, and practise until the moves become second nature. Over time, we will add more of the arts until you are as good as any boy or samurai.'

Fukano smiled, her grin spreading over the bottom half of her heart-shaped face. 'I would like that. I want to protect my okasan and Yui when you are away.'

'Arigato, Ka. After many years of training with your father, you can protect us if needed. Until then, concentrate on learning and do not act foolishly. I cannot live if something bad happens to you,' Cecelia sighed.

After several minutes of silence, Junsaku announced, 'It is time.' His brows pulled tight. 'I do not want to go, but I am obligated to return to Edo.' Dressed in black riding pants, a black coat, and a black belt, Junsaku stood, grabbed his swords, slid them into the sheaths attached to his obi, and said softly, 'Come. See me off.'

Cecelia, wearing a red and yellow silk kimono with white cranes, and Fukano, dressed in a wrap dress embroidered with bright pink cherry blossoms, stood from the table and followed Junsaku. As they exited the house and approached the front gate, Cecelia and Fukano tried to hold back the tears threatening to overflow from their emerald eyes.

'Do not be sad. I will return soon with presents!' Junsaku said, bending down and tickling Fukano underneath her armpits. He picked her up and raised her to face him, her thin body hanging in the air. 'Now, you be good and take care of your mother,' he instructed, kissing both cheeks. Then, he set his daughter back on the ground, her wooden sandals making a muffled tap as she met the cobblestone street, and he went to Cecelia. Junsaku embraced his wife, holding her tightly against him. She nestled her head on his shoulder, inhaling his familiar, musky scent. 'Aishiteimasu, Cecelia,' Junsaku whispered, lightly squeezing her body. 'You are my world, and I expect to return to you in five lunar cycles.'

'I will count the days,' Cecelia replied. 'I love you, too, Junsaku, with all I am.'

FORTY-THREE

JUNSAKU BOWED before approaching Fusakage Shogun.

The military leader sat in a heavy, wooden chair, the sleeves of his kimono draped over the armrests, the red silk almost touching the floor. 'Junsaku, welcome back. I am sorry for the loss of your boy.'

'Domo arigato gozaimasu, Fusakage-sama. Ninjas attacked us in the middle of the night, and when Nobushida tried to help me fight, one of the assailants killed him with a poison dart.'

'He acted bravely. How old was he?'

'Ten, almost eleven.'

'Did any of the attackers escape?'

'All three dead by my swords.' Junsaku frowned and lowered his head. 'It has been difficult for my family as they witnessed the boy's death.'

'Any idea who sent these ninjas?'

'Though many would like to see me gone, I suspect the Daichi clan of the north is behind the attack. They continue to be a threat and think getting rid of me will weaken your army. As you can imagine, my family is frightened, but I have taken steps to ensure their safety. Daimyo Yukiko offered guards to watch over my wife and daughter.'

'Ah, yes, your wife,' he sighed, his words drifting off. 'I have been meaning to discuss her with you.'

Junsaku stood taller, rolling his shoulders back, his cheeks reddened. 'What about my wife?' he asked harshly.

'I am told she is not Japanese.'

'That is true. My wife is from Europe, a country called Lithuania,' Junsaku replied, his voice a low and deep rumble, dripping with irritation. 'Who has shared this information with you?'

'A fellow samurai told me of your marriage situation. I suspect he hoped I would punish you. As you know, it is not customary for a samurai, especially in your rank, to marry a non-Japanese woman. Did you consider how this would be perceived?'

'Hai, Fusakage-sama, I thought of this, but I had no choice. If I did not marry her, I would have rather died. Being with her, married to Cecelia, feels as natural as breathing.'

The shogun stared at Junsaku, his posture rigid and commanding. 'I should remove you from your rank, Junsaku. Not marrying a Japanese woman disrespects our empire and the shogunate.' Junsaku puffed out his chest, his muscles tensed and strained, his eyes blackened as anger coursed through his veins. 'However,' Fusakage Shogun continued, 'you are my best samurai, and I know bushido is your life. Even though I will not punish you, others want you to pay for your disrespect. Though I find your decision to marry a non-Japanese woman objectionable, you are too important to my army to let this interfere. But Junsaku, watch your back. Though many want you dead because you work for me, they may also want to see you die for marrying a gaijin.'

Junsaku hated the word gaijin. He breathed deeply, brought his lower lip between his teeth, bit down slightly, and then exhaled, the air escaping like a hissing snake. Junsaku kept his voice calm and steady. 'You can rely on me to always be your devoted protector.'

'Hai. Protecting me is your priority, Junsaku, even above your family.'

'Understood, Fusakage-sama,' Junsaku obeyed, his throat tight as he swallowed.

As Junsaku poised himself to bow, a ghostly figure appeared out of nowhere behind the shogun's seat. The eight-foot-tall phantom cast a dark shadow over the leader, enveloping him in the inky darkness of its billowing cloak. Junsaku gazed over Fusakage's shoulder at the spectre, a look of bewilderment on his face, and the shogun shifted uncomfortably in his seat, puzzled by Junsaku's odd behaviour.

'What are you staring at?' Fusakage asked, glancing behind him.

Junsaku, as though in a trance, watched the ghost, its hood drifting side to side as if he was shaking his head in disagreement. With a chill coursing through him, Junsaku looked at the shogun, who stared back, his eyes narrowed, scrutinizing his general. When Junsaku slowly returned his gaze to the ghostly figure across the room, the spirit slowly dissipated before him, like wisps of smoke vanishing on the wind, leaving him with a strange sense of foreboding.

FORTY-FOUR

NINE YEARS had passed since Nobushida's death, and, just like her brother, Fukano committed herself to following the principles of bushido and martial arts training. One afternoon after school, Kasai, a fellow student, positioned himself defiantly before Fukano, puffing out his chest to appear more muscular beneath his grey cotton jacket. 'You think you are so strong, but you are just a girl, Fukano. You can never beat a man,' he challenged.

Fukano's hands rested on her narrow hips, and her relaxed fingers showed that she remained calm and cool-headed. 'Kasai, you must be careful, or I will cut you down like a tree.' The boys surrounding Kasai stifled their laughter at the idea of this slim, four-teen-year-old girl, half-Japanese, half-Lithuanian, challenging their sixteen-year-old friend. 'Not only can I beat you in a fight, but I can also run faster than you, you slug,' she quipped, goading him on.

'Ha!' Kasai replied, tipping back his head, chuckling. 'Gaijin, we will race to your house, and you can suck my dust along the way.'

'Japan is my birthplace, and my father is Japanese and protects the shogun, you *yowamushi*, so do not call me gaijin. And, when I beat you in this race, coward, I will take those shoes you wear and add them to my collection.' Fukano smiled coyly.

'Alright. But Fukano, know this; I will take *your* shoes, and your samurai father and gaijin mother will be disappointed that you could not beat a man,' Kasai finished, crossing his arms at his chest.

'Kasai, you are delusional; I will beat you. Now, let us race. I am anxious to add your waraji to my display. That will bring my total to eleven pairs of shoes, or maybe twelve. There are so many, I have lost count!'

One of the boys near Kasai suddenly erupted into laughter. Kasai's head whipped around, his face contorted into a fierce scowl resembling an angry bear, and he glared at the teenager who laughed; the boy's eyes widened, and he froze, halting his laughter in an attempt not to provoke Kasai further.

Kasai and Fukano stood side by side on the cobblestone road, prepared for their running race. Fukano wore a light-blue wrap dress that reached her ankles, tied at the waist with a canvas belt, a gift from her father, and a plain, white robe underneath, with flat, straw-rope sandals with tabi socks on her feet, the same kind of shoe worn by Kasai. They waited for the signal to start the race.

'*Iku!*' yelled a boy, and the race began.

Fukano and Kasai ran, their arms pumping like the drive rods of a locomotive. Moments later, Kasai paced more than two steps in the lead, a grin on his long face. However, his smile faded as he witnessed Fukano's light blue dress fly past him. As Kasai tried to speed up, his breathing became difficult, and his pace slowed as a stabbing pain struck his chest. When he finally arrived at the finish line, Fukano's house, he found her waiting at the wooden gate, leaning against the door, her arms folded at her chest. Moments later, the other boys clumsily approached as Fukano extended her right arm towards Kasai, palm up, and said steadily, 'Your shoes.' Everyone watched as Kasai removed his sandals, handed them to Fukano, and stood in his tabi socks on the cobblestone street. Fukano inclined her head slightly and said, 'Arigato, Kasai. And do not rechallenge me; your parents will not appreciate it if they have to keep buying you shoes.'

Kasai huffed as Fukano turned away with his waraji dangling in her fingers and passed through the gate to her home, disappearing behind the stone wall.

On the other side, in her family's garden, Fukano placed Kasai's straw sandals at the base of the wall near her other trophies. Fukano stood back, admired all the shoes she had won, and quickly tallied: she counted thirteen, smiling at the thought of showing her father her spoils when he arrived home later that day.

Fukano entered the house and went to the kitchen. 'Konnichiwa, Okasan.'

'Konnichiwa, Ka. Would you like a cup of *hōjicha?*'

'Hai, tea sounds nice,' Fukano said, grinning at her mother. She watched as her okasan gracefully added roasted green tea leaves to the pot perched above the open fire, thinking about how she resembled her mother: five foot nine inches, lean and toned, with the same jade-green eyes that curved up towards her temples. 'Oh, and I won another pair of *waraji*, Okasan,' Fukano bragged.

Cecelia placed her hands on her hips, her palms pressed against her bright yellow silk kimono. 'Fukano, what will we do with all those sandals piling up? If you keep this up, the villagers might begin to dislike us.' Cecelia picked up the teapot and carried it to the table, setting it down on a metal trivet. 'I should be upset with you, but honestly, your strength and courage make me proud. Do not ever change.'

'Arigato, Okasan,' Fukano said, bowing her head. 'I hope Otosan will be proud, too. He should be arriving soon, right?'

'Yes. I expect your father sometime today,' she replied. Then, Cecelia bent over and coughed, covering her mouth with her open hand. Seconds later, she quieted, stood upright, wiped her lips, and smiled at her daughter.

'Okasan, are you ill?'

'No, Ka. Just a cough. Nothing to worry about. I will be fine.'

***

AS THE GOLDEN sun descended behind the towering mountains that surrounded the village of Kakunadate, Yui served herself, Cecelia, and Fukano a meal of miso soup, pickles, and grilled mackerel at the low dining table. Halfway through their dinner, the clip-clop of horse's hooves on the cobblestone street outside interrupted the women's conversation.

'Otosan is here!' Fukano screeched, springing from her seat on the floor.

Cecelia stood gracefully and followed her daughter out the front door and into the courtyard. Fukano threw open the wooden gate and found her father tying the horse's reins to a metal loop in the stone wall.

'Otosan!' she exclaimed, her tanned, pink cheek squished against his chest as she hugged him tightly.

'I am glad to be home, Ka,' he said to his daughter as he stared at his wife standing close, her yellow kimono hugging her body. 'Cecelia, my love,' he whispered, stretching his arm towards her, beckoning her to take his hand.

Fukano let go of her father. He walked to Cecelia, embraced his wife, and kissed her. 'I have returned to my favourite place,' he said.

'I missed you,' Cecelia said, her arms holding him close. Suddenly, she let go, backed away, put her palm over her mouth, and coughed. 'Sumimasen,' she said. 'I have a tickle in my throat, that is all. Are you hungry? Thirsty?'

'Hai. I rode my horse for many hours without stopping. I just wanted to be home as soon as possible.'

Cecelia coughed again, this time the heave accompanied by a moist rattle that seemed to originate from deep inside her chest.

'Cecelia, you are sick; you need rest,' Junsaku said concernedly, his thick, black eyebrows angled towards the bridge of his nose.

'Junsaku, I am fine,' Cecelia assured him, weaving her arm with his.

Fukano approached her father, and together, the family entered their house.

FORTY-FIVE

FUKANO WOKE to birds chirping and the sound of her father's feet sliding across the tatami mats in their dojo, alerting her that the time had come to train. She put on her gi, slid open the fusuma doors, and entered the dojo. As she stepped inside the room, she watched her father executing katas with precision and power, admiring him as he moved swiftly across the tatami-covered floor. His feet seemed to float across the surface of the mats as the fabric of his gi rustled and created a swish sound that filled the room. Junsaku stopped, closed his eyes, lifted his hands above his head, and pressed his palms together. He inhaled deeply and exhaled loudly, slowly lowering his hands to the front of his chest, and when he opened his eyes, he saw Fukano watching him, her hands at her sides. They bowed to each other.

'Come, Ka,' Junsaku said. 'We will train here in the dojo and then go to the meadow where you will ride my horse and practise archery.'

'Osu, Sensei,' she replied obediently, now in the role of student rather than daughter.

'Hajime,' Junsaku stated, and they began their exercises.

While Fukano mirrored her father's movements, Junsaku became distracted by Cecelia's wet cough echoing from the kitchen. As Fukano focused on demonstrating the kata, Junsaku stopped abruptly. 'How long has your okasan been sick?' he asked.

'Not long, Otosan. I only heard the cough days ago, and she said she had no fever or other symptoms.'

Sharp creases formed above the bridge of Junsaku's nose. 'After I return to Edo, fetch the doctor if her symptoms worsen or do not go away. Also, send a message to me immediately. Do you understand?'

'Of course, Otosan,' she confirmed. 'Okasan is strong. This will pass soon.'

'Unfortunately, I cannot stay long on this visit. The shogunate is under serious threat, and I must return to the castle as planned, so I am relying on you to make sure your mother regains full health.'

Fukano shook her head, reassuring her father.

Junsaku positioned himself into a punching stance and pulled his left arm towards his chest, tucking his left fist below his armpit while extending his right arm. 'We start again. Hajime.' He punched the air before performing a block, Fukano following his movements precisely.

Cecelia came to the dojo wearing a lavender silk kimono with a white shawl wrapped around her shoulders. She watched her husband and daughter from the doorway, her cheeks the colour of ripe peaches.

'The sun has risen,' Junsaku said, smiling at his wife. Then, sharply inhaling as though trying to regain his breath, he stated, 'You are the most beautiful woman in the world, Cecelia.' As he sensed his daughter's gaze from behind, he glanced over his shoulder and looked at her. With velvety-soft eyes, he said apologetically, 'Sumimasen. I meant mother and daughter are the most beautiful women in the world.'

Fukano giggled, and a radiant grin spread across Cecelia's face, both women's eyes shining like polished emeralds.

'Will you two come to the kitchen and have something to eat?' Cecelia asked.

'Iie, Cecelia,' Junsaku said, draping his heavy arm over Fukano's shoulders. 'Fukano and I are going to the meadow to train using a bow and arrow while riding a horse. Afterwards, we will come back for a mid-day meal.'

'Fine. Yui and I will have it ready when you return.'

Junsaku walked to Cecelia and embraced her, his arms encircling her torso. 'And, when I get home, we spend time together, alone,' he whispered in her ear.

'Of course,' she replied, softly kissing his cheek.

Junsaku released his wife and clapped his hands. '*Watashi-tachi wa iku!* We go, Ka,' he announced, smiling broadly.

Junsaku's short, stalky, long-haired *Kisouma* stood quietly at the front of the house, bits of hay littering the ground where the horse had eaten earlier. Junsaku mounted first, then pulled Fukano onto the horse's back behind him. 'Cecelia,' Junsaku yelled, 'would you please fetch Fukano's archery set? I forgot to bring it from the dojo.'

Moments later, Cecelia exited the house, her wooden sandals tapping the stone walkway. She coughed as she handed the equipment to Fukano.

'Goodbye, Okasan,' Fukano said, sliding the wooden bow and the arrow-filled container over her right shoulder.

'Goodbye, Ka. *Kiwotsukete, kudasai.*'

'I will be careful,' she moaned.

Then Junsaku said to his wife, 'You must rest and get rid of that cough.'

'Do not worry, Junsaku. I am fine. But if it makes you feel better, I will lay down.'

Junsaku puckered his lips, sending an invisible kiss toward his wife. With a gentle squeeze of his legs, his horse began to walk down the road, its hooves clicking on the stone pavers, while Cecelia stood at the front gate, watching as Junsaku and Fukano disappeared over the rise in the road.

***

AS THEY RODE to the meadow, Junsaku and Fukano spoke in Japanese.

'Ka, have you been practising archery?' Junsaku asked.

'Hai, Otosan, I practise often. I even killed a wild boar last week and cleaned the animal myself. Also, did you see all the shoes I have won? I stacked them in the garden, near the wall.'

'Ah, hai, Fukano. I did see your trophies and apologise for not congratulating you yet. I assume you won those in a running race?'

'Hai. No one is faster than me. No one,' she boasted.

'You, my daughter, have strength, speed, and intelligence and can do everything a man can. You could have been *onna musha* and fought alongside me as a samurai. However, today, a girl is expected to be a wife and mother, not a warrior.' Junsaku paused momentarily, then said, 'It will be hard for you to get married. Do you know why?'

'Because you will never believe anyone is good enough for me.'

'Clever girl!' he exclaimed loudly, his voice booming in the warm spring air. 'No man is good enough for my daughter.'

'Anyway, I want to train in martial arts and be with you and Okasan. I am not interested in marriage.' Fukano's green eyes shimmered with determination.

When they reached the grassy meadow bordered by large evergreen trees, Junsaku dismounted, saying, 'Stay on the horse and slide onto the saddle. You will ride alone while I watch. I want you to gallop across this field and shoot at the trees, hitting the trunks, until you have used all the arrows. *Wakarimasu ka?*'

'I understand,' Fukano replied, her eyes aimed straight ahead as she prepared her mind and body for the task. Finally, Fukano pressed her heels below the kiso's ribcage, and the horse galloped, the rider's shoulder-length, sun-streaked brown hair bouncing in sync with the horse's mane. Fukano let go of the reins and grabbed an arrow from the pouch over her shoulder. With the bow in her left hand, she secured the shaft, pulled the bowstring with her right hand, and tightened her legs around the horse's sturdy belly, locking herself in place. She let go of the bowstring, and the arrow propelled towards the trees surrounding the meadow. Fukano hit her target, the tip piercing a trunk ten metres away. As the horse continued to gallop, Fukano shot arrows, her thighs gripping the horse, her heart pumping. Finally, when the pouch emptied, Fukano grabbed the reins and pulled them lightly. The horse's gait slowed, and Fukano turned the animal around and trotted toward her father, who waited at the meadow's edge. When she arrived where he waited, she could see her father's dark eyes sparkling with delight

'Yoku yatta, Ka. You destroyed the army of trees,' he joked. Then, with a more serious tone, he said, 'Though you may not have the samurai title, you have the skills. You did not miss one shot. I am proud of you.'

Fukano dismounted the horse, a bright smile on her face. 'Osu, Sensei,' she responded, her eyes sparkling with vivid brightness, blending with the green meadow stretching out behind her.

FORTY-SIX

WITH THE PEARLY glow of moonlight filtering through the window, Cecelia nestled next to Junsaku, her head on his chest, comforted by the rise and fall of his breathing. She kept her hand near her cheek, poised to cover her mouth if she coughed, the weight of their impending separation pressing on her heart like a heavy blanket.

'Cecelia, you need to get better,' Junsaku whispered, stroking his wife's back.

'When Yui and I went to the doctor today, he prepared a mixture of tea and herbs, and I am already feeling better. I still have several more days that I need to take this medicine, but honestly, there is nothing to worry about.'

Junsaku groaned and said, 'Cecelia must grow old with me to go to the next life together.' Then, Junsaku took a deep breath and held it momentarily, silently contemplating his situation before saying, 'I am considering not returning to Edo. I should stay with you and Fukano and ensure you are both safe, but I am obligated to the shogunate. I am not sure what the right choice is.'

Cecelia sat upright and held the blanket near her chest. 'You are a general, and there are new threats to the shogunate. Plus, I know how much bushido and your commitment to warrior life means to you. Go back to the shogun as planned. Fukano and I will be fine until you return. We have Yui, friends in the village, and the support of the daimyo to help protect us when you are away,' Cecelia reassured her husband.

'Cecelia, do you ever think it is a mistake to protect and kill for the shogun?'

'What is your opinion?' Cecelia purposely avoided answering his question. Acutely aware of the years her husband devoted to his training to achieve his rank of general, she felt uncomfortable offering her opinion because, if she influenced his decision to stay or leave the shogunate, she feared he might resent her one day.

'I am torn. I have devoted countless hours of hard work to achieve my rank, but lately, something feels wrong. I feel a sense of deep foreboding, especially when I am away from you and Fukano, and right now when you are sick, I am even more unsure.'

Cecelia put her hand on Junsaku's muscled upper arm. 'Firstly, I am not sick. I only have a passing cough. And secondly, you are a devoted samurai, as well as a wonderful husband and father.'

'But...' Junsaku began.

'No 'but'. Please do not give up everything you have worked hard to achieve just because I have a cough. I am taking the herbs, and my health is improving. I will be perfect when you return, and so will your daughter.'

Junsaku remained silent for several minutes, then said, 'Cecelia, I did take an oath to protect the shogun, and I should return to Edo until the threat of the Daichi clan in the north has ended.'

'How long will you be gone this time?'

'I am not sure. There is the possibility of battle.'

'I hate war,' Cecelia replied. 'Please make sure you do not get hurt. Come home to us.'

'No need to worry. I win every fight with barely a scratch.'

Junsaku held Cecelia close, her flat belly pressed against his hip. He stroked her hair, humming the tune Sakura until she fell asleep, an occasional, wet cough escaping her chest.

***

AFTER BREAKFAST the following day, Junsaku slung his travel bag over the back flanks of his horse. 'My beautiful wife and daughter, I must leave now, but I will return soon. Ka, give your otosan a hug,' he said, his dark eyes lacklustre.

She ran at him, took him in her arms, and squeezed hard. 'Please return soon, Otosan. Next time you are home, we will practise with the sword.'

'Bokken, Ka,' he responded calmly, patting her back. 'Only a wooden sword for now. It is not time for steel.'

'Osu, Sensei,' she said, moving away and bowing towards him.

Junsaku placed his hands on Cecelia's shoulders and gazed into her eyes. 'You must promise me that if your symptoms worsen, you will see the doctor immediately and have a message sent to me in Edo so I may come home.'

'I promise,' Cecelia replied with a tight smile. 'Now go. I will be fine, besides missing you terribly. Please come home as soon as you can. I miss you already.'

As Junsaku hugged his wife, Cecelia swallowed hard, suppressing the cough that clawed at her throat.

FORTY-SEVEN

JUNSAKU RODE for five days, taking a few breaks on his return trip to Edo. When he finally arrived at his second home in the capital city, tired, dirty, and thirsty, he had a choice: go to the castle and report for duty or visit his favourite inn, Kurakura, where he could eat stuffed squid, drink sake, then take a long, hot bath at the local onsen. Junsaku decided the shogun could wait and went to the inn.

After dinner, Junsaku bathed in a private outdoor hot spring, soaking his weary body in thermal, mineral-rich waters, the sweet taste of squid and rice wine lingering on his lips. Suddenly, Junsaku no longer felt alone, and a shiver ran down his spine, causing the hairs on his neck to stand on end. Then, Junsaku heard a man's deep voice say, 'You still have not learned.' He looked in the direction of the sound. Junsaku could see the hooded spirit floating amongst the trees, his black cloak and generous hood making him nearly invisible in the shadows. 'Learned what? You are not the first spirit to tell me this, and I still do not understand!' Junsaku's voice echoed with frustration and anger, his hands clenched into fists below the surface of the hot water, his patience at a breaking point.

A swirling mist enveloped Junsaku as the steaming water of the hot spring mingled with the crisp chill of the night air. Junsaku's gaze fixed on the apparition gliding toward him, its dark figure shrouded in the thickening fog. For the first time in his life, he felt the cold grip of fear as the ghostly figure approached, shrouded in blackness, the vision seeming to absorb the light from the moon and stars. The spectre stopped next to the edge of the onsen pool and stared at Junsaku, and, as though the voice emanated from deep inside himself, Junsaku heard a man's voice say, 'You are on the precipice.'

As Junsaku opened his mouth to speak, the air thick with tension, the spirit began to retreat into the surrounding woods as though pulled by an unseen force. Junsaku watched in awe as the figure dissolved into the darkness, the forest trees swallowing the spectre, and he felt unsure like never before, his body tense with anxiety and dread.

***

WHEN JUNSAKU reported to work the next day, he met with the shogun in his private room, his mind a whirlwind of thoughts from the previous night's events.

'Junsaku,' the shogun demanded, 'pay attention!'

Junsaku shook his head, forcing himself back to the present moment. 'Gomennasai, Fusakage-sama,' he replied, bowing his head.

'Where is your mind?' the shogun snapped.

'My trip was tiring, but I am here now.'

'Sit with me. We need to discuss the upcoming battle,' the shogun replied, lowering himself onto a floor cushion and tucking his legs beneath him. 'My spies have told me the Daichi clan is waiting for me in the Mutsu Prefecture. I received a message from the enemy that read, 'Fight or die a coward.' The shogun's jaw tensed. 'Junsaku, we must defeat the Daichi clan swiftly.'

'Hai, I understand, Fusakage-sama. Your army is ready. We leave tomorrow to teach these insurgents a lesson.' Junsaku clenched his fists tightly at his sides, his nails digging into his palms.

The shogun leaned forward, staring intensely at his general, his hands resting on his knees, and stated gravely, 'Junsaku, we must win. If we lose this fight, all is lost.'

Junsaku straightened his posture. 'We will be victorious. I will personally remove the clan leader's head and force his army to submit to you.'

***

WEEKS LATER, Junsaku and the shogun sat on horseback, perched atop a hill in the Mutsu prefecture. From their hidden vantage point behind thick foliage, the two leaders silently observed the shogun's warriors in the valley below, lined up and prepared for war.

As Junsaku stared at the battle-ready soldiers, he whispered aloud, his words weighted with confusion and sorrow, 'Why do we do this?'

The shogun turned sharply, his expression an angry frown, and glared at Junsaku as he answered with annoyance, 'To live in peace, General.'

Junsaku doubted the role of peace over power in the war they were about to undertake. However, he knew he needed to keep his opinions to himself and maintain a respectful composure, regardless of his scepticism.

With a stern tone, his speech clipped and direct, the shogun asked, 'I need to hear your detailed plan for winning this war,

General.'

'Fusakage-sama, before our arrival, I sent samurai to search for any clan spies with instructions to kill. I am confident my men destroyed anyone with a message or information before it reached their leader, so our enemy has no intelligence to aid their planning.' Junsaku turned his attention to the battle lines in the valley below, estimating as many as fifteen thousand enemy fighters, with foot soldiers in rows one hundred deep and another sixty rows of soldiers on horseback. He could also see the shogun's visibly smaller army facing the enemy lines, waiting for the fight to begin, with only forty rows of samurai on foot and thirty rows of soldiers on horseback. Pointing at the battle-ready troops in the valley, Junsaku said, 'Fusakage-sama, notice how our army appears outnumbered. We did not put all our samurai into the first wave because part of my strategy is to make the enemy believe our army is small and weak, causing the Daichi clan to become overconfident.'

The shogun rubbed his chin.

'As you can see,' Junsaku explained, 'we only have five thousand samurai prepared to fight in the valley, or at least that is what the Daichi clan believes. The clan cannot see that thousands of foot soldiers and mounted samurai hide in the surrounding forest trees, awaiting my signal to join the battle. The only risk with my plan is that our casualties could be high in the initial surge.'

With lifted brows, the shogun spoke in a voice devoid of emotion, saying, 'Such is the nature of war.'

Junsaku continued, 'There are only three ways to access this valley: from the north, south, and west. As you can see, the east side is impenetrable because of the cliff walls.' Junsaku took a breath. 'My plan is in three stages. In stage one, I will enter the battle from here, the south, join our seemingly small and weak army on the battlefield, and issue the command to begin the fight. The enemy does not know that four-thousand-foot soldiers hide in the flanks on the north side of the valley and will join the fight shortly after it starts.' Junsaku paused and then looked at the shogun, who offered a subtle nod, signalling for Junsaku to proceed. 'Naturally, the enemy will want to push our army towards the cliffs in the east, backing us up to the sheer rock walls and trapping us. And we will let them,' Junsaku said confidently, the boldness of his statement catching the shogun off guard.

The shogun pursed his lips. 'Explain.'

'Fusakage-sama, we will allow the enemy army to believe they have our backs to the wall and that we are trapped, and then, I will alert my captain in the west. On my signal, he will lead six thousand mounted samurai into the valley, who will ambush the enemy from the rear, and our samurai army will surround and annihilate every one of the rogues and ensure our victory.' Junsaku paused momentarily, allowing the shogun to absorb everything, then summarised, 'With the full force of your samurai warriors engaged in battle, the enemy will be surrounded and destroyed.'

'You never cease to impress me, General. For today's battle, where is my position in the fight?' the shogun asked.

'I prefer if you do not engage in battle, Fusakage-sama. This war will be our biggest test, and you must live.'

The shogun waved his hand, indicating his agreement and the start of combat.

Junsaku spurred his horse and rode down the pathway to the battlefield, positioning himself in front of the shogun's samurai soldiers. Then he removed his katana from its scabbard, raised his sword, and yelled, *'Tatakai!'* initiating the start of war.

***

SOLDIERS ON both sides collided and fought for their lives. As Junsaku's second wave of foot soldiers entered the fight from the flanks, blood spread over the fertile ground as men were impaled by arrows and spears, cut by blades, and trampled by steel-shod horses' hooves. As Junsaku killed a foot soldier with his katana, slicing through the man's neck, he watched emotionless as the enemy's helmeted head rolled off his shoulder and hit the grass, followed by his body collapsing like a wet noodle.

Junsaku noticed the enemy gaining ground and knew the time had come for stage three. He rose from his saddle, balanced himself, and stretched his arms wide, signalling to the mounted samurai hiding in the surrounding forest to unleash their assault. Moments later, thousands of the shogun's samurai warriors charged from the west, the cacophony of their running feet and the thundering of horses' hooves echoing through the valley. The sudden chaos caught the Daichi warriors off guard; the mounted samurai horses pranced with agitation as their riders tried to regain control, while the foot soldiers spun in frantic circles, attempting to make sense of the situation. A satisfied and slightly arrogant smile unfolded on Junsaku's face. His flawlessly executed strategy caused immense self-confidence to flow through him as he recognised the shogun's army had gained the upper hand.

As Junsaku gazed across the vast battlefield, he saw the clan leader on horseback. He watched as the man thrust his spear and impaled one of the shogun's warriors with deadly precision. Junsaku tightened his legs and raced his steed forward, thinking, *'I will fulfil my promise to the shogun and remove the clan leader's head myself.'* When the clan leader saw Junsaku rapidly approaching, he held out his spear and charged the general on horseback.

Junsaku galloped forward on a collision course with the enemy leader. As Junsaku neared the man, he pulled on his horse's reins, forced a sharp left turn, launched off the steed, and landed on the ground, rolling over his right shoulder. Junsaku came onto his knees, drew his wakizashi sword, and removed the horse's front leg below the knee, sending the horse and rider crashing to the ground with a sickening thud.

Junsaku stood above the clan leader. 'I can see you have a broken back, you coward. You are defeated.' Then, Junsaku grabbed the man by his topknot, pulled his head upward, and used his sword to cut through his neck, fulfilling his promise to the shogun. As he tossed the enemy's head beside him onto the blood-soaked grass, an unsettling cold enveloped him, and he sensed the hooded spirit looming behind him. 'Not today,' he whispered, refusing to turn around, ignoring the ghost who haunted him. Normally hyper-focused, Junsaku's mind clouded as though a storm erupted inside him, and when he glanced at the clan leader's decapitated head lying on the ground, the dead man's eyes still open wide, he felt uncertainty, almost remorse, for killing the man so viciously. With new feelings rising inside him, causing him to question his life's ambition, he raised his sword above his head, feeling the weight in his hand, and released a painful cry, raw and primal. Sweat beaded on his forehead as he surveyed the maimed and dead bodies strewn around him, their blood soaking into the ground, and Junsaku had an overwhelming feeling that, after today's battle, his life would never be the same.

FORTY-EIGHT

HOURS AFTER the shogun's army paraded back into Edo, Junsaku met with his captains at the local inn to celebrate their conquest. 'Kanpai!' Junsaku cheered, lifting his sake glass and dumping the chilled nihonsho down his throat, the crisp, slightly sweet flavour lingering on his tongue. 'To victory, the shogun, and Japan!' he proclaimed.

A girl dressed in a red silk kimono with a white belt perfectly tied around her waist poured more rice wine into Junsaku's glass as a teenage boy dashed towards him. He stopped before Junsaku and, with his eyes aimed at the ground, he said, 'General, I come with an urgent message.'

'Speak up,' Junsaku ordered.

'It is from a person named Fukano. The message is you must return home immediately.'

The colour drained from Junsaku's face as his eyes blackened. The cup slipped from his fingers and clattered against the table, and sake erupted from the vessel, splattering the wood. 'Captain Sekigawa, tell the shogun I must go to my family. I will be back when I can.'

'Of course, Junsaku,' the captain replied, his brow furrowed with concern. Then, he leaned forward and said sincerely, 'Blessings to you and your family.'

Junsaku jumped up from the table, grabbed his swords, and ran from the inn. Outside, he untied his horse's reins and, without hesitation, sprang into the saddle, applying pressure near the horse's ribs. As Junsaku galloped through the vibrant city streets, the citizens stepped aside, creating a clear path for the samurai to pass.

***

THREE DAYS later, after enduring a gruelling twenty hours of riding each day with only short breaks to eat, drink from mountain streams, or have a brief nap, Junsaku finally approached the familiar front gate of his home in Kakunadate. Before his horse came to a complete stop, Junsaku slid off its back, sprinted through the weathered wooden gate, and burst through the front door, not even removing his shoes.

'Cecelia.' he bellowed, waiting for her to respond or appear before him. However, his wife's name hung in the still air, and the only answer given to him was an unsettling silence.

Fukano appeared from the dimly lit hallway. She stopped and gazed at her father, the rims of her green eyes bright red. With lips curved downwards and cheeks stained with tear marks, Fukano did not have to say a word; Junsaku could feel his daughter's agony. Junsaku's legs buckled, and he fell to his knees on the wood floor, his back hunched over.

Fukano came to him, knelt, and gently touched his cheeks with her palms, hoping to comfort him. 'She passed peacefully, Otosan.' After a short pause, Fukano continued, her words choked, 'I am so sorry you were not here. Okasan's health seemed to improve, and the cough disappeared. But it returned, worse than the first time, and then she developed a fever. We summoned the doctor immediately, who gave her medicine, but she could not keep it in her stomach. She was barely awake for three days and could not eat or drink, but I thought she would get better.' Fukano's voice cracked like dry leaves. 'I regret I did not send for you earlier, but she told me she would be fine, and so did the doctor. I honestly believed her health was improving.' Fukano sniffled, taking her father's hands in hers. 'Otosan, on the day she passed, I could sense that her spirit left hours before her body died, and right before that moment, Mother told me to tell you she loves you and she will be waiting for you.'

Junsaku sobbed, pulled his hands from Fukano, and used them to cover his face, trying to shield himself from the overwhelming wave of despair washing over him. Fukano cried softly with him while Yui stood quietly in the threshold, her eyes swollen and red, before she retreated to the garden, leaving what remained of the family alone to grieve.

'What about you, Ka?' Junsaku said, staring curiously at Fukano, his teary eyes glistening like polished obsidian rock. 'You cannot stay here without your mother. You are only fifteen.' Junsaku averted his gaze, casting his eyes to a shadowed corner in the room. As though speaking to an invisible person, he said aloud, his voice quivering, 'What will I do? She cannot live with me in Edo.'

'Father, I will live here with Yui.'

'No, Fukano!' he snapped. 'You will not stay here with Yui. You must be with family.' Junsaku sobbed, struggling to catch his breath, each gasp a reflection of his shattered soul, until finally, he inhaled deeply and stated, 'Fukano, you will go and live with my sister, Etsuko, in Okinawa.'

'But Otosan, I do not want to leave Kakunadate! Why can't I stay here or live with you in Edo?'

'Fukano, do not argue with me!' he barked. Even the sharpness of his tone surprised Junsaku, not remembering a time when he had spoken to his daughter so angrily. However, he carried on, forging through the explosive atmosphere. 'You should be with family, and you cannot live with me in Edo while I am still committed to the shogunate. I must trust my sister, your obasan, to raise you. I have made my decision. You will live with your aunt and uncle in Okinawa. I will send the message to them today and let them know you are coming.'

Fukano sensed she should not challenge her father. 'Hai, Otosan,' she surrendered, wiping away the tears that streamed down her soft, velvety cheeks.

FORTY-NINE

JUNSAKU WASHED and prepared Cecelia's body, including wetting her lips and giving her a last taste of water. He dressed her in the red kimono embroidered with white cranes and purple neckline he gifted her when they first met under the cherry blossom tree next to the river in Edo, then placed straw sandals on her feet to travel to the next realm.

That evening, just after sundown, Junsaku and Fukano walked up the leaf-covered pathway of the cemetery on the outskirts of Kakunodate, followed by Yui, each carrying a candle-lit lantern, lighting their way in the moonless night. Four low-ranking samurai followed, carrying Cecelia's wooden casket to the burial site beneath a cherry blossom tree. Fukano's green eyes were puffy and reddened from grief. Junsaku forced himself to appear calm as he tried to hide his agony from his daughter, and, silently in his mind, to cope, he repeated the phrase, *'Death is a part of life, and we will be together again'*. Despite his unwavering confidence that he would reunite with his wife, he still felt excruciating pain deep within, like a thousand swords sliced his heart and soul. Junsaku wanted to die rather than be without Cecelia; however, walking alongside his daughter, listening to the soft rustle of leaves and the chirping sounds of crickets and frogs reminded him that his journey had not ended.

When they arrived at the gravesite, a man dressed in a tall hat and ritual robes placed small carafes of sake on a black lacquer table. Before the ceremony began, Junsaku, Fukano, and Yui each drank a cup of rice wine. Junsaku filled five more cups and gave one to the monk and the remaining four to the samurai who had carried his wife's coffin. The men bowed, drank the nihonshu, and returned the cups to the table. Junsaku filled one last polished tin cup and carried it to Cecelia's coffin, which sat on the grass, not yet lowered into the earth. He lifted the vessel in the air and poured the sake onto the top of the wooden casket, causing a dark spot to form where the liquid stained the solid wood. Then Junsaku covered Cecelia's casket with a three-tail banner embroidered with the words: *With death comes rebirth.*

The monk spoke ritualistic words in the chilly air, bowed, and clapped ceremoniously as Junsaku, Fukano, and Yui stared at Cecelia's coffin. When the monk finished, Fukano reached into a bag and pulled out a terracotta bowl, an item from their kitchen symbolising earthy nourishment. Fukano lifted the vessel and threw it hard at the coffin, and the bowl shattered into a multitude of shards, the act signifying her mother would no longer need the implements of the living. Fukano looked up at her father, tears streaming down her cheeks, and Junsaku reached out and pulled her close, enveloping her in a protective embrace.

When the ceremony ended, Junsaku and the four samurai lowered Cecelia's coffin into the ground. After filling the grave with dirt, they placed a tall stone monument with *Cecelia Aoyama* etched in the white rock and a kanji inscription by Taiheiki that read:

There is no death.
There is no life.
Indeed, the skies are cloudless,
and the river waters clear.

Fukano carefully placed tinder and delicate sandalwood chips into a small, hollowed space carved in the headstone, and Junsaku ignited the incense using a steel flint. The rich, sweet aroma of sandalwood filled the air, the scent meant to soothe Cecelia's spirit, and as the fragrant smoke spiralled upward in the evening sky, Junsaku and Fukano bowed to her burial site before walking home, their fingers interlaced.

FJFTY

ONE WEEK after Cecelia's burial, Junsaku and Fukano left Kakunadate to go to the island of Okinawa. They travelled on horseback to the port of Kagoshima in Kyushu, Southern Japan, escorted by two labourers driving a four-wheeled, ox-drawn cart that carried Fukano's belongings. Upon their arrival at the bustling docks three weeks later, Junsaku sold the livestock and carriage, paid the workers their wages, and put the remaining money in a drawstring bag. Asserting his position as the shogun's general, Junsaku swiftly arranged immediate passage to the island of Okinawa, and hours later, he and Fukano began their ten-day journey aboard a two-sail trading vessel destined for the Ryukyu Islands.

Much like her mother's ocean journey when she travelled from Europe to Indonesia and then Japan, Fukano found herself captivated by the mesmerizing brilliance of the bright blue sea. The surface sparkled under the sun, dotted with deeper navy-blue patches that concealed vibrant coral reefs teeming with life just below the waves. From the sailboat deck, Fukano's eyes widened in wonder as she observed the smooth, glistening shells of sea turtles on the ocean's surface as they poked up their heads to breathe in the salty air. Playful dolphins leapt and tumbled near the ship, and she even spotted humpback whales gliding serenely through the water, marvelling as they eyed the boat before diving, vanishing into the blue depths.

When the ship arrived at Naha Port in Okinawa, Junsaku's sister, Etsuko, her husband, Onishi, and their small Japanese terrier, Nikka, waited with a hired driver and an open, horse-drawn carriage to transport them to Fukano's new home in the Urasoe Prefecture, three hours away.

As Junsaku and his daughter approached, Etsuko, Fukano's aunt, felt a pang of jealousy at her niece's captivating beauty. Tall and lean, with light olive skin, hair the colour of rich cocoa, and green eyes that curved towards her temples, Etsuko recognised her unique beauty and noticed her husband's cheeks flush as he stared at Fukano before bowing to Junsaku, who stood before him.

'Stand up, Onishi,' Junsaku commanded.

Onishi stood and smiled wide, revealing a large gap between his thick front teeth. 'Irasshaimase, Junsaku-san. Welcome! We are honoured. Konnichiwa, Mei.'

'Konnichiwa, Ojisan,' Fukano replied. 'Konnichiwa, Obasan,' she said, smiling warmly towards her aunt.

With a thin line formed on her lips, a smile that did not reach her eyes, Etsuko tipped her head toward Fukano, gripping the small dog close to her chest.

Fukano admired the terrier's white-furred body, contrasted with its black-haired head and raven-black eyes, and looked forward to playing with the animal. 'What is your dog's name?' she asked.

'Nikka,' her uncle replied.

'Is it a boy or a girl?'

'A female,' her aunt replied curtly.

'Can I pet her?' Fukano requested, her voice sweet and melodic.

Etsuko reluctantly placed the small terrier on the weathered wooden dock planks. Fukano bent down, and the dog ran to her. As Fukano petted Nikka, her fingers sinking into the dog's soft, stubbly fur, the little dog wagged its tail exuberantly.

'The dog likes you, Fukano,' Junsaku announced. 'Consider Nikka your first friend on the island!'

Fukano smiled brightly at her father and then picked up the terrier, who gave her a gentle lick on her chin before settling comfortably in her arms and panting lightly.

Dismissing her annoyance with her dog's immediate connection to the girl, Etsuko walked towards her brother with small steps and bowed. 'Konnichiwa, Onii, or am I to call you General?'

Junsaku closed the space between him and his sister and hugged her, squeezing and lifting her feet off the ground, her slightly plump body limp in his embrace. 'Sister, even though I am a general, I am still your older brother, your onii,' he answered, releasing his hold on her. 'Now, let us go to your house. We will catch up along the way.'

'Sumimasen,' Fukano said, turning the group's attention to her. 'May Nikka ride with me?'

Etsuko's lips pursed as she prepared to deny Fukano's request. Yet, when she noticed the broad smile on her brother's face, she decided approval was her best option. While her brother remained on the island, he was in charge—but she knew Junsaku would depart soon, and she would be free to manage the girl as she saw fit. 'Hai,' Etsuko replied brusquely. 'Let us leave now.'

Etsuko and Onishi sat on the front bench beside the driver, and Junsaku and Fukano settled in the back with Nikka, the dog nestled comfortably in Fukano's lap. As the carriage lurched forward, leaving the bustling port behind, the passengers felt the gentle bounce over gravel and dirt roads, accompanied by the rhythmic clip-clop of the horses' hooves. With a sense of wonder, Fukano took in her new surroundings. Lush, emerald-green plants and tall trees swayed in the warm breeze. Flowers decorated the landscape with vivid colours of bright pink, fiery blood orange, and electrifying yellow. Rugged, jagged grey limestone walls crisscrossed the hillsides, contrasting with the vibrant green, rolling hills, and, in the distance, Fukano could see the Pacific Ocean's aqua-blue waters, the waves sparkling like diamonds. Fukano put her lips near the dog's ear and whispered playfully, 'Nikka, do you like living here?'

The dog's ears perked up, and she lifted her head, looked at Fukano with eyes like shiny, black glass, and barked loudly.

'Nikka, iie!' Etsuko stated sharply, turning from the front seat and tapping the dog's skull firmly. 'Fukano, do not encourage her to misbehave.'

'Gomennasai, Obasan,' Fukano replied softly, rubbing Nikka's head as the dog buried its nose under Fukano's forearm.

'Etsuko,' Junsaku stated loudly, diverting his sister's focus from his daughter, 'tell me about your life.'

His sister stared at the road ahead as she spoke. 'Well, Junsaku, we live in a small house on the outskirts of the village. Ours is a modest life, not a lavish and adventurous one like yours. And, unlike you, we were unable to have children. Why is it you only have the girl? Your late wife could not give you a boy?'

Junsaku sighed loudly. 'Before I met Cecelia, I became a

caregiver to a boy, Nobushida, after his father died in battle. I loved him like a son, and so did Cecelia. After Fukano was born, Nobushida died trying to protect our family during an attack.' Junsaku clenched his hands tightly in his lap and shook his head slowly. 'After his death, Etsuko, we wanted more children, especially a boy, but sadly, it did not happen.' Junsaku noticed Fukano's jade eyes were glossy, and he reached out and stroked her soft cheek. 'Lucky for us, we had Fukano and love her beyond words. She has the grace and beauty of a woman and a warrior's fighting spirit.'

'Arigato, Father.'

Junsaku leaned towards the front bench, his eyes sparkling with mischief. As he inched toward his sister's head, he noticed the delicate wisps of her thinning black hair pulled tightly into a neat bun, barely concealing the pale skin of her scalp that peeked through. He lowered his voice, a teasing lilt in his tone. 'Etsuko, do you remember that time you smacked me with your toy?' He pointed to the mark near his lip. 'I still have the scar.'

Etsuko turned and met her brother's gaze, her eyes lifeless as unlit coal. 'Iie, I do not remember,' she replied, her voice flat and emotionless.

'So, Etsuko, I am not the only one who suffers your occasional cruelty?' Onishi joked.

Etsuko's face reddened, and she did not respond, turning her attention back to the horses at the front of the carriage.

Onishi grinned, his cheeks inflated like tiny, red balloons, and he said directly to Junsaku, 'Etsuko is a good wife. Though, as you know, she has a temper.'

'Onishi, enough!' Etsuko snapped, her tone destroying the lively conversation. 'Brother, I need to ask you something: how long will the girl stay with us?'

Junsaku's demeanour shifted, his once-playful expression becoming a mix of irritation and arrogance. 'Etsuko, my daughter's name is Fukano, and I expect you to call her by her name. And, sister, she will stay here until I command otherwise and when I no longer serve the shogunate. Edo is not a place to raise my daughter, especially without her mother.'

'Hai. It is a tragedy that Fukano lost her mother and you, your gaijin.'

Fuming at his sister's blatant disrespect, Junsaku moved so close to Etsuko that she could feel his hot breath against her neck. In a tone low and threatening, each word dripping with menace, he said, 'Never call Cecelia that again, or I will forget that we share the same blood.'

'Gomennasai,' Onishi whimpered, his brown eyes round as a big-eyed fish. 'My wife meant no dishonour, Junsaku-san. Isn't that right, Etsuko?'

With her hands folded in her lap, Etsuko closed her eyes and sluggishly inclined her head without saying a word.

Junsaku, enraged, gazed off to the side of the road, trying to balance his energy. As he focused on a massive banyan tree with many thick, brown trunks covered in olive-green leaves, its aerial roots cascading towards the ground, he saw the ghost materialise from the tangled web of branches as though exiting a maze. The spirit floated towards the road, draped in a flowing black cloak. Junsaku squinted his eyes, trying to see its face obscured beneath a deep shadow cast by the hood. Suddenly, Junsaku felt an intense sense of dread. Fukano reached out tenderly and took his hand in hers, and, at that moment, the ominous spirit dissolved slowly, its shadowed figure merging with the gnarled roots, leaving Junsaku's mind full of doubt and questions.

'Otosan, your thoughts have taken you far away. What is it?' Fukano asked.

'Nothing, Ka.'

'You look like you have seen a ghost.'

'I saw something in the trees. It must have been an animal.'

Suddenly, Junsaku questioned his decision to bring his daughter to live with his sister, a woman he had not seen or spoken to for years. But then, he reminded himself that while employed by the shogun, his daughter would not be safe with him in Edo and should be with family, even if that left his only option for his daughter to live with his estranged sister in Okinawa.

***

HOURS LATER, the carriage finally stopped in front of a rustic, single-level house with wooden walls, long, sliding lattice-shaped wood frame and paper shoji doors at the front, several windows with tightly closed shutters, and a thatched roof made from bundled grasses and reeds that sloped downwards from the roofline. Junsaku slipped off the bench and stretched his hand out to assist Fukano, who carefully stepped down from the carriage, holding the terrier close to her chest. Onishi jumped out of the cart, ran to the house, and quickly opened the shoji doors, allowing the refreshing sea breezes to fill the home with the aroma of salt and seaweed.

'Come to the kitchen,' Etsuko insisted as she walked briskly towards the house. 'The driver will unload Fukano's belongings while we have tea.'

'Nihonshu for me, sister. And, in case you have no sake, I have brought my own,' Junsaku said, pulling a small, pounded copper flask from his pocket.

In the kitchen, Onishi scurried to a cupboard, opened it, and pulled out a jar of amber liquid with a snake coiled inside. 'Junsaku,' he said, holding the container like a precious newborn, 'I have something you might enjoy even more than sake: *Habushu.*'

'Hai, habushu! I have only enjoyed habu sake once before, and it was *oishii*. Fukano,' Junsaku said to his daughter, pointing at the snake floating in the jar, its mouth open, fangs exposed, 'this drink, made from the deadly habu snake, is unique to Okinawa. Do you see the snake there?'

'Hai, Otosan, and it is disgusting,' she replied, squinching her nose.

'Iie, Ka. The look deceives you. The drink is delicious; sweet, and spicy. It is also called Okinawan snake wine.'

'Junsaku, this is a very good habushu, the highest quality. Should I get four cups?' Onishi questioned.

'Ka, would you like some?' Junsaku asked Fukano.

'Will I die?'

'No, Ka, this is not deadly like the snake's bite.'

'Hai, I will try it.' A lopsided smile spread across her face, revealing her hesitance.

'Etsuko, forget the tea. We will all have habushu.' Onishi declared.

'Not for me. I drink tea,' Etsuko said as she pulled three small brown ceramic cups from a shelf and placed them on the table.

'Junsaku,' Onishi said, 'allow me to pour for you.' Junsaku held his cup as Onishi poured. Then Onishi turned to Fukano. 'Mei, I will pour for you,' he said as he looked at his niece. A softness filled Onishi's eyes, speaking volumes of his affection for her even though they had only just met. Fukano held her cup with her fingertips as he poured. When he finished, he said to Fukano,

'Mei, please pour for me.'

'Hai,' she responded, filling his small cup, her hand gently gripping the jar as she poured. 'And Ojisan, please call me Fukano. I prefer this over mei, even if I am your niece.'

Onishi smiled and said, 'Of course, Fukano'.

Nikka, the terrier, lay on the stone floor with her body pressed against Fukano's leg while she scratched the dog's belly.

Etsuko came to the low table carrying a pot of hot tea. When Etsuko saw the dog relaxed beside Fukano, she exclaimed, 'Out of the kitchen, Nikka!'

'Oh, please, can she stay?' Fukano pleaded.

'The dog is fine, Etsuko,' Onishi stated boldly. However, when he glanced at his wife and saw her narrowed eyes, he quickly diverted his gaze and picked up his habushu, drinking the snake wine in one gulp.

'Fine,' Etsuko said, dropping the teapot onto the wooden table, the liquid inside sloshing loudly.

'Obasan, may I pour you habushu?' Fukano asked her aunt.

Without looking at Fukano, Etsuko answered, 'Iie. I am drinking tea. And Fukano, do not call me Obasan. It makes me feel old. Call me Etsuko-san.'

'Hai,' Fukano replied, quickly glancing at her father, noticing how one of his eyebrows arched high on his forehead, indicating his shared curiosity about her aunt's unpleasant behaviour.

Junsaku shrugged. 'Etsuko, while Fukano lives with you, I want you to continue to ensure she is learning. Outside of school, Cecelia taught Fukano languages, provided her with a European education, and taught her to be a lady. But now that she is here, she must go to the village school, and you can instruct her on how to be a proper wife.'

'Otosan,' Fukano protested, 'I do not want to be a wife! I want to be a warrior.'

'Ka,' Junsaku responded, his tone steady and reassuring, 'you can train like a warrior, but you cannot be a samurai. And, when you meet a man who captures your heart, your desire will take you on a different path—just as it did for your mother and me.'

'Unlikely,' she moaned, crossing her arms tightly over her chest.

'Teenager,' Junsaku remarked with a playful grin, shifting his attention to his sister. 'Etsuko, Otosan told me you always wanted to be married, even when you were young. He told me you learned the ways of a wife, so please teach my daughter.'

Junsaku's words caused Onishi to choke on the habushu he had just sipped. Snake wine shot from his mouth and splattered the table, and he quickly grabbed a rag and wiped away the liquid on the wooden surface.

'Onishi, do you have something to say?' Etsuko challenged her husband, her tone ice-cold.

'No, Etsuko. You will be an excellent teacher on the skills needed to be a good wife,' he commented sarcastically, his bravery bolstered by the alcohol.

Junsaku spoke again, this time with a more serious tone. 'If Fukano ever does decide to marry, her future husband must meet my approval, which will be difficult. Maybe impossible.'

Fukano huffed, then changed the subject. 'Otosan, must I stay here until you leave the shogunate?' Fukano realised how rude her statement sounded and immediately apologised. 'Gomennasai, Ojisan, Oba...I mean, Etsuko-san. I am grateful for your hospitality. I will just miss my father,' she said sincerely.

'Understandable,' her uncle replied.

Junsaku shifted in his seat. 'Ka, how long you live here depends on how many more years I must remain in service to the shogun.' The crease's on Junsaku's forehead deepened as he spoke, his words tinged with worry. 'Until then, you must stay with family.' He looked at his sister and brother-in-law and said bluntly, 'I have money for her care, and I will give you more as needed.'

Onishi's back straightened. 'Brother, we will treat her like a daughter. We never had children, so it will be good for Etsuko to raise a girl.' Onishi caught himself staring at Fukano as he spoke, and with a few rapid blinks as though coming out of a trance, he returned his attention to Junsaku. 'We will do our best to guide and protect her.'

'You will be given money for Fukano's food and schooling and to buy her dresses, hairpins, and other things she needs or wants. I will leave money with you on this trip and bring more each visit. My daughter must want for nothing.'

'Otosan, there is no need to leave money for silly hairpins!' Fukano quipped, her face scrunched in disapproval.

Junsaku reached into his jacket, pulled out a canvas bag the size of his fist, and dropped it onto the wooden table. Onishi and Etsuko's brown eyes stretched wider, becoming nearly perfect circles as the pouch hit the surface with a dull thud.

'Junsaku, these coins will suffice for now,' Etsuko stated, a sweet smile on her rosy lips as she dragged the pouch towards her and secured it in her lap.

FIFTY-ONE

AFTER ONLY five days in Okinawa, as the sun rose and painted the sky soft shades of gold and pink, Junsaku and Fukano stood on the grainy sand of the local beach. Nikka sat obediently at Fukano's feet, panting lightly, her folded ears relaxed. They waited for a hired fishing boat to deliver Junsaku to Naha Port to board a larger vessel destined for mainland Japan.

'Otosan, please return as soon as you can,' Fukano said, tasting light saltiness on her lips, a mix of sea air and tears. She reached out and embraced her father, her cheek pressed against his leather chest cover, and whispered, 'I miss Okasan so much, and now you are leaving me, too.'

'Ka, I will be back as soon as I can. Trust me, I have no words for how sad I am to leave you,' Junsaku said quietly, his eyes glossy. 'But we must stay strong. Remember everything your mother taught you about life and being a powerful, independent woman. Be true to yourself, Fukano, and never do anything that you believe is not right or just.'

Fukano sighed.

'And Ka, always be aware of your surroundings. We live in dangerous times, and you must stay alert.'

'I understand,' Fukano replied, releasing her embrace and standing before her father.

Junsaku cupped Fukano's shoulders. 'Lastly, listen to your ojisan and obasan while you are here. Find happiness. Continue your martial arts training. Make friends but be careful of boys.'

'Otosan, my only interest in boys is beating them in a race or even a fight. You do not need to worry about me.'

Junsaku tucked a strand of his daughter's hair behind her ear then hugged her. As he held her in his arms, he could see over her shoulder a wooden fishing boat approaching the shoreline, rowed by four men. The small boat stopped just outside the wave break, and the captain rang a bell, signalling for Junsaku to board.

'My beautiful girl, *watashi wa anato o aishiteimasu*. I love you, Fukano,' Junsaku said, gazing into his daughter's green eyes.

'I love you, too, Otosan.'

Junsaku kissed Fukano's forehead, then turned and walked towards the surf line. Fukano picked up Nikka and cuddled the dog as she watched her father enter the lapping water, dragging his legs through the small waves. When Junsaku met the fishing boat, he threw his leather travel bag and swords over the rail, climbed on board, and sat on an empty bench facing the beach, looking at his daughter as she stood on the shoreline, the sunshine haloing her tall figure.

As the boat gradually pulled away, Fukano watched intently as her father, who grew smaller and smaller with each stroke of the oars, faded into the distance and finally vanished from her sight altogether.

Alone in a strange place, Fukano began the twenty-minute walk back to her aunt and uncle's house with a heavy heart as the dog pranced beside her. Along the way, Fukano listened to the chirp and warble of birds, inhaling the fragrance of Okinawan pine, moss, and sea salt as her tears began to dry.

When Fukano arrived at the house, her aunt told her to prepare to eat lunch.

'Come, sit,' her uncle said, a lascivious grin on his face as he patted the floor cushion next to him, his cheeks the bright pink of dragon fruit, a shade lighter than his bloodshot eyes.

Fukano knelt on the cushion and Nikka lay down on the floor next to her, stretching her small, compact frame along the cool stone.

'Fukano, you will begin school tomorrow. A village boy will escort you,' Etsuko said loudly from the kitchen, stirring a pot of miso.

'Arigato, Etsuko-san, but I do not need someone to walk me to school. I will be fine on my own,' Fukano replied.

Etsuko whacked the spoon on the metal pot, alarming Nikka and causing the terrier to spring to her feet. 'Do not tell me what you need, girl. Learn your place,' Etsuko snarled. 'You will go to school tomorrow with a boy named Haru. He is a local boy and is your age. He will walk with you to ensure you stay out of trouble.'

Fukano frowned. 'Hai, Oba...I mean, Etsuko-san,' she responded, her green eyes stinging from tears waiting to erupt.

Etsuko dropped a bento box in front of Onishi and another in front of Fukano, each section filled with pickled vegetables, seaweed, and a chunk of fire-cooked goat. Then she sat at the table and poured Onishi a cup of tea and one for herself.

'Etsuko-san, may I have tea?' Fukano asked politely.

'Get it yourself,' Etsuko responded before taking a sip from her cup.

As Fukano poured herself tea, her uncle asked, 'So, Fukano, would you like to go to the beach for a swim?'

Fukano blushed. 'Uh, I would like it if all three of us went together,' she answered, her eyes drifting toward her aunt, who stared down into her lap at her tightly clenched hands.

'Your Obasan does not like the seawater so she will not join us. However, I will take you and ensure your safety,' Onishi said.

Fukano clenched her jaw and tried not to openly cringe at the thought of being alone with her uncle. 'Etsuko-san, will you please come with us to the beach?' Fukano pleaded.

'I do not swim.'

'You can just enjoy the shoreline, Etsuko-san. The sun is good for you. Could you join us? I think it would be appropriate for you to be there.'

'Come on, Etsuko,' Onishi coaxed. 'Stay on the beach while Fukano bathes in the warm water. It will be her first time in the ocean.' Then, Onishi's eyebrows lifted, and he asked, 'Fukano, can you swim?'

'Hai, Ojisan, my mother gave me lessons at Lake Tazawa near our home, and I am a strong swimmer,' she bragged, lifting her chin.

'Etsuko, you will come?' Onishi questioned his wife.

'Fine,' she mumbled.

'It is settled. We will all go to the sea, and Fukano will have a swim,' Onishi said, slapping his beefy thighs.

When she finished lunch, Fukano excused herself and went to her sparsely decorated bedroom. The only items inside the tight space were a futon mattress, folded and tucked away in the corner, a short table, a faded watercolour of a mandarin duck on the wall, and Fukano's unpacked belongings. Fukano opened one of her trunks and took out a short-sleeved, brown-coloured *jinbei* jacket and short pants for her beach visit, her excitement growing at the thought of swimming in the warm island waters. Then, a voice on the other side of the sliding doors interrupted her imagination.

'Fukano, are you ready to go?' asked her uncle.

'Yes...uh, hai, Ojisan. One minute,' Fukano replied, tying a tan belt around her slim waist. When Fukano opened the door, her uncle stood unusually close, and to her left, at the end of the hall, she could see her aunt leering at her. Fukano pushed past her uncle and stood facing her aunt, standing obediently, her arms at her side. 'Etsuko-san, will this be appropriate clothing for the ocean?'

'Hai. Now let us get this over with,' Etsuko replied curtly, going to the front entrance and sliding on her sandals before exiting the house.

FIFTY-TWO

O N HER first day attending school in Okinawa, Fukano chose one of her father's many gifts: a peach wraparound dress embroidered with pale yellow flowers. While she dressed, a vivid memory came to life, and she felt viscerally transported back to the kitchen of her house in Kakunodate. Fukano heard her mother's melodic voice, and she could even smell cedar and burning coal, matcha tea, and her mother's scent, the fragrance of sunshine and morning dew. Fukano smiled as she heard her okasan telling her father to stop bringing home so many dresses for his daughter because she was running out of storage.

Then Fukano's thoughts were interrupted by her aunt yelling, 'Come, girl. Haru has arrived to take you to school.'

'I do not need to be walked to school. I am not a baby,' Fukano muttered. 'He is lucky if I do not show him who should be protecting who.' She slid open the fusuma panels of her room and stepped out, walking in socks on the wooden floor. When Fukano neared the front door, she saw Haru standing at the threshold, his posture rigid. Their eyes met, and they stood at an equal height of five feet nine inches. Fukano noticed his broad shoulders and tapered waist below his dark navy jacket, paired with matching pants made of heavy cotton, and, on his feet, straw sandals with ties that wrapped around his ankles.

'Konnichiwa, Fukano,' Haru said politely, bending in Fukano's direction. 'Thank you for allowing me to walk with you.'

'Konnichiwa,' Fukano said, returning the greeting, bowing slightly, a sour expression on her face. 'And I had no choice,' Fukano added, slipping on her wooden sandals in the genkan before storming past him with Nikka at her heels.

'Ignore her, Haru,' Etsuko stated. 'She does not yet know her place. Her mother was from Europe and taught her poorly. She is a work in progress.'

Etsuko's harsh words caused a visible furrow to form between Haru's thick, dark eyebrows. He bowed slightly to Etsuko, then turned and left the house, strolling towards Fukano, who leaned against a tree with folded arms as Nikka danced in place near her feet, the dog's spindly legs jittery with excitement.

Standing in the threshold of the sliding doors at the front of the house, Etsuko shouted, 'Nikka, come!' The dog stopped momentarily, tipped her head, and looked back and forth between Fukano and Etsuko, undecided on whether or not to obey. 'Come, dog!' Etsuko roared. The terrier's floppy black ears lowered. As the little dog inched towards the house, her backside nearly dragging on the dirt, she occasionally twisted her neck to glance back at Fukano, whose expression appeared equally sad to be separated.

Haru approached Fukano, who started walking quickly towards the school. Haru had to speed up to catch her, and when he reached her, he asked, 'How do you like Okinawa, Fukano?'

'I do not like it,' she replied sharply. 'I want to return to my village.'

'Oh, but I do not think that is possible at this time. I understand your father has placed you here?'

'Hai. He abandoned me here, and he was wrong. He should have left me in Kakunodate. I could have taken care of myself.'

'Well, maybe you will come to like island living,' he suggested encouragingly before shifting the conversation to a different topic. 'You might enjoy school. The subjects are reading, writing, history, maths, astronomy, science, and martial arts. Actually, only the boys learn martial arts. The girls learn tea service, flower arranging, and sewing. Have you studied any of these things?'

Fukano released a loud, bellowing laugh. 'Are you kidding me, Haru? I will not be serving tea, sewing, or arranging flowers. I am the daughter of Japan's greatest samurai. I can read, write, and speak Japanese, English, Lithuanian, and Dutch, and my mother also taught me science, maths, and astronomy. And martial arts? Do you think the daughter of the shogun's general would not know how to protect herself?' she stated, staring him straight in the eyes, her expression defiant. Then, with her index finger raised and held closely in front of Haru's face, Fukano stated, 'I warn you, Haru. Do not get on my bad side, and feel free to warn the others.'

Haru's eyes widened. 'Hai, Fukano, I will warn everyone to be as scared of you as I am now.'

Fukano tightened her lips, fighting the urge to smile. 'Yoi. Good.'

Twenty minutes later, they arrived at the school, a single-level, rectangular wooden building with a deck wrapped around two sides and bamboo shutters covering the windows. Stepping inside, Fukano noted the dark wood floors, thick, exposed wooden beams along the ceiling and clay walls, and long tables with benches where the students sat facing the teacher, who used sandstone to write on a slab of black slate mounted on the wall.

The teacher approached, and Fukano bowed respectfully, her gesture reciprocated by the man, who inclined his head slightly. A short, lean Buddhist monk, Fukano's teacher wore a brown outer robe, loose-fitting pants a shade lighter than his jacket, and a light brown rakusu, a traditional Japanese garment that hung around his neck like a bib. The rakusu signified that he received dharma transmission, giving him authorisation to teach. 'Welcome. I am Nakayama-san,' the monk said to Fukano, his amber eyes narrowing as he studied her intently. 'You must be Fukano Aoyama, the general's daughter.'

'Hai,' she responded, her green eyes glimmering with pride.

'I have heard tales of him, even here in Okinawa. His fame is great.'

'Yes, my father is a legend. He has taught me martial arts, as well, and I have excellent skills. My otosan says that I am good enough to be a samurai.'

With a slight smirk, he replied, 'As I am sure you have been told, at this school, we prepare the boys to become warriors and the girls to become wives.'

Fukano winced as frustration surged through her, bordering on rage, and she bit her tongue, forcing herself not to speak.

With a wave of his hand, the teacher instructed, 'Fukano, sit next to Haru.' Then, he turned his attention to the other students and commanded, 'Everyone, time to begin. Take your seats.'

***

IN THE AFTERNOON, Sensei Tanaka, the martial arts instructor, entered the classroom, dressed in his gi, and stood quietly with his hands clasped at the waist.

The monk, Nakayama, who had been discussing Japanese history with the class, rapped his cane on the desk. 'This ends our lesson for the day,' said the teacher. 'Girls, head to flower arranging instruction with Azusa-san in the crane room, and boys, you will join Sensei Tanaka for karate practise.'

The girls left the classroom, and Fukano remained inside, standing beside Haru and gathering with the boys. The group stood frozen, their eyes wide with astonishment, as Sensei Tanaka's gaze locked on Fukano. 'What do you think you are doing?' he asked smugly.

Fukano straightened her posture. 'I am joining karate training.'

The boys broke into boisterous laughter, except for Haru, who remained silent, watching his new friend with awe and admiration.

'This girl is *kuruoshī*,' proclaimed Rin, the class bully.

'*Damatte!*' Sensei Tanaka scolded. Dead silence settled in the room, and Sensei Tanaka glared at Fukano. 'Are you joking? Are you that stupid or just deliberately disruptive?' Fukano inhaled, ready to answer, but the sensei cut her off before she could respond. 'You may think you are special because your father is the shogun's general, but that holds no weight here. Girls do not and will never practise martial arts in this school or my dojo. Now, join the girls and learn how to be a proper wife before you feel the sting of my bokken across your back.'

Fukano slowly began moving her feet into a fighting stance when she felt a tug on her forearm. 'Fukano, come,' the slim, petite female arts teacher demanded, trying to pull her away from the group. With the woman still clasping her arm, Fukano turned, looked at Sensei Tanaka, and stated confidently, 'Sensei, one day, you will meet my father when he comes to visit me, and then you can deal with him.'

FIFTY-THREE

ONE BRIGHT morning, on their walk to school, Fukano questioned Haru about her aunt and uncle. 'How long has your family known Etsuko and Onishi?'

'My parents have known them for many years. Truthfully, my okasan does not care for your uncle. She told my father there is something about him she finds bothersome. She describes him as a panda. She says he is seemingly friendly with his round eyes and bulging belly, but beneath his exterior is something unpredictable, even menacing.'

'That is a good description. If my uncle tries anything with me, I will make him regret it.'

'If he ever bothers you, Fukano, tell me. I will protect you.'

'I can protect myself, Haru. Anyway, want to race to school?'

A wide smile spread across Haru's slim face, and he abruptly announced, 'Ready, set, go!'

Before Haru could take off running, Fukano grabbed his arm and stopped him. 'Wait! We should have a bet.'

Haru chuckled lightly. 'Alright. Same bet as you make with the other boys; whoever loses must give the winner their shoes.'

Fukano let out an exasperated huff. 'Collecting shoes is for babies, Haru. This time, when I win, you will practise karate and the way of the sword with me.'

A smirk tugged at the corners of his lips as he replied, a hint of sarcasm in his voice, 'Fine, daughter of the greatest samurai to ever live in this world or the next, I accept your bet. However, there is a caveat: if I win, you must deliver a hand-made flower arrangement to my house every Saturday morning for one year.'

Fukano responded lightning fast. 'I accept your bet, Haru. And, because you made fun of my father's reputation, you will feel the pain of my bokken across your legs on our first day of training.'

Fukano's arrogance momentarily eclipsed Haru's confidence. However, as he took deep breaths and focused his mind, his self-esteem gradually returned.

'One, two, three,' Fukano roared, and they ran towards the finish line.

When Haru arrived at the school, his chest heaving, he found Fukano lounging beneath a tree, pretending to be asleep, her long legs outstretched on the grass. Her bright, green eyes opened wide as he approached, and she fluttered her eyelids and said, 'Haru, I thought you would never arrive. I considered sending out a search party. I even thought I would pick and arrange flowers while I waited.'

'Haha, very funny,' Haru grumbled.

Fukano stood up and cupped Haru's shoulders. 'I will see you at the old temple grounds on Saturday for your first lesson.'

Haru gritted his teeth. 'We need to get to class before we are late,' he announced, walking quickly towards school, annoyed by his loss.

FIFTY-FOUR

EVERY SATURDAY, regardless of the weather, Fukano and Haru dedicated themselves to hours of rigorous training on the temple grounds. Fukano admired Haru's skills, especially in Karate: The Art of Empty Hand. Haru also showcased his abilities with various fighting weapons from the Ryukyu Islands. He shared with Fukano the history of Okinawan karate and explained how the early masters crafted weapons from everyday farming tools, transforming simple instruments into lethal weapons.

Haru excelled with the *nunchaku,* a pair of short, heavy wooden sticks linked by a sturdy chain, which he adeptly swung around his body with mesmerizing speed. He also expertly wielded the *sai,* a three-pronged dagger, holding one in each hand, the weapon featuring two sharp, pointed outer prongs designed to stab, with a taller central prong that could catch and redirect incoming blades.

Haru found himself equally impressed with Fukano's skills, especially with the wooden sword. Her movements were fluid and precise, and each strike with the bokken resonated with a power that defied her slender frame. Astonished by her ability to learn and master new katas and weapons techniques of Okinawa, each of Fukano's movements flowed as if she had been practising them for decades rather than months. Haru believed Fukano was a freak of nature and felt genuine gratitude for having her as a friend, careful to stay on her good side.

One Saturday, Haru conducted a lesson using a *bō*, gripping the long, slender staff confidently, while Fukano used her bokken, her wooden sword, to fight back. 'Focus,' Haru said, readying his bō, a six-foot-long stick that could be deadly in the hands of a master. Though Haru knew he was highly skilled with the bō staff, he felt his familiar insecurity, which he masked with bravado as he looked firmly at his opponent and said, 'It is today, Kohai, that you will be defeated.' The term 'kohai,' which meant junior, rolled off his tongue with a taunting flair, and he knew the word would annoy Fukano.

'Kohai is ready, Sensei,' Fukano responded flippantly, her bokken held low at her right side. She lightly gripped the hilt, ready to explode into action, her green eyes shimmering with fierce determination as Haru raised his bō staff high, his muscles tensed, prepared to knock his opponent off her pedestal.

***

AFTER TRAINING, Fukano and Haru sat on the sandy beach. Covered in dried sweat and stained, deshelved clothes, they stared at the vast expanse of ocean as they relaxed, steadying their breathing after hours of rigorous exercise. Nearby, Nikka, who accompanied Fukano everywhere except school, sprawled out on the sand while Haru rubbed her belly, her tail wagging contentedly.

'You almost won that one, Master,' Fukano teased as she brushed a loose strand of hair away from her face.

'Can we drop the 'master' charade, Fukano?' Haru replied,

wiping the dirt from his pant leg. 'Just admit I had you confused with my feint. I went low for a moment, expecting you to anticipate my move, and then arched my body, planning for my bō to come down on your overly inflated head. I still cannot believe it. I was sure I was going to crush you.' Haru sat in stunned silence, then continued, 'As I wielded my bō, I thought you were doomed. Then, the next thing I knew, your bokken smashed into my right knee, which still hurts; thank you very much. And worst of all, before the pain in my knee even registered, I noticed your weapon resting on my left temple: a death strike.' Haru shook his head. 'You did it again; you won. And, in the name of all that is sacred, what move was that? I have never seen anything like it.'

'That technique is called the cyclone, named after a famous samurai who invented it to combat someone highly skilled with the bō. When done correctly, my Haru, it is unbeatable.'

'My Haru! She just called me 'my Haru',' he thought, heat rising in his body, losing himself momentarily in her meaning, his face flushed. Then, he blinked rapidly, forced his mind back to the present moment, and said, 'Let me guess; the famous samurai who invented it is your otosan, the great General Junsaku Aoyama?'

'You are wise, Kohai. You have guessed correctly,' Fukano chuckled, jumping to her feet. 'Come, Nikka, time to go home or Etsuko will not feed us.'

'See you tomorrow, Fukano,' Haru yelled as she walked briskly towards her house.

Fukano raised her hand above her head and fluttered her long fingers, shouting, 'See you tomorrow, Kohai!'

Haru watched Fukano's tall figure walking away before she disappeared behind the grove of tropical trees that lined the beach, leaving him alone with the soothing sounds of lapping waves, chirping birds, and his steady breathing.

FIFTY-FIVE

NIKKA BARKED in the genkan, her chocolate-brown eyes lively with curiosity as her tail wagged vigorously, causing her hindquarters to sway.

Fukano heard the commotion, ran to the front of the house, and threw open the sliding doors. 'Otosan!' she shrieked as her father dismounted his horse. 'Finally, you are here!'

Junsaku moved quickly towards her. He embraced his daughter and lifted her off the ground until her feet hovered over the stone path. 'How I have missed my Ka,' he whispered in her ear. He set her down, kissed her forehead, and stared into her green eyes. 'You grow more beautiful every day.'

'I have missed you so much, Otosan. How long will you stay?'

'Half a moon, and I must leave. The shogun is under threat by a clan in the south, near the castle at Kumamoto. Anyway, enough. I did not come to discuss work. I came to see my daughter, so let us enjoy our time together. Where is my sister?'

'She is in the kitchen. She must not have heard you arrive.'

'We will go inside,' he said, sliding his arm over Fukano's shoulders and drawing her close as they walked into the house. Inside, he shouted, 'Etsuko, it is I, your onii, Junsaku.'

Etsuko set a metal teapot directly on orange-glowing wood coals in the firepit at the centre of the kitchen and bowed slightly. 'Junsaku,' she said solemnly.

'That is as much excitement as you can show me, sister? I thought you would be happier to see me.'

Etsuko tightened her lips into a semblance of a smile. 'Of course, Onii,' she replied mechanically. 'Sit. Would you like nihonshu?'

'Hai.' Junsaku folded his legs below the low table. 'And where is Onishi?'

'I expect my husband soon,' Etsuko responded, setting a small cup in front of Junsaku and filling it with sake.

'You want some, Ka?'

Fukano's eyes danced. 'Hai!'

'Etsuko, pour sake for my daughter and have some yourself.'

As Etsuko carefully filled each small cup with rice wine, Fukano settled near her father, crossing her legs beneath the low table while Nikka stretched out on the stone floor with her back gently touching Fukano's hip. Noticing a tight scowl on her aunt's face, Fukano glanced at her father and saw him looking at his sister, his bushy black eyebrows lifted on his forehead, and Fukano could see her father also found Etsuko's expression odd.

Etsuko joined them at the table. Junsaku poured sake for his sister, lifted his glass, and cheered, 'Kanpai!' Both women returned the gesture and sipped the chilled, slightly sweet sake. 'How have you been, daughter? Tell me about your school,' Junsaku said.

'I am fine, Otosan, and school is adequate.' Fukano's face contorted into a scowl. 'However, I am not allowed to do martial arts because I am a girl.'

'Ah, this is not good, but these are the rules. While I am here, we will train together daily. Are you ready?'

'Hai. I still practise often, either alone or with my friend, Haru,' Fukano replied. Then she took her father's hand in hers. 'Otosan, I miss you terribly. Why can I not return to our old village and live with Yui?'

Etsuko cleared her throat. 'I am going to the kitchen. I need to prepare more food now that we have an extra mouth to feed,' she stated coldly before standing and leaving Fukano and her father alone at the table.

Junsaku frowned. 'Fukano, I have told you. You must be with family, and until I leave the shogun's service, only Etsuko can look after you. Sister, is my daughter behaving?' he shouted to Etsuko, who cut vegetables in the kitchen.

Etsuko's eyes focused on the cucumber she sliced as she answered, 'She is no trouble.'

'Is she helping you around the house? Is she learning to be a proper lady? And someday, a married woman?'

Fukano let out a short, dismissive snort. 'Otosan, how often must I tell you? Marriage is not important to me. I may never marry.'

Junsaku smiled, tiny lines fanning out from the corners of his eyes. 'I should be upset by that statement, but I am not. No man is good enough for my daughter.' With fatherly affection, he reached out and slipped his hand behind Fukano's neck, squeezing lightly. 'At least be ready to manage a house and potentially a husband, Ka. You may find someone you love deeply—someone I agree is worthy of your heart.'

The house's front door slid open, and Onishi entered carrying parcels. 'Ah, Junsaku-san, you have come for a visit,' he said cheerfully, bowing before walking towards the kitchen. 'You must miss your beautiful daughter so much. She is a pleasure to have with us and is helpful to my wife,' he chirped as he unpacked fresh vegetables from a basket. 'Also, she is doing well in school.'

'This is good news, Onishi,' Junsaku replied. 'I wish I could be near my daughter every day and that she could live with me, but it is unsafe.'

'She can remain here as long as you require,' Onishi replied, winking at Fukano.

Fukano fidgeted, and as her father and uncle continued to chat, Fukano could see her aunt in her peripheral, her eyes narrow as daggers.

***

DURING HER father's two-week visit, Fukano did not go to school. Instead, she stayed with her otosan, spending hours each day training in martial arts, practising katas, tai sabaki, sword fighting with her wooden bokken, and archery.

One mid-day, after training on the beach, Fukano asked her father, 'Otosan, would you like to meet my friend, Haru? He is the person I train with at the temple on Saturday's. We can go to the school and walk home with him.'

'Of course,' he agreed.

Father and daughter returned to the house, changed out of their gis, and walked to the school to meet Haru. As Junsaku and Fukano approached the school, they heard the unmistakable sound of bokken striking bokken.

'They are practising in the outside dojo!' Fukano said excitedly. 'Hurry, Otosan. You can see Haru's skills. He is the best in the class.'

Junsaku smiled at his daughter, keeping pace with her as she moved briskly in the direction of the training ground.

Haru caught sight of Fukano racing towards him wearing a brown jacket cinched at the waist, matching pants, and straw waraji sandals, with half of her long, sun-kissed brown hair tied in a tight bun at the top of her head, the remaining strands cascading down to her mid-back. Then, Haru noticed Junsaku trailing a few paces behind. He wore a striking red jacket with the symbol of the shogunate embroidered with gold and blue threads on the breast of the coat. The sight of the samurai general caused Haru to grow nervous, especially because of the man's long and short swords in his belt and the fierce expression on his face, which set his heart racing.

Distracted, Haru heard his instructor shout, 'Haru, what on earth are you looking at?'

'Sumimasen, Sensei Tanaka. We have visitors,' Haru stammered, pointing towards Fukano and Junsaku approaching.

'I do not care if...' the teacher began before stopping abruptly. Sensei Tanaka saw Junsaku standing at the edge of the training field and commanded, 'Students, line up! We have an honoured guest.'

The students formed an orderly line with their instructor.

'Ojigi,' ordered Sensei Tanaka.

All the boys bent at the waist in Junsaku's direction, frozen like statues. Junsaku bowed in return and instructed the boys to stand upright before he walked to the centre of the field.

'You honour us with your presence, General,' Sensei said, bowing again.

'Do not let me interrupt your instruction. I will observe,' Junsaku commented, glancing at the students before strolling to the edge of the training grounds.

With hesitancy in his voice for fear of offending Junsaku, Sensei Tanaka asked, 'General, would you give the students a technique lesson?'

Just as Junsaku prepared to decline, he saw a look of earnestness in Fukano's widened green eyes, her eager expression almost pleading. Junsaku thought of Fukano's martial arts skills and how Japan banned girls from training in school, and this inequity motivated him to accept the request at once.

'Hai, Sensei, I will demonstrate a technique. Hand me a bokken.' Junsaku removed his steel swords, handed them to Fukano, and accepted a wooden sword from the teacher. Then Junsaku gestured for the sensei to step forward. 'Are you skilled in the crane step tai sabaki counter?' Junsaku knew the teacher would answer no, considering he invented it and had only taught the moves to the shogun's highest-ranking samurai and his daughter.

'Iie, General,' the sensei replied timidly.

'Well, now is a suitable time to learn. Take your stance, attack me with a downward right-side crescent strike, and assert your full force,' Junsaku instructed. 'Do not hold back. Understood?'

'Hai, General,' the man said with a respectful nod.

As Junsaku watched the sensei prepare himself, he sensed unease from the teacher, his movements lacking confidence. 'Wait,' Junsaku instructed, raising a hand. 'I want to watch your form as you strike, so I will choose another partner to accept your blow.'

The students exchanged anxious glances, filled with trepidation, whispering to each other in hushed tones. None of them had ever encountered this technique before, and they were all gripped with a sense of uncertainty and fear, knowing someone could be hurt or, even worse, lose their life.

'Fukano, come here,' Junsaku roared, his voice cutting through the low hum of chatter amongst the all-male students.

Fukano leaned her father's swords against a tree trunk, rushed forward, and bowed to him. 'Osu, Sensei.'

'Fukano, take this bokken and ready yourself.'

Fukano nodded and forced herself to look serious, tightening her lips to hold back her smile. She had been practising this technique for years and was confident she would excel in the demonstration.

'I must protest!' Sensei Tanaka argued.

Junsaku moved as quickly as a cheetah and stood directly before the teacher, the man's head barely reaching Junsaku's shoulders. 'You forget yourself!' Junsaku said, his booming voice causing birds to flee the tree branches. The teacher dropped into a deep bow. Before Sensei Tanaka could apologise for being insubordinate, Junsaku stated, 'Nothing has changed with this new opponent. As I instructed, you will attack with your full force and dedication. If you pull your strike or deviate from your path, be warned; you will deal with me.' Junsaku took a deep breath before returning to the edge of the training grounds. 'Now, face each other, bow, and take your stances.'

As the sensei looked at the tall, lean girl standing before him, his anger and boldness grew. Instructed to apply full force to his opponent, Sensei Tanaka thought, *This girl is no match for me. I will humiliate her and her arrogant father.*

'Hajime,' Junsaku ordered.

Sensei Tanaka raised his bokken, sped forward, and violently struck downward, shocked when his weapon whizzed through the air and collided with nothing, including Fukano.

Moments before Sensei Tanaka attacked, Fukano anticipated the teacher's move and responded, her body flowing effortlessly as though her feet floated above the ground. Before the sensei reached her, Fukano shifted her body out of the way, avoiding a whack to her head. As the teacher's sword cut downward, Fukano dodged his blow by sliding her left foot forward, slightly to the right of her attacker. Then she pivoted to his right side, shifting her body, and maneuvered herself just behind his right shoulder, effectively placing herself in his blind spot. As Sensei Tanaka poised his wooden sword at waist level, Fukano made her move. She aimed for Tanaka's right wrist, striking with incredible accuracy, causing a sharp, echoing snap before Tanaka's bokken slipped from his grip and fell to the ground.

Fukano slid backwards and came to a standstill.

'Yame. Face each other, bow, and then bow to me,' Junsaku commanded, signalling the end of the practice match.

With total silence settling on the training ground as the students stared, awestruck and stunned, Junsaku approached the sensei. 'Show me your injury.' The teacher held out his arm. Junsaku examined his wrist and stated, 'This is a minor break. It will heal quickly. Luckily, your partner showed restraint, or this blow could have ended your teaching career. Now, you go to the doctor and have your wrist wrapped. I will continue instructing the class on this technique with the assistance of my best student, Fukano.' Junsaku lifted his hand and gestured for the teacher to leave, which he did, his head hung.

***

AFTER PRACTICE, Fukano shouted, 'Haru!' as he left the training grounds. 'Come here. We will walk home with you.' Haru approached, his posture straighter than usual, his heart beating quickly, and Fukano introduced him to her father. 'Haru, I would like you to meet my otosan, Junsaku-san.'

Haru bowed to Junsaku. 'Konnichiwa, General. It is an honour. Thank you for your training today.'

'You may stand, Haru,' Junsaku replied, smiling. Junsaku placed his hand on Haru's shoulder and said, 'My daughter calls you her friend, and you demonstrated great skill during our training, so relax and breathe.'

Haru sighed as his lips curved upward, a soft smile reaching his eyes.

'Let us head home and have some food and sake,' Junsaku grinned.

As the three strolled on the sunlit dirt road towards home, they spoke like old friends, the air smelling of salt water and pungent seaweed.

'How long are you staying, Junsaku-san?' Haru asked.

While Haru awaited the answer, he saw Fukano's lips curve downward.

'Sadly, I must go at dawn,' Junsaku answered. 'The shogun has troubles in the south, and I must be there to advise him and fight if needed.' Junsaku's brown eyes darkened to the colour of black ink. 'Haru, I trust you will take care of Fukano, ensuring no harm comes to her?'

'I will, Junsaku-san. However, we both know Fukano can take care of herself.'

Junsaku squeezed Fukano's hand. 'As her sensei, I can vouch she is an excellent student of the martial way and a warrior at heart, even if she is a girl,' he playfully teased, a proud smile illuminating his face. Fukano slapped her father's upper arm as he continued, 'In all seriousness, Haru, come and find me if anything happens. I try to keep Fukano informed of my whereabouts, but if she is unsure where I am, go to the castle at Edo and send a message to me.'

'Otosan, stop it!' Fukano demanded. 'Nothing will happen to me.'

'Hai, hai. I am sure you will be fine, Daughter.'

Junsaku looked at Haru and gave a subtle nod. Haru knew precisely what his gesture meant, clear in his understanding that he would help to protect Fukano while she lived in Okinawa, and if Fukano needed her father, he would be the one to fetch him.

FIFTY-SIX

FUKANO SAT cross-legged on a cushion, an open book resting in her lap. The air around her was peaceful and quiet, and the only sound in the room was rustling paper as Fukano carefully turned each page.

Suddenly, the serenity was interrupted when her uncle entered the kitchen. 'Where is your aunt?' Onishi asked.

Nikka lay next to Fukano. At the sound of Onishi's voice, the terrier's floppy black ears lifted. She looked up at Fukano and cocked her head to the side.

'She went to the village,' Fukano responded bluntly.

'And what are you doing, sweet girl?'

'My name is Fukano, and what does it look like I am doing?' She glared annoyingly at her uncle.

'Why not take a break from your reading and sit with me? We can talk.'

'Iie. I need to finish my schoolwork,' she huffed, placing her hand on Nikka's course fur.

Onishi approached Fukano, closing the distance between them and sending a cold chill through her body. He stood above her, staring at the crown of her head, and in a lowered voice, said,

'You can go back to reading soon. Have a cup of habu sake with me.'

Fukano scooted away. 'No, Uncle. Do not interrupt me while I do my schoolwork, or I will tell Etsuko of your behaviour.' Onishi abruptly sank to his knees beside her, his breathing loud near her ear. Fukano slammed the book shut. 'What are you doing? Get away from me, or else!'

Onishi slowly reached his right hand towards Fukano, and, with incredible speed, she grabbed his wrist with her left hand and clamped it, applying pressure at his pulse point and, at the same time, pressing down on the top, causing his hand to bend.

Onishi yelped in pain as Etsuko appeared at the front entrance, holding a paper-wrapped fish. 'What is going on?' she demanded, her voice sharp and authoritative.

Fukano released her hold, and Onishi scrambled to his feet, his cheeks flushed. 'Fukano is struggling with her schoolwork. I helped her.' Onishi stared at his wife, blinking rapidly.

Fukano looked at her aunt and saw Etsuko's eyes glowing like hot coals.

'She does not need your help, and if she does, it will be from me,' she snapped, storming past Fukano and Onishi. Stopping suddenly, Etsuko fixed a piercing glare on her husband, her lips curling into a tangled smirk. 'She leads you on, Onishi, and you act like a teenage boy.'

'That is not true, Etsuko.' Then, after a momentary pause, he said softly, 'I will not help her with her studies again,' before exiting the kitchen and leaving through the front door.

'Etsuko-san,' Fukano said earnestly, hoping to find an ally in her aunt, 'I did not ask for his attention. I never do anything to encourage his actions, and I do not want to be alone with him. I had to defend myself.'

'Do your work, and stop causing trouble in this house,' Etsuko chastised. 'As long as I continue to receive money from your father, you can remain here. But I warn you, girl,' she continued, leaning forward slightly, 'if you cause more disruption, you will regret ever stepping foot on this island.'

Though naturally brave, a wave of fear washed over Fukano, and her self-confidence retreated like a turtle hiding in its shell. Her heart raced as Etsuko scooped Nikka off the ground and left the room.

***

LATER IN the day, wearing her gi, Fukano arrived at the old temple prepared for her weekly training session with Haru. As she practised a kata, voices from the road along the edge of the temple grounds interrupted her concentration, and a booming voice yelled, 'Look! The gaijin thinks she is a karate master!'

As three boys approached Fukano from the road, each carrying a wooden sword, Fukano recognised the teen at the front— Rin Tsunabe, the local bully. Fukano loathed Rin and instantly knew it was he who called her gaijin.

On her very first day of school, Rin bullied her, calling her crazy, pushing and shoving her when no one was looking, and even dropping a fistful of dirt into her bento box, making her lunch inedible. After enduring weeks of torment, the straw finally broke when Rin sneaked up from behind and used a small knife to take a lock of her hair. When Fukano realised what he had done, she got up from the bench, faced him, and stated calmly, 'Today is the day you learn your lesson in humility, Rin Tsunabe.' Just as she prepared to deliver a strike, the monk stepped between them and ordered them to stop their argument and return to their studies.

On the temple grounds today, Rin approached Fukano, who stood tall and confident. He stood before her and glared. 'Go away, half-breed,' he said bitterly, his words drawing laughter from his two disciples who exchanged glances as though they shared a private joke. 'No one wants you here. You are not one of us.'

Fukano clasped her hands at her belly. 'You are right, Rin. I am not one of you. And do you know why I am unlike you and your idiot friends?' Fukano looked at each boy and continued, 'Because I have a brain, and I do not look like the back end of an ox.'

Out of nowhere, Nikka appeared from inside the temple, teeth barred, and she charged Rin. With the dog within his range, Rin batted her away with his wooden sword. Nikka's stocky body rolled across the hard ground before a boulder stopped her, causing her to yelp and then lay motionless.

Fukano's temper went from annoyance to rage, and she picked up her bokken. 'Prepare yourself, cowards.' Fukano launched herself at the boys, catching them completely off-guard as she unleashed a rapid succession of powerful strikes.

Fukano's attack surprised the boys, who quickly retreated. After a short huddle, the teens returned to the fight. 'That was a mistake, girl,' said Yutte, the largest of the three. He rushed Fukano with his wooden sword, aiming for the side of her head. Fukano smirked at his clumsy effort, thinking the boys would have been wiser to attack her as a group rather than lose the fight as individuals. As Yutte's bokken dropped towards her head, Fukano moved to her right, pivoted left, and delivered a powerful downward strike to Yutte's head, sending him crashing to the ground. With Yutte sprawled on the hard dirt, unconscious, Fukano spun back to her right, holding the hilt of her bokken with both hands. She pointed the wooden sword directly at the two other boys, who stood with a surprised look on their faces, shocked that a girl had defeated their brawny friend so effortlessly.

Rin whispered to the remaining boy, Hiroto, and Fukano could not hear what he said. Then, the two boys attacked in unison with their bokkens, one approaching from Fukano's left, the other from her right, striking high and low, showing no mercy. Fukano parried and performed tai sabaki, continuously avoiding their strikes and positioning herself to deliver counterstrikes. She toyed with her adversaries and practised her moves, confident in her skills, knowing she could end this fight at any time. Then, Rin landed his first blow and hit Fukano on her right shoulder. Fukano's rage became a bonfire, and, seeing Rin's satisfied grin, she felt a surge of adrenaline as she struck him on his ribcage, listening to his bones crack and the wind escaping his lungs. Rin dropped to his knees and was about to raise his hand in defeat when they all heard male voices nearby, the sound coming from behind a grove of trees at the outer edge of the temple grounds.

'It is Amoto and the three Satama brothers,' Hiroto announced. 'They are coming here!'

Rin rose from the ground, his eyes narrowed. With a rough tone, he said, 'Now you will learn your lesson, gaijin.'

Fukano's heart beat faster. She knew she could not win the fight alone but would not give up. She gripped her bokken, resolute in her vow that Rin would not leave the temple grounds unharmed, no matter the cost. As Rin and his entourage waited for the others to join the fight, Fukano's mind raced with strategic thoughts: *'First, the bully Rin will hit the ground and not get up, and then I will inflict as much damage on the rest of them until I go down. My plan is the way of a samurai.'*

Fukano waited, listening to the rustling trees and the crackling of leaves underfoot as Amoto and the three Satama brothers headed towards her, ready to enter the fight. Fukano watched the four boys exit a dense thicket of trees, running in her direction, bokkens in hand, and she had to take deep breaths to balance her energy. Suddenly, Fukano observed another figure emerge from the dense canopy of trees, and she recognised him instantly: Haru. With a look of fierce determination, he ran toward the new assailants, and she could see he had come to her aid, ready to confront the threat head-on.

Spinning his six-foot-long bō staff like a propeller, Haru charged Fukano's assailants, and, in a blur of motion, he expertly incapacitated two of the Satama brothers in mere seconds, leaving only two still standing.

With Haru helping to defend her, Fukano did not hesitate to strike Rin. She leapt in the air and came down with a savage kick to the side of his left knee. Rin screamed in agony from his newly damaged knee, the bone poking out from beneath his skin, writhing in pain as tears streamed down his face. Fukano's lips curled into a smirk as she stared at Rin helplessly on the ground. 'Oh, Rin, you cannot possibly walk home now! I would offer to carry you, but as you can see, I am just a girl,' she taunted.

Fukano turned to Hiroto, the only original attacker still standing. 'He is not walking out of here,' she stated, pointing towards Rin. Then her green eyes tightened, and with a threatening tone asked, 'In what condition would you like to arrive home today?'

The boy dropped his wooden sword, and before it even hit the ground, he took off running.

Worried for Haru, Fukano rushed to his aid, ready to help him. However, she saw Haru approaching with his bō slung over his shoulder, gently holding Nikka in his arms. In the middle of the field, Fukano saw four bodies lying on the ground, each one squirming from injuries, and the sight filled her with relief.

When Haru reached Fukano, he embraced her with one arm, the other lightly gripping the dog. 'Are you hurt?'

Fukano allowed Haru to hug her briefly, feeling his breath on her neck, then pulled away. She took Nikka from him, kissed the dog on the top of her head, and answered, 'Just a few bruises, but I am fine.' Then she smiled and said, 'Haru, I think we have had enough training for today,' nodding towards the defeated boys who lay scattered on the ground, their limbs splayed in different directions as they struggled to stand up.

***

ON THE WAY home, Fukano and Haru discussed the fight at the temple. When they were close to Haru's house, Fukano changed the topic, telling Haru what had happened between her and Onishi earlier that day.

'I told you,' Haru said. 'My okasan said she does not like your uncle. She is right. Onishi cannot be trusted.'

'Maybe it was nothing.'

'Fukano, what do you feel? What is your inner voice telling you? Ask, and listen to the answer.'

Fukano took a deep breath and let the question linger in her mind, the answer becoming clear. 'Hai, Haru, he is not acting appropriately. I must steer clear of him, especially to avoid the wrath of my aunt.'

'Should you tell your father?'

'If I do, Onishi might die. Before I tell my otosan, let me try to handle it myself to avoid risking Onishi's life.'

'Alright,' Haru shrugged. 'But if you need me, you get me, no matter what. I will defend you.'

FIFTY-SEVEN

THE DAY after the fight at the temple, Fukano and Haru sat at a wooden table, waiting for class to begin. Rin walked in using two long sticks for support, his leg wrapped with stiff bandages.

'What happened to you?' the teacher asked.

'Nothing. I am fine,' Rin mumbled, briefly glancing at Fukano, his eyes the colour of smouldering embers.

'You look like you have been in a fight, Rin.' A brief silence like a weight hung in the air. Then, the teacher stated, 'I will be right back.'

He left the classroom and returned several minutes later with Sensei Tanaka. 'Join me outside, Rin. We need to talk,' the sensei ordered. Rin followed his martial arts teacher from the room, limping. After several minutes, during which the students waited quietly, barely breathing, the teenager returned to the classroom, followed by Sensei Tanaka.

Sensei Tanaka frowned at Fukano. 'Outside, Fukano,' he demanded, gesturing towards the door.

Fukano looked at Haru with wide, unblinking eyes before standing and exiting the building behind her teacher.

Sensei Tanaka stood beneath a Japanese willow tree, his hands clasped in front of his waist, his eyebrows furrowed. 'Fukano, Rin told me you caused his leg injury.'

'In self-defence.'

The sensei's lips pressed together in a thin line, and a rumbling growl came from deep within his chest. 'Under no circumstances are you to fight,' he warned. 'It is improper behaviour for a girl. I will not tolerate it.'

'And I will not stand for bullying,' Fukano responded boldly, rolling back her shoulders.

The sensei's hands tensed like claws. Infuriated, he said, 'I do not care what you think, girl. You will listen or no longer be allowed at this school or any others in Okinawa.'

'Are we done?'

'Know your place,' he hissed, his cheeks bright red. 'Now get back to class!'

***

'ETSUKO, WE have a visitor,' Onishi called out from the entrance. 'It is Yasua-san, the headmaster of Fukano's school. He is requesting to speak with us.'

Onishi directed the man dressed in a dull green kimono to the sitting room, and the two men sat on cushions at a low-wooden table.

Etsuko entered and bowed slightly, saying, 'Yasua-san, irasshaimase. Welcome. May I bring you tea?'

'Iie,' the headmaster murmured.

Etsuko knelt on a cushion. 'And what is the reason for your visit?'

'It is regarding Fukano, the girl who lives with you.'

'Hai, my brother's daughter,' Etsuko frowned. 'What has she

done now?'

'Is Fukano alright?' Onishi questioned concernedly. 'Is she hurt?'

'No, nothing like that,' the headmaster replied, his tone irritated. 'She is causing trouble at school, and you need to address it immediately.'

Red blotches spread to parts of Etsuko's face and neck. As she opened her mouth to respond, Headmaster Yasua cut her off. 'Despite being prohibited, she has tried to insert herself into martial arts training with the boys. Also, she has been in fights. Her behaviour is unladylike and entirely out of place. Fukano is an embarrassment to our school and our martial arts program, and it must end now.' The headmaster inhaled loudly, then said, 'We allowed this girl to enrol in our school solely because of her father's rank in the shogunate, but she disobeys orders, acts insubordinate, and even fights when she should be performing womanly duties. A woman of pure Japanese blood would not behave this way, and I am here to tell you we will not tolerate it. You must stop it, or we will ban her from school.' The headmaster stood and began walking briskly towards the front door. Onishi and Etsuko popped up and followed him. As the man slipped on his shoes in the genkan, the last thing he said was, 'I expect you to fix this.' Then he left, forcefully closing the sliding shoji doors behind him.

With the headmaster gone, Etsuko flew into a rage. 'Onishi, find the girl now and bring her to me.'

'She is out walking. I do not know where she has gone,' Onishi replied timidly, his eyes downcast.

'Then find her, you useless drunkard!' She pushed past him, shoving him aside. 'She is ruining my good name, and it is time she learnt how a real Japanese woman behaves.'

***

ONISHI FOUND Fukano at the beach, practising katas. 'Fukano, I need to speak with you,' he said, struggling to keep his balance, the sand shifting beneath his feet.

Startled, Fukano assumed a fight stance. 'What do you want?'

'You need to get home this minute. Your aunt is beside herself with anger.'

'Why? What has happened?'

'The headmaster of your school came to the house and complained about you. He told us you have been misbehaving and fighting. He said you are an embarrassment to the school, and now you have enraged Etsuko because you are harming her good name.'

'Good name? What a joke,' Fukano thought. With a smirk, Fukano said, 'Fine, let us go.'

As she followed her uncle home, Fukano said nothing, keeping her distance. Just as Fukano reached the house's front door, Etsuko flew out of the doorway and lunged at her, wielding a long stick in her hand. 'I will teach you some manners if it kills me!' she roared.

Fukano stood in place, waiting for her aunt to swing the stick and, when she did, Fukano performed tai sabaki and moved to her right, avoiding the first blow. Fukano continued to avoid her aunt's subsequent three attempts to strike her.

Fatigued, Etsuko placed the tip of the stick on the stone pathway and leaned on it, saying breathlessly, 'You will stand still and take your punishment, gaijin.'

'I will not be hit by you or anyone else, especially when I have done nothing wrong,' Fukano stated firmly. 'And I am not a gaijin. I am the...'

Before Fukano could finish, Etsuko interrupted, her voice full of mockery; 'Hai, hai, you are the daughter of a great samurai,' she sneered. 'I've heard you brag before. Now, go into your room and stay there. You will have no food or drink for the rest of the day. Tomorrow morning, you will see the error of your ways.' Fukano did not move, listening to Etsuko's loud breathing. Then, Etsuko banged the tip of the stick on the ground and snapped, 'Get out of my sight!'

'Whatever you say, Obasan,' Fukano answered sarcastically, fully aware that referring to Etsuko as 'aunt' irritated her. Fukano turned on her heels and walked towards the front entrance rather than down the hall to her room, with Nikka following happily.

'Nikka, stay!' Etsuko shouted. The small dog's eyes drooped, and the terrier sat in place, watching as Fukano left the house. 'This is not over!' her aunt yelled. 'If you cause further trouble for me, at home, at school, or in the village, you will be sorry you ever came here.'

'I am sorry every day,' Fukano thought as she walked towards the beach, hoping to find a way to escape.

FIFTY-EIGHT

WITH FUKANO at school and Onishi working at the local furniture shop, Etsuko left the house wearing wooden sandals and a tan kimono that bulged from her aging curves. She walked for twenty minutes until she finally arrived at a modest clay and wood house with a thatched roof tucked behind a maze of banyan trees. She opened the wooden gate, walked into a small yard landscaped with boulders, neglected wild bushes, and high grasses cut by stone-paved paths, and knocked on the latticed shoji doors.

A woman in her sixties slid open the door, her black and grey-streaked hair pulled into a bun. 'Etsuko-san, come in,' she said with a bow before moving aside, making room for her guest to enter.

'Arigato gozaimasu, Aneko-san,' Etsuko replied, bowing back. She removed her wooden shoes, placed them neatly in the genkan, and entered the house.

'Come into the kitchen,' the older woman said, gesturing.

Etsuko entered a room where a small fire burned in the fire-pit in the centre of the stone floor.

'Sit,' Aneko said, bringing Etsuko a small wooden stool.

'Would you like tea?'

'Iie. The reason for my visit is brief, and I will not take up much of your time.'

When both women were seated, Aneko asked, 'What can I do for you?'

Etsuko inhaled deeply, a gentle smile on her lips as she met Aneko's gaze. 'You may have heard of my brother, Junsaku Aoyama, the shogun's top samurai, a general feared by all? Well, recently, his wife died, and he sent his teenage girl to live with me, asking me to care for her.'

'Hai, I have heard of your brother and that you now care for his daughter. Very kind of you, Etsuko.'

'As you can imagine, I care deeply for my niece and am committed to protecting her from harm.'

Aneko nodded, saying, 'Naturally.'

'But, because of my brother's position with the shogun, I am afraid our family here in Okinawa is threatened by those who wish him dead. Recently, I saw a strange man lurking near our home with swords hanging from his waist like a samurai. But this man was no samurai. I believe he may be a ronin who wants to hurt Fukano, and I am fearful, Aneko-san!' Etsuko covered her face and forced her hands to tremble for effect.

Aneko pressed her palm on her chest. 'This is not good, Etsuko. Do you genuinely believe this man would try to harm the girl? We must tell the villagers to see if someone can help identify this person.'

Etsuko looked directly at Aneko. 'Iie. That would not be wise. Even Onishi believes he is a masterless samurai. We do not want to anger this stranger, draw more attention to our family, or frighten the girl,' she said. 'I have the perfect plan to protect my brother's daughter and warn the enemy not to threaten us. Would you like to know how you can help, dear friend?'

'Hai,' the woman answered. 'Tell me.'

'I need poison for my plan to work, and you have it,' Etsuko stated plainly.

'I do not know what you are talking about,' the woman stammered, her head swaying in disagreement.

'You do know, Aneko. Do not worry. If you give me what I need, what you did to your husband will stay our secret.'

Aneko shifted on her stool. 'I do not understand your meaning, Etsuko. I cannot help you.'

Etsuko cleared her throat. 'Aneko, I know the truth. Your husband, Isamu, was young when he died, and hours before his death, he was the picture of health. I have never told a soul, but I saw how you killed him.'

Aneko gasped, then clamped her lips, saying nothing.

'I was walking near the beach where the men, including your husband, were working on repairing a boat. I saw you lurking in the trees, near where the workers hung their leather drink bags.' Etsuko leaned closer to Aneko, feeling the woman's hot breath on her face, and lowered her voice. 'I was about to yell out when I saw you empty a vile into Isamu's container and then run off. I was confused by your behaviour, but it became clear to me when we heard the doctor visited your home the next day and pronounced Isamu dead; you poisoned his drink.'

Aneko coughed, then said quietly, 'He died of natural causes.'

'You and I both know that is a lie,' Etsuko stated smugly. 'There are stories of generations of your family mastering the use of deadly herbs and plants, and, after your husband's untimely death, everyone was suspicious that you had something to do with it, but they had no evidence or proof. If I tell others what I saw that day at the beach, they will believe me and turn against you. Do not have me ruin your life, Aneko. Not at your age.'

Aneko's eyes watered.

'I remember you telling me Isamu was violent, so I understand why you killed him,' Etsuko said empathetically.

'Etsuko, it has been over ten years since Isamu died. No one will believe your story now,' Aneko said weakly.

'If I tell the villagers what I saw, confirming their suspicions, who do you think they will believe? You will be shunned, alone until the day you die, or worse, the elders may expel you from the village and ship you off to one of the local islands as a criminal.' Etsuko gave Aneko time to digest what she heard, then stated, 'I promise you I can be convincing.'

Aneko dropped her head and looked into her lap. 'What are you asking for, Etsuko?' she whispered.

'Wonderful. Here is my plan,' Etsuko announced gleefully. 'After you give me poison, I will invite this stranger into my home, showing him hospitality like I would for any guest. He will believe he has successfully managed to get close to our family and closer to the general's daughter and whatever revenge he seeks. Then, I will offer the ronin umeshu plum wine laced with poison. I will not let the man die, though. I am not a wicked person,' Etsuko boasted. 'Before it is too late, I will call the doctor, who will save his life. I will show grace by giving this ronin a second chance at life while also reminding him not to attempt any harm to the family of Junsaku Aoyama,' she grinned. 'Aneko, you do not need to feel responsible. You will be loyal to Japan by protecting the daughter of a high-ranking samurai, and the ronin will not die.

He will just receive a strong warning.'

'You are wise to protect the girl,' Aneko responded. Then, after a long pause, she said, 'Etsuko, I will help you and give you what you need because I believe in your mission. But know this: depending on the quantity, it will be deadly unless treated within days, sometimes even hours. I would only advise putting a droplet in the plum wine, enough to scare the man but not kill him.'

Etsuko grinned. 'Hai, that is good advice. And how much will I pay you?'

'If you promise not to share horrible rumours with the villagers, I will give it to you for free.'

'I would not take anything from you without payment, Aneko,' Etsuko replied. 'You are helping me, so let me help you. How can I repay you?'

'Let me see.' Aneko pondered the question. Then her eyes brightened, and she said, 'I would like a new wooden stool from the furniture shop where Onishi works.'

'Fine,' Etsuko agreed.

'I will go into the village tomorrow and talk to Onishi, and he can give me the stool as payment.'

'Iie!' Etsuko exclaimed nervously. Then, she ran her palms down the front side of her kimono, smoothing the fabric, stating calmly, 'Even though Onishi is aware of the threat from the ronin, I do not want him involved. Onishi has a big ego, and he will be embarrassed he did not have such a clever idea. You understand, right?' Etsuko asked, tilting her head. Then, almost laughing, she continued, 'Onishi believes he can protect our family, but if in a fight with a ronin or any man, I am afraid Onishi would lose. Between us, my husband is weak. So, Aneko, I want to keep this secret from him for now.'

Aneko nodded. 'I understand. Then, instead of a new stool, I will come to your house and take pickled vegetables and dried bonito fish if you have them?'

'Hai, Aneko, I have those. But give me the poison now, and rather than you coming to my home, I will personally deliver your requested items to you here tomorrow.'

'Fine, Etsuko.' Aneko stood, entered the kitchen, opened a cupboard, and retrieved a small vile.

Etsuko rose from the stool, and Aneko handed her the poison. Both women bowed before Etsuko left the house, humming as she strolled home.

FIFTY-NINE

'I HAVE received word, Fusakage-sama. Daimyo Kawabata has been overthrown and killed. The Sekiguchi clan has seized control of the castle at Yatsushiro in the south. We have no choice but to declare war.'

'Hai, Junsaku. How large is their battalion?' questioned the shogun.

'Only a fraction of ours,' replied Junsaku. 'If we attack now, we will hinder them from increasing the size of their force and destroy them. I will travel with five hundred mounted samurai to Kyushu and join forces with Daimyo Shibata. As one unified army, we will be large enough to squash the invaders like ants.'

***

FIVE HUNDRED mounted samurai supplied by the shogun joined forces with Daimyo Shibata's samurai in Kumamoto Prefecture, bringing the size of the combined army to twenty-five hundred, eleven hundred on horseback and fourteen hundred on foot. Daimyo Shibata listened as Junsaku laid out the strategy for the attack on the Sekiguchi clan.

While they met, samurai warriors prepared for battle, clad in stiff leather and iron-plated uniforms with the kamon of Shogun Fusakage's clan painted in gold on their lacquered breastplates. The horses shuffled their feet as they waited, and cloth banners strapped to the backs of foot soldiers flapping lightly in the breeze. When Junsaku's meeting with the daimyo ended, he issued the command, and the samurai army moved silently towards Yatsushiro, confident they would crush the Sekiguchi clan quickly.

Several hours later, Yatsushiro castle emerged in the distance, its silhouette visible in the twilight sky. Junsaku signalled for the army to camp, posting sentries and ordering the soldiers to sharpen their weapons and prepare for the brutality ahead. Junsaku slept for several hours, then rose and met with his captains and the daimyo. They finalised their strategy and began their advance.

When they arrived at Yatsushiro Castle, the samurai surrounded the fortress and awaited the general's command. Junsaku rode towards the fortress's main entrance, accompanied by five mounted warriors, one of the samurai holding a white flag, an offering for the clan to end the fight before it began. As the small group approached the entrance, an arrow whistled through the air and struck the ground just inches from the left side of Junsaku's steed. Junsaku's horse startled, but, like his seasoned rider, the animal quickly regained its composure, unfazed by battle.

Junsaku spoke loudly, his powerful voice resonating across the landscape, his volume amplified by the castle's rock walls; 'I am General Junsaku Aoyama, advisor to the shogun and leader of the greatest military force in Japan. Send out whoever is in charge to speak to me now.' An enemy soldier perched on a turret near the main gate, his bow nocked, looked straight at Junsaku and then scanned the horizon, seeing the formidable samurai army surrounding the area. Junsaku sighed and then shouted, 'I will not ask again.'

The soldier disappeared behind the building's stone wall. Moments later, Junsaku heard the sound of the rolling drawbridge. He and his men watched as the deck pushed out from the castle's main entrance, creating a bridge over the moat. A man in full armour wearing a tall, bronze helmet and riding a white horse exited the castle and approached Junsaku, stopping only metres away.

Junsaku spoke first. 'I will make this easy for you,' he said, not even bothering to ask the man's name. 'Leave your weapons and vacate the castle immediately, and you can live.'

The man on horseback boomed with laughter. 'I am Yagyu Tadamori, leader of the Sekiguchi clan, and I do not care who you are. You cannot reclaim this castle even with an army your size.'

Junsaku stared into the man's bloodshot eyes for several seconds, then stated, 'I have changed my mind. You are arrogant, stupid, and disrespectful, so here is my new offer: tell your men to lay down their weapons and leave, and you will kneel before me and take your own life.'

'Ha!' Tadamori scoffed, a smirk on his thin, angular face. 'All I have to do is raise my hand, and my archers will kill you on the spot.'

'That will bring you more dishonour, ronin,' Junsaku replied, exaggerating the word for masterless samurai. 'When you meet your end, remember this day. Never forget I gave you the option to save your life and the lives of your men, but your ego caused you to choose poorly.'

Junsaku turned his horse, and the other five riders in his group followed him as Tadamori yelled, 'You will never breach these walls, General! I look forward to the battle and, most of all, killing you.'

When Tadamori and his small entourage stepped through the castle's entrance, the heavy, wooden drawbridge rolled back, the chains creaking as they worked. As Junsaku made his way back to his troops, he smiled. He felt confident, knowing that four of his most trusted and skilled samurai already hid inside the fortress.

The prior night, under the cover of darkness, Junsaku sent highly trained samurai wearing black ninja uniforms and carrying their daisho swords to sneak into the castle grounds. Daimyo Shibata had told Junsaku about an unknown entrance leading to the fortress's interior, so Junsaku assigned four of his best soldiers to the task. In the dim light of a crescent moon, Junsaku cast a watchful eye over his men as they moved silently through the shadows, slipped into the moat, and swam to the secret entrance in the stone foundation to carry out the plan. Junsaku's scheme was simple; the soldiers were to stay hidden until the signal, and then they were to kill the guards at the gate and roll out the drawbridge.

Back with his army, Junsaku dismounted his steed and approached his soldiers. 'Men, today I fight alongside you,' he shouted, raising his bow.

The archers, hidden behind devilish metal face coverings, grunted loudly. Junsaku set his arrow in his bow before giving his fellow archers the signal, and the samurai army began their assault. Junsaku released his bowstring and sent his wooden shaft flying as thousands of other projectiles propelled around him, the arrows jetting towards the openings in the walls of the castle and the fighters on the turrets. Junsaku listened to the unmistakable whizzing sound as more arrows flew past him, realising that the enemy had started to shoot back. Junsaku lifted his fisted left hand, and a fiery arrow shot into the air on the general's signal, alerting the samurai hidden within the castle grounds to execute the plan. Junsaku continued shooting arrows while he waited for the castle drawbridge to appear, and finally, after a few minutes, the rolling deck pushed out from the main gate, the wooden platform sliding on rails as his men inside turned the wheel.

Junsaku and Daimyo Shibata led the mounted samurai and charged the castle. As riders attacked, galloping through a barrage of arrows, several soldiers were wounded or killed. Fortunately, because of the expertise of the foot soldiers shooting arrows by the thousands with deadly accuracy, most of the mounted samurai survived, reaching the castle entrance within minutes. The samurai army stormed the castle in force, and the general watched on horseback as his army killed and maimed the enemy with skill and efficiency.

In under one hour, the once defiant and determined clan rebels found themselves overwhelmed by the might of the highly-skilled warriors of the shogun and the daimyo. The men dropped their swords on the blood-stained pavement and awaited their fate. Junsaku dismounted his horse and surveyed the carnage, looking for Tadamori. As he searched, two of his samurai guards came forward, their hands gripping the arms of the slender clan leader, and they forced the man to his knees before Junsaku, who towered over him.

Junsaku outstretched his hand towards one of his samurai guards. 'Give me your *tanto,*' he ordered.

The samurai handed Junsaku his knife, and Junsaku placed the weapon on the ground before the kneeling clan leader. 'I will not take my life for the likes of you,' Tadamori said, spitting on the straw-rope sandals covering Junsaku's feet.

'Then you will die as the coward you are,' Junsaku said, drawing his katana.

Suddenly, Junsaku felt a frigid chill, and a shiver ran down his spine. Junsaku looked up and saw the hooded ghost standing on the ledge of a high wall directly across from him. As Junsaku stared at the spectre, squinting his eyes, the soldiers surrounding him noticed the general's odd expression and tense facial muscles, and they turned their attention to where he stared but saw nothing unusual, wondering what had come over their fearless leader.

Below the ledge where the ghost stood, projected on the castle wall, Junsaku saw the image of his family. Gathered around the kitchen fire, Junsaku watched as Cecelia laughed with their children, her arms wrapped around Fukano and Nobushida, and then the vision disappeared. The hooded apparition's shadowy gaze continued to lock on Junsaku as the samurai general vigorously shook his head, trying to dispel the images that haunted him. Then, Junsaku stared at the ghost and raised his sword; Junsaku knew he needed to finish what he had started, and with his eyes still glued to the phantom cloaked in black, his blade sliced the air. He cut through Tadamori's neck, sending his enemy's head to the ground with a heavy thud. As Tadamori lost his lifeblood, Junsaku heard a man's voice whisper in his ear, low and gruff, the sound coming from within arm's reach, 'Learn from my mistakes.' Though Junsaku heard the words clearly, the voice, disturbingly close to his left ear, lacked any warmth of breath. When he turned to see who spoke, no one was there. Then, he heard a loud clang, and Junsaku glanced down, shocked to see his katana lying on the ground, keenly aware that, for the first time in his life, he lost his grip on the hilt of his sword. Without picking it up, Junsaku returned his gaze to the hooded spectre, still standing on the ledge of the castle wall. He watched as the spirit turned his back to Junsaku before vanishing, his body absorbed into the grey rock. Junsaku felt utterly alone as his samurai soldiers stared at him, puzzled, trying to make sense of the general's behaviour.

SIXTY

A S PROMISED, Etsuko delivered the items to Aneko before returning home. The house was empty, with Fukano at school and Onishi at the furniture shop. Etsuko went to the storehouse in the backyard and entered the small wooden building. She removed the vile of poison hidden behind boxes and then grabbed the bottle of umeshu she had made the past summer from unripened plums. She removed the cork from the plum wine bottle and poured the entire contents of the lethal concoction into the umeshu, far more than a few drops Aneko had recommended using to avoid killing a person. Then, shaking the bottle, she blended the liquids until the plum wine's sweet and sour flavour overpowered the poison's bitter taste

Looking at the bottle in her hand, she asked herself, 'Can I go through with this?' thinking about the gravity of her choice. Etsuko felt momentarily anxious and uncomfortable. She shut her eyes tightly and inhaled deeply. Suddenly, her eyes sprang open, and her lips curved upwards at the corners as she placed the bottle on the shelf behind the stack of dusty boxes, ensuring no one would find it, confident in her decision.

***

IN THE EARLY afternoon, while Etsuko prepared dinner, Fukano entered the house, followed by Onishi, who kept his distance.

'Konnichiwa, Etsuko-san.' Fukano said politely.

Etsuko glared at Onishi and Fukano. 'I see you two found each other.'

'She was ahead of me as I walked home from work, Etsuko,' Onishi stated nervously. 'It is just coincidental.' Then, Onishi barked, 'Fukano, bring me sake.'

Fukano's brow furrowed in frustration as she walked briskly to the kitchen. As she reached into the cupboard to get a cup, her elbow inadvertently brushed against her aunt's arm. Etsuko, who cut a daikon radish, flinched as her knife grazed her skin, leaving a thin, crimson line across her forefinger.

As Fukano opened her mouth to apologise, Etsuko yelled, 'Stupid girl!' and attempted an open-handed slap to her niece's face.

Fukano's left hand shot up instinctively, and she delivered a forearm block to Etsuko's right arm.

Livid, Etsuko attacked again, this time with her left hand. With a swift motion, Fukano raised her arm and blocked her aunt's strike once more.

'Stop this at once!' Onishi demanded, grabbing Etsuko by her shoulders, holding her back.

'Get your hands off of me!' Etsuko boomed, twisting and turning, trying to break free of her husband's hold.

Fukano stood tall, her shoulders squared. Her gaze locked on Etsuko, and, with a steady voice, she stated, 'Do not attempt to strike me again.'

'Or what?' Etsuko asked, enunciating each word.

'I will defend myself.'

Onishi moved between his wife and his niece. 'Fukano, go to your room,' he pleaded, trying desperately to ease the tension.

Fukano turned her back on her aunt and said, 'Come, Nikka.'

Nikka popped up, her tail wagging side to side, and the dog followed Fukano out the front door and into the warm, tropical evening.

Etsuko spun on her heels and moved quickly towards Onishi, closing the space between them. With the tip of her nose almost touching his lips, she declared, her words as sharp as a sword, 'How dare you stop me!' Her eyes became thin slits, and she spoke with deliberate slowness. 'I am sick of you sticking up for the girl. I am ending this.' With that decisive declaration, she shoved Onishi aside and left the kitchen.

Onishi stood frozen, his complexion drained of colour. He wondered what his wife meant when she said, 'I am ending this.' Would she dare anger her brother by sending Fukano back to mainland Japan? He desperately hoped she would not be that foolish.

SIXTY-ONE

AFTER SUNSET, Fukano and the dog returned home. As Fukano approached the kitchen, she noticed the low table had three place settings. A wave of relief washed over her; it meant Etsuko would not be depriving her of dinner. Fukano could see her aunt in the kitchen, her jaw tight. Concerned that her aunt might still be angry, Fukano felt relieved when Etsuko glanced at her and smiled.

Onishi entered the room from the hallway. 'Is it time to eat?'

'Come and sit,' Etsuko directed Fukano and Onishi, and both took their seats at the table.

Etsuko went into the kitchen, returned with bento boxes filled with cooked cod, pickled daikon radish, mozuku, and tomago, and set them on the table.

'Pass me my bento, Fukano,' her uncle asked.

She felt repulsed as she slid the box towards Onishi, angling her body to create an invisible barrier between them. About to withdraw her hand, a sudden jolt of shock coursed through her as Onishi reached out and let his rough fingertip graze the delicate surface of her hand, his unexpected touch making her jump.

Etsuko quietly approached Fukano from behind, carrying

two bowls of miso soup, and set them on the table. Turning her attention to Onishi, her nose wrinkled in disgust as her husband shovelled the mozuku, strands of slippery brown algae, into his mouth with his chopsticks, she instructed, 'Fukano, fetch your uncle a carafe of sake.'

Fukano went to the kitchen then returned with rice wine in a small carafe, placing the container in front of Onishi.

'Pour for me?' he asked, holding his cup towards Fukano.

Bitterly, she poured sake into the ceramic cup and then placed the carafe loudly on the table.

Onishi grinned and dumped the liquid down his throat. 'Fukano, would you like some nihonshu?'

Fukano clenched her teeth and replied, 'no,' in English.

With a bright smile lighting up her features, Etsuko spoke, her tone unusually cheerful, saying, 'Onishi, excellent idea! Fukano has had a difficult day, and I want to apologise for my behaviour earlier. I know that it was an accident that I cut myself.' Etsuko looked directly into Fukano's jade-green eyes. 'Fukano, I have something special for you, better than sake. I made umeshu plum wine with fruit from our tree. I will bring you a cup.'

Etsuko grabbed a large clay cup from the cupboard and left through the backdoor, heading to the storehouse. She entered the small building and spotted the bottle of plum wine just as she had left it, the deep golden liquid glistening in the dim light. Etsuko hummed as she returned to the kitchen carrying the poisoned wine. She felt confident in two things: first, the plum wine's sweet and sour flavour masked any taste of poison, and, more importantly, she was making the right choice.

At the table, she set the cup of umeshu before Fukano. 'Here you are, Mei.'

Fukano smiled and replied, 'Arigato gozaimasu, Etsuko-san. You do not usually call me Mei, even though I am your niece. It is nice.' At that moment, Fukano felt a glimmer of hope that perhaps her relationship with her aunt could finally transform from its usual tension into something more harmonious.

Etsuko forced a closed-lip smile. 'Enjoy your special drink.'

'Kanpai,' Onishi said, lifting his glass towards Fukano.

Fukano did not respond to his gesture and turned to her aunt. 'Will you join us?'

'I will sit at the table to eat, but I am drinking tea.'

Fukano tasted the plum wine, and the flavour burst on her tongue, sweet and slightly sour.

'Do you like it?' Etsuko asked caringly.

'Hai. I like this very much.'

Fukano drank two cups of umeshu during dinner and then helped to clear the table. She took the bento boxes to the wash basin, feeding Nikka a small piece of left-over fish, and then a sudden, sharp pain shot through her belly. She hunched over and pressed her palms on her stomach.

'Fukano, what is it?' her uncle asked.

'I just felt a stomach pain. It has passed now.'

Her aunt twisted a dishrag in her hands. 'Maybe you should go to bed early tonight? You need to be healthy for school tomorrow.'

'But I should help you wash the dishes,' she said, pouring well water into the large tub used for cleaning. A peculiar, high-pitched sound suddenly erupted from Fukano's mouth, and she bent over, pressing her abdomen with both hands.

'You need to rest,' her uncle said. He slid his arm around her waist and used his opposite hand to grip her elbow. 'I will help you to your room.'

Fukano's green eyes stretched wide at her uncle's unwelcome touch. 'Iie. I will go alone. Good night,' she said, shuffling towards her bedroom.

When Fukano disappeared from sight, Onishi whispered, 'Etsuko, we need to call for a doctor. She is Junsaku's daughter. We must make sure she remains healthy.'

Etsuko moved close to Onishi and looked up at his face. 'You would like to ensure more than that, Husband,' she hissed. 'Ever since the girl arrived, you have desired her. I see it in your eyes and hear it in the words that spill from your mouth. I even saw you touch her hand tonight at the table, you pig!'

'What? Etsuko, that is not true!' he insisted. 'If I touched her hand, it was an accident. Fukano is Junsaku's daughter; I would never do anything to anger your brother.'

'My brother! My brother? Is that all you care about, you imbecile? What about your wife? Where is your honour? In front of me, you have not hidden your desire. You disgust me, Onishi, and I hate the girl.'

'She has done nothing wrong, and you exaggerate, Etsuko. I admit Fukano is beautiful, and what man does not look at youthful beauty? Just because I look does not mean I would ever dishonour you or my brother-in-law.'

'She will not be a problem much longer,' she said, walking across the stone floor to the bento boxes still needing to be washed.

'What does that mean?'

Etsuko stopped with her back to her husband, standing motionless in the kitchen.

'Etsuko, what are you saying?'

'Come outside. We will talk there.'

They slid open the shoji doors, exited the house, and entered the humid night air. Darkness cloaked everything, and the cloud-obscured moon dimly lit the garden, casting dull shadows in the yard.

'It is too late,' Etsuko stated.

'Too late for what? Do not speak to me in riddles and tell me; what have you done?'

'I did nothing. Onishi, this is on you. The girl will be gone soon,' she replied, looking directly into Onishi's wide eyes.

'No, Etsuko. Fukano stays with us until her father tells us it is time for her to leave.'

'You are wrong, Onishi. She is on her way.'

'On her way to where? You are not making sense. Fukano is staying. We promised your brother.'

'No,' Etsuko said brazenly, her chin raised defiantly.

'I will not risk sending her away, you stubborn woman. Junsaku will kill us.'

'She is ill, Onishi. Could you not see the way she acted in the kitchen? She will be gone within days.'

'What?' he said, a knot forming in his stomach. He drew a deep breath and leaned closer, whispering, 'Etsuko, what have you done?'

'I have poisoned her, Onishi. Because of your lust, she will die, and you will not do anything to save her,' she growled. Then, softening her tone, she said, 'Do you know why you will not help her, Onishi? Because, Husband, if you tell anyone I poisoned her, I will tell them you are a liar, and I will inform my brother that it was you who killed his daughter. I will tell Junsaku you are to blame, and he will kill you instantly.'

Etsuko cackled, her sharp, piercing laugh chilling Onishi to the bones. Onishi's hands began to tremble as he grappled with the shock of Etsuko's revelation. He stood motionless, his mouth hung open as he gazed into his wife's dark eyes, and he asked, bewildered, 'You poisoned your brother's daughter, your flesh and blood? What is wrong with you?'

'What is wrong with me? Her fate is your fault, Onishi, no one else's. Unless you want to be killed by my brother's sword, you will go along with me, and we will tell him she became ill and died. That is, if she dies. Sometimes the poison only causes paralysis.'

Onishi shook his head in disbelief, a wave of nausea washing over him. 'How could you do this?'

'I have done nothing, Onishi. This is all your fault.'

SIXTY-TWO

WHEN THE sun rose the following day, Fukano stayed in bed, hidden behind closed fusuma panels. Onishi sat at the kitchen table as Etsuko boiled water at the firepit in the dimly lit kitchen.

'You need to check on Fukano,' Onishi told his wife.

Etsuko placed the kettle on a wooden board, walked down the hall, and slid open the door to Fukano's room. She looked at Fukano, who lay underneath her blanket, her eyelids twitching, strands of hair stuck to her sweaty forehead.

'Fukano, time to get up for school.'

Fukano's head swayed slowly from side to side. She mumbled a string of disjointed words as she partly opened her eyes. With a flicker of awareness, her irises the colour of a primeval forest, she whispered weakly, 'Etsuko-san, bring the doctor.'

'Do not pretend to be sick just to avoid school. Get dressed and come to the kitchen.'

'Wait!' Fukano pleaded as her aunt closed the door and disappeared.

When Etsuko entered the kitchen, Onishi asked, 'How is she?'

'Go find out for yourself!' she snapped. 'You would like to go to her room, wouldn't you?'

'Etsuko, just tell me her condition,' Onishi said with a heavy sigh, running his hand over his thinning hair in frustration.

'She is ill, Onishi, just as I hoped. She requested to be seen by a doctor, but I will give her herbs and tell her they will make her better. She will trust me.'

Then came a knock on the door.

Onishi went to the shoji, slid open the panel, and saw Haru standing there. 'Come in,' he said.

'Ohayō,' the boy said, looking beyond Onishi, searching for his friend. 'Is Fukano ready?'

'She is still in her room,' Etsuko said, approaching him from the kitchen. 'She is pretending to be ill. I have told her to get up, but I don't know how long she will be or if she will even get out of bed. Do not wait for her. Go ahead, Haru. Walk to school without her.'

'I still have time. May I wait to see if Fukano decides to go to school today?' Haru asked politely.

'You may wait a few minutes, but I think she will not budge,' her aunt replied anxiously. 'Plus, Onishi and I will not be here much longer, Haru, so when we go, you will have to leave at the same time.'

'Would you prefer I wait outside?'

'No, of course not.' Etsuko replied, exasperated. 'However, as I said, I think it best if you go on to school without her. She is a good actor and will likely fake sickness all day.'

'I will wait a few minutes more and see if she comes out of her room.' Haru crossed his arms at his chest.

'You may be waiting for a long time.' Onishi said.

'May I check on her?' Haru asked.

Etsuko exhaled sharply.

Then, Onishi said, 'Haru, you can knock on the door of her room and see if she is ready.'

'But do not be surprised if she pretends to be sick for you, too,' Etsuko stated, her eyes blazing with anger as they bore into Onishi.

'Hai,' Haru replied.

Haru walked on the wood floor of the corridor to Fukano's room and knocked lightly on the partition. No one answered. He tapped the panel again with his knuckles, this time forcefully. 'Fukano,' he whispered loudly, 'it is me, Haru. Are you ready for school?' Again, no response. With trepidation, Haru decided to crack the door. When Haru peered into her room, he saw his friend under the covers, her eyes closed and her face moist with sweat. He looked down the hallway towards the kitchen, wondering if he should tell her aunt and uncle that she looked legitimately ill. Instead, he decided to go inside the bedroom. He approached the futon and knelt beside Fukano, lightly touching her forehead, feeling her burning heat, then gently nudged her shoulder and whispered, 'Can you hear me?'

'Haru, I am sick,' she moaned, her eyelids barely cracked open. 'You should not be near me.'

'Your aunt says you are pretending. Are you acting?' he asked, genuinely confused.

'Do you think I could act this well?' she scoffed, her voice tinged with frustration. 'I cannot pretend to make myself this hot, like my insides are boiling. I am genuinely unwell, Haru, and I would rather be at school than in this house.'

'When did you start to feel this way?'

'After dinner last night,' Fukano replied. Following a momentary silence, she said quietly, 'Maybe it was the umeshu.'

'You drank plum wine?'

'Yes. My aunt made it.'

'Did she also have a glass? Did your uncle?'

'No, she did not want any, and my uncle drank sake. It was only me drinking umeshu,' Fukano responded.

'What about the rest of the meal? Did you eat the same things?'

'Hai. We all had the same food, but it was only me who drank plum wine. Maybe I drank too much.'

'How many cups did you have?'

'Two.'

'Fukano, two cups of plum wine will not make you this ill,' Haru said. 'Tell me your symptoms.'

Fukano took a deep breath. 'Though I am sweating, I feel frozen. It is hard to stay awake, and I have strange dreams when I sleep. Also, my breathing is difficult.' Fukano closed her eyes. 'Haru, I have a terrible feeling I am dying.'

'Were you bitten by a snake?'

'Of course not! I would know if a snake bit me.'

'Yes, but I know of a person bitten by a snake who had similar symptoms. Are you certain?'

'Hai, Haru, I am certain nothing has bitten me,' she replied, rolling her half-open eyes.

Haru lowered his voice and asked, 'What about your uncle? Do you trust him? We know he lusts for you.'

'Hai, I know his feelings for me. However, I do not think he would hurt me because he knows my father would kill him.'

'What about your aunt?'

After a short pause, Fukano's eyes widened as a new aware-ness flooded her consciousness. 'She has been more venomous towards me lately,' she said quietly. 'I have tried to stay away from my uncle to prove to her I am no threat, but she hates me more each day, no matter what I do. Yet, last night, she called me Mei, which is strange as she never calls me this, and she even gave me her special umeshu.'

'Fukano, your aunt told me she does not think you need a doctor and that you are acting. I can see you are not acting. Honestly, I am fearful she or Onishi have done this to you.'

Fukano closed her eyes as she struggled to breathe, a strained wheezing sound filling the air. 'Haru, you must go now. You need to get my otosan,' she mumbled, her body shivering despite the sweltering heat that filled the room. Even as sickness attacked her youthful body, sapping her strength, her mind remained in check, and she knew she needed her father by her side.

Haru's sleek, jet-black eyebrows furrowed, forming faint lines on his forehead as he gazed worriedly at his friend. 'I cannot leave you alone. You are too sick.'

'The sooner you fetch him, the sooner he can help me. I need my otosan here. Do this for me, Haru,' Fukano pleaded.

'Where is your father? Do you even know?'

'He is with the shogun at the castle in Kumamoto.' Fukano inhaled sharply and clutched her stomach, the pain cutting her gut like a knife. 'Go, Haru. Tell him of my condition.'

Haru shook his head. 'You should have listened to me when I told you not to trust them. Now I am afraid to leave you. What if you die?'

'If I am dying, I need my father even more. Stop talking and go!' Fukano demanded.

Haru leaned in closer and stared into Fukano's half-open eyes. He reached out and put his hand on her forehead, feeling the heat and dampness of her sweat on his skin. 'I will find him and bring him to you, Fukano. I will go as fast as I can.' Haru glanced at the bedroom door to make sure they were alone, and the others weren't spying. Then, he moved his lips close to Fukano's ear, almost touching her skin. 'While I am gone, be careful,' he whispered urgently. 'If they bring food or drink, offer it to Nikka first and see how she responds. If the dog hesitates even for a moment, do not take it.' Then Haru backed away slightly and cupped Fukano's shoulders. Staring into her eyes, he inhaled deeply, suppressing the rising fear inside him, determined to shield his friend from further anguish, and stated calmly, 'Do not trust anyone. Do you hear me?'

'Hai,' she sighed, looking at him with green eyes dulled like antique bottle glass. 'Find Junsaku, Haru. Bring my otosan. I need him.'

Haru took her hand and clutched it lightly. 'Hang on until I return. And, when I pass through town, I will tell my mother you are very ill. She will send over a doctor. I am sure of it.'

'Arigato, Haru. You are my best friend.'

Haru squeezed Fukano's hand and exited her room. He walked down the short hall and saw Etsuko and Onishi standing near the front entrance.

'I am going to school now,' Haru said, quickly putting on his shoes in the genkan.

'That is best,' Etsuko replied, her hands clasped tightly at her waist. 'I am certain Fukano will attend school tomorrow, Haru.'

SIXTY-THREE

'**O**KASAN!' HARU shouted, storming into the house.

'Why are you not at school?' his mother questioned as Haru raced into the kitchen.

'Fukano, my friend, the daughter of the samurai general, is extremely ill. Etsuko believes she is pretending, but I know she is not!' he said, his words spoken with rapid fire.

Haru's mother's lips pursed. 'Son, if Etsuko believes the girl is faking sickness, she probably is. Children do this when they do not want to attend school, and it is not your business.'

'Okasan,' he implored, 'she is genuinely ill. She is as hot as the summer sand and cannot stay awake. If we do not help her, I fear she might die. I agreed to fetch her father in Kumamoto. I have no option. She is my friend. I must help her.'

Haru's mother's expression tightened as she stared at her son. After momentary silence, she finally said, 'Haru, we will go together to their house, and I will find out from Etsuko what is going on.'

'Hai, Okasan. Hopefully, they will be home. They said they were going out.'

Haru and his mother left the house and walked quickly to Onishi and Etsuko's home.

***

AT THE FRONT entrance, Haru's mother knocked. Nikka barked from inside, and after a few minutes, the doors slid open.

'Konnichiwa,' Haru's mother said to Etsuko, who stood in the doorway with Nikka sitting by her feet, her tail wagging furiously, the dog doing her utmost to remain in that position despite the excitement of unexpected guests. 'I apologise for this intrusion. May we come in?'

Etsuko looked at both of her visitors and then stepped aside and dipped her head, allowing them to enter. 'We will go to the kitchen and sit,' Etsuko said politely.

Haru and his mother sat cross-legged on the floor cushions around the wooden table. Etsuko carefully lifted the heavy iron kettle from the fire in the kitchen and brought the teapot with three cups to the table before sitting with her visitors. As she poured tea, she stated, 'Haru must have told you Fukano is sick, Kasumi. He is a caring young man. She is lucky to have such a friend.'

'Then you know she is sick?' Haru challenged, his eyebrows pinched. 'I thought you said she was acting?'

'Respect, Haru,' his mother scolded. Kasumi turned and faced Etsuko. 'Gomennasai. I apologise for my son's rudeness.'

'He tells the truth, Kasumi. At first, I believed Fukano was acting, faking to be sick. However, now I can see she is legitimately ill. I have sent Onishi to fetch the doctor. After she receives medicine, she will be fine. She is strong.'

'Oh, poor girl,' Kasumi sighed. 'Well, that is good news. See, Haru, you have nothing to worry about,' Kasumi reassured as she sipped tea. 'The doctor will be here soon, and your friend will be fine. You do not need to fetch her father.'

Etsuko's head tilted backwards, and she peered down her nose at Haru. 'You planned to tell my brother?'

'Fukano asked me to get Junsaku and bring him here.' Haru faced his mother. 'Okasan, Fukano is very sick. Shouldn't her otosan know this? Wouldn't you and father want to be informed if I were ill?'

'Well, hai,' his mother stated. Kasumi faced Etsuko and said, 'In my opinion, Junsaku should know about his daughter's condition. Do you agree?'

Etsuko paused, took a deep breath, rested her chin in her hands, and replied, 'At first, I thought my brother should know. But, because I am confident the doctor will be able to cure her, I decided against it. With his general's rank, Junsaku is extremely busy protecting the shogunate, so I do not want to burden him until we know more. If Fukano does not get better after the doctor's treatment, I will send a courier to inform him immediately. That is, if I can even figure out where he is. He travels and battles so often,' she sighed.

'I know where he is!' Haru declared. 'He is in Kumamoto on Kyushu in southern Japan. Do not worry, Etsuko. I will leave today and bring Junsaku back here. He will want to be with you and help ensure Fukano regains her health.'

'Son, that is excellent,' Kasumi said, placing her hand lightly on Haru's shoulder. 'I am proud of you, and I know Etsuko welcomes your support,' she finished, nodding towards Etsuko.

'I do not think this is necessary, Haru. I will alert my brother when the time is right.' Etsuko's words were full of apprehension as she crossed her arms defensively. 'Let us first get the doctor's diagnosis. I do not want you to go through all this trouble for nothing.'

'It is no trouble,' Haru responded confidently. 'I will leave immediately for Kumamoto.'

As Haru finished his sentence, Onishi entered the house, followed by the doctor. When Onishi saw Haru and his mother, his eyes bulged in shock at the unexpected guests, and the skin on his face reddened. Then, he composed himself and pointed to Fukano's room, directing the doctor where to go to treat his patient.

'Onishi, Haru and his mother were kind enough to come and check on Fukano,' Etsuko said, followed by a quiet huff. 'I told them you were bringing the doctor and that she would recover soon. Yet, Haru insists on going to the mainland to tell her father about her sickness. I have tried to convince him this is unnecessary.'

Onishi stiffened, his thick eyebrows raised as he blinked several times, then stammered, 'Ah...um, yes...she will be fine now that the doctor is here, Haru. You do not need to bother her father with this.'

'It is not a problem, Onishi. Besides, I do not want to break my promise to Fukano.'

Onishi took a deep breath and exhaled loudly. 'Haru, telling Junsaku is not a good idea. He does not need to know! I mean, not now. Let us first see what the doctor says,' he finished.

Etsuko flashed a fierce look at her husband before her expression softened. 'Disregard Onishi's response. He is worried about Fukano, and his mind is foggy. He cares deeply for his niece.'

'Hai, hai, she is a wonderful girl. I want her to recover, and I get anxious thinking that her father may believe we made her sick,' Onishi said, the pace of his words fast and sloppy. 'Children get sick, right, Kasumi?'

Kasumi's lips tightened, her expression reflecting disbelief. 'What an odd thing to say, Onishi. Why would Junsaku ever think you or Etsuko made Fukano sick?'

Etsuko chimed in. 'What a silly thing to say, Husband. Your worry is affecting your brain. Go for a walk on the beach. By tomorrow, Fukano will be healthy, I am sure of it.'

Onishi bowed then bolted from the room.

'I am sorry for my husband's poor choice of words, Kasumi. Onishi cares too much for everyone and hates to see anyone in pain.'

'Hai, your husband seems like a caring man,' Kasumi remarked, her voice dripping with sarcasm as she raised an eyebrow. 'Haru, let us leave. The doctor is here. Etsuko, tell us if we can be of any more service.'

Etsuko nodded thoughtfully. 'Of course.'

Kasumi and Haru bowed politely and bid their goodbyes before heading out of the house.

**

ON THE WAY home, Haru asked his mother, 'Okasan, do you agree something is off? Fukano's aunt and uncle are behaving strangely.'

'I have never liked that Onishi. There is something not right about him.'

'Fukano told me he misbehaves with her and that he tries to, ah, do things with her. Do you understand?'

'Certainly,' she replied. 'I have more years of life experience than you do, and being a woman, I understand how men can behave inappropriately around women, particularly those who are young and attractive.'

After a moment's hesitation, Haru inquired, 'Okasan, do you believe her aunt or uncle caused her illness?'

'What do you mean?'

'Well, could they have given her something that would have made her sick? Fukano informed me that Etsuko served her two cups of homemade umeshu during dinner last night, and shortly after consuming it, she fell ill. Such a small quantity of alcohol cannot make someone as sick as Fukano. It makes me suspicious.'

'Be careful of accusations without facts, son,' Kasumi cautioned. Yet despite her calm demeanour, deep down, her son's comments filled Kasumi with a strong sense of unease. After minutes of walking silently, listening to birds chirping and their footsteps tapping the pebbled road, Kasumi finally spoke. 'We will get you on a boat to Kyushu this afternoon, and I will give you money for a horse. You will find Junsaku; tell him his daughter is extremely ill and that he must come to Okinawa immediately.'

Haru breathed deeply, the air filling his lungs as a wave of relief washed over him. 'Arigato, Okasan.' His heart swelled with gratitude for his mother's support.

SIXTY-FOUR

DAYS AFTER departing the shores of Okinawa, Haru stood on the ship's deck, the salty breeze pulling on strands of hair that escaped his topknot as the sailboat glided gracefully into Kagoshima Bay in southern Kyushu. Once disembarked, he haggled with a vendor over a horse with a dull brown coat. After successfully purchasing the mare with a handful of shiny *mon* coins from his worn leather pouch, Haru secured his bag behind the saddle, swung himself onto the horse's back, and asked a male passerby, 'Kudasai, what road is fastest to get to Kumamoto castle?'

The man with shiny, black hair pointed down a cobblestone street lined with dark wooden houses and shops. 'Stay on that road. With few stops, you should arrive in Kumamoto in three days.'

'Domo arigato gozaimasu,' Haru replied as he urged his horse forward to find Junsaku.

***

HARU NAMED his horse Kage, and they travelled for twenty hours on the first day with only brief stops for eating, drinking, and resting. On the second day, tired and needing a break, Haru spent an hour bathing in a natural spring, an onsen, relaxing in the hot water that bubbled up from deep within the earth before continuing his journey on Kage. On day three, Haru rode into Kumamoto and saw the majestic silhouette of Kumamoto Castle on a hill surrounded by the bustling city.

Haru weaved his way through the city streets. As he neared the castle, its sloping stone walls towered over him, the complex perched high above the ground. Haru took note of the samurai stationed everywhere, their sharp eyes scanning the surroundings with unyielding vigilance. At the threshold of the main gate, a samurai guard pointed the tip of a sword at the centre of Haru's chest. From behind a leather and iron menpō mask that covered the lower half of the warrior's face, hiding his mouth behind a twisted sneer, Haru heard the question, the voice low and gravelly, 'What is your business?'

'I am here to see General Junsaku Aoyama on behalf of his daughter, Fukano. Tell him it is urgent.'

***

IN THE LANTERN light of the grand hall, Junsaku and his colleague, Ren, sat on the floor savouring freshly made rice cakes, pickled vegetables, and barley shochu, discussing their recent triumph. 'Our army was too powerful for them,' Junsaku boasted, lifting his ceramic cup. 'They did not stand a chance.'

'Kanpai,' Ren replied, toasting their victory before downing the alcoholic drink in one satisfying gulp.

'They should have known not to fight us. Those ronin were weak in combat and weak in mind.'

'Hai, I agree, Junsaku.' Ren's cheeks flushed a vibrant shade of red. 'We should go to the inn tonight, celebrate our success, and let the women help us relax.'

Junsaku smiled knowingly, his voice warm yet firm. 'I am happy to join you at the inn for entertainment and drink, Rin, but I am not interested in anything else with the courtesans. Only one woman possesses my heart and soul, and until we are together again, I remain faithful to her.'

As Junsaku and Rin prepared to leave the castle for the inn, a low-ranking samurai rushed into the hall, bowed, and said, 'General Aoyama, there is a boy at the castle's main gate who requests to see you. He says he brings news about your daughter.'

Junsaku sprinted forward, his heart pounding as he bolted past the guard, charging towards the gate. Spotting Haru standing near a brown mare, the leather reins held tightly in his fist, Junsaku could see a misty, reddish-orange aura clinging to his skin, the colour of a blood orange. Junsaku marched straight to him, grabbed his upper arm firmly, and demanded, 'Speak!'

'It is Fukano. She is sick. She is asking for you.'

After a brief pause, while Junsaku processed Haru's words, the tension in Junsaku's face melted away, replaced by an expression of amusement. He gripped Haru's shoulders, squeezing lightly. 'Haru, she is almost sixteen and as strong as a bear. Neither of you need to worry. If she is sick, it will pass. Tell her not to be scared.'

Haru sighed deeply. 'But Junsaku-san, something is wrong. Her illness is not normal. When I left her, she could hardly breathe or even move, and her temperature was as hot as the sun. I am suspicious that, well, her uncle, Onishi, he, um...'. Haru's sentence trailed off.

'What about her uncle? Why are you suspicious, Haru?' Junsaku growled, his face contorted, deep lines forming all over his face, making him look as fierce as a lion.

'I do not know if her uncle has done anything, but I do not trust him. Neither does my okasan. Did you know Onishi is attracted to Fukano and has even tried to touch her when they are alone? Fukano told me your sister, Etsuko, is angry and blames Fukano for Onishi's advances. It is pure speculation, Junsaku-san, but based on her symptoms, I fear someone may have poisoned your daughter.'

'Poison? Could it be a snake or spider bite?'

'Fukano said it is not a bite, and she said there are no marks on her skin,' Haru replied.

Junsaku's eyes flared like a bonfire. 'We must go.' Junsaku motioned with his hand, and a guard ran up to him. 'I need a horse, water, food and sake for three days – now!' he demanded.

In less than fifteen minutes, a samurai delivered a fully tacked black stallion, the saddle adorned with the shogun's symbol. A well-stocked leather bag hung over the horse's flanks, holding the supplies requested by Junsaku. Junsaku mounted the horse and, with a burst of energy, horse and rider surged out of the castle grounds, the hooves thundering against the cobblestones while Haru rode behind, trying to keep up.

***

THREE DAYS after leaving Kumamoto Castle, Junsaku and Haru reached Kagoshima Bay in the early morning, the air filled with the salty scent of the sea. They boarded a sturdy, three-masted sailboat bound for Okinawa, welcomed aboard by the ship's captain, who assigned them a cabin with two cots.

'Haru, tell me again what Fukano said about her uncle,' Junsaku asked as he lay in the bed staring at the ceiling, his eyes as black as the inside of a well, the sound of waves lapping against the boat's hull echoing in the cabin.

Haru sat on the edge of his cot, facing Junsaku. 'Fukano told me Onishi makes her uncomfortable. She said he looks at her funny and often tries to be alone with her. Fukano told me one night, when she was asleep in her bed, she awoke and found her uncle in her room, standing near her futon, staring down at her.'

Junsaku snarled.

'Fukano told me that Onishi asked her not to say anything about entering her room that night. He told Fukano he came to check on her, but she knew he was lying. After that, Onishi never came to her room again, but he often tries to touch her, and she either moves away or blocks him.'

'He will learn,' Junsaku hissed. 'What about her aunt? How does she act towards my daughter?'

'Honestly, she is unkind, Junsaku-san. She does not speak to Fukano and only gives her orders. Fukano believes Etsuko knows of her husband's attraction because she looks at them as though they are guilty of wrongdoing.' Haru paused briefly, gathering his thoughts. 'Junsaku-san, Fukano has tried to manage the situation. She did not want to worry you because she thought she could handle it alone.'

With words weighted so heavy it seemed they could sink to the bottom of the ocean, Junsaku asked, 'Haru, do you believe that because Onishi cannot have Fukano, he would rather see her dead?'

'I do not know. But Fukano became sick quickly, eating the same food as Onishi and Etsuko, except for two glasses of umeshu that only she drank. Fukano said your sister made the plum wine herself. Maybe, somehow, the umeshu became toxic or poisoned?' Haru hesitated momentarily, then reluctantly said, 'There is folklore on our island about mixing deadly plants and herbs with venom from the habu snake for poison.'

'And these mixtures kill?'

'According to legend, it is said that more often than not, they do, Junsaku-san.'

'Wretched boat! Can it not travel faster?' Junsaku bellowed, his voice bouncing off the wooden walls, every muscle in his body coiled like a tightly wound spring.

SIXTY-FIVE

A S JUNSAKU and Haru stepped off the boat in Okinawa,
Junsaku dashed ahead. The people at the dock moved aside,
clearing a path as they bowed awkwardly, a mix of respect and
surprise at the samurai general's urgency. Junsaku found two
horses tethered to a weathered post and grabbed their reins, un-
challenged by any bystanders. He tossed a set of leather straps to
Haru, and together, the men mounted the horses. With a shared
look of determination, they pressed their heels into the horses'
sides and galloped towards Junsaku's sister's house.

After two hours on horseback, they finally reached their destination. Junsaku tugged on the reins, feeling his horse beginning
to slow, but before the animal could stop, Junsaku leapt off the
saddle and hit the ground running, rushing towards the entrance.
He roughly slid open the door, cracking the shoji's outer wood
frame, and hurried inside, not bothering to remove his shoes. He
stepped over Nikka, who jumped and barked at his sudden intrusion, yelling loudly, 'Fukano!'

His sister emerged from the shadows of the kitchen, dressed
in a dark olive kimono with a black lace scarf covering her face.
'*Goshūshōsama desu,*' she said, bowing.

As though someone had kicked him squarely in the chest, Junsaku lost his breath. 'You are sorry for what loss, sister? Where is Fukano?' he demanded, turning in small circles, searching for his daughter, a desperate expression painted on his face.

Onishi approached from the corridor, dressed in a black kimono. He bowed and then stood meekly behind his wife.

'Where is my daughter?' Junsaku asked, his voice a low growl, the air thick with tension. Etsuko lowered her gaze to the ground and motioned towards the backyard. Junsaku stormed past her, roughly pushing Onishi aside as he charged out of the house. As he approached the garden, anger surging through him, his eyes were drawn to a newly formed mound of earth just beyond the garden's edge. Slightly longer than his daughter's height, a sudden rush of coldness gripped him and tightened his lungs, making each breath feel laboured and shallow, the pressure like being trapped in freezing water.

Junsaku's eyes blazed with fury as he returned to the house. With loud footsteps, he crossed through the kitchen, grabbed Onishi by the back of his neck, and pushed him forward, forcing him to the ground. Next, Junsaku moved behind his sister and kicked the back of her knees, causing her legs to buckle and her kneecaps to slam against the hard rock floor. 'What have you done?' Junsaku shouted, the anger in his voice rolling through the house like a clap of thunder.

'Brother, you are upset. It is understandable. But why are you treating us this way?' Etsuko's piercing gaze fixed on Haru. 'What falsehoods did the boy tell you?'

'Haru tells no lies, but I know you do. Now is your chance, Etsuko. I will allow you to tell me the truth and live, or you will die here.'

Etsuko's eyes glistened with unshed tears. 'Brother, we brought a doctor for Fukano right away, but despite our efforts and the doctor's care, the sickness was too strong. She fought like you, like a warrior, but ultimately, she could not survive the illness.'

Junsaku's mouth twisted into a sinister scowl, a murderously intense look in his dark eyes. 'And how did she become sick, Etsuko?'

'How should I know? People get sick and die. You know better than anyone that death is a part of life. Brother, be reasonable,' Etsuko begged.

Junsaku turned and looked down at Onishi, still crouched on the floor, beads of sweat on his forehead. Junsaku's eyes were dark and intense, like a dark abyss, as he glared at his brother-in-law. 'So, Onishi, you had feelings for my daughter?' Did you believe you could trade your wife for her?'

Onishi whimpered, his bloodshot eyes opened wide. 'Junsaku-san, listen to me. There is a misunderstanding. We gave Fukano food, shelter, and everything she needed, just as we promised.'

Junsaku pulled out his long sword and gripped the handle as he stared down at his sister on her knees. Then, Junsaku turned to Onishi and said, 'I will spare your life if you tell me the truth, Onishi. Do you want to live or die?'

Onishi swallowed, his words barely audible. 'I want to live.'

'Fine. Then tell me, how did you kill my daughter?'

Onishi inhaled and looked at his wife, whose eyes were glossy and desperate.

Junsaku pressed his blade under Onishi's chin, forcing him to look up. 'Tell me directly, coward. How did you do it?'

Onishi's eyes darted nervously. 'I did not do anything, Junsaku-san. I am innocent,' he replied, his voice quivering. Then, he blurted out, 'It was Etsuko. Your sister was jealous of Fukano's beauty and poisoned her.'

Etsuko moaned like a hurt animal and leapt to her feet. 'You liar! How dare you blame the girl's death on me,' she cried.

Standing before his sister, Junsaku lifted his sword and sliced through her body, cutting Etsuko from her right collarbone to her left hip, sending her torso to the floor, a pool of blood and entrails splattering the ground.

Haru, shocked, covered his mouth. He saw Nikka inching towards the bloodied floor, and he swept the dog into his arms, holding her close to his chest as he watched Junsaku turn to Onishi.

'Brother, please! Spare my life,' Onishi snivelled. 'I would never hurt Fukano!'

Junsaku placed the blade of his sword on the side of Onishi's neck. As tears streamed down Onishi's swollen red cheeks, Junsaku pulled his sword towards him and sliced the man's carotid artery. Onishi's hand shot up to the wound. As he tried to stop the bleeding, his chubby hand doused in blood, he finally weakened and fell to his side, his head smacking the wooden leg of the table.

Junsaku's eyes were raven black as tears cascaded down his tanned cheeks, gliding over the crescent-shaped scar near his lip. Junsaku went to where his sister lay dead and used the sleeve of her kimono to clean his blade. He sheathed his sword, left the house, and walked to the garden with Haru trailing him. He went to the mound of dirt where Fukano had been buried and stared at her grave, sobbing. Then, Junsaku sniffled loudly, wiped the tears off his face, and said sternly, 'Haru, bring me matches and straw. I will burn these treacherous dogs and everything they had so they leave this world with nothing, including their honour.'

***

HARU RETURNED thirty minutes later. 'Junsaku-san,' he called out, running towards him, 'I have what you asked for.' He held out a small bundle of matches, little sticks of pinewood with sulphur tips, and pointed to a wheelbarrow filled with golden straw.

Junsaku softly pressed his lips to the tips of his fingers and placed them against the earth of the burial mound. He then walked to Haru, took the matches, and strode purposefully towards the wheelbarrow. 'Haru, stack straw near the house wall. Pile it high. I want the fire to reach the roof as quickly as possible.'

After Haru finished stacking the straw, Junsaku lit a match and held it close to the dry grass. He watched the colour of the stalks turn from gold to charcoal as the orange-yellow fire crept up the walls, the flames dancing and flickering, growing in intensity until, finally, the fire reached the top of the house, and the thatched roof burst into flames, the dry grass and reeds crackling as they burned. Then, the wooden rafters of the ceiling lit up, carrying the destructive fire to all the walls until, within minutes, flames engulfed the house, dark smoke billowing towards the blue sky.

As Haru stood frozen in place, mesmerized by the inferno devouring the house, thick, acrid smoke filled the air, stinging his eyes. Meanwhile, Junsaku walked to Fukano's grave, each step heavy with grief, and as he sank to the ground next to her gravesite, the ghost emerged directly in front of him.

The spectral figure, wrapped in a black flowing robe that seemed to absorb the smoke and ash around it, tilted its head gently toward Fukano's grave, the spirit's facial features obscured by its billowing black hood. Junsaku cast a fleeting glance at the cloaked apparition, its shadowy figure fixated on the ground where Fukano's lifeless body lay, and thought, *'Not now. I have no time for your riddles,'* hoping the spirit could sense his energy. Then, Junsaku said aloud, his tone firm, 'Haru, it is time. I must move my daughter to be with her mother and brother.'

SIXTY-SIX

THE FIRE destroyed the house within hours, leaving only bits of burnt wood and ash on the patch of blackened landscape where it once stood. Amidst the ash and smouldering embers, the only discerning clues that people had ever inhabited the destroyed structure were the melted, twisted remains of the kitchen's metal pots and utensils and the bone fragments of Etsuko and Onishi. As the scent of smoke wafted through the air, overpowering the smell of tropical flowers and the salty sea, villagers hurried to the spot of the fire, their wide eyes a mix of curiosity and trepidation. Haru addressed them with a commanding yet calm tone, informing them that General Junsaku Aoyama was in charge of the situation, urging the villagers to return to their daily routines and insisting they speak no further of the event. Even the village elders and authorities understood the unspoken rule: questioning one of the shogun's top samurai would only invite disaster.

Haru stayed nearby, sitting under the shade of a palm tree, while the general sat beside his daughter's grave, lost in thought, almost as though he meditated. After several hours, Junsaku finally stood and approached Haru. 'I have one last favour to ask;

can you arrange a casket, horse and wagon, and men to assist with the exhumation of my daughter?' Junsaku reached into his pocket, pulled out a sack of mon coins, and handed them to Haru. 'For payment.'

'Of course, Junsaku-san.'

'Make sure the casket is beautiful, Haru, and befitting of Fukano,' Junsaku said tenderly.

Haru nodded, and both men looked at the burial mound. Nikka perched on top of the dirt, her hairy chin pressed against the earth. The dog's charcoal-coloured eyes were wet, her eyelids heavy, as she gazed at the men, not lifting her head.

Junsaku sighed loudly. 'You will need to care for the dog, Haru. Fukano loved her very much.'

'Hai. I will bring Nikka to live with my family.' Haru bent down and snapped his fingers. 'Come, Nikka.'

The dog lifted her head, raised her floppy ears, and then dropped her snout back on the grave, releasing a loud puff of air through her nose. Haru walked to the mound, picked up the dog, and settled her into his arms.

'I will take Nikka to my house, get the items you requested, and be back shortly,' Haru said.

***

WHEN HARU returned with the gravediggers to unearth Fukano's body, Junsaku told them to be careful. The men grabbed shovels and began removing dirt. Within minutes, a shovelhead hit a hard object, and the men carefully removed more dirt until a plain, flat slat of wood, dusted with dark-brown sediment, became visible.

The workers paused their dig, sweat glistening on their brows. A labourer with wild black hair turned to Junsaku and asked, 'With permission, we will remove the lid, take your daughter's body from the box, and move her into the casket,' pointing towards the rectangular, white marble box resting solemnly in the back of the horse-drawn wagon, its surface gleaming softly in the fading afternoon sun.

'Hai,' Junsaku replied, the word sticking in his throat.

A man jumped onto the wooden coffin, landed with a dull thump, and then used a prybar to remove the lid. Junsaku glimpsed the outline of his daughter's body inside, wrapped in light-tan fabric, shrouded from head to toe like a mummy, and the sight caused his chest to tighten, making it hard to breathe.

Haru placed his hand gently on Junsaku's shoulder.

'Leave us,' Junsaku demanded. 'Haru, you may stay.'

The workers hurried out of the grave, went to the wagon, and waited.

Junsaku stepped on the edges of the pine-wood coffin, balanced himself, and then bent and lifted Fukano. He carefully slid his daughter's stiffened body over his shoulder, then reached up with his left hand to allow Haru to help him climb out of the hole in the ground. Junsaku lay Fukano's body down on a patch of soft grass near the garden and, using his knife, cut away the fabric that covered her head. Removing the cloth, he saw his daughter's face, her expression calm and peaceful in the soft orange glow of the setting sun. Her eyes were closed, her mouth curved slightly upward, and her skin lacked its usual lustre, dulled and paled, faded of the brightness of her short life. Junsaku gazed lovingly at Fukano's face as the truth presented itself, forcing him to confront reality; it was his fault that everyone he loved and promised to protect was gone. For as long as he could remember, he dedicated his loyalty to the rulers of Japan. Now, as anger raged within him like an electric storm, he found himself at a crossroads.

Junsaku was confident about his path; his next steps were clear, even if it was too late. Junsaku poured water from his canteen onto a clean piece of fabric and washed Fukano's face, wiping her cheeks, eyes, and mouth. He squeezed water droplets on her lips to ensure she did not feel thirsty as she journeyed to the next life, then lifted her still-wrapped body in his arms. He carried her and then gently placed her corpse into the stone casket at the back of the wagon, holding the nape of her neck as her body settled inside.

Junsaku lowered his head and whispered prayers while Haru and the workers silently reflected. When Junsaku finished, he stated quietly, 'Seal it.'

On the count of three, the men lifted the lid and placed it on top of the casket, hiding Fukano's body for eternity.

Junsaku brushed his palms over his cheeks, clearing away tears, and told the workers, 'Arigato. You may go. We will manage the rest from here.'

The men bowed and disappeared down the dirt road.

'Haru, I will ride to the port in the morning, load the casket onto a ship, and arrange for transport to the mainland to deliver my daughter to her mother and brother.'

'Come to my house and rest for the night, Junsaku-san.'

'Iie, Haru. I will stay here with my daughter.'

Haru hesitated momentarily, then stated, 'I can go with you to deliver her.'

'No, Haru, you must finish school and be with your family. Now go.'

Reluctant to leave Junsaku's side, Haru's eyebrows lifted as he faced Fukano's casket and bowed. He began to walk sluggishly towards his home in the village, glancing over his shoulder multiple times, wanting to stay with Junsaku, but then his pace quickened, and he disappeared.

Junsaku, alone, went to the casket. He pressed his war-torn hands on the top of the casket. 'My precious Ka, why didn't you tell me sooner? I could have protected you. I cannot live. I can no longer breathe.' He coughed, choking on salty tears, then cleared his throat and said, 'We will all be together again.' Junsaku lay on the ground, his body drained of energy, and he crawled under the wagon to rest. With his hand tightly gripping the hilt of his sword, he closed his eyes.

***

JUNSAKU WOKE to a pink and violet sky and the raucous chirping of birds. He rolled out from under the carriage and saw Haru sitting beneath a nearby palm tree, a small fire burning before him. Over the fire, Haru grilled rice balls on wooden skewers, rotating the sticks. The flame heat should have turned the white rice to a golden-brown colour, but instead, the rice burned to almost black, and Junsaku realised Haru was not a skilled cook.

Junsaku went to him and patted his head, chuckling. 'I guess you are hungry?'

'Ohayō, Junsaku-san,' Haru said, smiling. 'These are for our breakfast.'

'You did not need to bring me breakfast, Haru.'

'I did not come just to bring you food, Junsaku-san. I am coming with you to the mainland to deliver Fukano to her mother and brother.'

'I am not sure this is a good idea.'

'Of course it is, Junsaku-san. She was my dearest friend.'

Junsaku inhaled deeply, held his breath momentarily, and said, 'Fine, Haru. Get in the wagon so we may leave.'

Both men stepped into the wooden carriage and sat next to each other on the front bench. Junsaku grabbed the reins and said, 'Haru, from now on, we no longer mention her name. We do not want to cause her to return to the physical world.' Junsaku lightly flicked the leather reins, and the horses moved forward. 'Also, as we travel through Japan to reach the cemetery, Kurodani, where Fukano's mother and brother wait for her, in honour of my daughter and for your protection, we will continue your martial arts training. I will be your sensei.'

'Domo arigato gozaimasu!' Haru exclaimed, his voice raised an octave with excited gratitude.

SIXTY-SEVEN

JUNSAKU AND Haru set sail from Okinawa with Fukano's casket secured deep within the ship's hull. After a journey marked by calm seas and blue skies, they finally arrived at Kagoshima Bay. After disembarking at the bustling dock, Junsaku raised his hand commandingly, and a local samurai hurried over, spotting the emblem of the shogunate embroidered on his jacket. Bowing deeply in respect as he addressed Junsaku, the warrior asked, 'General, what do you need?'

'There is a casket on this ship. Find me a wagon with horses to transport it to Kakunodate in the Akita prefecture. Make sure you are gentle when you place it in the wagon's rear.' Then, turning to Haru, Junsaku said, 'I must get a message to the shogun. While I am gone, prepare enough food, water, and sake to last an entire moon cycle.'

Junsaku left Haru to organise the trip details and ascended the hill towards the port office. As he stepped into the confines of a small room, a petite Japanese man stationed behind a polished wooden counter dropped his pen, startled by Junsaku's arrival. As soon as he saw the samurai general, he bowed, his eyes aimed at the ground.

Junsaku wasted no time, launching right into his order. 'You will arrange delivery of an urgent message to the shogun at the castle in Edo.'

'Hai,' the clerk replied nervously. He picked up a goose feather pen, touched the tip to the ink, and waited for Junsaku to tell him what to write.

As Junsaku dictated his message, his index finger tapped the gold cord wrapped around the hilt of his long sword. Junsaku's words flowed effortlessly as the clerk dipped and re-dipped his feather pen. When Junsaku finished, the man blew on the parchment, rotated the sheet, and invited Junsaku to proofread:

> *Fusakage Shogun,*
>
> *Due to personal reasons, I must resign my position, effective immediately. The time has come for me to follow my conscience and right my wrongs. It has been an honour to serve you and all of Japan.*
>
> *General Junsaku Aoyama*

Junsaku grunted approval and tossed a coin on the counter. Then, he leaned closer to the clerk and said, his voice low and serious, 'Remember, you must have this message delivered within three days, or I will return and send you to your next life.'

'Hai,' the clerk replied, his voice shaky. Then, he bent into a respectful bow and remained in that position until Junsaku vanished.

Junsaku walked down the hill and saw Haru standing beside two chestnut-coloured, muscularly built horses harnessed to a four-wheeled cart. Fukano's stone casket rested in the back of the wagon, its polished lid reflecting the bright sun like a beacon

When Junsaku strode up to Haru, he asked, 'Is everything

ready?'

Haru nodded. 'Hai, Junsaku-san.'

Junsaku smiled slightly and gently squeezed Haru's shoulder. 'Subarashī. Let us go.' Junsaku and Haru seated themselves on the front bench. Junsaku grabbed the reins as two uniformed samurai approached and stood quietly at the back of the carriage, eyes forward. 'Iie,' Junsaku said, waving his hands at the soldiers. 'You are not to come with us. We go alone. Return to your duties.'

The men looked at each other in confusion, and then one samurai said to Junsaku, 'Our lord, Daimyo Matashichi, has told us to escort you and follow your command, General.'

'Iie, that is not necessary,' Junsaku snapped. 'Now leave us and tell your daimyo I told you to go. I no longer work for the shogun.'

The men shrugged and walked away.

'Junsaku-san, I mean no disrespect, but why would you tell them you no longer work for the shogun?' Haru asked.

'I have sent a message to Edo castle relinquishing my rank so I may focus on reuniting my family.'

A look of surprise flickered across Haru's face, but he remained quiet, unsure how to respond.

As they bounced in the carriage, the horses moving forward in a perfect, four-beat gait, Junsaku said, 'Now that I am a masterless samurai, challenges are imminent, Haru. Over-confident men will see my swords and want to fight. I pity any man who tries because he will die.' Junsaku turned and looked Haru in the eyes. 'But you, Haru, can be killed, so I will teach you to protect yourself.'

***

AS JUNSAKU and Haru pressed on towards Kakunadate, Haru

could not stop thinking about Junsaku's ominous words. He felt apprehensive and even afraid of the threat of attack and fighting with roadside thugs, keenly aware that he had little chance of surviving without Junsaku. Without warning, Junsaku yanked the reins and steered the horses sharply to the left, leaving the road and driving the cart over grass and gravel.

'What are you doing, Junsaku-san?' Haru asked, confused by the change of course.

Junsaku gestured towards a cluster of tall pine trees in an open field, stating, 'We will camp in those trees tonight.'

'But Junsaku-san, it is still daylight. Shouldn't we try to cover more ground?' Haru asked, puzzled.

'First things first. I want to continue the martial arts training my daughter began to teach you. And then afterwards, you can cook our dinner,' he said, smiling, a playful sparkle in his eyes.

Haru tilted his head to the side, noticing the amusement when Junsaku mentioned he should cook their dinner. 'Why are you smiling?'

'To be honest, Haru-san, I hope your food is better than the rice cakes you cooked over the fire in Okinawa - I chipped a tooth they were so burnt!' Junsaku threw his head back, his laughter hearty and infectious, and jumped out of the carriage.

Haru chuckled and exited the cart, beginning to unload their supplies for the night. While Haru set up camp, he watched Junsaku, now in the open field, practicing complex sword patterns with his katana. Junsaku's feet moved as though he were skating on ice, and the blade moved with such speed that all Haru could see were glints of reflected sunlight on the razor-sharp steel blade as it cut through the air.

Junsaku stopped abruptly. He looked at Haru, bowed, and

straightened, saying, 'Get your bokken and come here. We will test your skills.' Haru grabbed his bokken from underneath the cart's wooden bench and walked to Junsaku, who waited in the field. 'Before we begin, Kohai, tell me of your martial experience,' Junsaku said, calling Haru 'Kohai', a term used to describe someone junior and less experienced.

'My father was a karate master, Junsaku-san, and I...' Haru began.

Junsaku interrupted and said firmly, 'Refer to me as sensei when we train.'

'Hai, Sensei,' Haru stammered. He took a deep breath. 'My grandfather was a karate master, and I started training in the art of empty hand when I was five years old, learning the weapon arts of the Ryukyu Islands.'

'Do you consider yourself a master in these disciplines, Kohai?'

'Iie, Sensei, I do not. However, I am highly skilled in the open hand technique and skilled with the bō, sai, and nunchaku,' Haru stated proudly, rolling back his shoulders and puffing out his chest.

'What about your skills with the sword?'

Haru momentarily paused as he considered Junsaku's question, his thoughts drifting back to his training with Fukano. He let out a deep sigh, his expression contemplative, and said, 'I spent four years studying with a master swordsman, honing my skills. I thought I had excellent abilities until I met a young girl in Okinawa and began training with her. She found fault in my techniques and beat me soundly in every sparring match.'

'Do not be too hard on yourself, Haru. My daughter was special.' Then, his lips curled upwards as he placed his thumbs on his chest, his eyes twinkling with pride and amusement. 'Plus, we cannot forget that she was trained by the best.' Junsaku removed his swords, set them aside, and retrieved his bokken from behind the wagon bench. He returned to the field and stood before Haru. 'Face me and ready yourself, Kohai.'

Haru squared his feet, held his bokken by his side, and bowed deeply from the waist. Junsaku exploded forward and shoulder-charged Haru, hitting him in the chest and knocking him flat on his back.

Junsaku stared down at Haru. 'I said to ready yourself.'

Haru gasped for air. 'You did not say hajime!'

'Kohai, there is no one saying 'begin' in real battle. You must always be ready for an attack, even when you sleep. Now, on your feet,' Junsaku barked.

Haru stood, centred himself, and held the hilt of the wooden sword firmly with both hands. He pointed the tip at Junsaku's chest, and Junsaku attacked, delivering slashes, thrusts, and high and low strikes. Haru defended himself by blocking and moving, trying his best to survive the onslaught.

'Yame!' Junsaku yelled for Haru to stop. 'Kohai, you are dead. You are taking too many steps away from me, as though you are retreating from the fight. You need to take one step back only,' he instructed. 'And remember to breathe, find your centre, and that place in your mind that calms you. You must find mush-in, meaning 'no mind,' and release your fear.'

Haru's eyes slowly closed as he took a deep breath, trying to calm his thoughts. As he focused on managing his breathing, a sudden sense of clarity washed over him like an ocean wave; Fukano was, or had been, the centre of his world. He felt an overwhelming sense of gratitude and love for her. She became everything to him and made him feel strong in the brief time he knew her, and he regretted never telling her his feelings.

As Junsaku watched Haru, he could see the boy's aura. As Haru focused, the energy around him calmed, and his aura transformed from a mess of indistinct colours into electric hues of yellows, blues and greens that flowed like a river around his body. Junsaku smiled when he knew that Haru had found his centre, and he attacked. This time, Haru's movements flowed. Haru effortlessly performed tai sabaki, dodging and avoiding his teacher's attempted strikes while controlling his distance from Junsaku. Then, applying all the techniques he had learned, Haru tried to land a blow on Junsaku but instead had to duck to avoid a strike to his head. When Haru came up, he performed an up-ward slash, confident he would hit Junsaku in the thigh, but as he attempted to hit his teacher, Junsaku spun in a circle, avoided Haru's strike, and landed a blow to the backside of his student's head.

Haru stopped, stood still, and sighed, knowing he had avoid-ed severe injury because his sensei pulled his strike.

'Yoko yatta na!' Junsaku said, congratulating Haru.

Haru's shoulders slumped. 'But Sensei, I lost,' he moaned.

'Your movements improved, and you had multiple chances of landing a strike. However, you hesitated. You have the skill but need to commit. I see immense potential in you, Haru-san. Tell me, what helped you find your centre?'

Haru took a deep breath and bowed deeply before Junsaku. With a steady and respectful tone, he declared, 'The thought of your daughter.'

Junsaku returned the bow and said with a broad smile, 'Ari-gato, Haru-san. She was a true gem, shining brightly for us all.

Now, time for you to make dinner and for me to drink sake.'

***

EARLY THE NEXT morning, while they ate a light breakfast, Junsaku asked Haru, 'Have you ever used a katana or wakizashi?'

'Iie. I have never used a real sword, Sensei. Only a bokken.'

'You have no choice now. Here,' he said, handing his waki-zashi sword to Haru. 'With this shorter sword, you can stab, slash, and cut a man's throat.'

Haru clenched the braided handle of the wakizashi just below the tsuba, the sword guard, and admired the weapon, slightly longer than his forearm, with a razor-sharp edge and a wavy grain pattern on the steel blade that mimicked rippling water.

'I want you to imagine your arm is a tree trunk that does not bend at the elbow,' Junsaku instructed. 'If you bend, you will lose the speed and force needed to kill. Keeping your arm extended and the blade's tip pointed towards the sky, imagine your entire arm is a sword as you cut, bringing the blade down on your enemy. Always have this wakizashi ready on your left hip, Haru. This road is treacherous and full of rogues. We will be attacked, and you will die if you hesitate or do not use the sword correctly.'

Haru's eyes dimmed to the colour of black coffee, his heart pumping fast, and he affirmed, 'I will be ready, Sensei.'

Junsaku walked to the carriage, stopped, and stared at the box holding his daughter's body. He stretched his hands wide, pressed his palms on the stone surface, and bent at the waist, touching the casket with his forehead, breathing loudly. After a few minutes, he stated, 'I can sense my daughter's spirit is anxious to be near her mother. We must go.'

The warm sun beat down on Haru and Junsaku as they climbed onto the wooden front bench of the horse-drawn cart.

Junsaku handed the reins to Haru, who took them and lightly snapped the leather straps. The horses started walking on the dusty dirt road leading to Kakunodate, stirring up small dust clouds with each step as the wind gently brushed against their faces.

SIXTY-EIGHT

HARU GLIDED the horse-drawn cart along the road while Junsaku slept upright on the wagon's front seat, his head hung, his chin almost touching his chest.

'Around the next bend, stop alongside the river,' Junsaku said quietly, his eyes still closed, not bothering to raise his head.

His words startled Haru. 'I thought you were asleep, Sensei.'

'Warriors never sleep, Kohai,' Junsaku said, yawning loudly as he stretched his arms above his head.

When the wagon rounded the bend, the sound of a flowing river behind a dense grove of trees surprised Haru. Haru wondered how Junsaku knew the river was there; he never heard the sound of moving water when they were on the road. Haru steered the cart, navigated the carriage over grass and through trees, and spotted the river. The water meandered gently, and on the opposite side of the river, Haru saw a vast bamboo forest stretching as far as the eye could see, the tall, slender stalks swaying in the breeze.

Junsaku pointed upriver. 'Take the wagon across and find a clearing in the bamboo grove.'

Haru carefully maneuvered the cart across the shallowest

point of the river. Once across, he steered the cart to an open spot surrounded by towering green bamboo stalks, jumped down, and started to unpack the wagon.

'Leave all of that, Kohai. We are not camping here. It is time to train. Grab your wakizashi and follow me,'

Haru grabbed his sword from under the cart's front bench and hurried after his teacher.

Standing before a giant bamboo plant, Junsaku instructed, 'Kohai, take a stance in front of a bamboo and, using your sword, cut it in half.'

'But Sensei, I have never done this before. I do not know the technique.'

'I have taught you how to wield the blade and hold your body and arms.' Junsaku locked eyes with his student and said, 'Focus, Kohai. Cut through the bamboo.'

Haru squared his feet, inhaled deeply, and struck. His wakizashi hit the bamboo, and the blade lodged in the shaft, the impact reverberating up his arms and through his shoulders.

'I said cut through the bamboo, not jam your sword into it.'

Feeling the sting of embarrassment for his poor performance, Haru dropped to a deep bow and remained in that position, eyes on the ground.

'Stand up,' Junsaku demanded. Then, he asked, 'Why did you fail, Kohai?'

'Sensei, I lack the power and skill.'

Junsaku let out an exasperated sigh. 'Wrong. You have the skill but set yourself up for failure by being fearful and not believing in yourself. Kohai, your mind is your most powerful weapon. Now, ready yourself again.'

With a sharp tug, Haru freed his sword from the bamboo

and approached another nearby, slightly larger bamboo trunk. Before Haru lifted his sword to strike, Junsaku tapped him on the back of the head with his jō and said, 'Let us start with a smaller tree, Kohai,' pointing to a plant with a thinner stalk. Haru moved to the bamboo that Junsaku pointed out, positioning himself in front of the plant. 'Find your centre, Kohai. Do not look at the bamboo. Instead, look beyond it. Imagine a pine tree on a distant mountain and visualise yourself cutting it down with your sword rather than concentrating on the bamboo before you. Do this in your mind as you strike.'

Haru focused. Beyond the bamboo, he imagined a tall pine tree on a distant mountainside. As he exhaled, he swung his sword, and the pine tree in his mind toppled over. However, the bamboo before him remained upright, and his heart sank. 'Gomennasai, Sensei. I have failed you again,' Haru apologised.

'Have you, Kohai?'

Junsaku tapped the bamboo with his jō. To Haru's amazement, he watched as the tall piece of bamboo broke in two, the top half toppling to the ground. Not only had he successfully cut the bamboo with his sword, but he also never even felt his blade slice through it.

'Now, Kohai, answer me this: do you have the skill and power to cut a piece of bamboo?'

'Hai, Sensei,' Haru answered, elated.

'And Kohai, do you also have the skill and power to kill a man with that strike?'

Haru avoided eye contact with his teacher. 'Even if I have the skill and power, Sensei, I do not know if I have the mental strength.'

'You will realise your strength when you are fighting for your life or the life of others. For now, you need practise, so we will keep going until the sun sets.'

For several more hours, Junsaku and Haru practised cutting bamboo. Haru's performance varied between either cutting bamboo stalks into pieces or prying his sword out of sturdy trunks.

When the sky turned to bold shades of orange and violet, Junsaku announced, 'Yame.' Haru stopped, exhausted, noticing hundreds of pieces of bamboo scattered on the forest floor. 'Well done, Kohai. Remember my lessons and those you received from my daughter. Never forget the mountain beyond. It is a calm place that will help you focus, especially in battle.'

'Osu, Sensei,' Haru replied, bowing again.

'Let us eat dinner and enjoy sake,' Junsaku said, grinning as he gave his student a hearty pat on his back.

SIXTY-NINE

HARU STEERED the cart the next day while Junsaku napped on the wagon's front seat. Haru could hardly believe he accompanied one of the greatest samurai Japan had ever known, and this man had now acted as his sensei.

Lost in thought, the horses suddenly spooked. Junsaku woke, and his hand grabbed the hilt of his sword while Haru tugged the reins, regaining control of the horses. With his right hand on the handle of his sword, Junsaku gestured for Haru to do the same.

'We are being watched,' Junsaku murmured, his voice barely above a whisper as he inclined his head toward a dense grove of trees along the right side of the winding road. 'Prepare yourself,' Junsaku advised, sliding from the wagon seat as smoothly as water over rocks.

Junsaku walked to the front of the cart, positioned himself with his back to the trees, and could hear the rustling of the underbrush nearby, a sign the attackers were close.

Haru leapt down from the wagon seat and hurried to Junsaku's side, his eyes darting nervously, scanning for movement. 'I do not see anyone, Junsaku-san,' he whispered.

'Even though you cannot see them, they are there. Ready

yourself, Haru. Step back five paces and find your centre. No matter how many attackers there are, I will fight them, but if any get past me, you must be ready to defend your life.'

Haru heard war cries as three men sprang from the trees and ran at them, their swords held high, their eyes focused like eagles hunting prey. Junsaku stood with his back to the approaching assailants, his relaxed expression conveying a sense of calm. Haru watched in fear as a burly man wearing tattered clothes attempted to attack Junsaku from behind. His sword arched downward, but before the man's sword struck Junsaku's skull, Junsaku turned, drew his sword, and, in a flash, cut through the assailant's shoulder with an upward strike, sending the man's dismembered arm, still clutching his sword, to rest on the dusty road. Junsaku continued fighting, his movements flowing. He redirected his blade and applied a straight thrust to the attacker's chest, and then, withdrawing his sword, his blow sent the enemy's body face-first onto the gravel.

As Haru watched Junsaku fight with a second assailant, Haru's mind struggled to comprehend the scene, the first life-or-death fight he had ever witnessed. Then Haru heard Junsaku yell, 'Behind you!' Haru spun around, sword in hand, and blocked a strike from the third attacker. As Haru continued to block his opponent's attempted strikes, his movements reflexive rather than skilful, he suddenly heard Fukano's voice say, 'Tai sabaki.' Haru moved to his opponent's blind side and counter-attacked, his movements natural and intuitive. When the rogue rushed him again, attempting another onslaught, Haru performed more tai sabaki, moving his body to the right and forward before spinning his left leg around, out of the line of the sword attack. Faster than his opponent could react, Haru swung his sword, and it came to a sudden halt, shuddering in his grasp as the sharp edge lodged into the upper part of the man's spine. The man let out a guttural scream as he fell to his knees, dropping his sword to the ground. Haru, fuelled by adrenaline and still gripping his wakizashi firmly in both hands, kicked the man in his left shoulder, and his blow dislodged the blade from the assailant's spine. The man fell into the dirt, and, without hesitation, Haru drove his wakizashi sword through the man's back, puncturing his heart and leaving the enemy lying motionless.

Frozen in place, his mouth slightly open, Haru stared hypnotically at the first man he had ever killed. Then, as though awakened by ice water hitting his face, Haru shook his head and turned to find Junsaku leaning against the wagon.

'Took you long enough,' Junsaku remarked casually, his arms crossed.

Haru exhaled slowly, feeling the weight of tension lift from his shoulders as he sheathed his sword, his heart still racing from the adrenaline of the fight. Grateful to be unscathed, he twisted his lips into a crooked smile and walked towards the wagon.

SEVENTY

WATERCOLOUR STROKES of vibrant yellow, orange, and purple brushed the sky as Junsaku and Haru finally arrived at the village of Kakunodate. When they reached Junsaku's home, Yui stepped out from behind the creaky wood gate. She wore a lavender kimono, and the silver streaks in her otherwise jet-black hair were the only sign that time had passed. When she saw Junsaku, she bowed.

'*Konbanwa*, Yui. Please stand,' Junsaku said kindly. Then, he walked towards her, reached out, and for the first time in his life, pulled her into a hug. Yui stiffened in his arms, confused by Junsaku's show of affection. When Junsaku finally released her, Yui could see past his shoulder and noticed a teenage boy approaching.

'Konbanwa. Good evening. I am Haru,' he said, bowing his head.

'Konbanwa, Haru-san,' Yui replied.

Surprised and confused by Junsaku's unexpected return to Kakunodate, Yui looked at the cart and noticed a casket in the back of the wagon, the polished surface of the white marble reflecting the colours of the evening sky, and she felt heat rise to her cheeks. With a slumped posture and trembling voice, she lowered her head and whispered, 'Fukano,' her words full of reverence as though she were praying.

Junsaku put his bent finger beneath her chin and gently guided her eyes to meet his. 'Hai, Yui, our beloved girl has gone to the next world, and I am here to bury her near her mother and brother. Tonight, I will take her casket to the shrine, pray for her soul at the altar, and then I will stay the night to guard and protect her. In the morning, just after sunrise, you and Haru come for her burial.' Junsaku swallowed hard.

Yui wiped a tear from her eye. 'Before you go, Junsaku-san, will you come inside and sit by the warm fire? I have sake, pickles, and fish.'

'Arigato, Yui, but iie, no. I must begin arrangements immediately. However, I will clean and change my clothes,' he said, entering the house.

Junsaku went to his and Cecelia's bedroom. He changed into an ink-black kimono with a long, black, sleeveless coat over it, then placed his two swords in the obi around his waist. When he finished, he went to the kitchen and found Yui and Haru drinking tea. 'I am going now. You both join me at the cemetery in the morning,' he stated.

***

UPON JUNSAKU'S arrival at the shrine, he spoke to a monk who swiftly gathered a group of labourers to move Fukano's heavy casket. The labourers carefully placed the stone, rectangular box in front of the temple altar, the *kamidana*, which resembled a miniature shrine, complete with a sloping rooftop and shelving inside that held *shinzō*, kami sculptures. Then, Junsaku and the monk lit incense and adorned the altar with evergreen trims and sprigs of cherry blossoms to honour his daughter.

'Tomorrow, we will have a ceremony before burying my daughter beneath the cherry blossom tree next to her mother and brother,' Junsaku instructed the monk.

'Hai,' the man replied, bowing before leaving Junsaku alone.

***

JUNSAKU SAT cross-legged on the cool floor near his daughter's casket, soft candlelight flickering around him as he focused and entered deep meditation. After only a few minutes, he sensed he was not alone and opened his eyes to find Koji seated before him, the monk who had guided him in meditation when he was younger. Junsaku knew Koji had died, but the figure before him seemed as real as himself.

'You are here,' Junsaku said softly, the man's presence soothing him.

Koji looked calm and peaceful, and his serene smile eased some of the weight that pressed on Junsaku's heart.

Then, Junsaku's emotions erupted, and he wept, crying out, 'Why?' searching for answers amidst the chaos surrounding him.

'Junsaku,' Koji said with the care of a loving father, 'think on this: 'The zen master said to his student, 'The world is vast and wide. Why do you put on your robes at the sound of a bell?''

Junsaku sat in silence for what felt like an eternity, working to harness his emotions and steady his breathing. His chest tightened as he stared blankly into his lap, thinking about the monk's riddle. Suddenly, as if cleansed by the cold flow of a waterfall, clarity swept over him. 'I have been blind, Koji-san. I lived my life following other's commands. I did not do things because I wanted to; I allowed others to control me. I gave up my freedom, and now I have nothing.'

'You have nothing?' the monk replied.

'I have the truth, but it is too late.'

'Junsaku, it is never too late.'

Junsaku looked at the monk, tipped his head, and said sincerely, 'Domo arigato gozaimasu, Koji-san. My path is crystal clear to me now.'

Koji faded away, his form dissolving into the candlelight. In the chilly, nighttime air, Junsaku moved closer to Fukano's casket and lay his body on the shrine floor. He thought of finding a blanket to cover Fukano and keep her warm but then remembered that only his daughter's physical shell remained and that she no longer suffered the cold.

SEVENTY-ONE

THE CHERRY blossom tree shaded Cecelia's and Nobushida's gravesites. Pink and white flower petals spotted the branches, and the tree's falling flowers blanketed the ground. Before sunrise, Junsaku and the labourers moved Fukano's casket from the altar to her burial site, where tiny white and pink flowers floated down and scattered on the surface of her stone casket.

Haru and Yui arrived for the burial as the morning sun warmed the earth. To start the ceremony, Junsaku, Yui, and Haru picked up ceramic water bowls from the grave's edge and held them steady, careful not to spill any water, as a short, slender monk wearing a tall, triangular hat chanted the purification of the soul. Just as the monk switched to chanting sutras, asking for Fukano's transgressions in this lifetime to be forgiven and to aid her in her transition to the next world and her eventual rebirth, he motioned for Junsaku, Yui and Haru to pour water onto Fukano's casket. Next, the monk removed a white cloth draped around his shoulders and handed it to Junsaku. Junsaku knelt beside the grave, laid the fabric along the top of the casket, and then stood, clenching his hands at his waist as he recited a death poem:

The setting sun, the rising moon,
the earth fragrant with cherry blossom,
you sleep to be awakened.

Junsaku knelt again, placed his forehead on the ground, and dug his fingers into the grass and dirt. After several minutes, he stood and said, 'It is time to leave. She is with the others now. Let us go to the house for nihonshu,' and he walked towards the main pathway, his jaw clenched. Despite the storm raging within him, he steadied himself, determined to do what he knew had to be done.

***

BACK AT the house, Junsaku, Haru, and Yui relaxed in the kitchen. They sat on cushions at the low table, drinking sake, sharing stories of Fukano, Nobushida, and Cecelia, careful not to mention the names of the deceased as they reminisced.

'You should have seen her as she walked off that enormous sailing ship. My wife looked confident and curious, her green eyes as sharp and round as an owl, her long brown hair ruffled by the sea air,' Junsaku said, grinning. 'I had never seen anyone with an aura as bright as hers. A stunning purple hue surrounded her figure, and her energy rippled with fireworks of yellow. She was the most beautiful soul I had ever seen.' Junsaku paused momentarily, then continued. 'The boy was another blessing in my life. So much spirit! He loved his sister with all his heart, and she adored him. And, my daughter,' he said, his voice soft and low, 'she came into our lives with the beauty of a woman and the power of a warrior. What a wonder.'

'I miss her,' Haru sighed. 'She was my best friend.'

'Only a friend?' Junsaku questioned, raising one bushy eyebrow.

'Hai, Sensei. I mean, Junsaku-san. I swear it. She was just a dear friend, that is all!' Haru stammered, struggling to find the right words.

'Calm yourself, Haru. She told me you were her friend. Just so you know, if Fukano wanted to be more than just friends, I would have approved.' Junsaku patted Haru's shoulder and then lifted his sake glass. 'Kanpai,' he proclaimed. 'To my beloved wife, brave son, and extraordinary daughter.'

Haru and Yui raised their glasses, repeated 'kanpai', and drank the rice wine.

'Tomorrow, I am leaving,' Junsaku announced.

'Will you go south with me?' Haru asked.

'Iie. You will be going alone. You will ride one of my horses, and I will ensure you have enough supplies and money to get home.'

'Will you return to Edo?'

'No, Haru. I am going somewhere else.'

'Junsaku, this is your home,' Yui said gently. 'You should stay here. I will find other arrangements.'

'Iie, Yui. This is your home now,' he replied, his relaxed smile reaching his eyes. 'You have been loyal to my family, and I am grateful.'

Yui's eyes expressed deep appreciation as Haru asked, 'Can you tell us where you will go, Junsaku-san?'

'There is no need for details. Just trust that I know where I truly belong.'

SEVENTY-TWO

JUNSAKU STOOD near the front gate wearing a white kimono, a black outer robe, loose white pants, tabi socks, and beige zori slippers with a wood lacquered base, stroking the horse's mane. 'Haru, remember to stay alert on the road and have your sword ready,' Junsaku instructed. 'Stay sharp and be cunning. Do not flaunt your money or supplies. And, if you stop at a village inn, do not show your mon coins.'

'Hai,' replied Haru.

Junsaku reached into his pocket, removed an envelope sealed with a vivid red wax stamp of Junsaku's three-leaf family crest, and handed it to Haru. 'This is for you.'

Haru took the envelope, noticing the name Hirokawa-san written on the paper in kanji. 'What is this, Sensei?'

'This is your chance to choose to become a samurai warrior if you want. This message is for my friend, Captain Hirokawa, who resides at the castle in Edo. This letter orders him to become your sensei and to train you to be a samurai. If you deliver this to him, he will not disobey my command.' Junsaku gazed intensely into Haru's eyes and said, 'With the right teacher, you have the potential to achieve greatness. You are at a pivotal moment in your life. You can either return home to island life or deliver this letter and become a samurai. The choice is yours.'

'Domo arigato gozaimasu, Junsaku-san.' Haru placed his palm on his chest.

'Whatever choice you make, Haru, always be true to yourself.'

'I will remember your advice,' Haru replied. Then he turned to Yui, who wore the hair comb given to her years earlier by Junsaku, and said, 'Domo arigato gozaimasu for your hospitality.'

'Enough of these goodbyes,' Junsaku announced. 'Go, Haru! Be brave, live by bushido, and practise honesty, sincerity, and devotion. Believe in yourself as I believe in you.'

Haru swallowed hard before he mounted his horse. He gently squeezed the middle of the horse's ribcage with his thighs. The animal walked forward on the cobblestone road, and Haru kept his eyes aimed ahead, forcing himself not to look back.

'Now, Yui, it is time for me to go,' Junsaku said. 'But before I leave, I need to wash my face. Please bring me water.'

'Of course. I will be right back,' she replied.

Yui walked to the kitchen and pumped spring water into a bowl. She then grabbed a piece of linen and returned to Junsaku, who waited on a boulder in the front yard. Yui knelt, placed the bowl on the ground, wet the fabric, twisted it in her hands, and handed the cloth to Junsaku.

Junsaku washed his stubbled face, high cheekbones, lips, bushy eyebrows, and deep-set eyelids, then announced, 'I am ready.'

He left the yard silently, shutting the wooden gate behind him, and Yui felt elated as she watched him depart; she knew his destination, which made her heart smile.

SEVENTY-THREE

JUNSAKU ARRIVED at the shrine and immediately went to his family's burial plot beneath the cherry blossom tree. On Cecelia's tall stone monument, a vase held fresh sakura branches with pink blossoms, and on Fukano and Nobushida's grave markers, incense of sandalwood slowly burned, filling the air with a blended scent of woodiness, spice, and creamy sweetness.

Junsaku sat on the grass and stared at Cecelia's grave, the canopy of the flowering tree shading him from the bright sun. 'Can you forgive me?' he questioned aloud, a tear sliding down his cheek. 'I am sorry I did not protect our family as I should have. You should have all been my priority.' Junsaku wiped his eyes, kissed his fingertips, and touched Cecelia's headstone, repeating the gesture on Fukano and Nobushida's grave markers. 'I am coming,' he whispered.

Junsaku moved to his knees, pulled the tanto from his belt, and placed it on the grass. He untied his sash, stretched open his robes, exposed his bare torso, and picked up the knife, pressing the tip against his flesh. Then, out of nowhere, the cloaked spirit materialized. Junsaku's heart thumped in his chest as the ghost glided closer, halting just inches from him. Deep inside the void of the apparition's black hood, for the first time, Junsaku could see the ghost's piercing blue eyes looking at him, sparkling like jewelled sapphires caught in the light. Junsaku moved the blade away from his stomach and set it on the ground. 'Why have you come?'

As though the powerful voice originated deep within his soul, he heard, 'I warned you.'

'You gave me no warnings!' Junsaku roared.

''Tis not true,' the spirit grumbled, his words shaking the ground below Junsaku's knees. 'I told you to learn from my mistakes.'

Behind the ghost, only faintly discernible in the bright daylight, Junsaku caught sight of a shadowy silhouette. As his eyes adjusted, he noticed the translucent image of an Irish wolfhound, its fur dry and mangled. 'Dog?' Junsaku said incredulously.

The ghostly dog barked, the animal's eerie woof echoing through the graveyard.

Junsaku's eyes stretched wide as he realised the spirit's identity. 'You are the boy who visited me when I was young!'

'Ay. And do you remember what I told you then?'

'Hai. You told me to learn from your mistakes. But you never told me what those were, so how was I to know?'

The eight-foot figure raised his arm and slid back the black hood that covered his head, revealing an ethereal, glowing, light-skinned face. 'Junsaku, think upon the last years. When did I appear to you?' he asked, a flicker like blue-winged butterflies shimmering in his eyes.

Junsaku tilted his head slightly, and then, after a moment's pause, straightened his posture, saying, 'You appeared when I questioned my devotion to the rulers of Japan. I know now that

I made the mistake of dedicating my life to the shogunate rather than my family. But why did you not stop me? If you would have told me to choose my family, I would have listened, and they might still be alive today.'

The spirit said nothing as his penetrating eyes bore through Junsaku.

'Speak, ghost!' Junsaku demanded. 'Why did you not tell me?'

The spirit transformed from shadowy black to radiant gold, bathing Junsaku and everything around it in an ethereal light brighter than the sunshine. 'Junsaku, you share my soul from a past life. During that lifetime, my name was Bartholomew. I was an executioner. I killed many people in servitude to the kingdom. For my entire life, I had little, and what little I had, I lost it in service to lords and rulers.' The ghost fell silent for a moment as if gathering its thoughts. Then, in a more sombre tone, it spoke again. 'As I learnt in that life, you needed to learn in this one. Unfortunately, you ignored the warning signs, the gnawing feeling in your gut, your soul's whispers, and even my warnings. Instead, you pledged your unwavering loyalty to rulers, even if it meant putting your family in great danger. And now, Junsaku, you stand alone, again, aware of the cost of your choices.'

Junsaku covered his face with his hands.

'You must remember this in your next life,' the ghost said.

When Junsaku removed his hands from his face, the phantom vanished.

Junsaku picked up the tanto and held it loosely as he thought about what the spirit told him. The words played in his head as he tried to record the message, imprinting it into his soul's memory. Then, clamping the wrapped hilt of his knife, he forced the blade into his stomach, sliced down, and twisted it back upwards, a groan escaping his throat. As he bled, his eyes wide open, his family appeared before him. Standing amidst delicate pink and white cherry blossoms that swirled around them in a mesmerising display, Cecelia, Fukano, and Nobushida held hands, all smiling at Junsaku. As Junsaku stared at his family, his energy seemed to burst from his body, casting a radiant and brilliant white light as he fell to the ground, lifeless, his soul finally free of the physical world.

Sincerest thanks for reading
His Name is Junsaku
book two in the series,
The Many Lives of Wolf.

If you liked the novel, please leave a review on
Amazon and Goodreads.

---

*For new book announcements, book reviews, travel,
leisure, and foodie recommendations, check out my
blog @TenkaraSmart.com.*

About the Author

Raised in San Diego, California, Tenkara Smart received a Bachelor of Arts degree in English Literature and a Minor in Creative Writing from San Diego State University. After two decades working for one of America's leading running retailers, Tenkara stepped down from her role as vice president and moved with her husband to Qatar and then to Australia. Tenkara's passion for travel has taken her to various places around the globe, including many visits to her favourite destination, Japan. Additionally, her husband, an accomplished, eighth-level black belt with extensive training in the art of Okinawan karate and a man who has lived a life of adventure, is a powerful source of inspiration in her writing.

www.ingramcontent.com/pod-product-compliance
Lightning Source LLC
Chambersburg PA
CBHW031116210626
46816CB00016B/1461